MP
ℛ ℘

ANGEL IN THE HOUSE

Another hilarious adventure from the king of comedy crime.

Angel, faced with impending parenthood, has to do the unthinkable and get a job. Working for Rudgard and Blugden Confidential Investigations, he has to plug the leak of stolen Botox from a supposedly secure laboratory, but he is distracted by a redhead with a passion for salsa dancing, a Russian sailor with a passion for old East German cars, an estate agent with a passion for Audrey Hepburn, and a redundant KGB officer trying to retrain as a gangster! Oh, and which brave soul is going to tell Angel's fearsome hippy mother that she's soon to be a grandmother?

ANGEL IN THE HOUSE

ANGEL IN THE HOUSE

by

Mike Ripley

Magna Large Print Books
Long Preston, North Yorkshire,
BD23 4ND, England.

British Library Cataloguing in Publication Data.

Ripley, Mike
    Angel in the house.

    A catalogue record of this book is
    available from the British Library

    ISBN   0-7505-2543-6

First published in Great Britain in 2005 by Allison & Busby Ltd.

Copyright © 2005 by Mike Ripley

Cover illustration © Old Tin Dog

The moral right of the author has been asserted

Published in Large Print 2006 by arrangement with
Allison & Busby Ltd.

Magna Large Print is an imprint of Library Magna Books Ltd.

Printed and bound in Great Britain by
T.J. (International) Ltd., Cornwall, PL28 8RW

Dedication

This one is for Minette Walters, Colin Dexter, Marcel Berlins, Philip Oakes, Paul Doherty, Catherine Aird, John Connolly, Ruth Dudley Edwards, Denise Danks, Rodney Wingfield, Janet Neel, Stella Duffy, Shelley Silas, Martyn Waites, Russell James and Mark Timlin, who all took heart from the fact that only the good died young in 2003.

But also for all my Phantom People in Moscow, and Captain Peter Corbett, under whatever flag he sails.

Chapter One

'Make yourself useful and look through these,' said Amy.

'What am I looking for?'

'Something suitable for a family home outside London, but not one of those boring executive homes called The Excelsior or The Evergreen or anything where the architecture came out of a catalogue. Something with space, with style, with character and maybe a bit of land. Near enough London to commute, far enough out to make people jealous. Catchment areas for schools may be a consideration but that's probably too advanced for you. Just limit your trawl to the ones you would fancy burgling.'

'I'll ignore that,' I said, mentally filing it away under Slights and Put-Downs for future revenge purposes, and picked up the pile of estate agency bumph she had dumped on the sofa next to me. And just to make sure I knew she meant business, she scooped up the remote control for the TV and DVD player and took it with her into the kitchen.

To the back of her head I yelled: 'Does *madam* have a price range?'

'*Madam* was thinking in the region of seven to eight,' she shouted back.

'Would that be the seven or the eight as followed by perhaps five zeroes?' I said, working it out quickly before I had to use my fingers.

'Tacking *four* zeroes on won't buy you much these days. Start sifting.'

'Have we got a seven and five zeroes?' I threw over my shoulder.

'What do you mean?'

She had come out of the kitchen and was standing behind me, so close her voice made me jump. I was going to have to buy her more chunky jewellery. Or a bell.

'I'm on it,' I said and grabbed a handful of sheets off the top of the pile. I seemed to strike lucky immediately.

'This one looks good, but what does "gated domain" mean?'

'Means it's inside a secured perimeter. High walls, regular security patrols, minefields, guard towers, machine-guns, that sort of thing.'

'Cool. Listen, it's a snip at 500K. Four bedrooms, swimming pool, maid service, gardener and gated domain.'

'Where is it?'

'Just outside Nice on the Cote d'Azur.'

'Dream on.'

'Can't we even...?'

'No. We've got jobs to think of.'

'*We?* What's this *we* shit? I thought I was a house husband, a DSO.'

'A what?'

'A Domestic Significant Other.'

'You really think I'd leave you in the South of France during the working week? You're out of your tree. Next.'

I screwed up that sheet and dropped it on the

floor, taking another from the pile.

'How about "Select Surrey"?'

'Is it an Executive Home?'

'Looks like it, but it does cost a straight million so that must mean something.'

'Not these days,' she said. 'That's about the going rate for a penthouse flat overlooking Chelsea Bridge.'

I noticed that Amy had helped herself to a glass of wine without offering me one. I filed that away too. The Slights and Snubs file was beginning to bulge.

'Impressive family house,' I read another, 'double garage, swimming pool, six bedrooms...'

'Where?'

'Stoke Poges.'

'No way. Not a serious address. It's so important to have a good address.'

'So number 3, Slaughter Lane, Blubberhouse, would be out of the question?'

'Tell me you're making that up.'

'I'm making it up.'

'Get back to the real ones, there are hundreds more to choose from.'

'They're all a bit pricey,' I said, flicking through them. 'What was the brief you gave the agents?'

'Oh, you know what estate agents are like,' she said, without realising that I didn't. I had never bought a house before. I had once blown one up, but I didn't think that would count for much in her eyes.

'I told them the price range was 700K to 800K, so immediately they try to offload everything on their books over a million.'

'I see what you mean – listen to this: "lakeside family house, six beds, billiards room, comes with a self-contained one-bed flat, a boathouse, a pier and your own harbour." Now how cute is that? Oh. Two and a half million cute, that's how much. Nice views over Lake Windermere though.'

'Cumbria?' she said like she was considering it. 'Nah ... too far to commute and anyway, I bet you don't get the lake for that price.'

'Well, not all of it,' I admitted. 'This is closer. West London town house designed by Erno Goldfinger in 1958. Fifty year lease. How about that?'

'You expect me to *lease?*' she drawled, in her cod Sean Connery imitation.

'No, Mister Bond, I expect you to *buy*... Or there's this, built in 1867 in the Strawberry Gothic style in ten acres of landscaped Hertfordshire: Hecton Manor. It looks huge and it's only a million.'

Did I just say *only a million* out loud, without gagging? Then I read the small print.

'Hold the removal van. That's just for the one flat inside the manor.'

'And that means a communal garden and I don't fancy that,' she said primly. 'I'm not sharing a garden even if it is ten acres.'

Which was a bit rich coming from someone who didn't even know if we had a shed or not at the bottom of our present garden.

'You won't like this then: Grade II listed manor in Oxfordshire. You can buy an entire wing for £2.25 million and listen to this: "you'll be joining a community of homeowners including Americans, who hold barbeques to celebrate Independence Day". That's nice, isn't it? Though I didn't think it was *that* good a film.'

'Hang on to that one,' said Amy from behind her glass.

'You cannot be serious.'

'I don't want to buy it. God, it sounds awful. But if we're ever stuck for somewhere to eat on the 4th of July, we could always drop in.'

'Do you suppose the Americans live in the West Wing?' I tried, but she wasn't listening, she was helping herself to the next sheet on the pile.

'Here's one for you,' she grinned. 'St Bueno's.'

'St Bueno's? What's that, a pipe tobacco?'

'It's a church, in Llanfaenor, Monmouthshire. Last service held there thirty years ago; became a bicycle repair shop and then tastefully converted in to a two-bedroomed house. No evidence of people being buried there. It's only £300,000.'

'No thanks, if not even the Welsh wouldn't be seen dead there. OK, my turn and the stakes are raised. Basement flat in SW5, completely transformed by "an architect fast becoming a household face on television". State-of-the-art heating, lighting and alarm systems which can be operated by a mobile phone.'

'Get real. You can't even manage text messages.'

She had a point.

'Yet you trust me to deal with estate agents?' I asked innocently.

'It's no more than they deserve, anyway, you ought to make yourself useful while you've still got time on your hands.'

Amy's decision to up stakes and move out of

13

London into that great green wasteland of countryside beyond the M25 had come as a bit of a shock. On my Richter scale of surprises it had scored about a 6, compared to the straight 11 she'd hit when she told me she was pregnant.

No child of hers was going to be brought up in the kebab fumes and litter, or crime and violence of London, having to dodge drive-by shootings whilst being delivered to kindergarten in the biggest 4x4 on the civilian market that wasn't actually a Humvee. I had asked her if she was sure she wasn't thinking of Manchester, rather than dear old Hampstead, when it came to drive-bys, as the last one recorded in our street had probably involved a cartload of Bow Street Runners chasing Dick Turpin or maybe a low-flying Stuka way off course in 1940. The Neighbourhood Watch, parking wardens and speed cameras had pretty much stamped out the habit in recent times.

She had pointed out that as I was registered to vote in Hackney, I basically had no room to talk. About anything. I didn't quite see the logic in that – and I wasn't registered to vote anywhere (that way you avoid jury duty) – as people obviously did bring up children in Hackney and there were lots of schools there which were always in the newspapers for 'failing', whatever that meant, but which could not help being good at languages as over 110 dialects were spoken there these days.

At that point she had reminded me that I had no room to talk about anything.

'So what am I supposed to do?' I asked, throwing a sheaf of 'particulars' as they call them, up into the air.

'Pick those up and sort them into three piles.'

'Ones I like, ones I don't like and ones we can't afford?' I offered helpfully.

'Don't be ridiculous,' she snorted. 'First pile: ones no more than an hour's drive from the West End.'

I was wondering when she'd think about the shops.

'You driving or me?' I smiled, but she ignored that.

'Second pile: houses that look possible but are in the wrong place.'

I thought I understood that – just.

'Third pile: rubbish houses, but the estate agents have a classy name. You know, "Snelgrove and Windsor: specialists in country properties since 1688", that sort of thing, that are based outside London. You can ring them up and say they've been recommended by Lord Cabot.'

'Who's Lord Cabot?'

'I have no idea, but they won't ask, they're all such snobs.'

'Won't we come across as pretty snobbish?'

'Yes, which is why they'll go out of their way to help us, find us the right place and maybe tip us off before things come on the market. The best places are always sold before the For Sale sign goes up.'

'You think they are that shallow?'

'Tadpoles-gasping-for-air shallow. So even you might manage a charm offensive.'

'Can't we do this on the internet?' I tried. 'Lots of people sell their houses on the net.'

'They say about 750,000 people *look* for a

house on the net but there's nothing to say how many actually buy. You put up about four million results if you just type "houses for sale" into a search engine. With your attention span, you'd probably buy one in Nevada by mistake.'

'Nevada? Instead of what – Surrey? It's an easy mistake to make – the desert panorama, the rattle-snakes, the neon-lit casinos shaped like pyramids, Englebert Humperdinck in permanent cabaret.'

'Well, that's ruled out Surrey. See what you can find wrong with all the other Home Counties. You've got two weeks, then I want to see some progress.'

Two weeks? I had been planning to spin this out for months until she gave up in despair and decided to stay in Hampstead.

'What's the rush?'

'These things take time and,' she patted her stomach, 'the clock's ticking.'

I realised that she had flat ginger ale in her glass, not wine, so I couldn't needle her on that. Once she had found out she was pregnant, we had both given up smoking immediately – or in my case the next day, when she told me I had. She had cut out alcohol completely as well, but had not included me in the pledge. There were, after all, limits.

'Hang on,' I raised a finger. 'Earlier ... you said I could do this house hunting quest whilst I *still had time on my hands*. What did you mean by that?'

'If we're buying a new house, we're going to need a new mortgage,' she said, like she was explaining it to a five-year-old. 'And even though you can get away with self-certification these

16

days, we'll be better off with two income streams, at least until we realise the equity in this place.'

I wished there had been a five-year-old to explain that to me, but there is never one around when you want one.

Then the mists began to clear and the awful truth dawned on me.

'I'm missing something here, aren't I? You're expecting me to get a job, aren't you?'

'Is that so unreasonable, darling?' she said sweetly, smiling and giving me *that* look from under her fringe.

'Be a bit tricky finding gainful employment in two weeks, with all this in-depth research into the housing market you want me to do.'

It was weak, I know, but I was floundering.

'Oh I wouldn't expect *you* to find gainful employment in two weeks...'

I could feel ice forming in my stomach.

'You've already found me a job, haven't you?'

'And you'll just love it.'

'That's what you said about venison cooked in Pernod.'

'Fair play, that was a mistake, I'll give you that, but you will like this.'

'I will?'

'You've always wanted to be a detective, haven't you?'

'What? Have you enrolled me as a Special Constable or something? It's your hormones, isn't it? You can't control them.'

She cuffed me playfully around the head.

'A *private* detective, you great div. You know, as in R & B Investigations.'

17

I relaxed. So much, I actually felt my blood pressure drop. It was winding me up: she was having a laugh.

I ... we ... did indeed know of Rudgard and Blugden: Confidential Investigations, of Shepherd's Bush. Not only had I been sort of responsible for introducing Stella Rudgard to Veronica Blugden about nine years ago, but I think I had foolishly claimed credit for teaming them up in the private detective business, with being an all-female agency as their unique selling point. I had actually done a few small jobs for them over the years, errands really, and offered some practical, masculine advice when they had found themselves out of their depth. Admittedly, the advice had not been very practical, instructive or, indeed, legal, and so I could not see even a ramshackle outfit like R&B being desperate enough to offer me a job.

'Bit of a problem, working for Rudgard & Blugden, darling. It's an all-female detective agency.'

'Not any more, that policy's been changed,' said Amy, avoiding my eyes.

'Since when?'

'Since the new owner took over.'

'They sold out?' I was feeling those cold icy fingers in my bowels again. 'Who to?'

'Me,' said Amy.

Amy's Hampstead house (it was Amy's when I met her and I had never made any claims to it other than a place to hang my car keys) was officially lodged with an estate agent at 9 a.m. the next day. It was not 'put up for sale' as that only happens in common areas and there was no ques-

18

tion of anyone putting a FOR SALE sign up in the front drive. This was, after all, Hampstead. In fact it probably wasn't lodged with an estate agent, but rather a Domiciliary Habitation (and Feng Shui) Consultant or suchlike. Either way, it wasn't really any of my business. Amy told me over breakfast and said I had one job that day and only one, and that was to get 'that piece of black crap' out of sight and keep it out of sight for as long as there might be people coming to view the property.

'Will I have to show people around the place?' I had asked.

Amy had put the expertly-manicured nail of her right forefinger under her chin, pointing up to her face.

'Do I look stupid? Is this my idiot face? This is a face that was born yesterday? *You* show people round the house? Are you insane? When we want them to give us money?'

There was a lot more in similar vein but by then I was out of the house and unlocking the piece of black crap parked in the driveway, which the manufacturers had called an Austin Fairway, but most people just said 'black London cab'. Only a privileged few knew his real name was Armstrong II and a very rarefied few knew what had happened to Armstrong I, and some of them were constrained either by the Official Secrets Act or just sheer embarrassment, so they would never talk about it.

Austin taxis of the old style, like the FS4 or the Fairway, not the snub-nosed TX or the boxy Metrocab, have always been my wheels of choice in London. What else blends into a London background better (or gets fewer parking tickets) than a black London taxi? They can turn on a sixpence and run on diesel, which makes them economic enough, though not as economical as they once were now that some busybody in the Green lobby has discovered that diesel is just as polluting as leaded petrol and the price differential now favours unleaded or low sulphur fuel.

I started the engine and pointed Armstrong roughly eastwards, aiming for Camden Town and Islington, skirting central London to avoid the hordes of sweaty tourists tramping the greasy streets of the West End in what was turning out to be one of the hottest summers for years. It was fast becoming the only topic of conversation: was this going to be as hot as 1976? The older Londoner, however, would pick up on the year and point out that the July and August of 1979 were probably hotter than '76. Had to be, didn't they, because 1979 was the year the pubs in the City ran out of lager. You wouldn't forget something like that, would you? That was the summer when one of the big breweries had to rush supplies of Heatwave Lager into the pubs as a stop-gap for the usual Heineken or Stella. The fact that this was just a basic pale ale brewed with a lighter coloured malt and served superchilled didn't matter. It was just what the hot and bothered City punter wanted and he didn't mind paying £2 a pint a for it. Any cabbie would tell you that story, with a real feeling of nostalgia. Well, face it, beer in London at *only* £2 a pint; those surely were the good old days.

I had not been over to Barking for some time and on the northern edge of Bethnal Green I actually pulled into the kerb to take a look at how the landscape was changing. All the old Sixties blocks of flats above four storeys high were being pulled down, and for the first time that I could remember, the local residents had a clear view across to the Canary Wharf towers on the Isle of Dogs. Sitting there, with the engine idling gently (210,000 miles on the clock and still running as sweet as a nut) I thought about the recording studio down Curtain Road near Liverpool Street station where I'd done many a gig as a session trumpeter and wondered what had happened to it. That was the trouble with London. Buildings and sometimes whole streets could disappear, and after about a month, no one would miss them. When they'd redeveloped Liverpool Street, some of us lost a damn fine basement wine bar (especially prized because mobile phones didn't work down there in the gloom), one of the last of Victorian oyster bars and the only non-porn secondhand bookshop for miles. But most people hadn't noticed and seemed quite happy with the McDonald's, the two Burger Kings and the host of sandwich shops and booths selling undistinguished microwaved baguettes at very distinguished prices, which they'd got instead.

Something flicked across my eyeline in Armstrong's wing mirror. About fifty yards down the road behind me, three young Neds, all trainers, tracksuit bottoms and Burberry baseball caps, came skidding out of one of the buildings. The lead Ned carried something shiny and metallic clutched to his chest: a VCR or a DVD player. The two behind were making good time despite carrying the weight of a large-screen TV between them. The lead one nodded his Burberry at me, tucked his prize under one arm, put two fingers in his mouth and whistled loudly, then put up a hand as if to flag me down. Cheeky little gits.

I let them puff and pant their way to within twenty feet before I put Armstrong into gear and pulled away.

Some things never change.

Duncan the Drunken (Probably the Best Car Mechanic in the World) had his emporium in a pair of converted railway arches at the end of a cobbled alley, which, thanks to the new relief road which cordoned off Barking station as if it had the plague, was almost impossible to find unless you knew it was there. There was no chance of Duncan attracting any new or passing trade as, apart from the double yellow lines painted down the alley, even the local council seemed to have forgotten about it since Victoria ruled. Not that the yellow lines seemed to affect his business. Judging by the number of Mercedes C180 Kompressors parked on them, business seemed to be booming.

I parked behind the fifth one and checked them all out, walking to the sliding metal doors. All five were new, or at least less than a year old, and all seemed to have legitimate registration plates (or 'index numbers' as the cops call them) and kosher tax discs. In years gone by I had seen cars at Duncan's which used the old-style label from a bottle of Guinness stuck in the corner of the windscreen. From a distance it might fool the naked eye, but these days there are cameras everywhere.

If business was this good, maybe Duncan wouldn't be interested in baby-sitting Armstrong for as long as it took for Amy to forget his existence which, with a baby on the way and a new house to buy, not to mention numerous tradesmen to bully, shouldn't be too long.

Inside the garage was another Mercedes with the hood up and the bottom half of a pair of overalls protruding, almost as if the car had, shark-like, fancied a mechanic for lunch. It certainly wasn't Duncan bending over into the engine, unless he'd lost about a hundred and forty pounds and changed sex, or had some really duff liposuction. I guessed it was one of his young apprentices on a jobseeker allowance.

Duncan himself was sitting on a swivel typist's chair that had lost its back rest, holding a pint mug of tea (he had the white china pint mugs shipped down from Yorkshire) balanced on his knee with one hand. In the other he held a magazine and was deep into an article entitled *How Gay Is Your Car?*

''Morning, Dunc,' I announced myself above the music coming out of the tape player in his tiny office.

'A Peugeot 206,' he said loudly by way of a response, but he was talking to the figure leaning into the Mercedes, not me.

'I wasn't far off,' mumbled the overalls.

'True, true. The new Mini comes second runner-up,' conceded Duncan.

''Morning, Dunc,' I said, really loud this time.

'Oh 'ello, Angel. Do *you* know what the Gay Car of the Year is – as voted by the Club Automobile

Rainbow of France?'

'Peugeot 206?' I said, playing along.

'Knew you'd know,' he said smugly.

'I thought it was bleeding obvious, with the new Mini close behind, so to speak?'

He consulted the magazine.

'And the new VW Beetle, the Jeep Wrangler, any VW Golf and the Porsche Boxer. Them two'll be for lesbians, I suppose.'

The overalls had straightened up and were wiping their hands on what had once been a red pinstriped shirt. No wonder you never saw them in the City any more. Blonde, blue-eyed teenage apprentice mechanics were using them as oily rags.

'You're not of the sensible shoes persuasion yerself, are you Jessamy?' said Dunc with all the sensitivity and political correctness which had ensured no female jobseeker usually lasted more than a fortnight.

'Not really, but if you bought me a Boxer, I'd help 'em out if they were busy at the week-end,' said Jessamy.

Maybe she would last the month. Duncan probably got tax breaks or grants for the 'apprenticeships' he offered, neither of which he needed as he was never short of work; he just liked winding up the younger generation. Hence the music playing at the moment on maximum volume: *Led Zeppelin: The BBC Sessions.*

He caught my frown.

'What's up with you? Heavy metal's back in fashion these days.'

'*The Darkness* and *Kings of Leon* are in fashion; this is time capsule stuff. They're probably using

24

it on the telly commercials for Peugeot 206s.'

'Nay, they wouldn't dare,' said Duncan, his accent becoming deeper Yorkshire as he thought I might be serious. Then the tape segued into the intro to *Whole Lotta Love* and Duncan dropped the magazine he was holding, planted his legs apart and took up the stance.

Even over the bass riff, I could hear Jessamy swear.

'Duncan!' I yelled. 'Put down the air guitar! Step away from the air guitar! Do not return to the air guitar!'

But before I could make any impression on him, Jessamy took matters into her own hands, stomping off into the office. The music ended abruptly with a loud click and then there was another one.

'Kettle's on,' she yelled.

'Good girl,' beamed Duncan. 'That lass'll make some man a damn fine mechanic one day. Now what can I do for you?'

'You can tell me that black London cabs don't feature in that survey.' I pointed to his magazine.

'Oh, I doubt that.' He picked up the magazine and ran a finger down the page, his tongue jutting out over his top lip in fake concentration. 'Let's see now... Ford Mondeos and any white van; they're raging heteros, but the Ford Puma and the Chrysler PT Cruise, they're both worth outing. Ah, here we are, the Austin Fairway de-licensed Hackney Carriage as driven by hooligans who've never grown up and who ought to know better 'cos they certainly can afford better ... they're down as "asexual" it says here, along with all Skodas.

Happy now?'

'You should be, you'll be driving it for the next month or so.'

'Will I now? Why's that? Has the lovely and talented Amy put her foot down?'

'How did you know?' I said far too quickly.

'You forget, my son, I'm married too. Though *I* have tried to forget; tried really bloody hard sometimes. They make you get rid of all your toys in the end.'

'She's not making me get rid of anything,' I defended myself. 'She just wants Armstrong out of sight for a month or so while her house is on the market.'

'Moving, are we?' Duncan feigned interest.

'Amy fancies a place in the country.'

'Bloody hell,' she pregnant or what? That'll be the flat in Stuart Street gone for a Burton as well. You won't be allowed to keep that on if you're building a nest out in the sticks out in the back of beyond, where it smells of cow dung and incest and the pubs still close in the afternoon, and they burn incomers in big wicker statues, stuff like that.'

I thought this was a bit rich, coming from a transplanted Yorkshireman, where you're never more than a stone's throw away from a wuthering height or a dale or a moor or similar.

'Hark at Mr Metrosexual there,' said Jessamy, reappearing with a cup of instant coffee for herself, but none for me. On what I'd seen to date, she would go far in the garage business. 'The man who daren't go into a Starbuck's by himself.'

Duncan had the good grace to start to blush and while he was distracted, I made my pitch.

'So, you look after Armstrong for a month and I don't mind you doing the odd bit of mini-cabbing, or the occasional wedding.' Duncan had done weddings in the past, in parts of Essex where the old black cabs were a rarity now, which was ironic considering how many real London cab drivers lived out towards Southend and Clacton and commuted in to work every day. 'In return, you lend me a set of wheels. Any of those Mercs you've got queuing round the block will do.'

'You can't have any of them, Jessamy's not finished ringing them.'

I had thought that the practice of 'ringing', turning back a car's hodometer, the total mileage recorder, to make the car appear younger had all but disappeared since people started recording their mileages when they taxed their motors each year. Duncan's flotilla of Mercedes looked new enough not to need such cosmetic surgery and as far as I knew, the practice had not exactly been legalised and Duncan could lose his business if he got prosecuted under some piece of Fair Trading legislation, though how any of that could ever be quoted in respect of second-hand car dealers was always good for a laugh.

'Should you be teaching your young apprentice such dodgy techniques, o wise master?' I asked him.

'Don't know that it's illegal to ring the mileage *up*. Ringing it down, now that'd be different.'

'So you're putting fake miles *on* to these cars?'

'Yep,' he said proudly.

'You're not having a senior moment, are you,

Dunc? Been sniffing the old exhaust fumes too much?'

'Bugger off, you cheeky sod. They're for export, aren't they?'

'Oh well, that's all very clear then, isn't it?'

'To Malaysia.'

'Where else? Barking to Kuala Lumpur, well-known trade route.'

'Straight up, these Mercs are being shipped to Malaysia,' he paused for a beat to hit home his winning point, 'where there's a massive import tax on new luxury cars, but no tax on used, second-hand cars. So Jessamy puts thirty or forty thousand miles on the clock, the paperwork gets done and at the other end somebody rings back to the genuine mileage, or perhaps slightly less. It's good money for a morning's work and valuable training for young Jessy. See, you've learned something now, haven't you, smartarse?'

'No day is wasted, Duncan. Now, can we do a deal?'

'I suppose so. Got something that'll suit you down to the ground, but it's not here, it's round the corner in my overspill car park.'

'That'd be the station car park, wouldn't it? With a fake ticket on it?'

'Don't worry, you can take off the Disabled stickers. Jessamy, my love, go and get the courtesy car for young Mr Angel, would you? Keys are on the desk.'

'It'd better not be a Peugeot 206,' I warned him.

It was a Peugeot 206.

Chapter Two

Thankfully, Duncan had not asked why I needed a courtesy car to replace Armstrong. If I had let it slip that it was in order to get to *work*, I would never have been able to live it down, and still ended up with a lime green Peugeot 206, Europe's gay car of choice. I could have been honest with him and said that I needed something which was registered for the congestion charge, could be parked, possibly illegally, in Shepherd's Bush during daylight and which wouldn't be missed if it was towed away, nicked or just set on fire. But I've always found that being totally honest with Duncan never really paid a dividend. He was a rogue who only liked dealing with rogues. Everyone else was a civilian.

With the natural luck of the blissfully ignorant, he had suspected Amy was pregnant and he had also touched a nerve when he had mentioned the flat in Stuart Street, but I don't think I had shown any obvious weaknesses there. Still, it was something I would have to sort out — the flat, I mean. The other thing was months' away and now that Amy had made up her mind, I wouldn't have much further input into that.

In the meantime, I had other things to worry about, like my first day at work, so I headed up west, crossing the border from Holland Park into Shepherd's Bush about noon. I reckoned they should have got the doors open and the kettle on by now. They had better have for I was not in a mood to be messed with. I was, after all, sleeping with the new boss, so I deserved a bit of respect. I planned to show my face, all teeth and smiles, log into my expense account and go for lunch.

The first time I had seen the front door to R & B Investigations, it needed to be re-hung and a new lock put on after some local wannabe gangsters from the Shepherd's Bush Road mafia had decided to turn over the business. It wasn't Rudgard & Blugden then, of course, it was a two-bit operation run by an ex-copper called Albert Block who had taken a young and innocent Veronica Blugden under his wing. I suppose I did too, after I realised that she shouldn't really be roaming the streets alone without an electronic tag or a huge ball of string played out behind her so that she could find her way home.

Her first case, flying solo, was to find the wayward missing daughter of a minor Home Counties aristocrat, which I helped her to do with only slight damage to a vintage car museum along the way. Veronica came out of it with her own business, due to the sudden early retirement of Albert Block, and a new partner in the shape of Stella (Estelle) Rudgard, now no longer missing, but still pretty wayward. I had last seen Stella at her hen party at Gerry's club on Dean Street just prior to marriage to some eligible (i.e. rich) society bachelor. It was quite likely that Stella had not bothered coming back from her honeymoon in the Caribbean (all of it) and as she no longer needed a job, or to see Shepherd's Bush Green ever again, she had probably sold her half of the businesses to Amy for a snip. Certainly Amy would not have paid over the odds for it, she was too good a businesswoman for that.

I had one other slight connection with R & B Confidential Ivestigations Ltd. Only a few weeks ago I had been sort of responsible for one of their up-and-coming trainee enquiry agents, young Steffi Innocent, getting the push. It wasn't that Steffi had the effrontery to follow both Amy and me around, I could live with that, after all she was only trying to earn a crust. Nor did I really mind that she'd copied my *modus operandi* by swanning around in a delicensed London black cab, even if it was a TX1 and not a proper model like a Fairway or a 4FS. Well, that did rankle a bit, but what had really marked Steffi's cards was her psychotic hatred of, and violence towards, cats and one cat in particular – mine. For that, she had to burn.

I let my finger hover over the bell push/intercom as the thought stuck me that they somehow might hold this against me. It was, after all, an all-female detectives agency, or had been up until now. But then, the staff turnover in west London was horrendous and, anyway, they might never have noticed she was gone. I pressed away and got an answering buzz followed by a voice strained through a cheese grater.

'R & B Confidential. Yes?'

'It's Angel,' I said leaning in to the voice box, 'I think I'm expected.'

'Too right you are,' growled a voice I didn't recognise and then, more distant and muffled as if she was covering up the intercom: 'Ronnie! The

31

axeman cometh.'

I tried to work out who it could be. The last time I looked, the agency employed Stella, who was still in the Caribbean probably trying to crash Johnny Depp's hotel suite; Veronica, sometimes called Ronnie by the sensible shoes brigade; the infamous Steffi Innocent, who was far from innocent of a lot of things, and had been let go; and a Mrs Delacourt, the mum of a Brixton chum of mine, Crimson, who could have advertised dark Jamaican rum on calendars in her younger days, assuming they had calendars back then.

Whoever it was buzzed the lock so I could push the door open and start up the stairs. Unlike the bare boards that had creaked all the way up the last time I was there, my trainers struggled to find a grip in a new, thick pile carpet. There was a time when if you still had stair carpet in Shepherd's Bush it meant you were overdue for a burglary. No burglars here, though. They wouldn't dare, not with the guard dogs they employed these days.

They weren't dogs of course, not even in the sense Duncan the Drunken might have called them 'dogs'. Certainly not in that sense. They were both in their early twenties (and even as I thought that, I sighed) and both above-average height, slim and curved in all the right places. They were standing at the top of the staircase, blocking my route and for a split second, from below, I thought they were a couple of Ninja assassins, but it was just a trick of the angled spotlighting. They both wore black cotton trouser suits, almost but not quite matching, and black Victorian style ankle boots with spiky heels which Amy would have called 'so 2003'.

'We wanted to get a good look at the new boss,' one of them said, but I honestly couldn't tell which one. They were like twins and one of them was a ventriloquist.

I stopped three steps below them, my eyes levels with their waists and did a slow double-take, looking behind me to see if anyone else had come in.

'Not me, ladies, I'm just reporting for duty to Vonnie Blugden.'

'You are Angel, aren't you?' said the almost-twin on my left.

'Last time I looked,' I said and flashed my best smile.

The almost-twin on the right was reading my T-shirt, which said *My Other T-Shirt's A Paul Smith.*

'Who's Paul Smith?' she asked me and I knew it was her because I saw her lips move.

'A guy I steal T-shirts from. Is Veronica in?'

'She's expecting you,' one of them said and then they separated to let me pass.

'So were you two,' I smiled. 'Whoever you are.'

'I'm Lorna and she's Laura,' one of them said confusingly. 'We have a bet on to see which one of us you'll fire first.'

'Ladies, it's obvious you don't know me. If anyone's going to be fired around here, it's going to be me. I didn't get to where I am today by not firing wastrels who avoid working, are not team players, cheat on their expenses and take sickies at the drop of a hat.'

Which confused them long enough for me to stride up to Veronica's office and enter without knocking, saying, very loudly before the door closed behind me: 'Ronnie! Darlink! You look wonderful. You haven't changed a bit.'

That wasn't strictly true; she certainly looked better than when I first met her. In those days when people questioned whether she was eighteen or not, they were talking about her dress size not whether she was old enough to drink. A few years of being her own boss and an independent professional woman in west London (even if it was Shepherd's Bush) had made her diet regularly, exercise occasionally, spend a bit of cash on her clothes and a spot of make-up and, most importantly, start to look people in the eye – especially men – and even answer them back. Though she never had any problem in that department when it came to me.

'And neither have you,' she sighed from behind her desk where her attention was utterly fixed on a PC flat screen showing a game of Spider Solitaire. It comes free with Windows XP and is supposed to be addictive. I've seen Amy waste hours trying to get a game to come out and I pity the weak-willed who get so easily hooked on something so pointless when there's 3D Pinball in the same software package; and that takes real skill to get over 5,000,000 without tilting.

'Thank you,' I said genuinely. 'I'll take that as a compliment.'

'It wasn't meant as one, but you might as well. You won't get many round here.'

I pulled out the visitor's chair and straddled it so I was sitting across the desk from her. I put my elbows on the desk and my chin in my hands and peeped at her around the flatscreen.

34

'Try moving the Jack,' I offered.

'How did you know that?' she snapped, as I couldn't physically see the Spider Solitaire screen.

'Just a hunch. I have to say I noticed a slight chill in the air when I came in. The Thompson twins out there were decidedly frosty.'

'Who? Oh, Laura and Lorna. They're not twins,' Veronica drawled absentmindedly. 'They were friends of Steffi Innocent's and I suppose they think you were responsible for us having to let her go.'

'Now why would they think that?'

'I might have given them that impression,' she said airily, hitting the keyboard and ending the game. I had no idea if she had won, but then neither had she.

'And why would you do that to an old mate who just happens to be coming to work with you?'

'I never said I'd done it to an old mate. It was just better for team-building and corporate morale to have somebody outside the office to blame. I'd no idea you were coming here to work. You are coming here to work, aren't you?'

She put her head on one side so she could look me in the eyes. I realised something else that was new about her; apart from the self-confidence transplant, she had traded in her thick tortoise-shell glasses with lenses like the bottoms of Pepsi bottles for rimless hexagonals with sidepieces so fine you could hardly see them. The effect was as if she was wearing the sort of *pince-nez* a secret policeman in a sci-fi movie would. They suited her.

'I'm told I'm here to work and I suppose it's

35

only right we should share the load, now that I'm a partner.'

Veronica sat back in her chair and linked her fingers across her ample bosom. It was a mark of how far she'd come that she remained totally cool.

'I believe Stella sold her share of the business to Amy May, which makes *her* my partner, not you. Even though you're her ... *partner.*'

She almost lost it there and started blushing, but she had right on her side and, unfortunately for me, she knew it.

'Now part of the deal – and my solicitor hasn't had a chance to go through the fine print yet...'

'Stella still on the lash in the Caribbean?' I tried to distract her.

'I believe Mrs Wemyss-Wilkins is still on honeymoon.'

Wemyss-Wilkins? Blimey. What sort of bloodstock was Stella tapping into?

Veronica saw my reaction to the name and for a second she was tempted, I knew she was, to share some juicy bit of gossip about the newlyweds, knowing that Stella and I had once been quite close. Close in the sexual frenzy meaning of the word, that is. There was absolutely nothing platonic about our relationship.

But Veronica was aiming for the high ground.

'As I was saying, part of the contract as I understand it, was that you were taken on as an employee of R & B Investigations. I repeat the word *employee* because I know it is a strange one for you, possibly completely foreign to you.'

Oh she was good; she'd been rehearsing this.

'And as I don't seem to have any choice in the

36

matter until my solicitor has access to all the papers, I suppose we'll have to find you something to do, so for the probationary month, you'll understudy one of our graduate trainees.'

'That'll be the Thompson twins?'

'It will probably be Lorna, she's the more mature of the two, but I told you, they're not twins. And who's this Thompson? Neither of them are called Thompson.'

'Skip it. Are they on work experience from school?'

Veronica screwed up her nose at me in disgust.

'They're our graduate entries for this year. Stella herself went around several universities on a recruitment drive, which they called the "milk round" for some reason. Laura and Lorna interviewed the best out of hundreds of applicants.'

'Any of them male?'

'The majority, funnily enough.' She seemed genuinely surprised by that.

'But none of them were up to Stella's exacting standards?' I suggested innocently.

'I don't know about that, but you seem to forget that we are – were – an all-female enquiry agency. That is the bedrock of our success.'

'Don't you have trouble with sexual discrimination?' I asked, giving her an opening for one of several dozen punchlines.

She settled for: 'Not until you arrived.' I think she could have done better.

'And they both got Firsts,' she added.

'In what, Media Studies?'

'One in Chemistry and one in Russian Language and Literature, if you must know, Mister

Smartarse. Now I suppose we'd better get you started, if we can't put it off any longer.'

'I thought I'd ease myself in gently, you know, hang about the place for a while, see how it's done. Young Lorna can *mentor* me if you like. That's what it's called these days, isn't it? I mean, it's not as if I expected to take on my first case this afternoon. I realise I might need some on-the-job training, but we can start right after lunch. By the way, how exactly do we claim expenses?'

Veronica sighed loudly and pulled a sheet of paper from the stack of plastic filing trays on her desk.

'Let's not walk before we can crawl, shall we? You need to read this, then I'll go over the Health and Safety stuff, then I'll give you some case files to read, then I'll show you Stella's office, where you'll be based, and by then it'll probably be time to go home so why don't we say your first day proper will be tomorrow, when you can come in at nine and be suitably dressed. I think a suit and tie would be best, don't you?'

She proffered the sheet of paper and I began to read. She had printed it off a website and it was headed Association of British Investigators and there was a roundel logo featuring a Union Jack. 'Code of Ethics' it read, and there were eight basic commandments about performing all professional duties 'with the highest moral principles and never be guilty of conduct which will bring reproach upon the profession of private investigator'. Most of it was in that vein, the stinger being paragraph six: *To conduct all investigations within the bounds of legality, morality and professional ethics.* Bloody hell. I hope she wasn't expecting me to join a club which had rules like that.

'Ah, the good old Association of British Investigators,' I flannelled just to show off the research I had done on the internet. Dates back to the British Detective Association, formed in 1913, you know. I assumed you were all members.'

Actually, all the respectable detective agencies were and most probably did abide, more or less, by their code of ethics. There was still no licensing system for private detectives in Britain, although one had been talked about for ages and was said to be coming into effect later this year.

I had found that out on the web too, along with details of an American firm at infidelity.com which specialised in divorce, checking on spouses' movements, alimony reductions and premarital surveillance, whatever that was. Their logo was 'The Truth Starts Here' – alongside Mistrust I presumed, but you never knew, so I'd made a note of their number.

'Do you think you can live by that Code?' Veronica asked.

'Of course,' I smiled sweetly. 'Now about expense claims...'

'I'll need your P60,' she said.

'My what?'

'Your P60 from the Inland Revenue, for your tax code and PAYE office.'

I must have looked blank.

'Or a P47 from your last employers?'

'I'm sorry. What would that be in English?'

'Do you know your National Insurance number?'

'Not off the top of my head.'

'Do you *have* a National Insurance number?'

'Yes. Probably. Doesn't everyone?'

'Do you think you could get one by tomorrow morning?'

I felt like saying I could get her an Irish passport by tomorrow morning if she wanted one and wouldn't ask questions about it, but I bit my tongue. It's never good to get on the wrong side of the boss.

Not before you've actually started work, that is.

Veronica's lecture on Health and Safety took about thirty seconds. It was the usual what-to-do-in-case-of-a-fire and the exits are here, here and there. And in the event that we did escape a raging inferno, our official meeting point was on Shepherd's Bush Common, and not in the nearest boozer, which was ridiculous as the traffic would get you trying to cross the road before the flames did.

Next came the new (i.e. she'd just made it up) Policy on Loos. There were three in the building, one in what used to be a bathroom when the place was a house and which was just across the landing from Stella's office. That one was reserved for clients 'in distress' whatever that might mean, and was not for the use of the likes of me. There were two others – one off the kitchen and one on the ground floor near the back of the building. Both had Ladies signs on them, but they would allow me to use the one downstairs at the back. I got the impression they didn't like going there themselves.

The office was, naturally these days, a No Smoking work environment, the only exception being a client 'in distress'. What the hell did she do to them so that they had to run for the toilet fumbling their packet of twenty Bensons and cheap Cricket lighter?

Then I was shown where the kitchen was, although it hadn't moved since the last time I'd been there, and most importantly, introduced to 'the only really vital member of staff' – the kettle. I must have passed some sort of test by recognising the Brita water filter jug, correctly identifying a jar of instant coffee (Free Trade) and guessing that the semi-skimmed organic milk was stored in the white metal thing which was probably a fridge.

Consequently, I was supremely qualified to make the coffee as it was now officially lunchtime and, right on cue, there were the Thompson twins holding identical white mugs with a map of the Underground system printed on them. I had a pair of boxer shorts with the same design.

The mention of lunchtime cheered me up briefly, until I realised that all three of them had plastic containers of pasta salad and tubs of fruits of the forest yoghurt stashed in the fridge and it became clear that lunch was intended to be taken standing up there in the kitchen, using plastic cutlery.

I muttered something about leaving my lunch in the car and said I'd be back soon. Nobody seemed to mind me nipping out.

Veronica wasn't half in a snit when I returned, but it was her own fault for not telling me that at R & B, 'lunchtime' equalled 'lunch hour' and they

41

took that, rather pedantically I thought, to mean just the one hour. She obviously had no idea how long it took to prepare a fresh green Thai curry or that service was notoriously slow at lunchtimes round Shepherd's Bush. She also muttered something about a house rule of no alcohol during working hours, to which I questioned whether she had ever tried eating a green curry without a couple of cold Singha beers?

To make matters worse, Amy had phoned the office to see how my first day at work was going. Almost certainly, it was to check that I'd actually turned up for work. She hadn't tried my mobile – or maybe she had – because once again I'd forgotten to switch the damn thing on. Not only that, I remembered that I had left it in Armstrong's glove compartment.

'Amy wished us all well on your first day,' said Veronica smugly. 'Not you, but us. Said she hoped we could cope. Oh, and by the way, she gave me your National Insurance number and tax code.'

'How the hell did she know them?'

'It seems she was your last employer.'

'She was?'

'She's registered as a Limited Company.'

'She is?'

'Amy May Designs. You, it seems are on the company's books as chauffeur and bodyguard.'

'Bodyguard?' Then the penny dropped. 'She's been writing me off against tax, hasn't she?'

'I wonder how she worked out the depreciation,' Veronica giggled, then bit her lower lip to stop herself. 'Has it come as a bit of a shock?'

'No, no, of course not,' I lied.

As soon as I got home, I was demanding a pay rise, but before that I distracted myself by giving Stella's old office a good going-over before I moved in. I found nothing much of interest. There were no files, as Veronica had removed them to her office for safe keeping, no book of contacts, no Roladex of police informers, no packs of incriminating negatives, no bottle of bourbon in the bottom drawer of the desk (square bottle so it didn't roll around). The top drawer did have something in it: multi-coloured paper-clips linked in a chain, a few pencils and a pack of Post-It notes (pink ones), an unopened pack of 'barely there' black 7 denier stockings and opened packs of Golden Virginia rolling tobacco and giant green Rizla papers; just about everything you might need in an emergency except for petty cash slips or expense account forms. They had to be here somewhere and, dammit, I was a detective now so I should be able to find them.

'Lorna! Where are the petty cash forms?'

One of the Thompson twins put her head around the door.

'We each have a PDF template spread sheet on our laptops if we need to claim expenses,' she said – or at least that's what I thought she said. She had confused me with the 'if' we needed to claim.

'When we're out on a job we just email them in. Vonnie or Stella would OK them,' she nattered on, 'and then the cash would be paid directly into our bank accounts on the last Thursday of every month with our salaries. It's all part of the move to the paperless office.'

'The cashless office more like,' I muttered

43

darkly, then instantly cheered up.

'We get laptops?'

'Of course,' said Lorna as if I had asked if she had any spare change.

'And salaries?'

That freaked her.

She frowned as if it was a really difficult question and began to slide out of Stella's workspace.

'You're weird,' she said. 'By the way, I'm Laura, not Lorna. But you're still weird.'

Lorna came to see me shortly after, just as I was beginning to feel lonely, staring at the wall.

'It's too late to do much today now,' she said, 'as I've got to transcribe a report from one of our operatives who is in the field. Mrs Delacourt – she says she knows you.'

'Crimson's mum? Sure I know her. What's she up to?'

'She's working undercover down at Gatwick in one of the franchise catering outlets which has an unexplained cash flow problem. She sent you a message saying Good Luck.'

'That was nice of her.'

'She sent me a message as well: Don't Trust Him.'

'Charming.'

'So, anyway, I think we might as well start fresh tomorrow morning and I'll go over our current client list, the overall business plan and the diary for the next month. If you like, I can show you a couple of my current case files and you can shadow me over the rest of the week. Are you feeling alright? You've gone quite pale.'

'Tomorrow you said?'

'That's right. Nine o'clock. Vonnie said not to forget the suit and tie in case any clients call.'

I had just realised the full horror of my situation.

This going to work business; they expected me to do it every day.

Chapter Three

My excuse for being two hours late the next morning was a good one. I had been having my car specially equipped with the latest high-tech gear which no private eye could do without and I was going to suggest to 'management' that my little Peugeot become an official company car for use by all operatives. I was taking a gamble there, on the fact that Veronica and the Thompson twins couldn't drive, and I was right. I did this all in a loud voice, making sure Veronica heard that 'Amy thinks it's a brilliant idea'.

In fact Amy had said nothing of the sort, because I'd had the idea sitting in a traffic jam after I'd left Duncan's garage that morning. The only thing Amy had said when she'd eventually arrived home and put my little Peugeot in the shade of her Freelander out on the drive, was: 'New car? How gay is that?'

The evening went downhill fast, especially when she asked what was for dinner and I said I couldn't be expected to have anything ready – her coming home at all hours – now I had a full-time job to go to. She'd just flicked her hair at me and asked if the pressure of working for a living had made me forget the number for Domino's Piazzas.

There was no point in talking to her in that mood, so I took a malicious delight in drinking a huge glass of wine in front of her while she sipped a tonic water. I thought about lighting up a cigarette, but I wasn't that brave.

I had to go back over to Duncan's place, to get my mobile out of Armstrong's glove compartment. While I was there, I transferred some other gear from the boot to the Peugeot. A brown leather 'Flying Tigers' jacket which I'd picked up at a charity shop for eight quid and which had a crude map of the Pacific printed on the lining in case I ever got shot down there, a pair of waterproof work gloves, a torch and my toolkit along with my latest toy, a JCB impact wrench which ran off the cigarette lighter and made light work of loosening the nuts on a car wheel. It being impossible to change a punctured tyre these days with just physical strength, as the wheel nuts on new cars are factory tightened under tremendous pressure, my impact wrench had already paid for itself helping out several damsels in distress who were stuck at the roadside with a flat, not knowing where the spare wheel on their new 4 x 4 was let alone how to change it.

Duncan spotted me transferring things and muttered that the JGB wrench could seriously damage his emergency call-out trade, but just to show he was keeping abreast of modern technology himself, he offered to fit a new version of the Road Angel into the Peugeot while I was there. If I liked it, he would transfer it to Armstrong when I reclaimed him and all for £300, which was less than cost price.

Now nobody actually buys a Road Angel because of its fully integrated GPS navigational system. If you see a black London cab with one, you should start to worry. London cabbies should know where they are going by a combination of vast experience and genetic selection, not with the aid of satellite tracking. (Mind you, I can think of a few mini-cab drivers who could use one.)

It's their *other* function which makes them so popular, the in-built laser detection system which tells you when you are approaching a police speed trap or speed camera; even a lone traffic bobby hiding in the shrubbery with a 'hair dryer' laser gun. If you are near danger zone, a picture of a camera flashes up on the LED and the thing – no bigger than an alarm clock on your dashboard – beeps at you so you can slow down to the speed limit if you can remember what it was. They even work on the A1, the Great North Road going out of London, where the speed cameras are placed in pairs after every stretch of roadworks, so just when you think you've cleared one and it's safe to put your foot down, the back-up one hidden round the corner snaps you. The Road Angel will beep at you a second time, saving you three points on your licence and sixty quid a pop fine. They were a wonderful example of the democracy of modern technology. 'Whatever became available to the forces of law and order would soon enough be available, legally, to the rest of us. It was only a matter of time before the technologies cancelled themselves out and they stopped cluttering up the countryside with ugly yellow speed cameras, though for most Londoners, who only managed an average of eight miles per hour (the same speed as a Hansom cab in Sherlock Holmes' day), their appeal was limited.

But to keep Duncan happy, I said I would give it a try and I made it back to Shepherd's Bush without getting either lost, or a speeding ticket, just in time to put the kettle on.

Laura, or maybe Lorna, made a point of looking at her watch but Veronica said nothing when I took her a cup of coffee in the *Lion King* mug which I'd found in the kitchen and I'd guessed belonged to her. And they all warmed to me when I produced a box of a dozen Krispy Kreme doughnuts, which had been well worth the detour up to Enfield. Lorna said she had heard of them, but never tried one as she hardly ever shopped in Harrods.

I didn't tell her that they had escaped the Knightsbridge ghetto as far as Enfield to the north and Canary Wharf to the east and it was only a matter of time before they took over the world.

'Angels' kisses,' Lorna murmured dreamily as she chewed.

'I'm sorry...?' I said, knowing it would embarrass her – and it did.

'Oh – er – it's something my Nan used to say about her scones, they were like angels' kisses on the mouth.' She licked her finger ends as quickly as she could and hid her face in her coffee mug to give herself thinking time.

'So what's it like, living with a fashion guru?'

she said, valiantly trying to change the subject.

'You ought to ask Amy that,' I said, which produced a smile from Lorna and a cross between a laugh and a snort from Laura.

'Yeah, right.'

'I'm serious, that's what Amy calls me,' I said. 'She values my input.'

Though that's not what Amy had said when she'd started throwing up in the mornings.

'She needs a man's approval for her designs?' sneered Laura.

'Not approval, no. Just a man's distance. Someone who can tell her, objectively, where a new design will fit into the fashion circle of life. Make sure she's on the right lines if she wants to appeal to one of the Magnificent Seven dress senses.'

'Magnificent Seven?' said Lorna in a whisper. 'Wasn't there an old film called that?'

I bit my tongue and kept my temper. I was dealing with children here and I had to remember that.

'OK then, call them The Seven Pillars of Fashion Wisdom,' I tried but that brought blank looks from both of them. Maybe I would have got a response if those two had done media studies at university, though somehow I doubted it. I soldiered on.

'When it comes to style there are basically seven types of women at the top end of the market, and you always design for the top end even if you make the real money further down the market in the High Street chain stores.'

'Which category do we come in?' asked Lorna with a childlike glee.

With both of them wearing their Top Shop

black trouser suits, with only their shoe size to differentiate them, I didn't like to say they didn't register on the scale.

'It's more a question of what you aspire to,' I deflected them. 'For instance, there's the Feminine Charmer who favours floaty dresses under long cashmere cardigans in ice cream colours and has a Me-O-Mi tote bag to carry her laptop to work. Or there's the Princess of Casual, who wears Joie jeans and Manolo Blahnik shoes.'

'Expensive,' breathed Laura.

'It gets worse,' I said. 'And there's the clearly identified type known as The Chameleon, who can switch between the charming chic and the casual. She's always sophisticated, never ever shows too much flesh and has been known to pay two hundred quid for a pair of Damaris knickers.'

Lorna whistled softly.

'Next comes the Chloe Girl, the epitome of urban cool – confident, sexy, feminine and slightly bohemian. Slightly older, she graduates to the Eternal Chic model – sweaters by Christina Oxenberg, fringed brown suede knee-length boots, probably from Chloe in Sloane Street, and ponchos. They're big with Eternal Chic chick, especially the alpaca and wool rollnecks and you don't get change from a grand for those.'

'That's five,' said Laura as I sucked in another Krispy Kreme.

'Mustn't forget the Glamour Queen – usually a single mum these days who goes for baby pink chiffon dresses from Verace, white trousers by Ceila Wis and sandals by Tod. Prefers hand luggage from Shizue.

'But at the top of the fashion food chain is the Uber Fashionista, the Great White of clothes buying. Can be just about any age as long as she doesn't mind forking out £350 for a pair of Dior Homme jeans and £1,600 for a Chanel jacket. Underwear is optional, but where thought necessary is bound to be expensive.'

I sat back and licked my lips several times. Doughnuts make you do that, I've found.

The Thompson twins were looking at me with a mixture of awe and respect, but mostly respect.

'So what's Amy working on at the moment?' asked Laura. 'If it's not a trade secret, that is.'

'Hardly. She's doing what all the other designers are doing at the moment, deciding what you'll be wearing on the beach and in the clubs on Ibiza next summer.'

'Huh! Dream on,' Lorna snorted.

'Chance would be a fine thing,' chimed her twin, 'with our student loans to pay off over, like, the next hundred years or so.'

'Push for a pay rise,' I suggested helpfully. 'I bet Veronica's got you on minimum wage – like me.'

'We're not complaining,' Laura came in quickly, her eyes flicking downwards to the floor. 'For inexperienced graduate trainees, we're on a very attractive package here.'

There was a good five seconds of silence until I said:

'Veronica's standing right behind me, isn't she?'

Well how was I supposed to know it was already nearly lunchtime? And I certainly didn't consider the morning a write-off. After all, I had found my mobile phone, gained a Road Angel, pigged out on top quality doughnuts and bonded with my two young co-workers; quite a productive day so far.

I didn't know that Veronica had a meeting with a potential client up the West End, did I? And how could I have known about the other client who was coming into the office at three o'clock? I mean, there wasn't any reason why I should know or even be interested in that, except for the fact that I now worked there and would have been expected to sit in and support Laura (or Lorna) who would be 'taking the meeting'. Alright, it probably was my fault that I'd forgotten to put a suit and tie on.

Veronica stomped off down the stairs and I wondered if she was in a strop because I had not offered to drive her up West. I would have done, without hesitation, if I'd had Armstrong there (it was better than sitting in an office), but I wasn't driving the little Peugeot anywhere I might be seen by somebody who knew me. As a parting shot, yelled over her shoulder, she asked if I had got round to familiarising myself with the suppliers' catalogues? I shouted after her that I was right on it, then turned back to the Thompson twins.

'What catalogues?'

'That big pile of stuff on your desk,' said Laura.

The pile was nearly two feet high. Big, thick illustrated catalogues with names like *Spyware, Electronic Eyes, Safe and Secure, Viewed From Above, Out of Sight and Sound* (which I thought was a bit cheeky), as well as a couple of back copies of *Police Review* with pages tagged with pink Post-It stickers and a flyer from *PC World* opened at the digital camera page. There was even a sales brochure from a company which made temporary fencing, barbed wire and electric fences which might have been called *Razor Wire Monthly*.

'What am I supposed to do with this lot?'

'Read and inwardly digest,' said Laura snottily. 'You are now the R & B technical expert and you're expected to advise clients on all aspects of indoor, outdoor, sight and sound surveillance and security, not forgetting that we can order and install all equipment with total discretion for only a twenty-five per cent mark-up on list prices.'

'I don't know how to install that sort of stuff. I have trouble with my mobile phone.'

'Don't worry about that,' soothed Lorna, 'Veronica has a little man down near Clapham Junction who does all that. You've just got to *sound as* if you know what you're talking about. Think you can mug enough to impress a prospective client?'

Client? Veronica had mentioned one of those.

'The client Vonnie's gone up West to see?' I asked hopefully.

'No, the one who's coming here at three o'clock.'

I looked at my watch; 12.05 p.m.

'We'd better have an early lunch then,' I said, taking an executive decision. 'There's an ace Indian take-away over in Loftus Road near the football ground. We can take my car.'

The chances of being spotted there by anyone who knew me were remote. The take-away I had in mind, called simply *Asian Food,* was halfway between Queen's Park Rangers' football ground and the BBC Television Centre up Wood Lane. I didn't know any QPR fans and the BBC's security staff knew me as a taxi driver – or thought they did.

Laura was a bit wary of leaving the office un-womanned but then she didn't trust Lorna and me to be out on our own, so we all trooped downstairs and round the corner to where I'd parked the Peugeot.

'What a dinky little car,' said Lorna. 'What colour is that? Teal?'

'Too dark,' said Laura, 'it's more like cyan, though they probably call it 'Aqua' or 'Moonstone' or something like that.'

As I was now the firm's expert on all things mechanical, as well as an acknowledged authority on fashion, I decided to nip the argument in the bud.

'It's slime,' I said.

I was beginning to warm to Laura; she was the one with initiative, the one who knew where the can of air freshener was kept. It proved to be needed after the three of us demolished the selection of curries and Nan breads I'd bought, the girls hoovering them up like they weren't used to hot food at lunchtime, which was probably the case.

Then Laura offered to dispose of all the containers in a black bin bag and zip around the whole office squirting Ocean Breeze, or some such smell, so that the air was clear in time for our visitor.

With an hour to go I said I wanted some peace and quiet to study the pile of manuals and sales brochures, so I shut myself in Stella's office, dumped all the catalogues in a filing cabinet, turned on her computer, brought up Google and typed in 'security and surveillance'.

There, with the magic of the internet, were 1,230,000 results. I was spoilt for choice and with only a dozen or so clicks of the mouse I was an instant expert. I knew everything there was to know (well, maybe not everything) about snake-head cameras, infrared illuminators and low light outdoor motion detector cameras with PIR, whatever that was, which recorded black-and-white pictures at a range of seventy metres. The American sites were the most outrageous, as they usually are, and I found one who would sell me, mail order, one of those door-frame metal detectors you have to walk through at airports. I was tempted to order one and install it in Veronica's office without telling her, see how long it was before she realised where all those bells and buzzers were coming from. I could put it on its most sensitive setting so that even the wiring in her bra set it off. But then I realised time was marching on and I had better concentrate. Because I had put the word 'security' into the search engine, the American sites naturally assumed I wanted a gun and I was half-tempted to join in an auction for a 'like new' Colt Anaconda. I seriously wondered how I could resist spending £350 with a guy in Kansas, to buy a full modification kit which would 'transform' my '10/22' (which I guessed was some sort of rifle) into an AK47 Krinkov complete with silencer, but then I didn't know a licensed dealer within the USA he could ship it to. I did, however, learn that you could fit surveillance cameras into smoke detectors and air filters and that a top-selling item for one London company was their 'Nanny Cam', a digital camera embedded in a stuffed teddy bear. You gave your kid the teddy bear and it kept an eye on the nanny or the au pair girl. Particularly popular in Knightsbridge and Kensington I suspected.

And there were also a couple of useful phrases I could learn, which I might be able to slip into a conversation with suitable gravitas: 'Digital video surveillance is quickly becoming the Gold Standard for home and business security' was one, and 'We can duplicate your eyes, ears and memory' was another. I was sure they would come in handy when I chatted up my first client. There was only one thing left to research.

'Laura! Who the hell is this client I'm expecting?'

'Olivier Zaborski,' she shouted through Stella's closed door, or at least that was what it sounded like.

'And in English?' I yelled back.

She opened the door and said: 'It's Hungarian actually.'

'Really? Nice skirt.'

She had put make up on and changed the trouser suit for a black velvet mini-skirt with black tights and ankle boots with kitten heels and, of all things, a white satin TALtop – one of Amy's earlier models – drawn into a V-neck to emphasise her small but enthusiastic cleavage. She couldn't resist smoothing both her palms down the front of her thighs at the mention of her skirt. It's an automatic response with women, almost as if they don't trust a compliment from a man and they just have to check that they have remembered to put a skirt on.

'Thanks. Lorna and I thought it would create a better impression if one of us dressed up for the client.'

'Good thinking. It's best if you do. I haven't the legs for that skirt.'

'Oh my God, it's not too much tits and leg is it?'

'Can you have too much? I mean, this Oliver Zelig is a bloke, isn't he?'

'*Olivier,* not Oliver. And it's Zaborski not Zelig. You'd better stick to Mr Zaborski, though, and only speak if you're spoken to.'

'Is that because I forgot to wear a suit?'

'That's one reason, but you've only been here a day – and you haven't spent much of that actually in the office.'

'And you've been here – what, several months?'

'More than one, anyway,' she sulked.

'And you've never been allowed to meet a client on your own, have you?

She looked down at her shoes, her bottom lip jutting out to such an extent it must have hindered her view.

'Tell you what,' I said, 'as I haven't a fucking clue as to what I should do, why don't you meet and greet Mr Zangwill and I'll stand in the corner and baffle him with the technical stuff if need be.'

'Do you know anything about the technical stuff?' She sounded doubtful.

'I can blag it, no problem. Don't worry, I'll behave myself. I'm sure Ollie Zee will be so charmed by you he won't even notice I'm in the room.'

'You'd do that?'

'Sure I would.'

Then if anything went wrong and we lost the client, Veronica couldn't blame me and it wouldn't get back to Amy.

Laura let rip a great big, beautiful smile and I almost felt jealous of our unsuspecting client.

'And his name...' she started.

'Is Mr Zaborski. I know and I said I'd behave. What's he do, this Mr Zaborski?'

'He makes drugs.'

'I'm warming to him already.'

When Lorna said, straight-faced: 'They're drugs, but not as we'd know them,' I burst out laughing and I could see she thought I'd flipped. 'What? What?'

'You sound like Doctor McCoy in *Star Trek*, you know: "They're drugs, Jim but not as we know them".' No reaction. 'When they found a new species of alien, he would always say "It's life, Jim, but not as we know it".'

'I don't have a television,' she said, still dead-pan.

'And I should get out more, I know. So what kind of drugs does Mr Zaborski push?'

'He doesn't *push* anything, he *manufactures*, and they're pharmaceuticals, not drugs. Well, pharmaceuticals are drugs, I suppose, but you know what I mean.'

'Things like medephanol?' I asked, more in hope than expectation.

'What's that?'

'It's supposed to be better than caffeine or any known amphetamine. It was developed in France, during sleep pattern research.'

'I don't think...'

'Or things like Vigel?'

'What's that?'

'You've heard of Viagra?' She nodded. 'Well, men are from the planet Viagra, women are from Vigel. It's supposed to stimulate the female libido and intensify orgasms. It kicks in immediately and the effects last up to two hours. It tastes of peppermint – so I'm told.'

Which might explain why Amy always bought peppermint flavoured toothpaste.

'I don't know about any of them,' said Lorna, refusing to be flustered, 'and it's not really our concern what Mr Zaborski manufactures in his laboratories. As long as he doesn't test things on animals of course.'

'Of course. Does he?'

'No he doesn't, we checked – got him to sign a disclaimer before we agreed to see him. All he wants is advice on the security of his premises.'

'That would be his secret laboratories high atop a fortified private mountain in the Swiss Alps, would it?'

'They're on an industrial estate near Cambridge, actually.'

'That doesn't sound very interesting, does it?'

'He mostly manufactures Botox,' she said primly.

'Now *that* is interesting.'

Mr Zaborski was about thirty-five, tall and thin and had five o'clock shadow which he would never lose no matter how many times a day he shaved. At first I thought he must have arrived by motor bike, dressed as he was in a leather jacket and tight stonewashed jeans tucked into brown rigger boots. Then he took off his jacket and hung it over the back of his chair, to reveal the nerd beneath the would-be biker and at this point, his coolness rating nosedived. I didn't need to be sleeping with fashion diva Amy May to know that short-sleeved shirts should *never* be tucked into the trousers (unless it's a plain white t-shirt and you're gay). And wearing a tie (of any hue or material) with a short-sleeved shirt was definitely suspect, unless you were going to a CIA reunion or auditioning for a job as a white-faced clown or mime artist. The clincher, though, was having one of those springy metal hoop things which hold three ballpoint pens clipped to the shirt's breast pocket. That said big time nerd, but for the moment, he was the nerd we called The Client and he could do no wrong.

Except he did, right from the off. In true nerd fashion, he totally ignored Laura's short skirt and welcoming smile. Even worse, after shaking her hand in initial greeting, he ignored the rest of her and spent the entire meeting talking to me as if she wasn't there, despite my constant staring at her legs in the hope that he would get the message.

He spoke Hungarian with a pronounced American accent, so I had no trouble following his drift.

'Mr Rudgard, I have a lot of money.'

'Please to meet you, Mr Zaborski, but I'm not

60

Mr Rudgard.'

'I am so sorry, but I thought Miss Blugden was a woman.'

'She is. What were you saying about money?'

'This is Mr Angel,' said Laura with a faint hint of desperation. 'He's our lead technician. Miss Blugden is one of our principles.'

'Oh, I see,' he said, not convincing anyone.

'Do go on,' I encouraged, 'about the money.'

Laura flashed me a killer look, but Mr Zaborski didn't seem to mind.

'Well, I have a lot of money...'

'And therefore you expect the best,' I said, getting my toadying in first.

'Absolutely. So I don't really care how much it costs, within reason, as long as you find out how the botulinus is being stolen from my laboratory.'

'We will need to know details of your present security measures, staff clearance levels, vetting procedures and so on, as well as physical barriers and restraints imposed on a day-to-day basis.'

This was Laura speaking. I was gobsmacked.

'Excuse me, but did you just say botulinus, as in ... like *The Satan Bug?*'

'Good Lord, I haven't heard that expression in years, but I know what you mean. Yes, what we manufacture is essentially a botulinus toxin, which is highly lethal. But diluted to the part per billion we work with, we have a drug which is safe and which is at the cutting edge of cosmetic technology. My company's ethos is to disprove that old saw 'By fifty, everyone has the face they deserve'. That is just not acceptable these days.'

'George Orwell will be turning in his grave,' I

said and when he blanked me, I added: 'It was George Orwell who came up with that old saw as you put it, that by fifty everyone has the face they deserve.'

'Who was George Orwell?' he asked, and it wasn't a wind-up. He wasn't particularly interested but he was definitely not winding me up.

'A writer,' I said with heavy heart and the determination to double Mr Zaborski's bill.

'*The Satan Bug* you mentioned. That was a book wasn't it?'

'Yes it was – and a film, actually.'

'Did Orwell write that? I don't read many books.'

'One of his best,' I said confidently. 'You should look it up.'

I was going to suggest he also try *The Guns of Wigan Pier* and *South by Animal Farm* but I didn't want to push it. We hadn't seen his money yet.

'I will,' he said, but he didn't look like he was taking notes. 'Now where was I?'

'A safe drug, for use in cosmetic surgery,' said Lorna, who was taking notes, thank goodness, on a shorthand pad.

'Correct. Now let's get something out of the way, right up front. Our base product is indeed Botulinum Toxin A, the toxin produced by the anaerobic micro-organism *clostridium botulinum*. The disease botulism is also the same thing, caused by an infection of the organism, which produces the toxin. It is thought to be the most lethal toxin known to man and one unit of Botox is defined as the median lethal intraperitoneal dose in mice.'

'Jesus! It's a Weapon of Mouse Destruction,' I

muttered, unable to stop myself. Mr Zaborski didn't seem to notice, but Laura had to bite down on her ballpoint pen to stop herself giggling.

'The fatal dose in humans is about one microgram – that's one-millionth of a gram – but I'm talking about the raw stew of botulinus. The material we use is exceedingly dilute and we purify using chromatography and centrifugation before diluting again with WFI.'

The *Wrestling Federation of India?* But this time I checked myself.

'WFI?'

'Water for Injection, so the drug can be used in syringes. It costs about £18 a litre. And once diluted and packaged under sterile conditions, you have a perfectly safe drug – the drug which has been called "the penicillin of the twenty-first century".'

I realised I was in the presence of a man who believed his own sales brochures.

'So it cures diseases, does it?' I asked. 'I didn't know that. I thought it was only used in cosmetic surgery to make actresses and television presenters look younger. I thought that explained why most actresses can't move their faces properly.'

I got some sort of a reaction to that. Mr Zaborski consulted his wristwatch, three grand's worth of Breitling Cosmonaute with so many dials and numbers on the face, he could have been reading off the latitude, checking how much oxygen he had left or even telling the time. I suspected he was merely gauging how many more minutes of his valuable time it would take for me to be suitably impressed by him.

'Don't believe what you read in the cheap news-papers, Mr Blugden.' I ignored him using the wrong name – an old lawyer's trick used to rattle witnesses. 'Especially about Botox being the 'pretty poison'. It's been around since the 1970s to treat spasticity, eye distortions such as strabismus, and neck stiffness. It also calms spasms in vaginal muscles which make sex painful and they've even done sweat control studies with it in Germany.'

I let that one go, even though Zaborski paused for a beat as if expecting a cheap crack.

'So it does have many medical applications, but I admit that its use in cosmetic surgery has increased by three thousand per cent in the last five years. Which makes it big business.'

'And you're worried that someone is stealing it from your laboratory?' Laura suggested.

'At $300 a shot, too fucking right I'm worried.'

Olivier Zaborski was showing emotion at last.

Chapter Four

'So you had your first client meeting?' said Amy that evening. 'And only twenty-four hours on the job; I'm impressed. I assume Veronica was?'

'Was what?' I was concentrating on opening a bottle of Montepulciano to go with the spaghetti Amy was cooking. It was a pity she couldn't have any, it was one of her favourites.

'Impressed.'

'She was out at another meeting and didn't

64

come back until after we'd all knocked off.'

Gone to the pub round the corner was actually more accurate, but something told me not to mention that.

'But you left her a Client Meeting Report – a File Note with Action Points – didn't you?'

'Of course. Give me some credit.'

I made a mental note to ring Laura as soon as I could use a phone alone, and get her to type up her notes from the meeting.

'So what's your first case going to be, then, Mister Private Dick?'

'Client confidentiality prevents me from naming names and dishing the dirt, I'm afraid.'

'Oh go on, give us a laugh. Tell me what the case is and I'll buy you a trenchcoat and a fedora tomorrow.'

'Do Prada do trenchcoats?'

'Almost certainly. Now who was your client? A mysterious blonde wanting somebody tailed? A rich widow wanting somebody bumped off.'

'That would be against the Investigators' Code, which Veronica made me learn. I remember quite clearly it said: Rule 3 – no bumpings off, and I'm sure there's something in the small print about mysterious blondes.'

'You never had much luck with blondes, did you?' she bitched gently.

'Not real ones, and the one today was not so much blonde as fair-haired, sort of mousey. And anyway, it was a him not a her and a bit of a nerd, really. A chemist, who's into the Botox business. Supposed to be Hungarian but sounded more Harvard Business School, but didn't look old

65

enough to go there.'

'Not Olivier Zaborski?' she said casually, bashing to death a couple of cloves of garlic with the flat of knife on the chopping board.

'How did you know that? I thought I was supposed to be the detective.'

'Hungarian origins, Botox, chemist, eligible rich bachelor with awards as Young Businessman of the Year. Of course I've heard of Olivier Zaborski. So would you have if you read the business pages instead of just the TV Guide. He's also been papped at all the best places, with some very sweet ladies on his arm.'

I was sure Amy had invented the verb to be 'papped', just to make me ask what it meant, but rather than give her the satisfaction I had figured out that it must refer to the *paparazzi* who photographed celebrities major and minor as they emerged, blinking in the flashlights, from nightclubs and restaurants.

'He didn't strike me as a lad about town,' I said.

'Then read the gossip columns. He's shagged at least half the models I use on a regular basis.'

'Doesn't look the type,' I sulked. 'Looks more like a second-year chemistry student pretending he's going to California for a surfing summer. God knows what your models see in him.'

'Yes, that is a mystery,' Amy said sarcastically, splitting a chilli open and de-seeding it with a flick of her blade. 'What could women see in a young, successful entrepreneur worth about three million – pounds not dollars – who has access to unlimited quantities of a drug which makes you look like you're thirty until you're sixty and then no more than forty until you're dead and nobody cares? What could a man like that possibly offer a woman?'

There was no point in arguing with Amy when she was in this mood, especially when she had a knife in her hand.

'Well he only had eyes for me this afternoon. I'm his main man now, his security consultant, his confidential...'

'So what's his problem?' She slammed a tin of tomatoes and the can-opener down in front of me. 'Open them while you tell me; it's called multi-tasking. You can do it.'

'I can't betray client confidentiality,' I said, but my heart wasn't in it as I watched her rip up fresh basil leaves with her nails.

'I think you'll find I have a substantial stake in the firm, and therefore the firm's business is my business.'

'And so I'm your employee now, although I discover I already was on the books as your ... what was it? Bodyguard? Chauffer? Dogsbody?'

'I wrote you a good reference,' she said, avoiding eye contact.

'Can you wangle a pay rise for me?'

'Don't push it, but you'd better start being nice to the boss.'

'Sure, boss. It seems your man Zaborski has bought himself a laboratory out in the wilds of Cambridgeshire, where he manufactures his pretty poison on a commercial scale. I didn't quite understand the chemistry, but until it's diluted, it's a serious biohazard. You drop a glass of that stuff on the floor and you wipe out Western Europe, but

Mr Cosmetics says that he only deals in the watered-down item, and if you smashed a glassful of that, all you'd do would be put a permanent smile on the face of the local farmers. Anyhoo – he reckons somebody is siphoning off his profits by stealing the finished Botox and flogging it on the black market. Not that I knew there was a black market in the world of cosmetic surgery.'

'Where've you been?'

'Obviously in a land without vain women.'

'Watch it.'

'He said eighty-eight per cent of Botox users were women.'

'What about the other twelve per cent?'

'Not sure. He said something about medical uses, oh, and sweaty Germans. It cures Germans who sweat too much.'

'Just Germans?'

'It's a very smart drug.'

'If there were smart drugs, you'd have them on prescription. I do wish you'd pay more attention. Any chance of some free samples?'

'I'm going up to the lab tomorrow, I'll ask.'

She stopped stirring the spaghetti sauce and gave one of *those* looks.

'That wasn't the right answer.'

'I assumed you meant for my mother, as a Christmas present,' I recovered quickly, but I only managed to jump from the simmering sauce into the boiling water waiting for the spaghetti.

'Have you told your mother?'

'Told her what?' I said without thinking, but this working for a living was really exhausting.

'Told her she's going to be a grandmother.'

'I'm choosing my moment,' I said carefully.

The moment I was choosing was one which involved me being in another country at the time, preferably one on another continent, although some free samples of Botox might well cushion the blow, come to think of it.

'I don't know what you're scared of,' said Amy, pushing spaghetti fronds into the boiling water until they wilted.

'My mother hasn't accepted that she's not still in her thirties, or a dress size 12 and she still thinks there's an outside chance the Beatles will get back together. What odds on the survival of the messenger who tells her she's going to be a granny?'

'What about your father then?'

'He wouldn't tell her. He hasn't seen her for years. Actually...' I paused as if the idea had only just occurred to me, '...he *would* tell her. In fact, he might just get a kick out of telling her...'

'But that would mean you telling *him*,' Amy pointed out with that strange unworldly logic which all women have and which is so difficult to contradict.

'Yeah, well, I will. Next time I see him.' I caught her look. It was difficult to miss. 'It's just I haven't talked to him recently.'

'It's been about five years, hasn't it?'

'Has it? Doesn't time fly. I could have studied to become a doctor. Don't worry, he'll get in touch when he needs money, or bailing out, or a taxi to take him south of the river when it's raining.'

'I always thought you had parental issues.'

'I do not! *They* have issues about *being* parents, I just try and stay out of range.'

69

And then she did the worst thing she could. She narrowed her eyes and simply said hmmm, to which there was no possible comeback for the subject was now closed. When I raised my glass to her and said 'cheers', her eyes were slits.

Over dinner she brought up the subject of work again – as if I hadn't had enough of the subject during the day, when I was there.

'So what exactly will you be doing for Zaborski Industries Inc., or whatever name he trades under?'

'His company is something called Tyler Pharmaceuticals, or at least that's the place he's bought and where he's set up his chemistry set. It's out in the wilds of Cambridgeshire somewhere. That's where they mix up the Botox, which is a refined form of botulinus toxin, but the really nasty biological stew is fermented somewhere in Wales apparently. By the time it gets to Cambridgeshire, according to Mr Zaborski, it's a low-risk chemical which is the greatest thing since aspirin, a real boon to mankind and, of course, womankind, who are willing to pay $300 a pop to have a laugh-line removed or a wrinkle straightened out.'

'So what's his problem?'

'He's convinced somebody is stealing quantities of the drug from right under his nose, so he's hired me to conduct a complete risk assessment of his electronic surveillance procedures and fire-walls, both hardware and software, to improve our chances of detecting the perpetrator.'

'Have you *any* idea what you're talking about?' Amy asked with an envious glance at my wine glass.

'Not really,' I said. 'I think it boils down to me seeing if his CCTV system is working or not. I go up there, change a fuse or something, picture comes back on, I put in a whacking great bill. Alternatively, I recommend a completely new system which we install at a suitably high mark-up.'

'Do you have the first clue about security surveillance systems?'

'Absolutely. Digital video surveillance is quickly becoming the gold standard for home and business security. Plus, did you know you can fit a digital camera into the eye socket of a kid's teddy bear?'

'As a Nanny Cam?' she said casually. 'To keep an eye on the nanny? Lots of parents have them. You just don't know who you can trust these days. We might be thinking on those lines soon.'

'Well for sure Mr Zaborski doesn't know who he can trust...' I started, then the double-take kicked in.

'We might have to get a nanny?'

'It's one option we may have to consider if I'm going to keep working.'

'Or an au pair, we could get an au pair,' I said helpfully.

'Only if she's called Frau Blucher and comes with references from the Bader-Meinhof gang,' Amy said in a tone which suggested this conversation didn't have long to run.

'Swedes make good au pairs,' I tried.

'Too cold, too rational. Forget it. Put the idea out of your tiny mind and get back to how you're going to blag your way through a security system risk assessment tomorrow.'

71

'Is that what I'll be doing?' It sounded good, I must try and remember it. 'What about an Italian?'

'Too Catholic.'

'French?'

'Too well dressed.'

'A Luxemburger?'

'Too few to choose from. I tell you, it's Frau Blucher from Transylvania or nothing, but don't lose sleep over it. You won't be on the interviewing panel. You'll be too busy selling closed-circuit cameras and digital recorders and you'll probably have to go to some technical institute to get an HND in using a screwdriver so you can install them.'

'Ah, now there you're wrong, because I'm an executive now. Rudgard & Bludgen have a little man down at Clapham Junction that does all that technical stuff. I'm going to take him with me to Cambridge. He can be my underling. I've never had underlings before.'

'So you're on top of things are you? Got everything sorted, so that nothing can go wrong?'

'I reckon so,' I said confidently. 'I've researched the problem, motivated my staff, called in specialist help, listened to the client and upheld all the principles of the Association of British Investigators. Well, apart from the one about not gossiping about a client's business.'

She was quiet for nearly a minute; just biding her time. Then she said:

'So you've done nothing about contacting estate agents?'

There are bits of London around Clapham Junction where they could still film the old Ealing comedies without recourse to blue screens and CGI. If they did, they would probably find a bit part for Frank Lemarquand.

Frank's Spy Shop – that's what it was called – was a shabby little establishment opposite the Lavender Hill post office. Its windows looked as if they hadn't been de-grimed since the trains heading for Clapham Junction ran on steam and burned coal. These days, no one in the neighbourhood under fifty had even a folk memory of a steam train and no one under thirty would recognise a lump of coal if it came through their front window.

Inside, the shop had a counter and not much else. There was no sign of any stock, though being a spy shop, I guessed that it was well camouflaged. There was a single video camera set up on a tripod and pointed at the door. It was linked to an ancient thirty-inch television resting on a low wooden table and under that was a VCR, but a model which Hitachi hadn't made for many a year. There was a flashing red light on the camera and one on the console of the VCR as I stepped through the door and then the TV screen crackled into life and I was watching myself in the doorway and then walking over to the counter to press the electric doorbell taped there with the helpful instruction 'Press for Attention' printed in thick felt-tip on a square of corrugated cardboard.

I heard footsteps coming down wooden steps and behind the counter, a black darkroom curtain guarding a doorway was pulled aside to reveal a small, thin, bespectacled sixty-or-so-year-old man, hair slicked into place with gel and dapper in a brown three piece suit with a wide pinstripe that would have been the bestseller in branches of Next round about 1985, and still was a bestseller in the Wandsworth Oxfam shop.

'Mr Angel?' he said in an accent I didn't quite recognise.

'Mr Lemarquand?'

'Yes, and thank you for pronouncing it correctly. The locals round here say Lee-McKand.'

I took a guess.

'Channel Islands, isn't it? Jersey?'

'Close enough. Alderney, actually, a long time ago.'

'I've never been there.'

'You haven't missed much. Veronica Blugden said you'd be calling.' He made a point of looking at his wristwatch. 'I assumed she meant first thing.'

It was only 11 a.m., which meant Veronica had been on the ball, though I'd never said anything about starting work at dawn's early light.

'I'm sorry, Mr Lemarquand, the message should have been that we were due in Cambridge this afternoon. I thought we could maybe stop off at a country pub for some lunch first, get to know each other, if we're going to work together. I'm sorry if that message didn't get through.'

I gave him one of my best you-just-can't-get-the-staff shrugs and, out of the corner of my eye, saw myself doing it on closed circuit TV. I looked good.

'Fine by me, said the little man, 'I've booked out the whole day to R & B, so I'll fit in with

74

whatever you've arranged. It's your grand.'

'A grand? A day?' I blurted out, taken off guard. We were paying him £1,000 a day?

The shareholders would go berserk. I was probably a shareholder.

Frank Lemarquand took of his glasses, large round black-framed things, produced a handkerchief like a magician and began to polish the lenses.

'Plus V.A.T,' he said calmly. 'That's my standard call-out fee.'

'I'm sorry, I was looking for someone who knew about security systems, not a plumber.'

'Ha, ha, very droll, or it was the first time I heard it. You pay top whack, you get top service.'

'That hasn't exactly been my experience of life, Frank,' I soothed, 'but then again, I've hung around the fashion business for quite a while. Shall we hit the road?'

Given his daily rate, I made an executive decision that he should buy lunch.

'I've been ready since eight o'clock this morning,' he said prissily. 'I just need to lock up.'

He motioned me to follow him through the curtained doorway and up a flight of a dozen bare and unpainted stairs.

'We'll take my van,' he said without turning round. 'It will make a better impression on the client than that tatty old Peugeot of yours and it has all my kit in it.'

At the top of the stairs he paused before what looked like a standard Victorian wooden panel bedroom door, and then he palmed something from his trouser pocket no bigger than a key ring,

75

which is what I half expected it to be. He pressed it and there was a high-pitched beeping noise from somewhere and then the bedroom door slid sideways into the wall with a metallic rumble, like the doors of an old Otis lift.

I was determined not to give him the satisfaction of being impressed, but I couldn't help it. That upstairs room had more electronic gear than the bridge of the starship *Enterprise,* and it all seemed to work. On a round table in the centre of the room were six or seven small colour monitors showing pictures of the staircase we had just climbed, the empty shop downstairs, the pavement immediately outside the shop door, and then there were aerial views of the junctions of Lavender Hill with Falcon Road and Latchmere Road. There was even a monitor showing the side street round the back where I'd left my car. I had wondered how he had had known I drove a tatty old Peugeot.

'Give me a minute to set the alarm,' said Frank.

As he turned to look at me, my face appeared on one of the monitors wearing a 'how the fuck did he do that?' expression.

'The camera's in your glasses, isn't it?' I said trying to sound confident.

He took off the thick black frames and the monitor picture showed a piece of the floor.

'Amazing what you can do with fibre optics, isn't it? A pity it's only vision and not sound as well.'

I was just relieved he couldn't tell what I was thinking.

He pointed to the monitor showing my Peugeot.

'That's from a camera on the roof. It can give

76

you a good five minutes warning when a traffic warden's coming, but you'd better move it if we're going to be gone all day.'

I was touched by his concern.

'Don't worry about it, it's got a Disabled permit.'

I didn't tell him they came as standard with every car provided *by* Duncan the Drunken.

'I'm impressed,' he said.

That made two of us.

Frank Lemarquand drove a brand new, red Mercedes Sprinter, the back of the van crammed with equipment until the paint job squeaked. In the front, screwed to the dashboard, was a small terminal not yet standard issue on a Mercedes (though it is probably only a matter of time) with various scart and jackplug sockets which I presumed would connect to the laptop and digital recording gear in the rear,

'Are we wired for sound?' I asked as I snapped on the passenger side seat belt.

'Mostly for vision, actually,' said Frank. 'Sound is relatively easy. Pictures require the best technology and the most memory, especially low light work. Of course, technology comes at a price. In the old days I used to have a microwave oven in the back, for those hot snacks on cold nights when I'd be sitting in the dark somewhere freezing my arse off. Can't do that with all these sensitive computers, but you do get better results and faster. There's a low light camera fixed just above one of the headlights. Plug it in there,' he pointed to the socket box, 'and you get an instant picture on the computer in the back. I've got a

Kodak printer connected which can give you a photographic print, or plug the mobile phone in and you can email it anywhere.'

'So no hanging about for a week waiting for your holiday snaps to come back from the chemist's.'

'Most of my clients wouldn't want their stuff seen by some lab technician in Boots.'

Frank started the engine and pulled out into traffic, heading for Wandsworth Bridge.

'Confidential, price-sensitive commercial intelligence, I suppose,' I said to keep the conversation going.

'Hardly. Only about ten per cent of my surveillance work is for what you might call the business community. Twenty per cent is divorce or R.I.C. work.'

'What the hell is that?'

'Relationship-in-Crisis. Same as divorce work, 'cept they're not married. Who's cheating on whom; who's screwing around or playing away.'

'People still hire you for that?'

'You'd be surprised. I'm in the security business and people will always pay to feel secure. Mind you, they also pay when they're insecure. Pay a lot, actually. About half my customers are what you'd call stalkers. They want to watch people they have no right to be watching. If they could buy half the stuff I've got in this van, I'd be out of business. Thank God most of it is prohibited on eBay.'

I was learning a lot in this new job of mine, just confirming *my* Rule of Life number 48: Every day's a school day.

Olivier Zaborski had given me an address for

Tyler Pharmaceuticals as simply 'The Shelfords' near '11/11', which was his way of saying Junction 11 on the M11, the motorway which goes north out of London to nowhere in particular, bypassing Cambridge and then simply disappearing into the flat East Anglian landscape. I almost wished I had brought the Peugeot as at least it had GPS navigation, but Frank Lemarquand's super spy bus probably had its own personal satellite. In any case, Frank knew where the laboratory was as he did quite a lot of work in Cambridge and had even scouted out the place before now, on the off-chance that they may one day call for his services.

'The Shelfords' turned out to be two villages, Great and Little, divided by a railway line and a level crossing. In one of them was a pub called The Square and Compasses, where Frank bought me homemade steak and kidney pie with green beans and mashed potatoes and a pint of Greene King IPA and himself an egg salad sandwich and an orange juice. He winced physically at the small amount of change he got from a ten pound note and then loudly demanded a receipt. I was beginning to wonder what he spent his grand-a-day fees on. It certainly wasn't clothes, or his stomach. Maybe he just lived to spy and it all went on equipment.

'Who are we going to be seeing at the laboratory?' Frank asked as I ate.

'Zaborski's Director of Research, a Dr Mark Sanger. He'll show us around the place and the security system. We take notes, go away and write a report recommending lots of new cameras, alarms, locks which work on palm prints or

retina scans, even guard dogs to patrol the perimeter if we can get commission on them.'

Frank made a face at his sandwich.

'I don't do dogs, they're redundant, not to
mention stupid and easily distracted. Anyway,
they're bound to have some rent-a-dickhead
uniformed outfit providing perimeter security. I
thought the problem was goods getting *out,* not
thieves getting *in.*'

'Well, yes it is, if you put it like that,' I said.

'How would you put it?'

'Like that.'

'Good, so we concentrate on internal security,
not external, but we don't let on that we suspect
it's an inside job. Does Zaborski trust his man
Sanger?'

'I guess so, I mean he didn't say he didn't.' But
then, I hadn't actually asked him.

'Let's not rule anybody out until we've done a
check on the employees with Zaborski's personnel people. I presume you've got that in hand.'

It didn't sound like a question, so I just nodded
as I chewed and wondered if anyone back at the
office had thought of that.

'What say you distract this Dr Sanger? Keep
him busy, do a bit of schmoozing.'

'Schmoozing?'

'Chat him up, ask him about his groundbreaking
research; that always goes down well with science
types. Do you have a problem with being charming for an hour, while I give the place a good look?'

'No,' I said confidently, 'I can do charming.'

'Good,' he said, glad that I would be of some
use after all. 'While I'm doing that, you might

80

find a use for this.'

He palmed something from his pocket on to the table in front of me. I put down my pint so I could examine it.

It was a small plastic pouch about six centimetres by four, with a Velcro flap on which was embossed the words Micro Precision. A short metal chain attached it to a key ring. I undid the Velcro and used the keyring to pull out the shiny metal object on the other end. Even I recognised it as a small digital camera with a side lever to raise the tiny square viewfinder and a button on the top edge to open the shutter. One lever and one button; this was a camera even I could operate.

'Where did you get this, Frank? Second-hand sale at the CIA?'

Frank shook his head.

'The Gadget Shop, Heathrow. Ten quid. There's enough memory on it for about eight shots. Keep it at chest height and see if you can get pictures of the production line or wherever it is they think their leakage is occurring, but don't let anyone see you doing it.'

'This is to test their present system, right?'

'Yeah ... something like that.'

I wanted clarification on that point, but then my mobile rang and while I fumbled for it, Frank took my empty glass to the bar and ordered a refill. I was warming to him and when I answered my phone, I realised I might need him as a friend.

'Angel?' I didn't recognise the barking tone at first.

'Possibly.'

'Angel, where are you?' It was Veronica.

'Cambridge, of course.' Well, near enough.

'I've just had a call from a Dr Sanger at Tyler Pharmaceuticals. *He* had a call last night from Mr Zaborski, who said you'd be meeting him at the laboratory and he was wondering where you were. *I* was wondering where you were.'

'Just turning in to the gate now, Von. I shouldn't really be talking on the phone while I'm driving.'

'It doesn't *sound* as if you're driving.'

'That's because I've just pulled over so I can talk to you.'

Was there no way of pleasing the woman? My steak and kidney was starting to congeal.

'What time were you supposed to be there?'

'I don't think I actually specified a time...'

'Well, you should have, and you should have put it in the office diary so we can transfer it to your time sheets for when we invoice Mr Zaborski.'

Time sheets? What was she on about?

'Look, Veronica, if I'm supposed to be checking out their surveillance systems and security procedures, surely it's better if they don't know exactly when I'm arriving. See my point?'

'I suppose so,' she said sulkily.

'How did you get this number, Von?' I said to keep her on the defensive.

'Amy sent me an email this morning. She said to give you a message.'

'Go on, then,' I said wearily, knowing that it wouldn't be good news.

'She said that as you were in Cambridge, you should look up Symington and Sedgeley. You'd know what it means.'

I had a damn good idea. More work, more hassle and little thanks.

Somewhere there was a devil working overtime to keep my idle hands busy.

Chapter Five

If the back of Frank's van was the bridge of the *USS Enterprise,* then Zaborski's laboratory outdid *Deep Space Nine.* Not that you would have thought that from the outside, where it looked like any one of a thousand single storey brick and black glass factory units built in the late Nineties on an out-of-town green field site just before the big supermarkets started doing the same and gobbled up so much land that even the local planning authorities started taking notice. As far as I could see, there were only two other units sharing the industrial estate with Tyler Pharmaceuticals: a mail order photographic developing and printing company that probably wasn't long for this world now that digital was replacing chemical film for your holiday snaps, not to mention homemade porn of the 'readers' wives' variety; and an off-shoot of a multinational confectionary company which made the packets of mints you buy to cover up the fact you've had a cigarette. Even though it displayed no brand names or advertising hoarding, it didn't take a detective to work that one out. You could tell it was a sweet factory by the smell of spearmint coming off the place, plus the fact that the people on a tea break (in the car park, having a fag and then a mint) all wore white overalls and hair nets or those stupid white plastic trilbies, and then there was a great smear of crystallised sugar running down the wall under the air conditioning vent, as if a thousand incontinent owls had decided to target the side of the building.

Tyler Pharmaceuticals didn't smell of anything in particular, but then I wasn't too sure what a pharmaceutical production plant was supposed to smell like. Dr Mark Sanger, on the other hand, arrived to meet us in the foyer exuding the aroma of Burberry Brit For Men, and was thus, obviously, American, as everybody in Britain had long since acknowledged that Burberry in all its forms had been hi-jacked by the ubiquitous street gangs of young neds and sengas and was therefore terminally naff.

'Pleased to meet you, Mr Blugden,' he said, approaching with a hand outstretched like an Olympic fencer demonstrating the lunge position.

'It's Miss Blugden, actually,' I said, then the look on his face told me that this was not clarifying matters. 'Of Rudgard and Blugden, who sent me. My name's Angel. I was the one who met with Mr Zaborski yesterday.'

'Do you have a card?'

'No, I'm afraid I don't. I suppose I should have, shouldn't I?' His face fell even further. 'I'm new, you see.'

Frank came to the rescue.

'I'm Frank Lemarquand, Dr Sanger. Surveillance and security consultant.' He did have a card and he flicked one towards Sanger. 'Do you just have the two cameras covering the car park? And the one co-axial one here in the foyer?'

As he shook Frank's hand, Sanger's eyes flipped to the whiteshirted man sitting behind the reception desk, who had released the electronic lock so the doors could slide open and let us in. The man in the white shirt was middle-aged and squinted at us over the tops of his glasses. He also wore a blue polyester tie done up in a small tight knot. He gave Sanger a weary nod, and in that one gesture I knew he was an ex-policeman.

'I think that's the case,' said Sanger, trying to look unconcerned, 'but Peter Sutton here is our head of security and he'll give you the inside track.'

Clearly embarrassed at having his perfect cover as a harmless receptionist blown, the man in the shirt and tie lumbered out from behind the desk to join us.

Once again, Frank took the lead, offering his hand.

'Frank Lemarquand, Mr Sutton. Would that have been Chief Inspector Sutton?'

'It was just Inspector, and that was a while ago, in another life. What can we do for you gentlemen? I've been told to offer you our full co-operation, though I'm sure you'll find all our systems are in the optimum place and working properly.'

'Perhaps you could show me your central control panel while Dr Sanger gives my colleague the official tour?'

Frank was so polite and charming that I almost offered to show him the central control panel even though I didn't know what or where it was. The former Inspector Sutton raised an eyebrow in the direction of the white-coated Dr Sanger, who nodded his permission. Sutton then indicated that Frank should follow him down the corridor. By the afternoon tea break they'd be swapping war stories and getting on like a house on fire.

'Are you and your personnel all ex-law enforcement?' Sanger asked me and now I was sure he was American as his voice betrayed a distinctly Southern lilt.

'What you might call Special Forces,' I said with a straight face. 'Frank was an electronics specialist and I myself was in what you might call transportation logistics and domestic security.'

I had my hands in my jacket pockets and my fingers felt the outline of the miniscule camera Frank had made me slip on my key-ring. I supposed I had to start looking for something worth photographing. But first, I had to *schmooze*.

'You ain't from around these parts, are you?' I asked Dr Sanger, resisting like mad the urge to add 'stranger'.

'I guess the accent gave it away, huh?' he smiled.

Actually it was the plaid shirt, leather waistcoat, stonewashed Levis and the Cuban heel on what looked suspiciously like cowboy boots showing under his open white coat which gave it away. There was no way an English industrial chemist could look so cool. They would probably keep their lab coats buttoned up to the throat in case they got a chill from the air conditioning, like their mums told them.

'Which part of the States are you from?'

'North Carolina. I did my graduate work at

Raleigh-Durham, in the research and technology triangle. Have you heard of it?'

'Oh yes,' I lied. 'It's highly thought of.'

'The technological hub of the New South – that's what they call it.'

'So what brought you over here?' I asked as we walked.

'My speciality is vaccine production. Container calibration, filling specifications, purification, sterilization, dilution processes and procedures, dosage measurement, packaging. Things like that. Not exactly the cutting edge of medical science, but a vital part I like to think.'

'A boring job, but somebody's got to do it.'

'Absolutely; doctors and their patients have to have complete trust in the vaccine products they use. They need to be sure that they contain the right drug, totally free from impurities and at the right concentration.'

'At the right price?'

'Price does indeed come into it.'

'There being no such thing as a free face-lift?'

Sanger paused in mid-stride.

'I thought only people who worked in medicine were so cynical about it.'

'Not in this country. We have the National Health Service, so we're allowed. Mind you, I don't think you can get Botox on the NHS, at least not for cosmetic purposes.'

'I know, I know, it's the Cinderella end of the market to most people, but it's where the money is. I did all my research and training working with 'flu vaccines aimed at the elderly and the poor. But guess what? There's no profit in that, so the

American drugs companies all pulled out of flu vaccines and moved into the prettier poisons. All our flu vaccines supplies were contracted out overseas – a lot of them to Britain – where production costs are cheaper, and that leaves pharmaceutical companies in the US free to concentrate on higher profits from drugs for cosmetic treatments or for E.D.'

'E.D?' I had to ask.

'Erectile Disfunction. You know that Viagra is the fastest selling drug in the world?' I didn't, but I wasn't surprised. 'Well, now its got competition from things like Levitra, Cialis and Uprima and there's also a female version which will be on the market in about three years. That's called PT-141 at the moment and it's taken nasally. It's supposed to stimulate desire in women.'

'But not if they have a cold?'

He ignored that.

'That's where the big bucks are these days: drugs to make you look good and drugs to help you exploit your good looks. We're not curing anything any more; this is the medical school of 'fix it before it's broke'. The only disease we take seriously is age.'

'But the paycheck helps cushion the blow to your ethics?'

'Ethics? Before Zaborski bought this place, it used to make a drug for cancer treatment, supplying hospitals in India.'

'A more noble calling?'

Dr Sanger seemed to think about that, then he produced a plastic card from the pocket of his lab coat and swiped it through an electronic lock on the wall.

'Not really. The previous owners went bust after filing fake insurance claims when a consignment of product went missing at Heathrow. That's part of the problem with the pharmaceutical business; they're almost impossible to insure against theft, so we have to stop the theft happening.'

A sliding door with a thick glass middle panel hissed open and Sanger, suddenly cheered up, smiled at me.

'I say "we" have to stop the theft, but, of course, I really mean "you" now you're taking the Zaborski dollar.'

The actual factory floor bit of Tyler Pharmaceuticals was much smaller than I had thought it would be. Sanger had taken me through two airlocks into a corridor with one side made of strengthened glass floor-to-ceiling, the only sounds being the hiss of the doors and the bass riff hum of the air-conditioning, which added to the science fiction scenario in my mind. Naturally, therefore, I expected the inside of the building to be bigger than the exterior, but of course it wasn't. The room we could see into was only big enough for about three employees, though they did look the part by being dressed in white space suits complete with plastic see-through helmets. They moved like television puppets, with a slow, exaggerated sweeping of the arms as they worked at a conveyer belt, packing small vials of clear liquid into square plastic boxes.

'The space suits are just for show, really,' Sanger was saying, 'in case we get a surprise visit from the Health and Safety people. What those guys are handling is the finished product and pretty harmless. If they dropped a batch, they'd be more at risk from the glass splinters.'

I had automatically leaned backwards away from the glass wall when I had realised what the spacemen inside were handling and I wasn't totally reassured by Sanger's claim that the vials of liquid were 'pretty harmless', though that would be a good advertising slogan for it given its main use.

'Let me get this straight,' I said. 'If a bomb went off in that room, there might be a permanent smile put on the faces of everyone in East Anglia but we wouldn't actually wipe out civilisation as we know it. Correct?'

He thought about that, then answered: 'Yeah, that's a fair summary. This is the final packaging stage. Those vials are a set, measured dosage and the filling of the vials is purely mechanical, calibrated by computer. And of course everything is under sterile conditions. I wanted you to see this stage because it is just about the only part of the process where humans have any contact with the drug before it goes onto the market.'

'So what happens after this stage?'

'Plastic frame packaging to hold a hundred units of vaccine, each of them shrink-wrapped, branded and bar-coded electronically. Each consignment is logged into the distribution chain about a million times – has to be. Do you know how difficult it is to get insurance on pharmaceuticals in transit?'

'You've mentioned that before,' I said to prove

I was paying attention. 'So you're sure your Botox isn't going missing once it leaves here?'

'That's about the only thing I am sure of. Every drop of vaccine which is shipped out of here is accounted for as it leaves here, when it's in transit and when it gets to the wholesalers. That's when we get paid and after that it's someone else's problem. There's never been a suggestion that what we ship doesn't get to where we send it.'

Sanger leaned forward and rested his forehead against the glass wall, as if tying to cool his brain.

'I'm not even sure we're losing material at all. I just can't see how it could be done.'

'But Olivier Zaborski thinks it's happening.'

'Olivier doesn't *think* that, Olivier *knows* it, he just doesn't know *how* and until he finds out, we're all under suspicion.'

'How does he know he's being ripped off?'

'Olivier has a fond memory for every dollar bill he's ever handled and sorts his nickels and dimes into piles on the night stand when he goes to bed.'

'So he's careful with his money?'

Sanger must have noticed my eyes flicking around the corridor.

'Tight as a dog's ass, as we would say. Don't worry, there are no cameras in here and it's totally soundproof. We often have confidential conferences out here in the 'alley' as we call it.'

'Put a bench seat and some ashtrays down the side and you have a staff rest room,' I suggested.

'Ashtrays? Oh, I almost forgot – you're English. You still smoke in this country. This is a no-smoking facility and we don't employ any smokers as

91

far as I know.'

Pity. Mingling with the smokers at lunchtime, usually outside in the howling wind, was a tried and true method of hearing all the gossip about a place and would have been a major weapon in my private detective armoury. My only weapon, come to think of it.

'So if we haven't got any smokers to suspect, who can we blame?'

I wasn't sure I was asking questions approved by the Private Detectives Handbook (Beginners), but Sanger took pity on me.

'Like I say, Olivier counts the pennies. He knows to the centilitre how much raw toxin he gets for his money and exactly what the dilution rate should be. Consequently, he knows, or he thinks he knows, to the last drop how much vaccine he should have to sell at the end of the day. He's convinced there's excessive wastage somewhere here in this plant. That wastage doesn't show up on any of our calibration or checking systems, and believe me we've triple checked and more. So, that means either he's being short-changed when he buys the raw toxin from the facility in Wales, which is unlikely as he owns it, or the material is being siphoned off in the course of its dilution and the sterilisation process here.'

'But it *could* be an industrial accident? I mean, it could be down to a simple leak in the pipelines or spillage or something like that?'

What was I saying? We were talking about the stuff that caused botulism, stuff so deadly that in bulk they kept it in Wales, along with other dangerous things like male voice choirs and Methodism.

And here was I, speculating that some of it was slopping out of the test tubes and probably being hosed down the drain by the cleaners every night. Which could mean that the sewage system of rural Cambridgeshire was awash with the drug, producing some very attractive rats.

'We've checked,' said Sanger, 'and don't think the local environmental department haven't gone over us with a fine tooth-comb. We handle a safe product here but as soon as you mention you're dealing in *clostridium botulinum*, everybody gets edgy.'

'People are funny that way,' I conceded.

'But there was something else which convinced Olivier, a real clincher.'

I made an effort to put on my Interested face. Perhaps I ought to be taking notes.

'All the glass vials or syringe bodies we use are manufactured with our trademark. It's not a trademark like the McDonald Golden Arches or anything, just a minute circle indent almost invisible to the naked eye. Certainly our consumers wouldn't see it.'

Of course they wouldn't. Most Botox 'consumers' are strapped to an operating table looking up the eye of a needle, if they were conscious.

'So what's the point of it?'

'Quality control. All pharmaceuticals are randomly hauled in and analysed to make sure they live up to their specification.'

'Checking that they do exactly what is says on the tin?'

'Excuse me?'

'Skip it. Carry on.'

'It's a serious business. There was a shortage of Botox in Florida in 1997 and they had to ration supplies. Backstreet cosmetic surgeons have been known to offer cut-price Botox which has turned out to be a mixture of liquid paraffin and industrial grade silicone as used in furniture manufacturing. So there are checks, and we welcome them as a company because we have a good product and we want to protect our premium price.'

'Olivier' – as I was taking his money, I felt I was on first-name terms – 'mentioned $300 a shot.'

'At the retail end, sure. But that's cheap when you consider a surgical facelift can set you back £4,500 – that's pounds, not dollars – and blepharoplasty alone can cost £3,000.'

'Wow!' I let out a low whistle and looked suitably impressed, but then I had to ask: 'What the fuck is blepho-ar-whatsit?'

'That's eyelid reduction to me and you.'

'Sounds awful. Whatever happened to growing old gracefully?'

'That's reserved for people with no money; it's the one freedom guaranteed to the poor.'

'So what was this "clincher" you mentioned which persuaded Olivier he was being fiddled?'

'It was a report from one of these independent quality control checks. Said our product had come through with flying colours; perfectly safe, completely up to specification.'

'And this upset him?'

'Sure did. The checks had been done by a research institute in Paris. We don't sell in Paris. France is not one of our licensed territories.'

'So you're saying there's a black market in the stuff?'

'Something that makes you younger, sexier, more confident? Yeah, I reckon there could be a black market in something like that, don't you?'

We met up with Frank Lemarquand and the security man Sutton in what they called the control room, which was the size of a decent built-in wardrobe, the back wall comprising entirely of 12-inch black-and-white monitors in five rows of four. Most of the monitors were on, showing various interiors and exteriors of the plant. Only three showed people and movement: the packaging room with the three spacemen which Sanger and I had been looking into; an exterior where two guys were loading boxes into the back of a white Transit van; and a small laboratory with large glass containers rather like tea urns which were being scrutinised by a ghostly figure with a clipboard. Despite the shapeless white trouser suit and hairnet, giving the impression of medical 'scrubs', it was definitely a female figure.

'What's that?' I asked, prodding the screen with a finger.

'That's the final stage of the dilution process, where we take samples for testing. We call them the 'washings' and so that is known as the wash room,' said Sanger.

'These three cameras,' the ex-copper Sutton took over, 'cover the three areas where there is human involvement in the production process.' He indicated the three monitors showing movement: the loading bay, the packing area and the wash room. 'The rest of the process is more or less fully automated, with in-place cleaning, so there's no human involvement needed.'

I stared at each of the monitors in turn in the hope that they would give me a clue as to what I should ask next. I was even conscious of Sanger and Sutton looking at me expectantly. Pretty soon they would be shuffling their feet and coughing discreetly, maybe even looking at their watches. Let them wait; I had been put on the spot by professionals like Amy before now. What could these guys do to me?

Fortunately, Frank Lemarquand had some professional pride and was determined to uphold the private detectives' charter.

'You seem to have all the sensitive areas covered by cameras,' said Frank, 'even if from only one overhead angle.'

'Are you saying that's a gap in our security?' challenged Sutton, taking it personally.

'It's a gap in your field of vision,' Frank soothed. 'And my job is to plug all possible gaps. In that case, I'll be recommending at least one extra camera, perhaps two, to cover lower angles and the doorway.'

'You've got your job to do, your commission to earn,' said Sanger, 'and it's Olivier's money at the end of the day.'

'But..?' I prompted, because he sounded as if there was a 'but' on the way.

'Let me show you something.' Sanger leaned over the control keyboard for the monitors and flicked a switch to turn on the console microphone. 'Would Dr Quinn report to the common room please?' he intoned severely as everyone does when using a tannoy system. (Though just the opposite is true with a Karaoke microphone.)

Sanger straightened up and stuck out a finger at a monitor on the second row from the top, which so far had remained blank. Then the screen flickered into life and gave us a ghostly image of a white-suited figure walking towards and then underneath the camera, and then out of shot. It was like watching a trailer for *Britain's Most Haunted* if there was such a show. (And if there wasn't, there would be.)

'You've just seen Dr Quinn leave the wash room through an air lock. The surveillance camera is triggered the moment the inner door starts to open,' Sanger was saying and getting an approving nod from Frank. 'The camera records everyone who goes in there and comes out. Every time. The camera doesn't lie, so it's fairly obvious, isn't it?'

He was expecting me to say something, perhaps to acknowledge that I knew what he was on about. Fortunately, Frank had been paying attention.

'She's not carrying anything.'

'Exactly my point,' Sanger smiled at the old man. I felt like saying I would have got there in the end, but it seemed churlish. 'Nothing gets carried in – in case of contamination – but likewise, nothing gets brought out, so there is no way anyone who works in the wash room can remove bulk quantities of vaccine. The people who work the packaging end of things are under constant surveillance and if a packed load went missing it would show up on our computerised stock control system.'

'So there's no chance a box of this stuff could fall off the back of a lorry whilst in transit, so to speak?'

Which I thought was a good question, but Frank just looked at me with pity.

'It might,' said Sanger, 'but we'd know about it pretty quickly. We run a proof-of-delivery checking system which makes enduser certificates in the arms industry look like petty cash receipts.'

'So who has access to this wash room?' I didn't care what Frank thought, my questions were definitely getting better.

'Dr Quinn and Dr Bob Harvey are our senior chemists. You can meet them both now.'

'Is everyone here a doctor of something?'

Sanger allowed himself a smile.

'Pretty much. British PhDs are cheap labour these days.'

'You mean they can't get jobs in the US as easily as they used to?'

'Something like that. As for the packing area, which we call Dispatch, we have six or seven guys on our books – that right, Peter?'

Sutton, once a policeman, ever a policeman, snapped to attention.

'Six at the moment, Dr Sanger. All what you might call semiskilled, all live fairly locally, all with good references, which we insist upon, and they've all been through an advanced Criminal Records check.'

'I thought those were only for people likely to be working with children,' I said.

'That's what they're *mostly* intended for,' said Sutton, his face impassive.

'I can have their names and personnel files emailed to you if it's any help,' offered Sanger. Over his shoulder, I saw Frank nod his head ever so slightly.

'That would be very useful, thank you.'

There: I had taken an executive decision and it hadn't been very hard. I now had something I could delegate to Lorna, or Laura. This management business was a doddle.

'No problem. What's your confidential email address?'

'My *confidential* one?' I stalled. Over his shoulder I could see Frank's face break into a smirky grin.

'Well, we are talking confidential personnel files here.'

Dr Sanger clearly couldn't understand why I was hesitating. From the look he was giving me I would have put money on my personnel file having a staff appraisal something like 'when his IQ reaches 50, he should sell', if he'd been writing it.

I made a decisive show of getting my mobile out.

'I need to phone the office to secure the link, would you excuse me?'

'You'll have to go outside into the car park to use that,' chimed Sutton, wearing his Mr Security hat.

'In case it interferes with the equipment in here?' I asked, as if I cared.

'They use a jammer,' said Frank, at which both Sanger and Sutton looked impressed. 'I noticed that as soon as we came in.'

'Standard procedure,' said the American. 'All phone calls are automatically recorded and we jam all mobile signals inside the building. If you want a tip, go at least five yards out into the car park and you should be OK. When you've finished, Peter here will bring you to the common room to meet the others.'

I've been escorted out of many places by policemen, and ex-policemen, in my time but never through so many airlocks and sliding doors. I didn't know whether to mention this to Peter Sutton or not, but he had something he wanted to ask me.

'Has Frank Lemarquand been with your company long?'

'He's done work for us before,' I said carefully, 'and is well thought-of, but I couldn't say exactly how long he's worked for us. Is it important?'

'Shouldn't think so, it's just the name rings a bell somewhere. He's not local is he?'

'Well certainly not local to here,' I said, assuming he meant rural Cambridgeshire. 'His business is in Clapham.'

'But he's not a Cockney, is he? Not with a name like that.'

'I don't think anyone from Clapham is a Cockney, but you can't tell by the name. I know born-and-bred Cockneys called Patel and Gupta. Originally Frank's from Alderney.'

I only told him that to see if he knew where it was. He did.

'Channel Islands, of course!' His ex-policeman's eyes lit up. 'About five years ago, big fraud case involving the Royal Bank of Jersey or Guernsey or one of the islands. An unauthorised withdrawal of electronic funds, was how they put it, but the details were hushed up so no-one could copy the method. Mind you, these tax havens are naturally bloody secretive, aren't they? Somebody called Lemarquand did time for it though, I'm sure they did.'

'It's probably a dead common name in the Islands. Maybe everyone on Alderney is called Lemarquand, all that inbreeding.'

'You could be right there, but my memory's not wrong either. It'll niggle me will that.'

'I wouldn't worry too much as long as you don't give Frank your PIN number.'

The outside door hissed and I strode five paces out into the car park, and then another five, just to make sure I got a good signal to call the office.

I was fairly sure it was Laura who answered.

'Hi, it's Angel, what's our email address and why haven't I got any business cards saying I'm a detective?'

'Usually it's the initials of whoever you're emailing, at Rudgard and Blugden Investigations, then dot "co", dot "uk". Just the initials though – and all in lower case.'

'So the address is *rabbi.co. uk?*'

'R-A-B-I, not Rabbi,' she said indignantly, not detecting anything remotely funny. 'And actually, I'm wrong. It had to be changed to Rudgard and Blugden Confidential Investigations – that's R-A-B-C-I dot co dot uk, so it wouldn't be confused.'

'With Rabbi, like I said.'

'No, no, not that. It seems there's a Reserve Bank of India whatever that is, and a Royal Agricultural Benevolent Institute. And there's sure to be a Royal Artillery something-or-other.'

'You know, I'm really sorry I asked,' I said, 'though I'm only doing the client's bidding. The top man here down at the lab wants to send some personnel files through for us – you – to go through.'

'Looking for what?'

I had absolutely no idea.

'The usual things,' I said confidently. 'Do you know how to run an advanced Criminal Records search?'

'Oh yes,' she gloated. 'Veronica showed me how when I first started.'

'Then we can all sleep easier. Try that for starters, then credit checks and so on; you know, the full routine. And you might keep an eye out for any link, however tenuous, with Paris, or France, or things French.'

'Why's that then?' she said, betraying an Estuary English accent I hadn't noticed before.

'It's what we field operatives call a hunch. May be something, may be nothing.'

'So what's it like out in the field?' she said dreamily.

I glanced around the car park and over the surrounding fields.

'Pretty desolate. It's flat and bleak round here, and the wind comes straight from Russia, which they always blame for the high suicide rate.'

'Not that sort of field, you dipstick. Oh and by the way, you do have business cards, they arrived at lunchtime. Veronica got them done for you.'

I was quietly impressed.

'I'll pick them up in the morning. Now where do I get these emails sent to?'

'You can send them to yourself. That'll be *fma@rabci.co.uk*. What does the M stand for, by the way?'

'What?'

'It's on your business cards: Fitzroy M. Angel. I never knew Roy came from Fitzroy, that's rather cute.'

'Well it follows on.'

'What does?'

'The 'M' is Maclean, as in Fitzroy Maclean.'

'Who?'

'Sir Fitzroy Maclean. Top Man. The soldier, the war hero, the author.' No response. 'The Scotsman. Chief of the clan Maclean or something.' Still nothing. 'He wrote a famous book called *Eastern Approaches* about the war in Yugoslavia and Marshal Tito.'

'Who?'

'Skip it. All you need to know is that when I was born, my father was reading that book and it inspired him. He's very impressionable.'

'You must resent him for landing you with a name like that.'

'Not at all. I was lucky really. The next book he got out of the library was *Mein Kampf*.'

'Who's that by?'

'Oh, come on Laura, per-leese!'

'I'm Lorna.'

'Next time I ring, I'm asking for the other one, but you can ask Veronica something for me. Has Frank Lemarquand got any sort of criminal record?'

'I shouldn't think so...'

But I'd had enough of her. I punched the Off

button and reached automatically into the chest pocket of my jacket for the emergency packet of cigarettes I always keep there.

Even as I tugged the zip, I knew the pocket was empty. Well, not quite. My emergency box of matches stolen from Soho House was still there, but empty. I opened it up anyway to see the word 'No' written in black felt-tip on the cardboard drawer.

The stress just kept coming.

Dr Sanger introduced them as Dr Cassandra Quinn and Dr Robert Harvey.

Harvey looked like a gangling teenager who dressed as if he had lost a fight in an Oxfam shop, said 'Call me Bob' and offered me a sweaty palm to clasp.

Dr Quinn, whom I had only seen before in ghostly black-and-white on a CCTV monitor, turned out to be a small but striking redhead. Without her white lab hat, her hair, the colour of newly baked brandy snaps, tumbled halfway down her back. She didn't stand up, or offer to shake hands. She just about acknowledged my presence but gave the impression she'd be happier if I called her Doctor Quinn, if I had to address her at all, and ideally did that from another room. Which was a pity, as what they called the 'common room' was the only part of Tyler Pharmaceuticals where they seemed to have anywhere to sit down. Nothing simple, like plastic chairs around a formica-topped table, of course, as you would find in any other works canteen, but three lowslung leather settees and a coffee machine which offered 'chococappucino'.

'I've been sent here by Olivier Zaborski,' I announced once the introductions were over, not because I wanted to drop names or pull rank, but because I couldn't think of anything else.

Dr Bob Harvey raised his eyebrows at the mention of the big man's name. The redheaded Dr Quinn sucked in air over clenched teeth, and looked totally under-whelmed.

'For how long?' she asked.

'I have no idea,' I answered hoping my honesty would be disarming. 'My company is doing a thorough health check on your internal security systems, so you'll be seeing my colleague Frank and I roaming the grounds, getting in your hair and generally causing trouble for a couple of weeks at least.'

'You think Olivier will let you run up the bills for two weeks?'

'Cassie! Please!' Sanger flashed at her, but not with any real venom. She took it well.

'Oh please what? Please don't disrespect our noble leader, The Great Zaborski? The Bill Gates of the cosmetic drug industry? Those two didn't get where they are today by not counting every penny along the way. If you don't get results in three or four days, which is about Olivier's attention span, Olivier will forget where he put his cheque book. And you won't get results. You won't find how the Botox is going missing from this place, because it isn't happening. We are not losing product. Olivier's calculations are wrong, which everybody here knows but nobody dare tell him.'

'We don't *know* that Cassie, because we don't

know the full production costs, only Mr Zaborski does,' said Bob Harvey nervously, but I got the impression he was more frightened of his redheaded colleague than he was of the big boss.

'Bollocks. Olivier's arithmetic is crap, or at least very simplistic. He uses a simple dilution factor – let's say 100 to avoid giving away industrial secrets. In his little black book, one litre of pure toxin is diluted to make one hundred litres of vaccine. If he doesn't sell one hundred litres exactly, then his books don't balance and so he must be being ripped off. It's as simple as that to him. The great entrepreneur is too busy doing strategic thinking to ever consider that down here at the coal-face we might have to adjust dilution levels for quality control, and he doesn't allow enough for the purification and sterilisation process, and, of course, he assumes that he gets a full litre of toxin to start with.'

Cassandra Quinn saw me looking at her and decided to dumb it down a bit by leaning forward on the sofa until she was pointing her cleavage at me and then speaking slowly.

'Think of a pub,' she said, bringing it down to my level. 'The landlord gets a barrel of beer from the brewery and serves it through pumps on the bar. Now if the barrel contains 280 pints, you'd expect him to sell 280 pint glasses.'

'Two hundred and eighty-eight,' I said.

'Pardon?'

'There are 288 pints in a barrel, which is an actual Imperial unit measure of thirty-six gallons. Eight pints in a gallon. Eight times thirty-six equals 288, not 280. But you rarely get barrels in a pub cellar these days. There are either kegs or firkins or pins, which are smaller.'

I realised that the common room had gone quiet and everyone was looking at me.

'Whatever,' said Dr Quinn. 'The landlord buys a barrel from the brewery and everyone expects him to get 288 full, fresh pints out of it, with no waste. But in real life we know it doesn't happen that way and even the taxman makes allowances for waste, and spillage, and evaporation.'

I could have mentioned the scenario where Marie, down at *The Spice of Life*, always slipped me a free pint when the landlord wasn't looking, but it might have clouded her thinking. Still, that was probably covered by 'evaporation'.

'Now come on, Cassandra,' soothed Bob Harvey, 'we are working in a controlled environment. Our whole business is one of fine calculation and accurate measurement to the *nth* degree, we don't go sloshing beer into glasses.'

'No, we don't,' she came back strongly. 'If we did, then you'd hear the words "piss up" and "brewery" mentioned frequently in the context of "can't organize".'

I noticed that Dr Sanger was carefully staying out of this spat and Sutton, the security man, was perfecting his bored policeman face, eyes pointed up at the ceiling.

'Could I just say,' it was good old Frank acting as referee, 'that Mr Zaborski's production and accountancy methods are not at issue here. His security is and our job is to make sure his security systems are watertight. As I understand it, this plant deals in a highly toxic poison and therefore

107

even a suspected leakage must be taken seriously, whatever its monetary value.'

Whatever Frank was being paid, he was worth it. Come to think of it: what was I being paid?

'Let me assure you,' Dr Sanger tried to assure us, 'our raw material, *clostridium botulinum*, is fully controlled and supervised from a secure facility in Wales. It undergoes an automatic dilution process before it is transported and on its arrival here is diluted again, into a perfectly safe aseptic solution. We are not, repeat not, talking about a possible terrorist interest here.'

That was a relief as it had never occurred to me that we were.

'No, Mark, we're talking theft.' Cassie Quinn's voice was almost a growl. 'Olivier Zaborski thinks he's got a thief working here siphoning off his precious profits and if it is happening inside this plant, then it must be somebody with automatic access to the production line. Which means it's one of four people; and those four people are all sitting in this room right now.'

It was quite a dramatic little speech.

I wondered if I should be taking notes.

As Frank drove the Mercedes van out of the car park, he said:

'Well, that was embarrassing. I thought little Miss Marple back there was going to do our job for us.'

'Give her a length of rubber hose and I reckon she could beat a confession out of one of them.'

'I know people over Wandsworth way who'd pay good money to see that,' Frank grinned.

'I know people down the Tottenham Court Road who'd pay to have it done to them,' I replied and I wasn't kidding. 'So who do you think she suspects? The ex-copper?'

'There's a good chance he'd have to be in on things,' Frank mused, 'as he is in charge of the CCTV cameras.'

'Don't they have anyone monitoring the monitors?'

'Of course they don't. Machines are far cheaper than people. You just get someone who likes a bit of power, like an ex-copper, who's prepared to go through all the digital recordings. You'll never catch them red-handed, but you'll have them on record.'

'And Sutton's pretty thorough?'

'Sure he is, he's got fuck all else to do all day. And, fair play to them, their system is pretty damn near perfect. They have all the important angles covered with motion detectors on the cameras. I can't see how anyone could walk in there and out again with a jug full of dope without being spotted.'

'But Sutton could turn the cameras off, couldn't he? For however long it took?'

'He could, but he'd have to fiddle all the time clocks and logs recorded on their central computer, which would also record any power surge if he tried to do a black-out. I don't think he has those kind of smarts. He's ex-Plod, not a hacker and that's a hacker's job.'

'So if not him, who's our usual suspect?'

'Why are you asking me?'

Because there was no one else in the van, that

was why, but I wasn't going to admit that.

'You've seen far more situations like this than I have.'

'You mean people in high-value, security conscious scientific industries?'

'Exactly,' I said, not sure if he was winding me up or not. What I'd actually meant was people in a self-contained *work* environment. That was virgin territory to me.

'It's usually the boss,' said Frank nodding sagely to himself.

'Dr Sanger?'

'No, you prat, Zaborski?'

'Zaborski's stealing his own Botox?'

'No way. It's probably an accounting fiddle or he's trying to affect the share price or something. There is no theft, no leakage, no *evaporation* – I liked that one – from that plant. It's not possible. The best magician in the world couldn't get in and out of those airlocks without being seen. I told you, they've got a bloody good surveillance system there.'

'You're not going to tell them that?'

'Give me a break, this is good contract work for me. I should think we can spin it out for two weeks, maybe three with installation of all the new gear I'll recommend.'

'Which they don't need?'

'Not really, but these big business boys don't feel they've got value for money unless they spend a lot of money. And I'm happy to take some off them. A couple of weeks out here in the country air will do me just fine. Think they'd run to putting us up in a nice country pub or a hotel in Cambridge?'

'Veronica might have something to say about that,' I said, and just the mention of her name reminded me of something – something I had forgotten to do.

Frank was heading back to the M11 through the villages both called Shelford. We stopped for traffic lights at a small crossroads, opposite a thatched cottage painted blue. In its front garden was a wooden sign saying it was for sale and there was the name of the estate agent handling it: Symington & Sedgeley, and a Cambridge phone number.

So that's who they were. I had finally detected something.

I pulled out my mobile and turned it on. The display told me I had missed five calls and had three messages.

Frank almost swerved off the road as I shouted 'I'm doing it! I'm doing it!' and began to dial.

Chapter Six

The next morning I drove the Peugeot into Shepherd's Bush hoping to get in and out of the office before Veronica noticed me, but she must have come in especially early to catch me as she was already prowling around her office with the door open at nine-thirty.

She stood to attention as I tried to sneak by.

'Oh, so you do work here after all,' she boomed, showing that she had picked up sarcasm from a correspondence course during a postal strike.

'Veronica, I'm so glad I caught you; and by the way, that dress is a stunner. You really have lost weight, haven't you?'

Though she probably fought the urge, she couldn't resist smoothing the black woollen material over her hips and glancing downwards with a proud little smile. It's a natural, almost automatic female reaction, as if they expect to see all those shed pounds in a pile at their feet. Now she was distracted, it was time to strike.

'Did Lorna get some personnel files from Tyler Pharmaceuticals? They should have been emailed to me yesterday afternoon.'

'Laura is working on them now, though I don't want you to think she's employed as your personal assistant.'

'Has she found anything?'

'Give her a chance. She will do a proper internal report and you can pick it up on your computer,' she said primly.

'I have a computer?'

'All operatives are issued with a lap-top and a password.'

'A password, eh? How cool is that?'

Veronica consulted a Post-It note stuck to the screen of her desk computer.

'It's Poirot.'

'What is?'

'Your password into the office intranet. Laura and Lorna chose that between them.'

'Why Poirot?'

'Because he's a detective and he's old. Well, that's what the girls said.'

I filed that one away for future references and retribution rather than rising to the bait.

'I left some messages for you yesterday,' I said, all businesslike and professional.

'You did?'

Well, I'd meant to.

'Nobody's told me how to claim expenses yet and nobody's actually mentioned what my salary was going to be.'

'Put your expenses in at the end of the month. There's a programme on your lap-top called Housekeeping. It's all in there. If you use your own car.'

'Do we have a company car?'

'No, we don't. So if you use your own vehicle, and the engine size is less that 1600ccs, whatever that means, then we allow 40p a mile which is the Inland Revenue approved limit. All journeys and mileage have to be logged, any out-of-pocket expenses above five pounds have to be cleared in advance with either Stella or me, and as she's still out of the country, that means me. The same goes for all expenses for entertainment. You are allowed a subsistence allowance of £7.50 per day when working away from the office. You must have receipts for everything.'

I was already sorry I had asked, but Veronica was only pausing to draw breath.

'As for your salary, it was agreed that it would be set by the three principles of the agency. That's myself, Stella and, of course, Amy May.'

'"Would be"? As in "will be" – when Stella gets back?'

I was right to be suspicious.

'No, as in when your three months' probation period is complete.'

'Three months' probation period?'

'That's perfectly normal.'

'Without pay?'

'Ah, now that's *not* normal practice,' she conceded, 'but it was proposed by Amy in view of your lack of employment experience. I'm surprised she didn't mention that to you.'

'I'm not,' I said.

The night before, when I had eventually got back to Hampstead after rescuing the Peugeot from Clapham Junction and fighting my way through the West End traffic, Amy had already eaten and was lying with her feet up on the sofa sipping Ginger Ale and reading a book called *Spiritual Midwifery,* so I knew I would get little sympathy from her.

In the kitchen she had left out a box of eggs, a bunch of spring onions and a chunk of dry and crumbly Red Leicester (just how I like it), which was nice of her, but she had also hidden the cork-screw, which was not. So I made myself a four-egg omelette and opened a can of beer, taking it all through on a tray.

Amy was still reading and there was a CD playing – one of the new breed of 'lounge jazz' singers: the over-hyped crooning generation who reckoned they knew it all but couldn't point to New Orleans on a map and thought that Nat King Cole was something to do with the miners' strike. I don't know why she listened to such stuff, as it only seemed to put her in a bad mood. Maybe she was doing it for the well-being of the developing baby, though I could have made a good case for whale song having more passion in the beat.

There was no 'Had a nice day?' or 'Busy day at the office, dear?' Before I had got the first forkful to my mouth she waded straight in with: 'So what did Symington and Sedgeley have to offer?'

I sipped my beer to give myself thinking time.

'I'm seeing Mr Symington himself tomorrow, in Cambridge,' I said, exaggerating slightly. I had mentioned I was from a detective agency no more than five times when fixing up an appointment, so I ought to get to see *somebody* in their Cambridge office.

'Behave yourself and be polite. They're supposed to be a very posh agency.'

'I don't have to pretend we need servants' quarters or stables for the polo ponies, do I?'

'Just try and look as if we have money, that always works with estate agents. Wear a suit, take the Freelander if you must. Don't for God's sake turn up looking like a cab driver.'

'I've deposited Armstrong with Duncan for the duration,' I said, probably failing to keep the bitterness out my voice.

'Well, that's something, but think about the suit.'

'Don't worry, I'll positively exude money. After all, now I've got a job, we've got two incomes, haven't we?'

That was when she could have said something; a perfect opportunity, but did she?

Not a word.

I had thought about asking Veronica if she minded if I took an hour or so off to visit Symington and Sedgeley, estate agents to the nouveau riche, but now I knew I wasn't actually on the payroll and she wasn't paying for my time, I thought: sod it.

From Stella's old office I phoned Frank Lemarquand's mobile number to find out whether he had left Clapham yet, only for him to answer from the car park of Tyler Pharmaceuticals in Cambridge. He was probably getting paid by the hour, he was so keen.

I told him to keep up the good work and that I would join him later in the day, without being too time specific. As I was talking to him I noticed a small box which had been left on the desk and taped to its lid was a sample of my new business card. There was no logo or particular style to it and, frankly, I could have done better for three quid on one of those machines you find in train stations. One of the Thompson twins had probably knocked them up on her computer and had forgotten to put on the spell check.

Fiztry MacLean Angel
R &B Confidential Enquires

Fitzry!
I was working with idiots and they were the ones getting paid, but I decided not to show any more weakness in front of Veronica. I stuffed a few of the cards into my wallet and stuck my head round her door on my way out.

'I'm meeting Frank back up at the laboratory,'

116

I said confidently. 'Did you get my memo about him?'

'Er ...no. What memo?'

I put on a pained expression, as if I might bash my head against the door frame at any minute.

'About Frank. Has he got a criminal record? One of Zaborski's security men seems to think he has.'

'No,' Veronica said uncertainly. 'Nothing like that has ever come up before and we've used him for several years. I'm sure Stella would have done a thorough check.'

'It would just be nice to know who I'm working with,' I said haughtily and, having scrambled back up the moral high ground, I turned and scurried down the stairs before she thought to ask why I needed to drive out to the country again.

But face it, without a salary, fiddling the mileage expenses was going to be my only source of income.

I got the little slimeball of a Peugeot up to 70 mph on the M11, though it didn't much like it and even then, coaches and overloaded lorries were zipping by me with disdain. At one point, where the nearside lane had been cordoned off by warning cones for no obvious reason, the Road Angel on the dashboard beeped loudly and the display showed an icon of a movie camera. I slowed to the temporary limit of 50 mph and in the rear view mirror I saw the car behind get flashed by a speed camera hidden behind a Road Works sign. So at least one thing on the Peugeot worked.

Frank was sitting in the driving seat of his van

as I drove into the Tyler car park and pulled up beside him. He was drinking tea from a gunmetal Thermos flask and listening to something on earphones. I toyed with the thought of trying to guess Frank's taste in music, but only for as long as it took me to take four strides and rap on his window with my knuckles.

He put a finger to his lips before lowering the window. From inside the cab came a distinct whiff of onions. Maybe Frank did have a microwave in the back among all the other equipment, or one of George Foreman's lean, mean grilling machines. The one thing his superspy van did lack was a decent sound system, because he wasn't listening to music.

He took off the headphones and twisted one side so he could offer me an earpiece and I leaned against the van door feeling slightly ridiculous in case anyone spotted us.

'There's no one around,' he said, reading my mind again. 'It's lunchtime and none of the CCTV cameras come this far out into the car park – can you believe that?'

Reassured, I applied my left ear. It definitely wasn't music and for a moment I thought Frank must have been ringing one of those 0909 numbers on his hands-free mobile kit. People who do ring those chat lines looking for a 'Hot Housewife' or, more basically, 'Quick Relief', usually prefer to keep their hands free. (So I'm told.) If he was paying premium rate for his heavy breathing then he was getting his money's worth from what I could hear.

'Mmmm ... uh-huh ...oh, yes ... Mmm ... I'm

there already...'

I realised it was one half, the female half, of somebody else's phone call and the call was coming to an end if not a climax.

'Promise me you'll take care, my little bear. I love you, Misha. See you on Saturday. Unos, dos, tres, kiss kiss.'

That was followed by the unmistakable beeping noise and metallic clack as a mobile phone was switched off and closed, then something less obvious: a rustling of paper and a tearing sound as if something was being unwrapped followed by *click-scrape, click-scrape*. I smiled, partly at the blissful memories the sound produced but also at the fact that I realised before Frank did that we were eavesdropping on the sound of a cigarette lighter flicked into action and a deep, satisfying, sensual, very audible exhalation.

Now that was what I called an erotic phone call.

Frank tugged the earphones from me.

'Get in and I'll play back the whole thing.'

'Who was that?'

'Dr Cassandra Quinn, the one you fancy.'

'What do you mean the one I fancy?'

'That camera I gave you yesterday. The disk was full of shots of her or bits of her body.'

I had given Frank the camera on the way home and had totally forgotten about it. In fact I'd almost forgotten to use it, and couldn't quite remember what I was *supposed* to be taking pictures of, and so I had just snapped away without aiming and no one had seemed to notice me doing so.

As I opened the passenger door to climb in,

Frank had to move a sheet of greaseproof paper on which lay the remains of an open three-cheese-and-red-onion sandwich.

'Those pictures are proper stalker stuff if you ask me,' he said.

'Look who's talking,' I snorted. 'You're spending your lunch hour bugging her office listening in to her chatting to her Russian boyfriend.'

'Why do you think that?'

'Well it wasn't her mother she was talking to, was it?' I helped myself to half his sandwich. You don't smell the onions so much when you're eating them yourself.

'No, not that, you dork. How do you know he's Russian? We couldn't hear *him*.'

'Ah, faithful Watson, that's why I'm the detective. I've got business cards to prove it now as well.'

'No shit, Sherlock?' he said with a gleam in his eye.

'You've just been dying to say that, haven't you?'

'Since yesterday morning,' he nodded.

'Okay then, she called him "my little bear" and then "Misha". Now I'm not exactly fluent in Russian, but I know that 'Misha' is a diminutive of Mikhail or Michael and it also means a bear, but a friendly one, not the sort that can hold you off the ground with one paw and disembowel you with the other.'

'What do they call that sort of bear?'

'The dangerous sort.'

'Oh, right, that's really interesting, I'm glad I asked. And anyway, I have not bugged her office.' He showed the earphones to me and the lead which disappeared behind his seat and into the back of the van. 'This is a directional microphone pointed at her shiny new bright red VW Beetle, which is parked about thirty feet away. She's sitting in her car having her lunch as well, so I thought I'd give the equipment a warm-up.'

Despite myself, I turned my head thinking that Dr Quinn must be in the next parking space, but that was a Porsche Boxer – Sanger's probably – and then there were two other parked cars before I spotted the familiar upside-down jelly-mould shape which, despite modern tweakings, remained as distinctive as the day Hitler laid the foundation stone for the VW plant in Wolfsburg in 1938.

I had to take Frank's word that Cassandra Quinn was in there, and the fact that she was a safe distance away was comforting considering we were intruding on her love life by the sound of things.

'Where the hell is the microphone?' I asked, in between bites of Frank's sandwich.

'It's in the roof rack. It's not really directional unless you move the van, but she just happened to be parked directly in line. I couldn't really resist.'

I had wondered – briefly – why the van, with all that room inside, had needed a roof rack attachment, especially as the last thing you would carry on the roof was sensitive electronic equipment, but the idea of long-range microphones inside the tubular steel frame had never occurred to me.

'I guessed that was where it was. Obvious, really,' I said just to keep Frank in his place. 'So what did she say to lover boy? Play me the tape, but just the juicy bits. Women who wear starched white coats to work like to get down and dirty when they're off duty.'

'I'll playback the *disk*,' sneered Frank, watching his sandwich disappear. 'Nobody uses tape anymore.'

'I knew that,' I said, breathing red onion on him.

There wasn't much to Dr Quinn's lunchtime telephonic tryst. In fact, as far as phone sex went, some of the old Directory Enquiries operators (when there was a Directory Enquiries and when it was staffed by humans not machines) doing the night shift were better value once you got them chatting.

'I'm as well as can be expected, Big Boy, considering I haven't seen you for weeks and weeks... Yes, I know that... Can't wait, I really can't wait... Now don't you let them bully you, 'specially not that drunk pig captain... You've got to keep practicing... Next time it's a mid-tempo conjunto... And are you listening to the Irakere I gave you? You should. It's as good as sex... No, of course it isn't, but what's a girl to do? A lonely girl at that, miles from the nearest port and missing her homecoming lover?... Her big, cuddly, oh-so-huggable lover?... I know... I know you can't talk for long... Now that's just rude... But I like it... Mmm... uh-huh ... oh yes... Mmm.... I'm there already... Promise me you'll take care, my little bear... I love you Misha... See you on Saturday. Unos, dos, tres, kiss, kiss.'

'What do you make of that, then?' Frank asked me.

'Apart from the fact that she has the hots for a salsa-dancing Russian sailor and she'll be over him like a rash come Saturday night, absolutely nothing, my dear Watson.'

Frank stared straight ahead through the windscreen of the van, not wanting to have to ask.

'Where d'you get the salsa from?'

'She was talking about him practising a "midtempo conjunto" which is a form of classic Cuban salsa, and listening to *Irakere,* a salsa band sometimes known as The Rolling Stones of Cuba. Also, the "one, two, three, kiss, kiss" is the way Salsa dance teachers get their students to know each other better. Is there any tea left in that flask?'

'It's coffee,' Frank sulked.

'Even better. Thanks.' I helped myself.

'How come you know stuff like that?'

'Because the voices tell me it,' I held the flask's metal cup to my mouth to give my voice a Ghost Train echo and rolled my eyes. But Frank wasn't spooked so easily. 'And also because I used to earn a crust as a session musician and I used to play stuff like that about seven or eight years ago, before it became fashionable. In those days, most people didn't know their *son* from their *guaracha,* but Dr Quinn, it seems, does. We could have ourselves a suspect, Watson.'

'A suspect? Based on what? Her love of spic music and a Commie boyfriend?'

'I don't think Russia's still communist, Frank, and maybe you should get out more. But be that as it may, having a dubious taste in men and music is more than we've got on anyone else at Tyler Pharmaceuticals at the moment.'

'And that's enough in your book is it?'

'It's a start. Anyway, why is she hiding out here in the car park to phone lover boy?'

'Because her mobile won't work in there. I told you that yesterday; they use a signal jammer.'

'Don't they have land lines?'

'Maybe she doesn't like making personal calls on the company's phones.'

'Yeah, right. Nobody likes doing that do they?'

'Fair point,' he conceded, 'especially when the company keeps records of all out-going calls.'

'They do?' I thought that was a bit sneaky and I hoped Rudgard & Blugden didn't do it.

'Well, it's really nothing more than what BT does when it sends you your bill, but the company can run a programme highlighting any fre-quently-dialled numbers they don't recognise. It's mostly used for catching blokes phoning their bookmakers on the firm's time.'

'Is nothing sacred? What about overseas?'

'Of course, that's easy.'

'Can you go back over, say the last six months, and see if anyone's been phoning Paris?'

'Paris? Well I *could*, but I'm supposed to be measuring up for new security cameras in the packaging area. Of course, you could do that, now you've decided to come to work.'

'Well of course I'd love to, Frank, but I've got another job on: a very important meeting with a posh estate agent in Cambridge.'

'And that's a matter of life or death, is it?' he said cynically.

'Yes it is, Frank. Mine.'

Symington & Sedgeley didn't really occupy offices, they inhabited a large, detached Edward-ian villa on Hills Road which, with a fresh coat of paint, could probably have gone on their books for a cool million. It had two gates connected by a semi-circular driveway, parking for several large Audis and the odd Lexus, and was within a cricket ball's throw of the Perse School, which put it one of the poshest catchment areas for schools outside of downtown Windsor. And for your medical convenience, at one end of the long, tree-lined avenue, was Addenbrookes, a genuine five-star hospital where rumour had it the night nurses put chocolate mints on your pillow. Way down the other end of Hills Road, which you could just about see with binoculars, was the railway line, some outstandingly grotty pubs and a wide selection of kebab and video rental shops. That was where the real people lived.

In a way I was grateful that they didn't have an office in the middle of the city as the planners had, long ago, ripped the old heart out of the city and replaced it with a traffic flow system which did everything but flow. At any given time of the day you were likely to sit in a traffic jam for up to an hour and then suddenly find yourself in a Left Turn Only lane. If you did manage to get into second gear at any stage, you were buzzed by dozens of kamikaze cyclists, like starlings mobbing a kestrel. I had unfond memories of cyclists in Cambridge and was far too sober to deal with them today, what with so many other things on my mind, including why both Cambridge and Oxford, our two premier league university towns, were total pants when it came to traffic. It was incredible really, when you thought about the sort of people who paid council tax there. Enough little grey brain cells to split an atom before breakfast, cure cancer before lunch, deconstruct the latest postmodern Icelandic novel in the afternoon, and then knock off a couple of sonnets in any Finno-Ugrian language (actually, there aren't that many) before nipping down the pub to break a war-winning code over a game of skittles. Oxbridge may have produced some of the finest minds known to M16 and the KGB over the years, yet when it came to organising traffic flow and parking spaces, the words 'piss up' and 'brewery' were not in the same sentence.

The heavy front door of Symington & Sedgeley's house was open, held ajar by an old flat iron with a brass handle and porcelain handgrip. That and the door knocker, a chucky brass representation of a religious saint holding what looked like a quill pen in one hand and an axe in the other, would both fetch a decent price in an antique shop and in Hackney, they would have been lifted and away long before now. In Hampstead too, these days.

I guessed the sainted door knocker to be St Jude, whom I knew was the patron saint of lost causes – and probably estate agents too – but did not use him, as all I had to do was push lightly on the door to find myself in a cool square hallway, which was probably bloody freezing in winter. There was a wide polished wooden staircase going up through two right-angles to the first floor and in the alcove formed by it, there was a single 'work station' perfectly tailored to fit the space.

At the computer keyboard was a perfectly tailored middle-aged woman with swept-back blonde hair and a double string of real pearls around the throat of a high-necked and amply-filled grey cashmere sweater.

'You must be Mr Angel,' she said in a voice which had brought a hundred WI meetings to order. 'Mr Symington expected you at twelve.'

I glanced at my watch to find I was only thirty minutes late. My, but they were sticklers for punctuality out here in the country.

I dug one of my new business cards out of my wallet to impress her and she held it by the edges, between finger and thumb.

'I'm grateful Mr Symington can see me,' I said politely, flashing her my best smile and pronouncing the first syllable like she had "sim" not "sime".

'He has to leave for a luncheon at one o'clock, but I'll tell him you're here.'

She came out from behind her high-tech pillbox and walked by me so closely I could smell she was wearing Ormonde, from Ormonde Jayne of Mayfair, which they say is made with black hemlock. She wore a brown suede skirt which worked well on her figure, black opaque stockings and brown designer shoes with gold decoration and a medium heel. I didn't recognise the designer, but after years of living with Amy, I could guess the price.

Her heels clacked up the stairs and she knew I was watching her rear, so she didn't hurry. It was only when she had held out a hand to take my card that I guessed she was probably nearer sixty than fifty – Amy always said it was always the hands which gave women away – though you couldn't tell from her face. Perhaps she was a Botox customer, though it probably wasn't polite to ask.

Her legs disappeared from view somewhere on the first floor landing and she was gone for nearly five minutes, which I spent hopping from one foot to the other, trying to stave off boredom by looking for the CCTV cameras, but unless they were built in to the dark wood panelling or the ornately carved banister, there didn't seem to be any. There were no photographs of houses for sale to look at nor descriptions of properties written in estateagentese, which was usually good for a laugh. No one had attempted to sell me an investment mortgage or explain, in less than two hours, how I could reduce my monthly payments by taking out an 'Australian' mortgage. What sort of an estate agent's was this?

'If you'd like to come up,' came the cut-glass voice from above me, 'Mr Symington will see you straight away, but he doesn't have long.'

I trotted up the stairs, hoping that she meant the boss man had an office on the first floor and that she wasn't going to show me into a darkened bedroom where the old boy lay dying in his bed, determined to make one last sale before he shuffled off to that spacious property with spectacular views (inspection advised) in the sky.

Mr Symington was old and nowhere near as well preserved as his receptionist, and he did have an office, not a bedroom; but everything else was as weird as I had imagined.

'Thank you, Jane,' he said to the woman who held the door open for me, 'and please telephone the Masonic Lodge and tell them I'll be late. Do come in, Mr Angel, I'm Julius Symington.'

He was standing behind an antique oak desk on which someone might have written dispatches for the Crimean War and they could have used the quill pen and glass inkwell there to do so. There was no sign of a computer or even a telephone and apart from two leather-seated Captain's chairs the only other furniture in the room was a grandfather clock and a single, green metal filing cabinet.

I remembered Amy's instructions to be polite and look as if I had money. Hopefully, Mr Symington couldn't see the Peugeot from his window.

I stepped into the room, holding out my hand.

'It's good of you to see me, Mr Symington,' I said.

'No, it's good of you to come and see us,' he replied. 'How did you know we needed a detective? Oh dear, that really is a stupid question, isn't it? You must get that all the time.'

'I'm not sure I'm following you, Mr Symington,' I said, totally confused but taking the chair he offered.

'Well, of course you knew we needed a detective, you being a Psychic Detective agency. I mean, you would have seen it coming, wouldn't you?'

Chapter Seven

'So my wife didn't send you?'

'I've never met your wife,' I said, more out of habit than anything.

'And you're not a psychic detective?'

129

'I knew you were going to ask that. No, I'm sorry, I'm not.'

'But your card...'

Mr Symington reached into the top pocket of his tweed jacket and produced a pair of bifocals, then he took my card off the desk and held it under his nose.

'Oh, I'm so sorry, I thought it said 'Psychic' but it's 'Fitzy' or something. Is that your name?'

'It should be Fitzroy. Those cards are badly printed, shoddy workmanship I'm afraid.'

Mr Symington shook his head.

'Oh, how embarrassing. Fitzroy Maclean, eh? Like that soldier chappie?'

'Exactly.' At least the old boy wasn't totally bonkers.

Symington took off his spectacles and holstered them back in his top pocket, then made himself comfortable on the chair behind the desk.

'I do apologise, you must think you've walked into a mad house.'

As far as I knew, all estate agents were like this, but I tried to give the impression that I could take it all in my stride.

'Not at all, in my line of work, the unusual comes as standard.'

'I do admit that talking to a detective is quite out-of-the-ordinary for me, but you see, I was sort of expecting one to call today. It was my wife's idea, you understand. In fact she was quite insistent about it and she was the one who was going to arrange it.'

'Mr Symington, I came here looking to buy a house. That was my wife's idea and she was quite insistent about it. She thinks highly of the reputation of your firm.'

He picked up my card again and narrowed his eyes at it.

'I wish I could say the same, Mr...Angel. I'm afraid I've never heard of Rudgard and Blugden, though I used to know a Rudgard – Sir Drummond Rudgard in fact, ran a sort of classic car museum over in Hertfordshire.'

'Same family,' I said knowing it would impress him. 'Sir Drummond's daughter is the founding partner of the company.'

'Not little Estelle? She was a very pretty child and quite precocious, not to say downright cheeky as a youngster.' No change there, then. 'But didn't something happen to Rudgard's motor museum? I seem to remember reading something in the paper...'

'I believe it burned down, but it was insured.'

Very well insured as I remembered, but Mr Symington was not really listening.

'So little Estelle is a detective, eh? But not, it would seem, a psychic one.'

This wasn't helping me to put together a list of houses which Amy could find fault with, but if I walked out now and told her what had gone down, she would never believe me.

'No, I'm not a psychic detective, Mr Symington. I'm not even sure what one is and I've no idea why you think you need one.'

'I'm not sure I have, Mr Angel.' He consulted his watch. 'I know this is an imposition, but could you spare me a few minutes of your time?'

I'm waiting for you to sell me a house for an obscene

131

amount of money, you old buffer, I thought as I said: 'Of course. And if I can help in any way, I'm sure I can rearrange my schedule.'

It wasn't like I'd be losing earnings, as I wasn't being paid anything.

'Splendid. One second.'

He jumped to his feet and walked out on to the landing, leaning over it to shout instructions down to the work station built in under the stairs. I wondered if anyone had ever suggested an intercom to him.

'Mrs Bond? Mrs Bond? Ah, there you are. Would you ring the Masons for me and tell them I'm unavoidably delayed. You know, pressure of work, that sort of thing. And then would you be an absolute darling and bring us two of your special sandwiches and the usual? That's so kind of you, Jane. Thank you.'

Back at his desk he asked me if sandwiches 'would do?' as he was keeping me from my luncheon – and he did say 'luncheon'. I said a sandwich would be fine as long as it wasn't cheese and onion, and he smiled at that before launching into his story.

'Comberton Manor, The Limes, Balsham Old Rectory and The Old Rosemary Branch, are all properties which have been on our books longer than they should. They're all old properties of character but they have been modernised. Tastefully, mind you, all I'm saying is they are perfectly sound, comfortable family houses with a bit of ground each, which you could move into immediately.'

Maybe I had misjudged him. Maybe this was

132

his sales pitch and he wasn't mad at all.

'And none of them look remotely haunted.'

Maybe not.

It transpired that Mr Symington had a wife who had become bored with riding, hunting, shooting, fishing, taxidermy and all those other traditional country pursuits, like straining cheap agricultural diesel through an old pair of tights stuffed with charcoal to remove the red dye so it could be used in the Range Rover without fear of detection. Worse, she had become hooked on daytime television shows on property trading, home improvement 'make-overs' and garden design, and became convinced that with her new-found knowledge and natural talent, she could add value to some of the slower-moving properties on Symington & Sedgeley's books. They had to have a certain amount of class to begin with, of course, and a potential selling price of at least £750,000 to make it worth her while. Most would, naturally, be quite old. Brand new five bedroomed 'executive' homes with a jacuzzi but no garden, slammed up by speculative builders, sold for over three-quarters of a million as soon as they hit the market as long as there was parking for the bread-winning executive's Lexus and the Mitsubishi Warrior for the little woman to blitzkrieg her way down to the village shop. But the larger, older, 'properties of character' got the Mrs Symington treatment.

Nothing major, of course; certainly nothing structural. Just the odd, feminine touch to make them more welcoming to potential purchasers. Freshly cut flowers, the garden neatened, a log fire laid in the Inglenook (made with scrunched up pages of the *Daily Telegraph* because it burns so much better than the tabloid newspapers), the Aga polished, the pot pourri refreshed – that sort of thing.

And it had worked. Houses that were thought to be 'long sells' shifted without having to resort to 'downward incentives' on the asking price. Until this year, that is, when certain properties given the Mrs S homely treatment didn't move at all, bucking her winning trend. Not only were they not selling, there were few, if any, viewers for them.

Mrs S couldn't believe she had lost her touch and so had immediately come to the conclusion that all her fine tuning and tweaking of the atmosphere, as she called it, had been sabotaged. On closer inspection, she convinced herself that her suspicions were fully justified. In more than one house, things were not exactly as she had left them – and Mrs Symington was nothing if not *precise* about where she had left things.

Furniture had been moved slightly, internal doors left open, curtains closed when they should have been open; in one case, a vase of flowers broken in the hallway, and in another, a tastefully built log fire had been lit and burned to cold ash. Perhaps most bizarrely, the dining room of one property which had been empty for six months – and had never had a single potential purchaser round to view it – distinctly smelled of *curry*.

Mrs S remained totally perplexed by these strange happenings until, that is, she saw an interview with a professional clairvoyant one morning on breakfast TV.

(I had already formed the opinion that Mrs Symington watched far too much television.)

The answer was obvious – to her. The houses were haunted or at least acting as bed-and-breakfast stops for restless spirits passing through Cambridgeshire. And that being the case, what was needed was a psychic detective. What else?

What I needed by this time was a stiff drink and spookily enough, I got one right on cue. The woman Symington had called Mrs Bond entered without knocking, bearing a silver tray on which were two plates of sandwiches and two flutes of a sparkling gold liquid.

'We can at least give you a bite to eat whilst you waste your lunch hour listening to this tom-foolery,' Mr Symington said graciously.

The sandwiches were smoked salmon on granary bread and came with a wedge of lemon. The liquid was champagne. I was sure Tom wouldn't mind being fooled more often.

'Mrs Bond, you are a treasure. If I'm allowed to say such things these days.'

Mrs Bond smiled at us both and I swear the brown suede skirt was an inch higher above the knee than when she'd showed me upstairs.

'I hope you don't think we're dipsomaniacs here, Mr Angel,' chuckled the old boy as we both raised our glasses. 'I'm maintaining a tradition of the firm that the senior partners allow themselves just the one glass of bubbly a day.'

'An excellent tradition,' I said. 'Are the other senior partners joining us?'

'I certainly hope not, they're all dead!' The chuckle became a dirty laugh. 'And I really would

135

need a psychic detective then, wouldn't I?'

'You were about to tell me why your wife thought you needed one.'

'Ah yes, there was this damned television programme with a clairvoyant on who was talking about how psychic detectives not only helped the police in gruesome murder cases, but how they could use the same skills *predicting* hauntings. Point them at a house where some violence has occurred or at, say, an accident black spot patch of road where somebody has been killed in a car and the psychic detective can judge whether that place is going to be haunted at some point in the future.'

'And what's the good of that, then?' I asked between mouthfuls.

'Well it would ... well, I'm not terribly sure, actually,' he said thoughtfully.

'Apart from keeping Mrs Symington quiet?'

It was a cheeky thing to say, but I'd finished the sandwich and he had said that the firm's champagne tradition only extended to the one glass. And, frankly, I'd had enough of this. I had an Amy to go back to who would want to know why I'd spent the afternoon listening to a cock-and-bull ghost story about empty houses.

Empty houses which were for sale.

'I hope that didn't sound rude,' I added quickly.

'Not at all, Mr Angel. The truth never comes out rude.'

I didn't disillusion him on that one.

'It's just that I'm not – my agency is not – in the psychic business. We do, however, specialise in security and surveillance. I could look at these

136

houses for you and see if it would be possible to install some remote recording devices which could be triggered by any unusual movement. It needn't be expensive.'

'Could you record psychic movement – ectoplasm, poltergeists, that sort of thing?'

He leaned forward clutching his glass with both hands so fervently I thought a refill might just be on the cards.

'Are any of the houses built on old Indian graveyards?'

'Good Lord, no.'

'Then I don't think so. We normally only detect human activity. Though, of course, if we can rule *that* out, then Mrs Symington may well be on to something.'

He closed his eyes for a second, then they snapped open as if he was inspired.

'I see where you're going with this, young man.'

'You do?'

'Yes, and it's an excellent plan. I'm being supportive of my good lady wife ... that's what you have to be these days, isn't it? Supportive, I mean. No matter how dotty the old dear's getting. I'm employing a respectable private detective agency, not some charlatan out of the *Psychic News'* classified ads. More than that, an agency with family connections to the Rudgards of Hertfordshire. That'll impress her. And if you find nothing, we can say she was right all along. By which time, hopefully, she'll have forgotten all about this business and taken up macrame or Tai Chi or something similar. Excellent, most excellent. You said not expensive.'

'I would have to see the houses in order to cost the equipment, time and labour, so forth. But I could get you an accurate estimate pretty quickly.'

Just as soon as I'd persuaded Frank to do a bit of electronic surveillance on the side.

'And your time? How much do you charge?'

I had no idea.

'A hundred a day plus expenses,' I said, but only because I'd heard James Garner say it dozens of times on reruns of *The Rockford Files*, though he was talking dollars not pounds sterling.

'Perfectly acceptable,' he smiled.

Damn.

'But as this is such a sensitive case, and one which might not do the agency's reputation much good, I think we should keep this arrangement ... discreet.'

'Absolutely, my boy, it wouldn't do Symington & Sedgeley any good if people heard we were *ghosthunting*. When can you start?'

'Well, I could look at the houses this afternoon.'

'And so you shall. Mrs Bond has copies of the property details and can tell you where they are. In fact, she'll drive you there – she knows the country round here like the back of her hand –and she can pick up the keys for you from my great-nephew.'

'I think the fewer people who are involved the better,' I cautioned.

'I quite agree. Don't worry about Mrs Bond, you can trust her with your life and it's perfectly normal for her to be showing clients around. You can pretend to be a prospective house buyer.'

His little eyes lit up at the brilliance of his own idea.

'But I *am* a prospective house buyer. That's why I came in here,' I explained slowly.

'Oh, I'm sure we can get round to that. Mrs Bond can take down your particulars as she drives you round our problem properties. Actually, they're not problems except for Mrs Symington. They're all perfectly good houses which will sell in time.'

I decided just to go with the flow.

'And who's this great-nephew?'

'Devon Sedgeley, a very *junior* partner in the firm.' So, no champagne for him, then. 'Who works out of our Shelford office. All the properties in question are on his portfolio: he's supposed to be in charge of selling them, but, frankly, he has too many interests other than work and I'm certainly not going to involve him in our little agreement.'

Agreement? I wasn't quite sure what I had agreed to, but he had agreed to pay me for it; which raised another problem.

'Your mentioning the Shelford office reminds me. I am duty bound by the Private Investigators Code of Ethics to warn you of any potential conflicts of interest.' I almost got to my feet and put my hand on my heart when I said this. 'I don't think there will be a conflict but I have to tell you that I am officially on another case in the Shelford area.'

'But you don't see a problem?' he asked anxiously.

'Not ethically, but it might look odd in other ways.'

'Other ways?'

'I was thinking, to put it bluntly, of how my office was going to invoice your firm for my time when I'm supposed to be here doing another job. It might look a bit odd.'

Mr Symington scratched his chin and thought about this. But not for long.

'An invoice might not look very good on our books, to be honest, as this is something I'm doing for Mrs Symington, who isn't actually employed by the firm.' He straightened his back and looked me firmly in the eyes. 'I think the best thing would be to dispense with invoices completely and let me give you a personal cheque. Would that impinge on your Code of Ethics?'

'I'd have to check the small print, but I don't think so. If you could make it out to F.M. Angel, that would be fine.'

'Ah yes, Fitzroy Maclean. Your parents must have held him in high regard to name you after him.'

'Something like that,' I agreed.

Mrs Bond agreed to show me the houses on Mrs Symington's 'most haunted' list, though I don't think the poor woman had any choice. She handed me four sheets of particulars, photocopied on to Symingron & Sedgeley headed notepaper, and told me to wait by the front door whilst she 'brought the car round' from the back of the house. I was rather glad of that, as she didn't seem to be the type to be impressed with a clapped-out Peugeot 206.

The For Sale particulars were written in the usual estate agentese but without the usual spelling mistakes, and all had basic directions keyed in to a map showing their proximity to Stansted Airport and to Audley End station, a plus point for commuters to London. There was no way these houses were being marketed at local farm labourers, if there were any left in Cambridgeshire, unless they had £750K stashed under the hayrick somewhere.

Two of the houses were in villages due east of Cambridge, and two of them due west. From their digital photographs, all looked substantial properties standing in their own grounds in 'delightfully private, rural settings'. I pushed the sheets back into the plastic folder Mrs Bond had provided so they would be nice and neat when Amy read them that evening and congratulated me on a job well done.

Then Mrs Bond drove round the corner and I was so glad we were taking her car instead of mine. I'd never been in a British racing green Aston Martin DB7 before.

'Nice car,' I said, snuggling into the leather seat. 'Is it yours?'

'It is now,' she said through clenched teeth. 'It was my husband's before the divorce. He used to call it his "babe magnet".'

'Hence the divorce,' I said.

'Hey! You really are a detective, aren't you?' she said without a smile. 'I also got the house, the villa in Spain, half his shares, all his jewellery, three Purdey shotguns and his wardrobe.'

'What did he get?' I had to ask.

'He got to live.'

She had put on some Gaultier sunglasses and

looked so stern I was impressed enough not to mess about when I got into the car. Now, as the V12 engine worked its way up through the automatic gearbox, I was prepared to be as quiet as a very impressed church mouse, especially as her foot was on the accelerator and I wasn't sure if the DB7 had a passenger airbag.

'Well, it's a very nice car,' I said trying to be soothing, rather than patronising. 'They say you are always the 'custodian' of an Aston Martin, not the owner.'

'So are you the *custodian* of that garish Peugeot 206?'

She'd seen it.

'More the *victim* really, but it comes in handy for covert surveillance sometimes.'

'Hah! I would spot you in an instant in that thing.'

'You probably would, but would you think the driver of *that* was any sort of threat to you? And would you remember the car or the driver ten seconds after seeing it?'

She made a so-so gesture with her head.

'I suppose the answer would be no to both questions.'

'Whereas, I would certainly remember *you* and this car – and not just because of the car.'

She thought about that and I was sure she was eyeing me out of the side of her glasses.

'If you're going to give me compliments, you'd better call me Jane.'

'Bond ... Jane Bond,' I breathed quietly.

'Don't ever say that again,' she said firmly.

Although the houses we were to visit were to the west and east, we headed south first, down to the Symington & Sedgeley satellite office in Great Shelford to collect the keys. It would have taken me the best part of half-an-hour to thread my way through the Cambridge traffic in the Peugeot, but in the Aston it seemed as if cars and lorries parted before us and every traffic light, even temporary ones, had to be on green by law.

For the blinking of an eye we were on the M11 – on at one junction and off the next. It was no more than three miles but I watched fascinated as the speedometer rose steadily. Mrs Bond read my mind.

'Top speed is supposed to be 165 mph, but the best I've managed is 120 without running into one of those bloody speed cameras.'

'I could sell you a little device which sits on the dashboard and warns you when a camera is coming up,' I offered, thinking that the Road Angel would be of more use in the Aston than in my borrowed slime bucket.

'Is it legal, and if so, how much?'

'Yes, and £500.'

She gripped the steering wheel even tighter, flexing the muscles in her arms.

'No can do,' she said. 'I may have got all his stuff, but my bastard ex-husband made sure he kept the cash he'd squirreled away. That's why I have to work for a living.'

'Life's a bitch like that, isn't it?' I agreed with her.

And then we were braking as we entered the village, sweeping majestically by the pub where

143

Frank and I had eaten the day before, finally slowing outside a small pink cottage which I must have driven by twice without realising it was an estate agents' office.

Mrs Bond parked on double yellow lines, killed the engine and took the keys with her as she climbed out, making no attempt to stop her skirt riding up but then there was no aesthetic reason why she should – no reason at all.

'You stay here,' she said.

'I'm under cover, am I?'

'Not really,' she shrugged. 'It's just I don't think you're quite ready for Devon yet.'

Then she closed the Aston's door and click-clacked her heels across the pavement to the pink house/office which had the name of the firm engraved in an arc across both ground floor sash windows, a bit like an old pub would have 'Saloon' and 'Snug' embossed.

I contorted myself so I could climb into the driver's seat and sat with my hands on the wheel, playing the sound of that famous engine over in my head and wishing the former Mr Bond had got the manual version so I could play at shifting up and down and, of course, utilizing the red button in the knob of the gear stick which operated the ejector seat. I did wonder, briefly, why she had warned me about Devon when we were in the middle of Cambridgeshire, then I remembered that was the name of Julius Symington's great nephew. I knew someone else called Devon – Devon Black – who ran a British style pub in New York. He'd been named by mad Anglophile parents and was rumoured to have a sister called Somerset.

Just as I was cornering at 100 mph with tyres screaming to avoid Goldfinger's henchmen in an old Mercedes saloon, one of them tapped on the window with a set of keys.

'Mrs Bond held the door open as I clambered out shamefaced with far less grace than she had. She said nothing, just handed me a set of keys and for a blissful moment, I was turning back towards the steering column. Then I realised they were house keys, four sets all crammed on to a Symington & Sedgeley plastic key ring.

I started to walk round the back of the Aston to the passenger door, not looking at her, keeping my eyes on the ground and hoping I wasn't blushing too much. And then suddenly, from the direction of the pink office came the most outrageously camp voice shouting:

'Oh go on, Jane, let him drive if he's old enough!'

I snapped my head up, targeting the voice, only to be distracted by Mrs Bond hissing loudly: 'Get in, we're leaving quick.'

'Don't we get introduced to the Toy Boy, then?' came the voice, even louder than before, and as I scuttled around the Aston I couldn't resist taking a look at our heckler.

He was youngish, certainly under thirty; short and slightly plump and had his hair shaved to the skull, though that wasn't unusual these days. He was wearing a double-breasted suit, which certainly wasn't unusual for an estate agent, standing with the jacket open, his hands in his trouser pockets. But instead of a striped shirt and sensible tie, he was wearing a t-shirt, which was unusual, as was the design on the t-shirt: a full-size head-and-shoulders image of Audrey Hepburn, complete with cigarette holder, in the classic pose from *Breakfast At Tiffany's*.

The V12 engine hummed into life as I pulled the passenger door open and Mrs Bond had the Aston rolling as soon as my backside hit leather, but just before I slammed my door, I could swear I heard the sing-song playground chant of 'Janey's got a toy boy; Janey's got...'

My blushes at being caught play driving the Aston were nothing compared to the crimson tide rising up Mrs Bond's neck and face.

We were almost out of the village before I managed to click my seat belt in place. I hadn't thought it wise to say anything until I was secure

'So that was Devon?'

'You'd better believe it,' she said, then relaxed, almost slowing to within 20 mph of the speed limit. 'But I'm glad you saw that, otherwise you wouldn't have believed me if I'd told you.'

'The black sheep of the family firm, huh?'

'Let's just say he has issues, lots of issues. And affectations – plenty of them, too. Oh, and a few obsessions.'

'The sainted Audrey being one? I noticed the T-shirt.'

'One of many. His favourite is one which just says *I love your funny face*. God knows what the clients think.'

'You let him near clients?'

'We can't really avoid it. He's the senior Sedgeley left in the firm and Mr Julius thought that putting him out here in the Shelford office would be a sort of damage limitation. It seems to have calmed him down a bit. We've had far fewer complaints in the last year, though he did cause a bit of a stir sending out Audrey Hepburn Christmas cards for the firm. Not to mention the Audrey calendar and posters on his wall; he's even got one of a portrait of her made out of Lego bricks, but at least we've stopped him playing *Moon River* in the office. His work has actually improved since he came out here and he's shifting a fair number of properties, though not the four we're looking at. They're all on his management portfolio, but he hasn't even shown anyone round for the last six months.'

'He's not frightened of ghosts, is he?'

'He certainly haunts my dreams,' she said quietly.

'You haven't got a thing about him being gay, have you? I'm only guessing about that, of course.'

'No I do not have any sort of *thing* about some-body being gay,' she scolded me. 'I have a son who is gay. Devon just plays at being the big drama queen to shock the locals. He likes pretending to be the only gay in the village, though you wouldn't catch him in any of the gay pubs in Cambridge. The camp act lets him get away with being a small-minded bully who was spoiled rotten as a child. *That's* what I've got against Devon. He's a pillock.'

'Oh well, that's alright then,' I said.

Neither The Old Rectory at Balsham, nor The Limes in the wonderfully-named village of Six Mile Bottom looked haunted, or even slightly

147

spooky, to me. Both were fine houses with period charm (said the particulars). The Old Rectory was a solid, stone-built Victorian pile ripe for modernisation (in other words: put some central heating in quick or the winter will freeze your nuts off), complete with four bedrooms, an impressive entrance hall, kitchen, lounge, dining room and even a conservatory leading out on to extensive lawns (which were actually big enough to land a glider on). Gloomy, and cold for sure, and it had obviously been unoccupied for some time, but not haunted.

The Limes was older, timber-framed and white-washed plaster, with low ceilings and exposed beams throughout: 5 beds., din. rm., sep. lounge, and even a 'study/library', which as far as I could see meant a room with fitted but empty book-shelves but sockets for telephones, broadband computer access and satellite television.

I made what I supposed were the right sort of noises for a prospective buyer as Mrs Bond showed me around both houses and even asked intelligent questions about the facilities and amenities in the local villages, of which there appeared to be none.

'So people round here make their own enter-tainment?' I asked my guide and mentor.

'My husband certainly did,' said Mrs Bond, biting her lower lip at the thought. 'But most people rent a video from Blockbusters.'

'There's a Blockbusters near here? And there was me thinking we were out in the sticks.'

'Oh you would be, make no mistake about that. Are you really looking for a house, or just stringing old Julius along?'

'Bit of both, really,' I said, which made her smile. 'I daren't go home without having done a bit of house hunting. We've taken the decision to move out of London, or so I've been told, for the sake of the children.'

'How many children do you have?'

'None, as yet, but there's one looming in the near future.'

'My two boys are now twenty-nine and twenty-seven and they're still looming. You'll find kids do that, they loom over your life like a cloud. Occasionally, the sun shines through but mostly it's solid cloud cover. I've told them I'm giving them until they're thirty, then I'm off. I'm selling up and becoming a SKIer – know what that is?'

'Spending the Kids' Inheritance?'

'Too right. I'm selling the house and the Aston and all the other stuff and buying a bedsit in Chelsea or Hampstead. Somewhere where there's some *life;* you know, late night binge drinking, streets which are no-go areas for the police, somewhere where they deliver pizzas along with the drugs.'

'Have you considered Hackney?' I suggested.

After looking at the two houses on the east side of Cambridge, Mrs Bond drove around the northern edge of the city and we crossed the M11 motorway heading briefly towards St Neots, and then zipped down a series of country lanes towards the other two houses on Mrs Symington's most haunted list, which happened to be only a mile or so apart.

I didn't have to read the particulars of The Old Rosemary Branch to know what it had once been.

'That's an old pub,' I said as we turned a corner in a sunken lane and I caught my first sight of the place, a tall, thin, three-storey white-washed lath-and-plaster house with a curved, rather than slanted, red tile roof.

'Is that you being a psychic detective?' asked Mrs Bond, turning into a gravel driveway big enough for several cars and perhaps a tractor or two.

'Just an elementary knowledge of East Anglian architecture, plus the fact that you can just about still make out a painted advert for the brewery's beers under the last six coats of whitewash on the end wall. Oh and back there on the main road there was a ghastly 1930s roadhouse pub called The *New* Rosemary Branch:, which usually means there was an old one somewhere nearby.

'I'm impressed, Sherlock,' she conceded.

'You're the second person to say that today – or something like it.'

As she led me inside, Mrs Bond told me that The Branch, as the locals of the village of Toft End called it, had been delicensed in 1933 by the then owners, the brewery company Lacon's of Great Yarmouth, which was miles away on the east coast of Norfolk. The pub had never had a proper pub sign, rather the golden eagle, which was Lacon's trade mark, had been painted in full colour and five times life size on the west wall. The brewery's 1920s paint job had outlived the brewery, which had gone out of business in the 1970s, but despite repeated attempts to obliterate it, that golden eagle was still faintly visible.

As a private, rather than public, house, The Branch had two huge lounges made from the old Saloon and Public bars, a generous entrance hall (which could have been a Snug bar), a study (the old 4-Ale Bar?) and two big bedrooms on each upper floor. The second floor was reached by a narrow, twisty staircase which, you had to open what looked like a cupboard door to find, but best of all was access to the first floor which was by two staircases, leading from each of the lounges. The dark dead space between them, running behind the central chimney which serviced the big fireplaces in both of the old bars, would have been where they stored the beer, for there was no cellar.

I stood underneath one of the large exposed beams and leaned with one hand on the brick-work of the fireplace in the larger of the two lounges.

'It's got character,' I told Mrs Bond.

'Built in 1662 we think. Operated as an inn from about 1720 and said at one time to be owned by the official hangman of Caxton Gibbet, which is not far away, and was the big eighteenth-century crossroads where they hanged highwaymen. There's a conservatory at the back beyond the kitchen and then a south-facing garden which has apple trees but, as far as I know, not a sprig, let alone a branch of rosemary. Shall I show you?'

I shook my head and patted the oak beam above my head.

'I'd rather just soak in the atmosphere.'

'Well, you may be psychic after all,' she said.

'How's that?'

'This is the only house of the four on your list which actually had a reputation for being haunted, back when it was a pub, according to local legend.'

'It was a pub, it would have been used to serving spirits.'

It was Mrs Bond's turn to shake her head, this time at my bad joke, then she looked pointedly at her watch.

'We've time to look at Comberton Manor and get back into Cambridge before the rush hour if you've seen everything you need to see.'

I was beginning to get the impression that she thought this entire exercise was less than a totally efficient use of her valuable time.

'When was the last time somebody viewed this place?' I asked, determined to impress her.

'About six months ago.'

'But Mrs Symingron's been in here since then?'

'Yes.'

'Doing a bit of tidying, ironing the curtains, arranging the logs in the fire grate?'

'That sort of thing,' Mrs Bond said, slightly irritated. 'Why?'

I bent over into the inglenook fireplace and reached into the neatly stacked birch logs in the dog grate, plucking something out which I then flourished.

'How long has she smoked cigars?' I asked Mrs Bond, waving a good two inches of crushed stub, complete with gold band, under her wrinkling nose.

The last house on our hit list was the biggest. The Manor at Comberton was a sprawling early nineteenth-century dark grey stone pile which had a touch of the Gothic about it and could have inspired the set designer for the Bates Motel in *Psycho*. If I'd had to guess, I would have plumped for the Manor being the one with the ghost. There was certainly room for someone looking around to have got lost and died before a search party could find them. This place not only had a library with actual books (although I suspected from their spines that someone had bought them by the yard just to make the place looked lived in) but even what the particulars called a billiards room, though the billiards table was long gone down the Antiques Roadshow. There were supposed to be eight bedrooms and two bathrooms upstairs, but by this time, I couldn't face another guided tour.

Mrs Bond and I made it as far as the kitchen, where I leaned against one of two deep 'butler's sinks' (which used to be much sought after by photographers developing their own 'artistic' negatives before the advent of digital) and tried to remember why I had given up smoking.

'I think even Mrs Symington gave up on this one,' said Mrs Bond. 'I don't think it's had a single viewer in the six months we've had it on our books. Though, funnily enough, this is the one which convinced her something strange was going on. She put flowers in vases in the hall, only to find one of them smashed all over the floor. Then this week she was convinced somebody had spilled red wine on the sofa in the lounge and that somebody had been sick in the billiards room, though they'd cleared most of it up.'

'Sounds like the ghosts were having a party,' I observed.

'I never get invited to parties like that,' she said.

'You will if you move to Hackney.'

'Why should I move to Hackney?'

'I might know of a flat coming free in the near future,' I said speculatively. 'You'd have to like cats, though.'

'Hey, let's focus shall we? I'm the estate agent here. Are we done or do you want to see more?'

'No, I've seen enough.' I wouldn't be recommending this place to Amy, it was far too gloomy as well as bloody cold.

I rubbed my hands up my arms and shivered.

'No wonder the ghosts round here like wild parties. They have to keep warm somehow.'

Mrs Bond glanced at the sheaf of printed particulars.

'The house has full central heating, but of course it won't have been on for quite a while. I checked the radiators actually and they're stone cold.'

I had a sudden 'Sherlock moment' (as I would later think of it) and turned so that I was facing the taps over the butler's sink and cranked on the hot tap. The water pipes burped once and then the tap gushed a steady flow of water. I gave it a few seconds and then stuck a finger in the flow. It wasn't boiling hot, but it was definitely warm.

'I hope the particulars make a special mention of the excellent insulation in this house. Keeps the water tank warm for months.'

Mrs Bond put her hands on her hips and looked me in the eyes.

'Just what *the fuck* is going on round here?' she asked politely.

Chapter Eight

For some reason, Frank was in a bit of a mood when I got back to the Tyler Pharmaceuticals car park, which was empty apart from his Mercedes Sprinter. I had thought he would have appreciated the faith I had shown in him by leaving him basically in charge of this stage of the Zaborski operation. The more difficult part – estimating the bill – I would, of course, take on myself.

But Frank seemed to have a bee in his bonnet about the fact that all the Tyler personnel had actually gone home for the day and he'd been trying to ring my mobile for the last two hours. I told him to take deep breaths and relax, offered to buy him a drink and promised to turn my phone on in future.

'Where the hell have you been all day?' he snapped, rather childishly I thought, as I climbed aboard his spy van.

'With a new client, taking on another case. There could be a bit of work in it for you.'

'Good for you,' he said but didn't sound grateful at all, 'because I've got bugger all else to do here.'

'You've finished doing all the … er … whatever it was you were doing?

'Yes. I've measured up for new cameras to cover all the blind spots in their system, but there aren't that many. Sanger, the boss man, he has the place pretty well covered and he won't like us suggesting there are gaps.'

'It's not up to him,' I pointed out. 'We'll do our report for Olivier Zaborski; he's the one with the cheque book. And anyway, there must be a gap somewhere as they're losing product.'

'God knows how,' said Frank. 'I can't see how anyone can get any quantity of liquid out of that processing room without being spotted. Certainly not enough to make it worthwhile, not even a mouthful and I don't know if you could do that. Do you know? What happens if you take Botox orally?'

'Is this leading up to a dirty joke?'

'No.'

'Then I neither know nor care. I should think you get to keep very youthful teeth and gums, but I really don't want to go there.'

I picked up Frank's stainless steel thermos flask from the seat next to me. 'How about...?'

'Not a chance. No one is allowed to take anything *in* to the wash room in case of contaminating the Botox, and apart from when the chemists change into their scrubs, they're under closed-circuit surveillance 24/7. Anyway, that sort of thing only happens in detective novels, you know, like the tea-leaf in the Turkish Bath.'

I stared hard at Frank but he didn't explain until I prompted: 'And in English?'

'It's a famous detective story from the 1920s, a classic actually. Man stabbed to death in Turkish Baths where all the suspects are stark bullock naked and there's no sign of a knife. Answer? The murderer smuggled in a pointed stake of ice in

156

his thermos, did the business and then left it to melt away. The giveaway was tea leaves in the melting ice water in the drain. Very clever.'

'Should have used a tea-bag.'

'I think you're missing the point,' he said sulkily.

'That's been said before,' I admitted. It had too, but usually the voice was female.

'You might have got a thermos flask into a Turkish Bath in the 1920s. There's no way you could get a flask into their wash room without it being caught on camera, in my not-so-humble professional opinion.'

'So how is the lovely Dr Quinn getting the stuff out?'

'You're sure it's her?' Frank seemed less convinced than I was.

'She's my number one suspect.'

'Why?'

'Alright then, she's my *only* suspect. Look at it this way, though: Dr Sanger is the obvious company man and far too clean cut to try and fiddle somebody like Olivier Zaborski. That ex-copper, Sutton, is dim but not that stupid, because if somebody is smuggling stuff out under the very lenses of the surveillance cameras, the bloke in charge of the cameras would have to be in on it. And the other chemist, whose name escapes me for the minute, doesn't strike me as the suspicious type. Our little Cassandra, though, she's well in the frame. She's female, and therefore knows all about Botox; she's a redhead, therefore prone to acting irrationally; and she has a Russian boyfriend. I rest my case.'

'That's a bit sweeping, isn't it?'

'Which particular bit? By the way, did you check the phone records?'

'Such as they are. They run a program which logs any numbers not on a recognised central list of contacts and customers. Sutton wouldn't give me the list of approved numbers; said they were commercially confidential, but he did give me a read-out of all those not on the list. Most of them were one-offs and mostly local. Sutton even admitted to being responsible for the calls to the local Domino Pizza place when he knew he was going to be late home.'

'Any Paris numbers? That'd be 00 33 code then 01 42 or 43, something like that, wouldn't it?'

'Probably, but there were none.'

'None?'

'Zero, zip, not a single hit for anywhere in France. But you shouldn't be surprised.'

'I shouldn't?' It was alright for him, this was my carefully thought-out scenario going down the pan and I didn't have any other bright ideas.

'No, because you know that Dr Quinn has a mobile phone, and she uses it quite a lot.'

I gave Frank a grin of admiration.

'You kept on listening after I'd gone this afternoon, didn't you?'

'I might have,' he said coyly.

'And you earwigged her phoning Paris?'

'No, she wasn't calling Paris as far as I could tell. I could only hear her, of course, I haven't got her phone tapped, you know.'

'So who was she phoning?'

'Eurostar. She was booking a ticket for this Saturday.'

'For Paris,' I said.

'Right on, Sherlock.'

Frank deserved a drink on expenses for that, so I told him to follow me to The Square and Compasses pub in the village, which was on our way back to London.

By the time he parked the Sprinter next to my Peugeot on the pub's forecourt, I was standing by the car I had parked next to, staring in disbelief that someone could have a more embarrassing set of wheels than me.

'Bloody hell,' breathed Frank as he joined me. 'What is it with you people who drive them things?'

We were standing gawking at a Peugeot 206, one of the new models but one with a paint job which I suspected was customised and not a regular production line finish, unless the French automotive industry was in a lot of trouble.

'What colour's that supposed to be, then?' Frank wondered aloud. 'Sickly flesh pink or prawn vomit?'

'I think it's called Roman Pink,' I said.

'How do you know that?'

'I'm the detective, right? Also that's the giveaway.'

I pointed to the corner of the rear window where there was a plastic sticker showing the famous 1953 Paramount studio shot of Gregory Peck astride a Vespa scooter, with a young Audrey Hepburn perched side-saddle behind him, arms clasped around his manly chest.

'It's from a film called *Roman Holiday*. It started

a craze for Vespas and Max Factor brought out a lipstick called Roman Pink, made a fortune, even though the film was in black and white.'

'And what on earth does that mean?' asked Frank, but he wasn't musing philosophical, he was pointing to a bumper sticker which read: REAL TEXTERS DON'T USE PREDICTIVE TEXT.

'It means the owner of this car has rather a lot of issues, not to mention affectations.'

'Do you know the owner?'

'No, but if he's in the pub, he'll be hard to miss.'

Devon Sedgeley certainly was in the pub, and not so much hiding his light under a bushel (whatever that was), as holding court, talking quietly to three other drinkers seated round a small table in the pub's bay window. That quartet were the only customers in the lounge bar, though it was still early and the pub had only just opened for the evening session. The idea of all-day opening had obviously not reached this far out into the sticks yet.

They were keeping their voices down and were obviously listening intently to young Devon. They could have all been from the same workplace, having a drink and a bitch about the boss before going home, but the three I didn't recognise didn't look like estate agents. Two were female and in their early twenties, one was dressed casually but expensively, pretending to be an impoverished student. But this was Cambridge and she wasn't fooling anyone. The other female wasn't attempting to fool anyone. She wore tight jeans and riding boots and a padded Barbour jacket, and that was genuine horse muck on the pub floor under her chair. The man in Devon's audience was much older, in fact as old as the three of them put together. He sat ram-rod straight in his chair, projecting an 'ex-military man' image from his tweed jacket and brown wool tie down to his khaki suede desert boots. He was sieving a glass of Guinness through his carefully clipped moustache whilst the two females were sipping white wine. Devon was sucking on the neck of a bottle of Holsten Pils and had a clear plastic shoulder bag hanging from the back of his chair. The bag was decorated with the blessed Audrey in full Ascot regalia from *My Fair Lady*. Come to think of it, he didn't look like an estate agent either.

Frank and I stood at the bar where the pub landlord pulled two pints of IPA and I splashed out and bought us a packet of dry roasted peanuts each.

'What's your interest in the wild bunch over there?' Frank whispered out of the side of his mouth.

'Later,' I hissed back. 'What time shall I meet you tomorrow?'

'Tomorrow? I told you, I've done my bit, the rest is report-writing and getting a quote together for some more equipment if you think the company'll go for it.'

'What's your mark-up on hardware?' I asked him, genuinely curious.

'Twenty per cent of list price. What's yours?'

'Mine?'

'Rudgard and Drummond usually stick their

161

end on top, but I've never known how much.'

I sipped my pint at the wonder of it all.

'So we're going to tell Zarborski that he needs some new spy-ware even though he probably doesn't, and it won't solve his problem, and if he went down Comet or PC World he could probably get it for half the price? And we even charge him a fee for telling him?'

'Welcome to the world of consultancy,' he said. 'Anything bothering you?'

I gave his question due and careful consideration for a full five seconds.

'Not a thing. This working for a living's turning out a lot less stressful than I'd been led to believe.'

Me and my big mouth.

'Well, hello. I do believe I spy strangers!' said somebody else's big mouth, so close both Frank and I came close to spilling our beer.

Devon Sedgeley introduced himself with a strong whiff of Hugo Boss for Men.

'Sorry to intrude, but a new face in this pub is rarer than the landlord announcing a Happy Hour.'

I grinned inanely, not really wanting to encourage him, and conscious of Frank bristling beside me and rapidly downing his pint. Maybe he had a thing about being approached by strange men in pubs, but Devon's tone was nothing if not polite and friendly – certainly nothing like the more-camp-than-Butlins screeching he'd displayed out in the street when he'd seen Mrs Bond earlier that afternoon.

'Didn't I see you with my colleague Jane Bond

this afternoon?'

I couldn't see any harm in talking to the guy; nobody had told me not to and it might distract him long enough for Frank to make a dash for the door. Certainly, I was conscious of three pairs of eyes from his table watching our every move.

'Yes indeed. Mrs Bond very kindly showed me some country properties.'

'Moving out of London?' he asked politely.

'Is it that obvious?'

'Most of our business comes from town rats wanting to be country mice,' he said, but with a smile he obviously thought was endearing. 'I'm Devon Sedgeley, by the way, of Symington and Sedgeley.'

He produced business cards from the breast pocket of his suit jacket and held up a fan of them like a stage magician doing the 'pick a card, any card' routine.

'I'm Roy Angel,' I said as I took one. There was no way I was going to give him one of my mis-printed 'Fitzy' ones. 'And this is Frank, a colleague of mine.'

Young Mr Sedgeley ignored Frank totally, for which I suspect Frank was grateful, and continued to size me up quite obviously. It felt like being measured for a coffin, or maybe being assessed as a mortgage risk, which of course is what the guy did for a living.

'Did Janey Bond look after you this afternoon?'

'She gave me a comprehensive tour of every-thing on offer,' I said and got exactly the reaction I thought I would.

'I'll bet she did,' he said, arching his eyebrows.

163

'We aim to give satisfaction and Jane is *very* experienced.'

I could sense Frank squirming beside me.

'I always was a sucker for fast women in vintage cars,' I said, straightfaced.

'I'd have thought it was the other way round in Jane's case, but one must be charitable,' he served back. 'What did you think of Comberton Manor?'

For a split second I wondered how he knew where we had been, but then I remembered Mrs Bond having to collect the keys from the Shelford office and that the properties we had visited were all on his 'portfolio'.

'A fine house – once. A bit on the cold and gloomy side for me, though. I preferred *The Old Rosemary Branch* myself, but really I'm just on a scouting mission for my other half. She's the one who will decide to join the country set.'

'I'm sure we'd be honoured if you did.' He did a half turn and gestured to his table of friends. 'Why not join this particular set right now? I'd be happy to buy you a drink.'

'Really should be going,' muttered Frank quietly.

'A small one, just a half of bitter, to be sociable. Mustn't put country noses out of joint before we even move here. They hold grudges, you know,' I said to Frank, turning to him so that Devon couldn't see and tapping my right ear with a finger and flicking my eyes to where I thought his Mercedes was parked outside. Frank just looked confused. 'But if you're keen to get off, don't wait for me.'

'I've got those ... er ... reports for you. In the van. I'll dig them out before I go,' he said, catching on to the fact that he had an escape clause and nodding a cursory goodbye to Devon before legging it towards the car park.

Goodness knows what he thought Devon was likely to do to him – or me – in front of the 'country set'. Perhaps he just had a limited experience of outrageous gays with an Audrey Hepburn fixation, which, if he had grown up on Alderney was understandable, but odd considering he now lived near Clapham Junction.

Devon ushered me over towards his friends by almost, but not quite, holding my elbow and once there, I got the impression that the over-the-top camp act was being toned down if not dropped. There was not an inflection or trace of a double-entendre as he said:

'These are my fellow Slops.'

'I beg your pardon?' Now I was the one sounding camp.

'We're all Slops – S, L, 0, P, S: Shelford Light Opera Society. Been going for years; well, the Slops has, not us of course. Let me introduce Colonel Colman.'

'I *have* been going for years,' said the military-looking man rising to his feet and proffering his hand. 'I thought I'd better say that before these young whippersnappers did.'

The two females made polite tut-tutting noises, telling the Colonel not to be so silly.

They both raised a hand and flashed a smile as Devon introduced the posh student as Gilly White and the horsey one as Scarlett Smith.

'And this is Roy Angel, who is looking for a house in the area, but apart from that is a man of mystery.'

'I'll bet Devon has been trying to recruit him even before he's moved here,' giggled the girl in the riding gear.

'Do you perform, Mr Angel?' asked the other one.

'Not on the stage, I'm afraid.'

'Do you play an instrument perhaps?' tried Colonel Colman. 'The orchestra pit always needs new faces.'

'Not a note, and I'm totally tone deaf,' I lied as I always did when approached by amateur operatic societies, Mormons, international terrorist groups and strangers wanting me to carry luggage through airport check-ins.

'Pity,' said the Colonel.

'Now come on, people, leave Roy alone. He's not even decided to move here but you lot seem determined to put him off.'

'That's alright. It's nice to see there's a bit of life in the local community. I thought it might be all jumble sales and fox hunting.'

As soon as I said it, the entire pub seemed to go quiet, even though we were the only people in the bar.

'Do you have anything against fox hunting, Mr Angel?' asked Scarlett – the one still wearing mucky riding boots.

I felt it was important to tell the truth, the whole truth and nothing but.

'I have absolutely nothing against fox hunting personally,' I said, keeping eye contact, and the

166

atmosphere around the table visibly relaxed.

I had told them I was no actor, so it was important to be sincere, and I had been. No one had ever chased me, personally, on horseback across a muddy field with a pack of dogs. Not yet, at least.

'Hey there, fellow Sloppies, no politics. Roy is down here on business, not to talk politics.'

I couldn't tell if Devon was fishing or not, but then he probably wasn't sure.

'Hardly business, I'm house-hunting.'

'That's serious business to me,' said Devon cheerfully, 'in fact it's my business to see that your hunt ends in a kill, so to speak. I'm talking houses, of course, not foxes. Jane Bond was showing Roy here around Comberton Manor this afternoon.'

'And what did you think of the old pile?' asked Colonel Colman with the air of a man who knows all the manor houses in the shire.

'He means the manor house, not Mrs Bond,' prompted Devon, getting the laugh he expected.

'I found Mrs Bond warm and charming, but the manor house bloody cold and rather gloomy,' I said diplomatically, which seemed to satisfy them. 'But I'm really just the advanced scouting party. I have to report back to my part ... other half, back in London and she'll tell me which house I like best.'

'I used to have a wife like that,' said the Colonel, almost to himself, but I ignored it.

'Which reminds me, I really do have to be making a move, so I'll say cheerio to you all.' I placed my empty glass on their table and nodded and smiled to each of them.

By the door, Devon Sedgeley reached for my

arm, but only the briefest of fleeting touches.

'You will let me know if you want to see any of those properties again, won't you? Or any others for that matter, just let me know your specifications. You've got my card?'

'Yes I have and yes, I will,' I said, opening the door.

He lowered his voice. Not much, but just enough to show he was serious.

'Better to deal with me direct than the Cambridge office if you want personal attention.' I didn't say anything and as I pulled the pub door open, he seemed to be distracted. 'Is that your car?'

It was too late to bluff him.

'It's a courtesy car while mine is being serviced,' was the best I could do.

'Nice wheels,' he breathed sexily.

Frank shushed me as I climbed in the front of the Mercedes next to him and passed over a set of headphones.

'They all started chattering together as soon as you were out the door. Plays havoc with my levels, that does,' he moaned.

The first voice I heard in the headphones was the Colonel's; and it was slightly unnerving that I could hear him as clearly as when he'd been sitting a table's width away, though now he was about thirty feet distant, out of sight and the other side of a brick wall.

'How serious do you think that chap is, Devon?'

'About the manor? Not at all. He told me he thought it the least interesting of the houses he'd

168

seen and he more or less said as much again when he was talking to you lot.'

'What other places did he look at? Were any on our list?' This from one of the women.

'They all were,' said Devon, 'but don't read anything into that. They're all houses that should have moved by now and probably would have if we were not using them, so head office naturally tried to unload them on the first likely buyer.'

'Is that chap a serious buyer?' This was the Colonel again.

'Shouldn't think so. Did he *look* like he could afford the manor.'

'You never can tell, these days.' A female voice.

'Well, he's not going to do anything before Saturday night, is he?'

'So we're still on?'

'Absolutely.'

I handed the headphones back to Frank, who had been listening in on a single earpiece.

'You up for a bit of overtime this week-end?' I asked him.

'You mean Saturday night, don't you, out at this manor they're talking about?'

'Nothing much gets by you, does it?'

'I'm quite happy to watch this one go by. My Saturday nights are precious to me. Why don't you do it?'

'Frank, I'd love to, but I'll be in Paris.'

'Paris? You can't go swanning off to Paris now you've got a job.'

Amy's reaction had been entirely predictable, so I went straight into my first line of defence.

169

'It *is* work, it's part of this case I'm working.' I thought that sounded quite professional. 'I won't be there to enjoy myself, I'll be following one of Olivier Zaborski's employees.'

I had already decided that the Association of British Investigators' Code of Ethics (Paragraph 3) pledge to respect the privacy of clients, did not apply to telling Amy anything she wanted to know if it meant an expenses-paid week-end break in Paris. After all, I had worked more or less non-stop for three days now. Surely I deserved a holiday?

'Zaborski has green-lit this trip?'

'Absolutely. We at Rudgard & Blugden spend our clients' money like we spend our own.' At least I hoped we did. 'He authorised the trip personally.'

He had too. When he had visited the office, he had left me his mobile phone number in case of emergencies (which I may have forgotten to tell Veronica about) and he had been happy to talk business even though when I had rung him it sounded as if there was a party going on in the background and I had apologised for disturbing him. He told me not to worry, as he didn't much like film premieres anyway.

Frank and I had not hung about for too long outside the *Square and Compasses,* just in case Devon and his tame chorus line came out to have a closer look at my sexy little car. I told Frank to follow me and drove out of the village towards the motorway, pulling in to the side on the slip road, hazard lights flashing, so we could have a quick

170

conference. It didn't take me long to convince Frank that I needed his unique skills for at least one more day out here in the countryside, as we were now working on two highly delicate investigations. Frequent use of the words 'bonus', 'overtime' and 'expenses' seemed to help, especially when preceded by the word 'generous'. Frank agreed to meet me at Tyler Pharmaceuticals the next day at first light – which on my internal clock would be about 11 a.m. – and we would finalise strategy then. This was assuming, of course, that I had the approval of the guy paying the bills.

That was when I had rung Olivier Zaborski. He was getting out of a limo at a film premiere in Leicester Square, I was standing next to a lime green Gayest Car in Europe on the slip road of a motorway in the middle of nowhere.

I told Zaborski (apologising profusely for phoning him out of office hours, but at the same time hoping he was noticing that I was still working) that we had completed the first stage of our investigation at Tyler and had come up with a possible lead, which of course I couldn't go into on the phone, but it involved Paris. That was all I had to say. He said he understood the need for discretion and I had his full authority to follow it up. Could I get a flight tomorrow? I told him that everything was in hand, as long as he was happy. He said he was very happy and I was to keep him informed. In fact, he would ring me for regular updates. I had actually said goodbye and ended the call before I began to wonder how he was going to do that as I hadn't given him my number; then it sunk in that by ringing him, I had given his mobile's memory my mobile number. Damn this modern technology.

Before I let Frank go for the night, I made him play me the recording he'd made of Dr Cassandra Quinn that afternoon. Not her cosy tête-a-tête with her salsa-loving Russian boyfriend, but a short, incredibly boring conversation with a travel agent somewhere in Cambridge, booking a ticket on the 0909 Saturday Eurostar from London Waterloo to Paris Gare du Nord, returning on Monday afternoon. Dr Quinn then read out a sixteen-digit credit card number and agreed to £86.90 being charged to it.

At that price, she was going economy. Zaborski had suggested that I fly over, but I thought it better if I caught the same train, which would save on the boss's expenses – even if I went first class.

'I have Olivier Zaborski's private mobile number,' I said in a desperate attempt to impress Amy, 'and he rings me regularly for updates on the case.'

'Perhaps he can get you to keep your phone switched on, then, because I sure as hell can't. Being so busy with *Olivier,* I don't suppose you had any time to do anything important like look for a house for us, did you?'

I could have pointed out that I would have had plenty of time on my hands if she hadn't insisted on me getting a job. There again, I could have suggested she take a chill pill or have the cigarette I knew she was screaming for, but I wasn't brave enough, drunk enough or stupid enough to do any of those.

'Actually I did find time to pop in to Symington & Sedgeley's Cambridge office,' I said trying not to sound too smug. 'I saw Julius Symington himself and he personally recommended four properties – just for starters, that is.'

I rescued the printed sheets of particulars from my jacket and smoothed them out as I handed them over.

'If there's anything there you fancy, we can run up there next week some time, or we could always refine the brief for them. They seem very thorough, very professional.'

Amy took the sheets and gave them a cursory glance, after examining the Symington & Sedgeley headed notepaper to see that it was genuine and not something I had just knocked up on the computer.

'I'll look at those while you're enjoying yourself in Paris.'

'I'm *working*, you know.'

'Then you can do some work for me; do some market research. It won't be too taxing, just take a camera with you and photograph some naked women.'

'Naked women?'

'Well, okay, then, not actually naked, more fully-clothed, and not real women, more sort of mannequins.'

'You want me to photograph some shop windows, don't you?'

'Look on it as industrial espionage, if that helps. I just want to see what a couple of the leading names are up to this summer.'

'I may not have time to wander the Golden

Triangle,' I told her.

The *triangle d'or* of Paris fashion is a triangular area where the apex is the Arc de Triomphe and the sides run down to the Place de la Concorde and the Place de l'Alma. Within that triangle are all the big fashion houses, including Givenchy, Chanel and Valentino. It was one of Amy's favourite hunting grounds.

'I *know* what's going on there,' she said haughtily. 'There are a couple of other places I want you to check out. I'll write them down for you, but one is *Le Mouton a Cinq Pattes* in the Marais market. They do last year's collections with the designer labels cut out.'

Now you had to admire the cheek of that.

'The other is *Zadig and Voltaire* in the Rue des France Bourgeois, famous for very trendy cashmere jumpers and cotton tops and perfectly cut trousers which make your arse look just stunning.'

'Want me to drop by *Sabbia Rosa* as well?' I tried.

I knew that *Sabbia Rosa* (on the Rue des Saints-Pères in the 6th Arrondisement) was the Ferrari of sexy female underwear shops, their speciality being made-to-measure basques. Unfortunately, Amy knew that too.

'No way, forget that. In fact you can forget *all* about that for a while.'

If that wasn't depressing enough, she showed she still knew how to kick a man when he was down.

'And I don't suppose you've given any thought to telling your mother she's going to be a granny, have you?'

174

'Give us a break,' I muttered, 'I've been a bit busy.'

'Or your father? How about telling your father?' she piled it on.

'I haven't spoken to him for over five years.'

'Maybe you should. It could be useful to have a title in the business; look good on the headed notepaper.'

If I was surprised it was only because she hadn't suggested it before this.

'Oh come on, he's only a life peer, which he got for sitting on dozens of committees and raising dosh for the Labour Party when it was really unfashionable to do so. It's not like he's a proper Lord or a Baron with estates and serfs and stuff.'

'When I first met you, you just said he worked in the House of Lords.'

'Well, he's supposed to. They call them working peers but from the gossip columns he seems to spend more time clubbing than he does debating fox hunting or whatever it is they do these days.'

'Did you see him in the papers at the weekend?' Amy said, suddenly moving closer in classic gossip-sharing mode. 'He was photographed at The Limelight dancing with Kim McIntosh.'

'Not Kim McIntosh the page three topless model?' I feigned surprise.

'The very same *19-year-old* topless model.'

'Cool,' I said. 'There's life in the old boy yet, then.'

Amy pretended to look shocked.

'That age difference, though: it can't be healthy.'

'Probably not, but if she dies, she dies.'

I got a punch on the upper arm, right on the

muscle where it hurts, for that and not just because it was the oldest joke in the book.

'She must be after his money.'

'Then she's even dumber than she looks. That all went a long time ago, though he won't have told her that.'

The last thing my father was, was forthcoming about money. Just ask my mother – ask her, and then retire to a safe distance.

'The gossip columns were seriously hinting about wedding bells,' Amy said as if she wasn't really interested.

'Does that mean I get to call Kim McIntosh "mummy"?' I said, wide-eyed and innocent.

'And does she know she might be becoming an instant granny?'

I allowed myself a malicious little grin, which I saw mirrored exactly in the evil smirk on Amy's face.

'I'll ring him first thing in the morning,' I said as we high-fived each other.

Chapter Nine

'And you think you're going to Paris, why?' stormed Veronica, first thing in the morning.

This time I really had got into the office early, not long after sparrow-fart, as it was Friday and the week-end started here. Unbelievably, the three witches were all at their desks by nine o'clock. What was it with these people? Didn't they have lives to go to?

I hadn't intended a confrontation with Veronica; that's why I had come in early – to leave her a note, to see if Laura or Lorna had dug anything out of the Tyler Pharmaceutical personnel files and to check if there was any petty cash available for my unscheduled trip to Paris. To my mind, that was a pretty full agenda and yet Veronica still gave the impression that she didn't think I was taking this work business seriously. There was only one way, in management terms, to smooth the path for my proposed course of executive action: pull rank.

'I have Mr Zaborski's blessing,' I said, trying not to sound too smug.

'I know. He rang me last night to tell me,' Veronica answered frostily.

'He did?'

'Quite late as a matter of fact, after he'd been to the cinema.'

I was quietly appalled. When did these multi-millionaire entrepreneurs ever sleep?

'So?'

'So I suppose I can't stop you going and I suppose Olivier Zaborski will be picking up the bill at the end of the day, but I still don't understand why you're going.'

'I'm on the case, boss, on the case. Tailing a suspect – our prime suspect.' I thought she would be pleased.

'And this would be who?'

'Dr Cassandra Quinn, one of the chemists up at Zaborski's factory who has direct, hands-on access to the Botox production line and also...' I paused for dramatic effect, '...a Paris connection.'

'Yes, Olivier seemed much taken with this Paris connection. What is the connection?'

I was prepared to give her the benefit of the doubt and assume she hadn't had time to read my report, but then I couldn't actually remember if I'd written it yet.

'She's going there this week-end.'

Even I thought this sounded a bit thin.

'And that's it?'

'Zaborski is convinced some of his missing Botox is being sold in Paris.'

'And that's it?' she said again.

'Frank Lemarquand has copies of the Tyler security tapes plus some recordings of phone calls he made of her on her mobile phone; they all point the finger at her.'

'I haven't seen transcripts yet, have I?'

She was right there because all the tapes Frank had given me I had left at home in Hampstead.

'Not yet,' I admitted.

'None of that will stand up in court, anyway,' she said gruffly.

'Who said anything about going to court?'

'We must conduct our business so that, if necessary, everything we do can be scrupulously examined in a court of law,' she said as if quoting something, which she probably was.

'Now you tell me. Is this a good time to ask for an advance on expenses before I go back out in the field?'

To my amazement, it was.

Not only did Lorna (or Laura?) provide me with

300 euros in crisp new notes, for which I had to sign three separate bits of paper, but she got on the phone to the local travel agent where Rudgard & Blugden had an account, and ordered me a Eurostar ticket which they would deliver to the office within fifteen minutes. I told her the outward train had to be the 0909 on Saturday, but the return could be any time on Monday afternoon, and to make it first class. She raised a plucked eyebrow at that, but didn't question it. Fortunately, Veronica wasn't within earshot. In the middle of calling the travel agent, though, she turned to me and asked if I knew where I was staying, which of course I didn't (a) because I had no idea whereabouts in Paris Dr Quinn was going and (b) I hadn't really thought about it. The travel agent, it turned out, could do me a two-night deal at a hotel to go with the Eurostar ticket and as it would be on the company's account, I said yes and told her to book it. If nothing else, it would be a bolt hole and somewhere I could sign the bills rather than pay cash. She said 'Yeah, fine' a couple of times, then quoted an account number (so rapidly I couldn't catch it), and when she had hung up, she said:

'You've got a room in the Hotel Austerlitz on something called the Boulevard de l'Hôpital. I've no idea where that is and if you think my French is bad, you should have heard the girl at the travel agent's.'

'That'll do nicely,' I said. 'It's bound to be down by the Gare d'Austerilitz somewhere. It's on the Metro. I'll find it.'

Whilst I was waiting for the tickets and the hotel

confirmation to arrive, I went over the Tyler personnel records with Laura (or possibly Lorna), asking her to concentrate on Cassandra Quinn and basically forget about the rest.

'If you insist, but she's the boring one if you ask me.'

'No, I didn't ask, and I wasn't going to, but now you just have to tell me why you think that.'

I couldn't afford to upset Laura, after all, I wouldn't have time to plough through the files myself over the week-end, I had a Paris to go to.

'Well, if you're looking for suspects,' she tapped her teeth with the end of a pencil whilst scrolling down the screen on her laptop, 'which I suspect you are, you might check out a few of the men before you pick on the only woman in the frame. Did you know that Dr Quinn is the *only* female employed at the plant?'

'She's also the only redhead,' I added helpfully, confusing her.

'I mean, doesn't that strike you as odd? Okay, so there are only twelve employees in total at the plant, but only one woman?'

'I'm the only male who works here,' I pointed out.

'That makes you one out of six if we count Stella and don't forget Mrs Delacourt, who's still out on a job. It's a better ratio than one out of twelve.'

'I'm surprised there are twelve. The place looked fully automated to me.'

She consulted her screen again.

'Three on the scientific management side: that's the American, Sanger, Dr Quinn and a Dr Bob Harvey. Then there's this chap Sutton, Head of

Security. He has a deputy, who seems to work night shifts and then there are five guys on the packaging and distribution side. That's it. All other functions – payroll, cleaning, catering, maintenance and engineering – are sub-contracted to outside suppliers and they change their suppliers every six months, which is probably a sensible security precaution.'

'Absolutely. That would be standard procedure,' I agreed confidently.

'So you haven't exactly got a lot of potential suspects who have access to the laboratories, have you?'

'No,' I said, but in fact, she'd just told me we had, technically, twelve, which was eight more than I'd been working on.

'But out of twelve, you zoom in on the only woman. Why?'

'She's the only redhead; I thought I'd told you that.'

I held her gaze in silence for two long minutes until she cracked.

'Okay, I'm only the office junior, I know, and you know something about her I don't and you're not going to tell me.'

Of course I did. I knew she was a redhead.

'So, anything unusual in her file?'

'Nothing out of the ordinary. First degree in chemistry at Sheffield, then a Masters and her Doctorate at Cambridge. Her PhD thesis was on 'Cleaning Technologies and Sterilization in Pharmaceutical Manufacturing', whatever that might be. First job with one of the big drug companies working on 'air handling' in passout ports. Joined

Tyler two years ago with excellent references. Doesn't seem to have ever taken a day off sick and doesn't take holidays.'

'Now surely that's out of the ordinary,' I said, but I was really thinking about what holiday entitlement I got with Rudgard & Blugden, and how soon I could take a 'sicky'.

'To be accurate, I should say she doesn't take chunks of holiday. She seems just to take long week-ends. Takes a lot of Fridays and Mondays off. She's got today and Monday booked as leave as a matter of fact.'

Somewhere a few inches above Laura's head a cartoon light bulb flashed on.

'She's going to Paris, isn't she?'

'I told you we can't trust redheads,' I said.

Laura tapped the side of her nose with pink fingernail and winked at me as if it was our little secret.

'Anything else in there?' I persevered.

'She's a fanatic salsa dancer.'

'It says that on her file?'

'The file has a copy of her e-mailed CV from when she applied for the job. She ran dance classes while she was at university. Mentions it several times; seems quite proud of it. It's supposed to be really good exercise.'

'The most fun you can have in public, standing upright with your clothes on,' I said.

'Is it?'

Now it was my turn to tap my nose with a finger and give her a long slow wink.

By the time I had waited for my train tickets to be

biked round (I had assumed they would use a motor-bike courier, not a pimply youth on a BMX bike), I was late leaving the office. Consequently, I was late getting down to darkest Cambridgeshire and once again Frank was sitting in his van in the Tyler car park having his lunch when I parked next to him.

'Sorry I'm late,' I said, helping myself to one of his sandwiches. It turned out to be pastrami and thinly-sliced gherkin on nutty, granary bread this time. I looked at the greaseproof wrapping but could see no sign of a price tag. 'These are really good. Do you buy them, or is there a Mrs Lemarquand doing a lunchbox for you?'

'No.' That was all he said, but he gathered up what was left, carefully re-folding the greaseproof paper parcel.

'All quiet here?' I asked, between mouthfuls.

'Far as I know, I've just been sitting here twiddling my thumbs,' sulked Frank. He was probably one of those people who simply weren't happy unless they were doing something, like working. I'd met several of them in the past and was nowhere near understanding them.

'Have you been in there yet?' I pointed to the laboratory.

'I was waiting for you. I'm not expected in there, like I said I've finished my survey and the report's all typed up. I've got it in the back of the van. You can take it in to them if you want to grab the glory.'

'Glory? They'll probably lynch me. We're basically acting as management consultants here and who likes consultants coming in and telling you you're not doing a proper job? Anyway, I suppose it ought to go direct to Olivier Zaborski. He's the one with the cheque book.'

'You're the boss,' he shrugged and I realised I probably was. 'Anyway, your favourite redhead's not here today, or at least her car's not here.'

'No, I know. She's taking a long week-end in Paris, where I'll be tailing her.'

Frank tried to stifle a giggle and failed.

'Tailing her? That sounds a bit rude to me. Make sure you put it down on the invoice as 'covert observation', it sounds better. Which reminds me, this job tomorrow, who gets the invoice for that?'

'That might turn out to be a cash-in-hand job, a bit of private business between me and you.'

If I thought that would please him, it seemed I couldn't have been more wrong.

'Hey, I run a legit business. It's not in my best interest to get the wrong side of the tax man, so I don't do it. I keep straight books, I declare everything and I even have an honest accountant.'

The indignation was almost totally convincing, then he said:

'Put me down for fifty quid an hour plus petrol and any equipment not recovered in working order is replaced as new. OK? Now where's this gaff you want me to wire up?'

'It's not far away, but I'd better show my face in here with Dr Sanger, keep the client happy, that sort of thing.'

'So this house job has nothing to do with the enquiry here at the Really Beautiful Drug Company?'

'No, it doesn't, but I like the name. We ought to suggest it to them.'

But he wasn't going to be diverted.

'So this house job, whatever it is, is basically a bit of moonlighting?'

'No shit, Sherlock.'

I was able to show Mark Sanger a beautifully typed and bound 25-page report on the short-comings of the surveillance systems operating in his 'facility' with a summary of recommendations to bring him up to state-of-the-art, which would, of course, cost a small fortune. In fact I didn't so much show it to Dr Sanger as wave it under his nose, never actually letting go of the one copy Frank had given me.

He didn't seem all that impressed. I had caught up with him in the staff common room where he was eating a sandwich and reading a book: *Isolation Technology, A Practical Guide (2nd Edition)*. I made a mental not to wait until they made the straight-to-video movie of it.

'What is it they say about management consultants?' he drawled, without looking up from the book. 'They borrow your watch so they can sell you the time?'

'Something like that,' I agreed. 'But all we've done is review your internal surveillance security operation and make a few suggestions.'

'Which will cost us how much? What's the bottom line, including your fees?'

'That's for Mr Zaborski,' I said proudly. 'He's our client and he has accepted our fee structure.'

Still reading his book, he said:

'Is there anything in that report which I couldn't have – or anyone who works here couldn't have –

told him for free?'

'Probably not,' I said, not keen to let on that I hadn't actually read it. 'But there again, would he have taken the advice seriously if it had been free?'

He couldn't answer that and for the first time I thought I was getting the hang of this working-for-a-living business.

I let Frank drive us into Cambridge in the van while I phoned ahead. I also felt happier at the thought of a Mercedes, even a van, in the car park of Symington & Sedgeley's head office, rather than my embarrassing Peugeot.

Mrs Bond answered my call and informed me that Julius Symington was out but he had been very pleased with the report she'd given him of our tour of the Cambridgeshire countryside yesterday and was glad I was making progress.

I was glad I was making progress, though not at all sure how, so I told her I wanted to borrow the keys to Comberton Manor just for the afternoon. I expected her to slap me down on that one right away, but she agreed to the idea immediately without asking any nasty questions such as why I wanted them.

She was waiting for us in the car park, rather than behind her machine-gun nest of a desk in the stair well, for which I didn't blame her in the slightest. You can command the attention of anybody (but particularly two men) when you're sitting casually on the bonnet of your classic Aston Martin, hair perfectly coiffured, wearing a crisp white pilot's shirt, khaki slacks like Katharine (not Audrey) Hepburn used to wear and Jimmy Choo shoes, much more than if you look as if you work in a cupboard under the stairs.

I introduced Frank as my 'security expert' and said I hoped we wouldn't get her into trouble if we had a snoop around the property. Frank only had eyes for the Aston until Mrs Bond bent over and leaned in the passenger side to get a bunch of keys out of the glove compartment. At that moment, Frank was secretly wishing he'd had a better shave that morning.

'I'm glad I caught you before you took them back to the Shelford office,' I said as she handed me a key with a parcel tag tied to it on which was written just the word 'Manor'.

'Worried in case Devon remembered you?' She raised an eyebrow.

'Oh I'm sure he remembers me. We ran into your huckleberry friend in the local pub last night.'

'Really?' She allowed herself a smile. 'Did he buy you a drink or was he too busy doing *Moon River* on the karaoke machine?'

'There's an image that will stay with me,' I said with a mock shudder.

'I've seen it for real – and it does. What was my huckleberry friend up to?'

'He was with his mates from the opera group and they seemed very interested in my choice of properties to view.'

'They would be; they're like vampires when it comes to searching out new recruits. Males especially, if they're under sixty and have both their original hips.'

'Well I told him I'm tone deaf and can't play a

note, but Frank here has a wonderful sense of rhythm and all his own body parts.'

Frank actually blushed as Jane Bond laughed.

'Now hang on a minute,' he spluttered, 'didn't you tell me you used to be a musician in a salsa band?'

'Yes, but I wasn't going to tell them that, was I?'

'Salsa, eh?' teased Mrs Bond. 'That's sexy that is. Probably best not to mention it to Devon; the very idea would just get him over excited.'

'He seemed very interested in my interest in Comberton Manor, so perhaps it would be better if he didn't know I was going for a second look.'

'What are you really going for?'

I saw no particular reason not to trust Jane Bond; a confident, good-looking, mature woman like that, with her own Aston Martin – of course I could trust her.

'To see if it's possible to wire the place so we can record any ghostly presence.'

'So you are a psychic detective after all?'

'If you've got a problem with ghosts, who else you gonna call?'

It was obvious she didn't get the reference and neither did Frank. Maybe I was losing my touch. Maybe I needed a holiday; say a nice long week-end with sights to see, good food, bars which never closed and, best of all, room service.

Yes, that would do nicely.

You can see the London Eye looming over you through the glass roof of Waterloo Station as you board the Eurostar. If you have a hangover, it can be quite unnerving early on a Saturday morning and it is all too easy to imagine a Spielbergian disaster movie scenario where the damn thing breaks off its hinges and starts rolling down the riverbank, crushing everything in its path. I had my own reasons to avoid the famous slow-motion ferris wheel, on which I was once trapped with a psychotic Welsh gangster in one of its observation bubbles on the sort of guided tour of London you wouldn't want to repeat.

I was determined not to let the shadow of the evil, all-seeing eye disrupt my much-deserved break in gay Paree. Amy had done quite enough already to put a damper on things, spending most of the previous evening harping on about why I hadn't phoned my father yet, to break the wonderful news that he was to become a grandfather. I just couldn't make her understand that these days I hardly had a minute to myself and anyway, the chances of my father being at home in his Westminster flat on a Friday night (especially if he was dating a nineteen-year-old topless model) were remote. Nevertheless, Amy had insisted I tried and she stood on my shoulder to make sure I did.

'Hi, Dad, it's me,' I said into the receiver. 'Yeah, fine, fine. She's fine too. Look, I won't keep you if you're going out, but I just had to tell you that Amy's pregnant...Yes, yes, it was a bit of a shock at first... No, she's fine, a picture of health... Oh, five or six months yet, no need to panic... No, I haven't told Mother, haven't seen her for a while... Well, if you don't mind telling her, that would be great! Yeah, okay ... yes, I've got to go too. Have fun. See you. Yes, later, dude.'

189

Amy had been in my face before I had put the phone down.

'You were talking to the answering machine, weren't you?'

'How did you know?'

'You didn't make a single crack about nineteen-year-old topless models.'

She knew me too well and got her revenge by making me repeat her instructions about which shops to check out over the weekend, even making me look up the addresses on an old street plan of central Paris, a souvenir from a previous visit. (My Rule of Life number 66 is: Never throw away maps of big cities. Local knowledge is so important when making up a fake address.)

And just to make sure I did what she wanted, she demanded photographic proof and presented me with an Olympus C-460 Zoom digital camera, charged up and ready to go, which I didn't even know we owned. She also gave me an instruction book which 'even' I could understand. I took it with good grace, regretting that I had given back the mini camera which fitted on a key ring to Frank. That only had one button to mess up.

Eventually she left me in peace long enough to pack a shoulder bag with the basic essentials and sneak off to bed, pleading an early start in the morning. When I had picked up my bag at 7.30, there was a luggage label tied to the zip fastener on which she'd written: 'No cigs. No booze. Turn your fuckin' phone on.'

The label accidentally fell off my bag somewhere on the Northern Line, and miraculously found itself tied to the rucksack of a Finnish student backpacker changing tubes at Leicester Square on his way to Heathrow.

At Waterloo I had plenty of time to buy a couple of film magazines and for a weak and overpriced cappuccino before I went down to the Eurostar boarding area, which regular cross-Channel commuters were said to call Platform Nine-and-three-quarters. I allowed a school party of French kids to jostle their way through the security funnel before I ran the gauntlet with a wave of my passport and a flourish of my first class ticket.

I wandered the length of the train, keeping the full width of the platform between me and the windows and the open doors, each guarded by a uniformed member of the train crew. When I reached the first class section at the front of the train, I hid behind one of the central pillars instead of boarding and looked back down the long platform. I almost regretted that I didn't have a trench coat, so I could turn up the collar, but I didn't need one. Not only would I have looked stupid on such a fine summer's morning, I really didn't require a disguise. Dr Cassandra Quinn was striding down the platform straight towards me. She was wearing a polo-necked top in white and pink hoops (ignoring the fashion mantra about horizontal stripes), bright, cherry red flared trousers and pink trainers, so she wasn't exactly trying to pass unnoticed but, to be fair, she had the figure to carry it off and I would probably have noticed her even if I hadn't been looking for her.

Two carriage lengths short of where I was hugging the concrete pillar, Dr Quinn showed her ticket to an attendant and hopped aboard, bouncing a Samsonite garment carrier with an extended handle up the steps behind her.

I gave her a good two minutes and when she hadn't reappeared on the platform, or passed along the train internally, I assumed she had found her seat so I went to find mine.

The Eurostar pulled out dead on time as I settled down behind a complimentary copy of the *Daily Telegraph*. I had worked out that Dr Quinn was actually three coaches behind me and so although I was supposed to be tailing her, technically she was following me, across south London then Kent, then into twenty miles of tunnel, at speeds of up to 130 mph.

Confident that she was unlikely to be getting off at any time before we were in France, I relaxed and, summoning the first class coach attendant, I ordered a Danish pastry, coffee and one of those miniature bottles of champagne which they give you on aeroplanes, but they sell you on Eurostar.

Still, I deserved a treat.

The first-time tourist arriving in Paris by Eurostar gets a pretty depressing view of the city as the train slips, almost apologetically, into the Gare du Nord, although the same could probably be said of the tourist coming the other way and seeing south-east London in all its glory.

As the train relaxed to a complete stop my fellow first class passengers disconnected their i-pods, grabbed their free newspapers as if they had a second-hand value among Parisians, and bolted for the luggage rack and the carriage door. Within less than a minute I was the only one in there, so I moved seats across the aisle away from the platform and facing the front of the train. That way, I could observe all the poor passengers from back in steerage class as they skipped down the platform towards the rather perfunctory passport control.

It wasn't long before Dr Quinn's cherry red trousers swished by the window, towing the Samsonite garment carrier behind them, and it was time to grab my own hold-all and go into detective mode again. I realised that I might be following a woman I didn't know across a strange city for several miles, which would be a first for me – professionally, that is. No one had ever paid me to do that before.

Once off the Eurostar platform, Dr Quinn marched across the station, following signs to the Metro, although she moved confidently as if she knew the route well. The station was busier than I had expected, given that it was a Saturday and, more importantly, about 1.20 p.m. when all true sons and daughters of France should be at lunch, not hanging around a station concourse.

Worryingly, the crowds thinned out drastically as I followed her down the tunnel to the Metro, so I dropped back to a good fifty metres behind her and kept my fingers crossed that she wouldn't turn round.

The different lines on the Metro are colour-coded, just like they are in London, but numbered rather than given names, like Jubilee or Circle Line. The trick of course, is to know which *direction* you need to go in, once you get the right line, and then you buy a ticket for the appropriate terminus. (And a lot of confusion could be avoided if they just said 'clockwise' and 'anti-clockwise' on the Circle Line.) Cassandra Quinn seemed to be heading for Line 5, colour-coded orange, and a quick look at a Metro map on the tunnel wall showed me that it ran from the wonderfully-named Bobigny Pablo Picasso in the 19th arrondisement, out towards Roissy and Charles de Gaulle airport on the north-west edge of the city, down through the Gare du Nord and the Gare de l'Est and due south, crossing on to the left bank of the Seine, with the other terminus at Place d'Italie. If she was going south, it would be really convenient for me as the Metro crossed the river at the Gare d'Austerlitz, where my luxury, four star hotel awaited me.

She paused at a ticket machine in the wall and fed in some change, taking her ticket and moving towards an escalator leading down to the subway platforms. I could hear the roar and rattle of the trains quite clearly, but the smell of burning rubber which I always associated with the Paris Metro from my first visits as a schoolboy, was missing. It had been something to do with ancient rubber wheels and primitive brakes, but like the once prevailing scent of Gauloises cigarettes in the cafes, it had been purged and I couldn't help thinking Paris had lost a little something in cleaning up its act.

I sprinted up the tunnel to the ticket machine and fumbled a ten euro note into it, opting for a Line 5 ticket to Place d'Italie as it was the longest journey, hurrying along not wanting to lose sight of her but, at the same time not wanting to go crashing into the back of her.

My luck was holding; in fact I was beginning to think that the whole business of tailing a suspect was a bit of a doddle. Cassandra Quinn had opted for the southbound train and just as those cherry trousers disappeared into one carriage, I hopped on board the following one just before the doors closed. I stayed at the back of the compartment, leaning against the door, so I had a good view of the platforms of each stop, despite being jostled by a group of over-excited Japanese teenagers.

My main worry was the first stop, the Gare de l'Est, a main line station where I could easily lose her if she got on another train, though I didn't think that likely. My luck held and no cherry trousers alighted and the train clattered off again.

At each station, I stuck my head out of the open doors and scoped the platforms, drawing a blank at Jacques Bonsergent, Republique, Oberkampf, Richard Lenoir, Breguet Sabin and Bastille, and suddenly the train was running over-ground and in the distance I could see the unmistakeable metallic spike of the Eiffel Tower.

And then we were rattling over the Seine and into the Gare d'Austerlitz, which the Metro enters almost as if it's coming in through the glass roof – it's a very Harry Potter moment, and slightly surreal when you get off the underground and then find you have to walk *down* two floors to get to street level.

Which is exactly what I had to do as it turned out, for Cassandra Quinn and her red trousers got off at Austerlitz station and walked down the platform passing within less than five feet of me. She didn't see me, I was sure, but I waited as long as I dared before jumping off the train – not wishing to get my arse nipped by the closing doors – and followed her to the stairs which were labelled *Sortie*.

This was moving towards the bizarre. Dr Quinn was getting off at *my* station and walking up the slip road towards the Boulevard de l'Hôpital, which was where *my* hotel was located. It was starting to unnerve me. There was only one thing to do.

Dr Quinn kept to the pavement, pulling her Samsonite behind her over the cobbles. As she walked alongside a rank of taxis (all of them empty of drivers, as it was still technically French lunch time), I skipped across the road and began to stride purposefully up the other side, over-taking her and being at least thirty metres in front of her by the time I got to the Boulevard de l'Hôpital.

I stopped and produced my street map of Paris, as if lost, although I could quite clearly see the sign saying Hotel Austerlitz from where I was standing.

The fact that there were so few people around certainly helped, as I could hear the noise her case made on its tiny wheels. As the sound got louder, I turned, still holding the street plan. She was about five feet away.

'Good God!' I said, 'Dr Quinn. What the hell are you doing here? You're not following me are you?'

Chapter Ten

'...?...'

She froze in her tracks and made a guttural choking sound in her throat in at least two languages and I could see from her eyes that her brain was racing through questions such as: was this a mugging, was she being propositioned and who the hell was I? I often have this effect on women and I suppose I should be thankful she wasn't carrying a can of mace.

'It's...?' she managed and I was both relieved and slightly peeved that she didn't remember me.

'Roy, Roy Angel. I did some work at Tyler Pharmaceuticals this week.'

'Oh yes, of course.' She relaxed as it all came flooding back to her. 'You're the security consultant.'

'Was,' I corrected, keen to stress the past tense. 'I've finished my report.'

'That was quick.' There was a gleam in her eyes now as her wits came back to her, and I suspected she had wits in abundance. 'So what brings you to Paris?'

'Bit of business, but mostly pleasure. How about you?'

'Just a week-end break, you know, get away from it all for a few days.'

'So pure pleasure then?' I said, not wanting to spook her, just keep her off balance.

'With any luck, yes,' she said, keeping eye contact. 'I'm meeting up with my boyfriend.'

'He lives here?'

'No, he's just coming in for the weekend as well. What sort of business brings you here, Ray?'

I let the name thing go.

'A bit of photography actually, if I can work out how to use a digital camera. It's for a project my wife's doing. Just normal touristy stuff: Eiffel Tower, Pompidou Centre, Notre Dame, that sort of thing. I'm tempted just to buy a selection of postcards and spend the weekend in a bar somewhere.'

'Do you know Paris well?' she asked in a tone which suggested she didn't believe a word I'd said.

'Well enough. The city centre's pretty small and it's easy enough to get around on foot. Damn sight easier than driving.'

I nodded towards the Place Valhubert just down the road, where six or eight lanes of converging traffic tried to do Le Mans style racing starts every time the traffic lights changed – and some times before they did.

'And I've got a good map,' I added as I was still holding it in one hand.

'Can I borrow it to find my hotel?'

'Allow me. What's the address?'

'It's called the Hotel du Jardin and it's supposed to be on the street of the Arenes de Lutece.'

I didn't want to patronise her map-reading skills but I couldn't help wincing at her accent.

'Don't need the map for that. I know it. Well, not the hotel, but I know the Arena; it's an old Roman amphitheatre on the edge of the Latin Quarter, on the other side of the Botanical Gardens which are just across the road. Ten minute stroll – tops. Let me show you, I could do with a walk after sitting on that train all morning. It's no trouble.'

'If you're sure,' she said.

'I'd be happy to.'

'Then thank you. It was really lucky I ran into you.'

'It's better to be lucky than good,' I murmured, mostly to myself.

We managed to cross the Boulevard de l'Hôpital without getting mown down by the traffic and walked towards the Seine and the main gates into the Jardin des Plantes where the biggest danger was either being mobbed by the huge, overweight crows that hop between the formal flower beds or tripping over a pair of teenaged lovers making out on the greensward. There were couples and whole families and even elderly ladies on their own enjoying picnics in the Garden. And these weren't the packet of crisps, damp egg sandwich and flask of tea picnics you saw in Hyde Park in the summer; these were *les picque-nicques,* with table cloths, bottles of wine, glass tumblers, creamy white cheeses and crusty bread affairs, even though the French didn't have a proper word for them.

I hadn't been spinning her a line, I really did know the Arenes de Lutece, a small but wonderfully preserved Roman amphitheatre hidden in a square island of green trees and hedges. It reminded me somewhat of Soho Square but instead of finding a wooden gazebo stuccoed with pigeon droppings in the middle of the square, here was a location where you could have filmed a small-scale version of *Gladiator*, built by the Romans to impress the uncouth local Celtic tribe the *Parisii*.

I walked Cassandra through it and apart from one old boy wearing a straw hat and sleeping off his lunch on the fifth or sixth tier of seating, we had the place to ourselves. The last time I had been there I had discovered it was the place where the Paris Fire Brigade's five-a-side soccer team came to practise between shifts and I had confirmed their suspicions that English goalkeepers were basically unreliable in penalty shoot-outs.

As we emerged through a small garden gate arrangement back on to the streets of the Latin Quarter, Dr Quinn had the manners to be impressed, if not particularly interested.

'That was impressive,' she said, 'and I would never have known it was there.'

'Not many people do, thank God,' I said and then pointed across the street. 'And there's your hotel.'

The Hotel du Jardin was an unflashy three-storey town house hotel, probably still family owned, typical of hundreds which still exist in Paris, offering basic comforts but no frills and if you don't mind the lack of room service and over-complex plumbing then the bill won't induce a heart attack.

A pretty dark haired girl behind a desk welcomed us and her smile widened as Cassandra said her name was Quinn.

'Ah, le Mighty Quinn...' she said reverentially to Cassandra's utter confusion.

'It's an old pop song by a band called Manfred Mann,' I whispered rapidly into her ear. 'And she's far too young to remember it – so are you – but it could have been one of her mother's favourites. It was very big in France and they still play it, they're a bit slow when it comes to pop music.'

They also thought Jerry Lewis was funny, but I didn't think that worth mentioning.

The desk girl checked her computer screen and told Cassandra that she had a double room reserved for two nights for her and that was right, wasn't it? Oh, and there was a message for her.

It was at this point that I realised that Dr Quinn might be hot stuff with a chemistry set and had at least three degrees to her name, but she couldn't speak a word of French, and so I added translator to my other jobs as map-reader and tourist guide. At this rate I was becoming indispensable.

I told the girl everything was correct and asked what *madame* should do about payment, then I translated.

'You've got a double room for two nights and she needs a credit card. You've also got a message waiting for you.'

'On the phone?' she asked me in English.

The desk girl understood that and told me it was just a note on the computer, from that morning when a 'friend' (and she said it with a twinkle in her eye) called Michel, though he certainly wasn't French, had rung to say he was delayed and would not be in Paris until Sunday morning. And by the way, my French was very good, much better than Michel's.

I thanked her for that and translated the relevant bits for Cassandra who looked down at the carpet and said 'Shit!'

'*Madame a dit: merde,*' I said politely for the desk girl's benefit and she smiled at me. I suspected she spoke perfect English but wasn't going to make the effort because Cassandra had not.

'I'm sorry if that's thrown your plans,' I said while she was still thinking it through. 'And I can't let you wander the streets of this brash city alone, so why don't I dump my stuff at my hotel and come back here and treat you to dinner this evening?'

'I had plans...' she said vaguely.

'Don't let me screw them up, for goodness' sake, but we all have to eat and that's one thing they're pretty good at in this town.'

'Nobody does it better,' said the desk girl quietly in French, her eyes riveted to her computer screen.

'Well I suppose I have to eat somewhere,' said Dr Quinn. 'Do you know a good restaurant?'

'In Paris?' I said loudly. 'Yes, I know a great one. Of course it's Italian.'

Cassandra Quinn reckoned she could find her room on the second floor without my help, so I offered to meet her in an hour when we could walk into the city centre, take in the sights and then eat. There was a moment of hesitation in her eyes, but only a moment's worth, as she weighed up the pros and cons of going around a foreign city with a strange man. On the one hand, she knew who I was and that I had been employed by Olivier Zaborski. She knew that I was married, because I had already volunteered the information, and that I spoke the language and knew my way around. I told her that I had a specific remit to visit clothes shops and discount fashion outlets. The last was, I think, the clincher.

As I retraced our route through the Botanic Gardens towards Austerlitz Bridge and Station, I began to have my doubts that she would be still in her hotel in an hour's time. But then she didn't seem to have anywhere else to go and the missing boyfriend was expecting her to be there, so why should she? I also wondered where my technique would come in the private eye's operational manual. There was probably a whole chapter on how to follow suspects by taking them out to dinner.

Which was something I was not going to do at the Hotel Austerlitz. I was given a key to a second-floor room and told there was a lift by the middle-aged Vietnamese *concierge*. Having a lift was about the extent of the hotel's luxuries. It had no restaurant other than a breakfast bar on the first floor, no room service except in cases of national emergency and no bar. Each room did have a television, though, with fourteen channels – all French.

No restaurant, French TV and no bar? I wondered if the Gestapo had been sad to leave in 1944.

I found my room, dumped my bag on the bed and shoehorned myself into the tiny bathroom to take a shower. The plumbing seemed to work and the water was hot but I had to fumble, almost blind, the bizarre screw handle which opened the window to release the fog of steam and condensation. From my bathroom window I would have had a clear view of the side of Austerlitz Station were it not for the large red neon sign saying *Terminus Bar* which ran down the side of the building.

Using the bedroom's large desk fan to dry off, I dressed in a grey seersucker shirt and black slacks, stuck Amy's digital camera in a pocket of my jacket and carried the jacket slung over my shoulder. With my fake Raybans on, I was sure I could blend into a summer Saturday in Paris, the art of which was to look cooler as the afternoon heat increased.

I definitely got a smirk of approval from the desk clerk back at the Hotel du Jardin, who buzzed Cassandra Quinn's room on the house telephone and informed me that *madame* would be down shortly. She was now wearing a badge pinned to her shirt above the right breast, saying her name was Prisca, and she made sure I saw it when she said:

'Madame Quinn is interested in sculpture?'

I must have blanked her, as the question caught me totally off guard.

'Madame has been asking for directions to the Museum of Open Air Sculpture,' Prisca said slowly as if talking to *un idiot.*

I gave her an all-purpose shrug of the shoulders which could have meant 'What do you expect? She's English.' Or just as easily 'Who can understand women?' You can do that in French and be immediately understood. It's a great language for shrugging in.

'It's down by the river, isn't it?' I asked her.

'Yes, though there's not much there. It's near the Batobus stop.'

I thanked her and gave her my second best smile, to keep her on my side but not encourage her. She had just given me an idea.

Cassandra appeared in the lobby with her voluminous red hair tied back in a thick pony tail. She was still wearing the cherry trousers and pink trainers, but she'd changed her stripey top for a loose, silky red thing with thin shoulder straps which she had trapped around the waist with a four-inch wide black leather belt. She had a huge canvas shopping bag slung over one shoulder and, for the first time in my presence, a smile on her face.

'Ready for the guided tour or would you prefer some extreme shopping?' I offered.

'How about a bit of both?'

'Good choice. Follow me, your *bateau* awaits.'

'My *what?*'

The Paris Batobus is the only way to travel and see the main city sights. If I lived in Paris I would insist on a job where I could commute by the Batobus, which plies a route from the Jardin des Plantes up the right bank of the Seine, with stops for the Hotel de Ville, The Louvre, the Champs Élyseés and then a long slow turning run under the Pont d'Iena to drop you at the Eiffel Tower. The rest of the circuit was along the Left Bank, offering staggering views from river level, of the foundations and walls of Notre Dame. Each glass-roofed Batobus comes equipped with the best sort of tour guide, the ones who say at the start of each journey: 'If you've heard all this before, tell me and I'll shut up.'

Cassandra said she had no qualms about boat travel, insisted on buying her own ticket and said she fancied the Eiffel Tower if we had the time. I said sure, we could be there in about twenty-five minutes and before I knew it she was pushing her way to the front of the queue for the stone steps down into the dark green Seine as the arriving Batobus – a sort of flat barge with a conservatory and fitted seating – nosed into view.

The tour guide on our boat shouted: 'Jardin des Plantes' and most of his passengers disembarked, leaving Cassandra the pick of the good seats at the rear, to where she rushed like a school kid without any encouragement from me.

For the next two hours she did the complete tourist deal, counting the bridges the boat went under (she made it sixteen), going 'ooh' and 'aah' in all the right places as the Batobus chugged around the stone walls of the Île St Louis and the Île de la Cité and the back end of Notre Dame, and she checked off famous names as she saw them on signs, as if she had an itinerary: Louvre, Tuileries, Place de la Concorde and, on the Left Bank, the Quai d'Orsay. When we docked at the landing step for the Eiffel Tower, she actually squealed and clapped her hands together.

Not even the massive queues for the entrances to the Tower damped her spirits.

'They're going to put an ice rink on the first

level,' I told her as we shuffled forward with the crowd, all of us looking up at the giant ladder of steel above us. 'And in their bid for the 2012 Olympics, they've said they'll put sand down here in between the four feet and hold the women's beach volleyball events.'

'I know,' said Cassandra, 'my boyfriend can't have mentioned it more than a hundred times since he heard he was coming to Paris.'

It was the first time she had mentioned him and I hadn't pushed it until now.

'Were you going to come here with him?'

'I thought about it, but he's been delayed and we'll only have one day together now.'

'Make him bring you tomorrow night, when they put the lights on. It's supposed to be dead romantic and there are no queues.'

'I might just do that,' she said and then gave me a typically English polite nod to thank me for the advice. A French woman would have kissed me.

We eventually made it to the ticket office where we each paid seven euros for access to the second floor, which was quite high enough to see all the sights – any higher was mountaineering, not tourism. From the viewing platforms I used Amy's camera for some vista shots and you have to admit, it's a pretty impressive set of vistas. I even persuaded Cassandra to pose for a couple of shots, looking out towards the École Militaire.

Using the camera reminded me of what I should be using it for and I explained to Cassandra that, if she'd seen enough, I ought to get back to Le Marais before the shops shut.

'What's Le Marais?' she asked.

'It used to be the Jewish quarter, now it's where the trendy boutiques and cheap clothes shops are. We can take the Batobus back to Notre Dame and walk over the bridges to the Île St Louis. I was thinking of eating there anyway.'

'Fashion boutiques, cheap clothes, restaurants...?' she said with a deliberate fluttering of her eyelashes, 'Are you sure you're not trying to chat me up, Ray?'

'I would, but I bet your boyfriend's bigger than me.'

'Oh yes, he is,' she said with a smile, 'but if you offer a girl things like that, you might be in with a chance.'

I grinned, but I didn't think so. It would mean her having to get my name right for a start.

We jumped off the Batobus at the Notre Dame stop on the Quai Montebello, climbed the concrete steps to street level and crossed one of the smaller Seine bridges to the tip of the Île de la Cite in the shadow of the cathedral. From there, I showed Cassandra the way across to the Île St Louis and then the Louis Phillippe bridge to the Right Bank and into the heart of the Marais district on the rue Vielle du Temple to the west of the Pompidou Centre.

'What are we looking for?' she asked.

'A shop called *Le Mouton à Cinq Pattes.*'

'What does that mean?'

'The Sheep With Five Legs.'

'Yeah, right, that's helpful.'

'It's taken from a French film of the 1950s, what the reference books call "a Gallic gem".'

'I'm no wiser,' she said happily.

'It starred Fernandel.'

'That doesn't help.'

'Never mind, it doesn't matter. The shop specialises in last year's designer collections but with the labels cut out.'

'Now I'm interested.'

She turned out to be far more interested than I was, fingerwalking the racks of party dresses and trouser suits with a mixture of rapture and reverence. She didn't even notice me taking half a dozen shots of the shop with her centre stage and of course none of the assistants minded because they thought I was her lovesick other half taking pictures of her. She even overcame the language barrier to have a detailed discussion with one of the shop assistants who was complementing her on her cherry red slacks, which were all the rage in Paris this summer and virtually every female under fifty was wearing them. Cassandra came away with a scrap of paper on which was written *Côte á Côte*, another boutique nearby which had been recommended by the staff as a place with even bigger discounts.

I made a mental note to tell Amy about that one, and the red trousers craze, but told Cassandra they would probably be closing up and she might like to come back tomorrow as Le Marais was the one area of Paris where all the shops tended to open on a Sunday. I suggested that we walked back to the Île St Louis for some refreshment.

'Good. I could murder a cup of tea,' she said, as English tourists always do.

'I wouldn't recommend the tea,' I said,

'anyway, it's six o'clock and that means only one thing in Paris. It's ice-cream time.'

At first she thought I was kidding, but as we crossed the bridge back on to the smaller of the two islands in the middle of the Seine, we began to see well-dressed French couples of all ages, even a few complete families, promenading along the quay, brandishing ice cream cones in every colour of an Impressionists' palette. I explained that this was a bit of an institution in Paris and that families would drive in from the suburbs and risk parking their cars illegally outside the Prefecture of Police just so they could be seen dripping ice-cream down their best clothes. Not just any ice-cream, though, it had to be from one of the famous Berthillon kiosks, where the queues started to form every evening at 6 p.m.

During the wait in the queue for the window kiosk she changed her mind four times but eventually plumped for a double cone with a scoop each of passion fruit and lime sorbets. I opted for pistachio ice cream because I've never tasted better than the French version.

We walked an almost complete circuit of the island as we ate our cones, a procedure, I explained, not so much to do with being seen by the other fashionable members of Berthillon's fan club, but to work up an appetite for dinner and contemplate which restaurant to visit.

I had already done that, of course, and steered her down the Rue St Louis en l'Île, the main street which bisects the island, and into *Las Castafiore*, where a tall, slim, blond maitre d' welcomed us in French, shook my hand and said 'Any friend of

Barry White is welcome here' to me, before showing us to a table near the rear of the restaurant, within reaching distance of the bar.

Cassandra squeezed into a chair with her back against the wall and I fitted the small table around her as the maitre d' slid two menus across the crisp white table cloth.

'You weren't kidding, were you? This really is an Italian restaurant.'

'Best one in Paris. Would you like a drink while we read the menu?'

'Just a fizzy mineral water, please.'

'Sure? I was thinking of having a *kir*.'

'I want to keep a clear head,' she said without elaborating.

For the first time in several hours, I remembered that I was supposed to be suspicious of her.

From the bar, the maitre d' produced a kir and a small bottle of Pelegrino with a glass full of ice on a small silver tray and took the one step from the bar to our table to serve them, telling me, in French, that they were with the compliments of the management.

'Thank you, Edward,' I said in English, and I used the English 'Edward' rather than the French 'Edouard'.

'He speaks English?' Cassandra asked in a whisper even though he had disappeared through the swing door with the glass porthole which led into the kitchen.

'Fairly well, for an American from Chicago.'

'He's American? But he speaks French.'

'An unusual combination I admit, but Ed has

211

lived in Paris for years and whenever Americans wander in here, he speaks nothing *but* French to them. I like his attitude.'

I had first wandered into *La Castafiore* the week the great Barry White, the singer with a Grand Canyon-deep bass voice, had died. Edward had been playing Barry White CDs in the restaurant all night long, in tribute. We had been speaking French and I had noticed his accent, which I couldn't really place, although I put that down to the amount of drink. And then I had mentioned Barry White's nickname, 'The Walrus of Love', but said that I couldn't for the life of me remember – if I ever knew – what the French for walrus was. Without thinking, Edward lapsed into American English, saying 'Neither the fuck do I' and his cover was blown. That evening had ended in hilarity (and more drink) when Edward had opened the door to the kitchen and asked the staff working there what the word for 'walrus' was, miming the animal by holding downward pointing fingers at the corners of his mouth and puffing his cheeks out. The chef, who was French, looked up from his chopping board and with a dead straight face said: 'How do you want it cooked?' When we had stopped laughing, we eventually decided that 'walrus of love' was *le morse d'amour*, though it's not a phrase you get to use often.

Cassandra laughed in all the right places as I told the story and she smiled sweetly at Edward every time he served us. She gave a good account of herself with the food, demolishing a dish of spaghetti with clams as a starter before moving on to chicken breasts wrapped into parcels with

Parma ham and cheese, leaving room for a crème brûlée. But throughout, she stuck to mineral water, leaving me to finish a bottle of wine by myself, and even refused a complimentary cognac with her coffee.

In the end, it was Edward who couldn't resist asking, and setting her up for one of the oldest gags in the world.

'Does madam not drink?' he asked her, in English, whilst opening another bottle of mineral water for her.

'No, not alcohol,' Cassandra replied, confident and not at all embarrassed.

'Not at all?' Edward persisted, knowing that I knew what was coming.

'No; I don't drink alcohol,' she said firmly.

Edward waited a beat, as was required by the laws of comedy, and then said loudly:

'You mean you wake up in the morning and that's as good as you're going to feel *all day?*'

Cassandra Quinn blushed, which is something I think she did sparingly and I, naturally, being the gentleman that I am, came riding to her rescue with subtle, diplomatic grace.

'Piss off, American imperialist scum or I'll start the rumour that you're converting this place into a Starbuck's. Now get me an armagnac, and the good stuff, mind.'

Edward put his hands on his hips and glared down at me.

'And what did your last slave die of?' he demanded in French for the benefit of the rest of the customers.

'*Ennui,*'I replied and he flounced off behind the

bar, all of two feet away, to get my drink.

'Is he not used to people not drinking?' Cassandra said, leaning forward over the table. I automatically leaned in too, making the neutral zone between us the smallest it had been all day.

'That's not just Edward, that's France, but don't let it bother you. I once took a black feminist vegan to a Japanese restaurant. Now there was a dinner date from hell; trust me.'

'You don't mind?'

'Why should I mind? So you don't drink and you don't smoke, (well she hadn't in my presence so far) but I'm sure you have some vices somewhere.'

'Actually, I do smoke occasionally, and I do have a vice, or at least my boyfriend thinks it is. Well, maybe not a vice, but an addiction.'

'But boyfriends are the worst people to judge things like that. You should only confess your vices and/or addictions to total strangers, or almost total strangers, that you happen to be having dinner with in a foreign city.'

'And only if in top-notch Italian restaurants,' said Edward from behind the bar, where he'd been eavesdropping.

I felt a twinge of sympathy for Cassandra. She might as well put all her thoughts and conversations on the internet, the number of people who were listening in on her on a daily basis. But it was a very small twinge. She was, after all, my only suspect, although she had said nothing remotely suspicious about her work all evening. Then again, I hadn't actually asked her any questions about her work, preferring to gain her total confidence first.

But she wasn't going to confess anything there

and then, at least not to me. She made a point of looking at her watch.

'I have to be going,' she said.

'Early night? It's not even dark yet outside.'

'There's something I want to do on my way back to the hotel. It's okay, I don't need a guide, I can find my own way back from here. Excuse me.'

I stood up to pull the table out so she could get out of her seat, but she wasn't leaving just yet. She shouldered her bag and jinked by me and then body-swerved Edward coming from behind the bar, to the door marked *Toilettes*.

A small glass bowl of armagnac appeared as if by magic on the table in front of me and Edward whipped his arm out of my sightline, as waiters in France are taught to do.

'And where is the lovely Amy?' he asked from somewhere behind me, in English.

'Back in London,' I said without turning my head.

'Ah, I see.'

'I doubt that.'

'Is the fashion scene in Paris too boring for her these days?'

'Not at all, in fact I'm here as a spy for her while she's busy being pregnant.'

'Oooh, pregnant, eh? Do you know who the father is?'

I raised my voice so the other customers could hear me and switched to French.

'Really, Edward, that's just typical of you Americans. The French are *not* "cheese eating surrender monkeys".'

'Keep your voice down, Angel, for God's sake,'

he hissed. 'American tourists might think I'm French but most of my regulars reckon I'm Canadian and I want to keep it like that. Nobody dislikes Canadians.'

'Except seal cubs,' I whispered, back in English.

'Don't go there, Angel.'

'Do you know what the French for "seal" is, Edward?'

'Yes I do, Mister Smart Arse, it's *phoque.*'

'But you didn't know what a walrus was, did you. I was really hoping you would have to ask one of your waitresses: 'I need the French word for a walrus and I suppose a *phoque* is out of the question?'

'Oh ha ha, very funny.' He made an O of his finger and thumb and held them in front of my face. 'Insert laugh here.' Then his voice dropped an octave. 'Although it might not be out of the question for you, you lucky son of a bitch.'

I turned my head to see what he had seen.

Cassandra was standing beside the tiny bar. In the toilet she had applied make-up and let down her long curls of red hair. She had taken off her jeans and unfurled the red silk top which now hugged her thighs to just above her knees. The pink trainers had joined her jeans and been stuffed into the shoulder bag, to be replaced by red shoes with three inch square heels, making her taller and showing off her legs. Her very good legs.

'I know what the lady wants,' said Edward. 'The lady wants to salsa!'

Chapter Eleven

Which just goes to show that if you want to know what's going on in Paris, just ask a waiter or a restaurant owner. As soon as he saw Cassandra's transformation outfit, Edward knew where she was headed.

'I know where *you're* going,' he chanted softly, playground style.

'The Museum of Open Air Sculpture,' said Cassandra, 'that's just down on the side of the river near the Botanic Gardens, right?'

'You mean the Salsa Club,' said Edward, 'Be there or be square. Once you're on the Left Bank, you can't miss them. You'll hear them before you see them.'

Now she had her dancing shoes on there was no holding her back. She insisted on paying half the bill and I insisted on accompanying her as it was, after all, on the way back to both our hotels. We both shook hands with Edward at the door of the restaurant. Cassandra got a kiss on the hand, I got kissed on both cheeks and told him not to try that back in Chicago.

We crossed the Pont de la Tournelle and descended the steps to the concrete quay which kept the Seine in check. The so-called Museum of Open Air Sculpture was little more than an unfinished municipal park of small clipped hedges designed to show off a few avant garde art works if

217

you got close enough to find them. Parisians had quickly discovered that on fine evenings, this nice, flat, traffic-free space could be put to better use as an al fresco ballroom. Actually, there were two ballrooms on different levels, one for beginners and one for those who already had their salsa pilot's licences. The whole thing was, remarkably, free of commercialism. In London, such a spontaneous event on the South Bank, say, would have attracted ice-cream sellers and burger vans within seconds, but here there was nothing, not even the Arab youths selling knocked-off bottles of mineral water from buckets filled with ice as they did on every other street corner of the city.

This was a free meeting of minds – the sort of thing the Left Bank used to do quite well but also a meeting of arms, legs and buttocks abandoned to the basic *son* rhythm which is the root of salsa music.

Cassandra's pace quickened as we neared the throng of gyrating bodies until her heels were clicking on the concrete quay like Morse code. Up ahead of us, I could see a crowd of perhaps two hundred people and beyond them, slightly higher on a raised part of the quay, about the same number again, and cherry red trousers were much in vogue. My ears could pick out a mixture of tunes and rhythms, a distant brass section (which as an old horn player made the hairs on the back of my neck stand up) and lots of soft, fast conga beats.

I felt Cassandra lean suddenly into my shoulder as a bicycle zoomed by us at great speed. A young French lad was standing up pedalling furiously.

218

On the seat of the ancient bike was his girlfriend, arms locked around his chest, laughing hysterically, her shiny blue dress pulled up around her waist, her legs splayed out wide to prevent her scuffing her best high heels on the bicycle frame and, in the process, giving much of the Left Bank an eye-popping view of her black stockings and white suspender belt.

'She's keen,' said Cassandra.

Which was rich coming from somebody who was almost running by now. And also, I noticed, holding my hand.

The first group of dancers were obviously the enthusiastic beginners and included several small groups being tutored by instructors. They all shared the same source of music, a large portable CD player which someone had rigged to a car battery. Next to it were perhaps two hundred CDs, many on labels I'd never heard of, some with sleeve notes in languages I'd never heard of either. Some I knew, such as Africando, the African salsa 'collective' which featured musicians from Senegal, as does the Orchestre Baobab de Dakar, and of course the Cuban masters like Chico Alvarez and Los Van Van, but there were piles of disks of salsa bands from Colombia, Peru and Puerto Rico and Afro-latino bands from the Congo, Benin, Mali and Guinea, which were new to me but very tempting. Amy had only outlawed fags and booze, she'd said nothing about bringing back a truckload of music.

'Stop fingering the records and come and dance,' Cassandra shouted in my ear.

'I'm not very good, I said.'

219

'Don't worry, I am.'

She was, too.

The basic rule of salsa is that it's a four-step structure, and if at least three of those steps don't land on your partner's feet, you're winning. The other good rule is to avoid the 'casino wheel' group moves of synchronised salsa which they sometimes try out on beginners and then the instructor will shout 'Camera!' at random moments, which means the group should freeze – in roughly the same position. Such things rarely look cool with novices. Keep it simple. Your cross-body turns should be smooth; if the female ends up with bruising on the breasts, something's going wrong. And above all, don't improvise, it will just look as if you've been stung.

During a slower number played by a big band with lyrics, ironically, bemoaning the exploitation of Cuban culture by outside forces, I confirmed what Cassandra already knew.

'You really are good at this, aren't you? Where do you practise?'

'In Barcelona, mostly.'

She laughed at the expression on my face.

'On holiday. They do these long week-end holidays to the clubs out there.'

'The waterfront clubs, like Salsa Buena Vista?'

'Why, yes.' She was impressed at my cosmopolitan knowledge, though it was an easy guess that a salsa club would be named after the legendary Buena Vista Social Club. 'There's also La Clave and La Habana, in fact there's quite a scene going on down there and the alternative back in Cambridge is the occasional course run in some draughty Community Centre attended by desperate housewives or butch lesbians who've been kicked out of an aerobics class. No men, or very rarely, and salsa is one of the two things a woman can't do without a man.'

'What's the other?' I had to ask.

'Change the wheel on a car at the side of a road, of course,' she said and waited for the follow up.

'I know lots of women who can change the wheel on a car,' I said, doing my bit for political correctness.

'You think I paid what I paid for this dress and these shoes to be left alone at the side of a road?'

'Fair play,' I acknowledged the point and, whilst she was in such a good mood and my arm was around her waist, I thought I'd try a bit of detective work. 'What does your boyfriend think about you zipping off to meet with the international mambo maestro set?'

'I met him in a salsa club in Barcelona.'

'This is Michel, right?' I said, remembering to say it as Prisca the hotel clerk had.

'Yes. He told me about this happening here most every night, which is pretty cool, you have to admit. And it's nearer than Barcelona.'

'Pity he couldn't make it. Sorry you're stuck with me.'

'Hey, I've danced with worse.'

Probably one of those butch lesbians expelled from box-aerobics for being too violent, I thought.

'No, come on, you deserve someone who knows what he's doing. Let's move up to the improvers' class next door. They've got a band.'

They had too, and it was a good one. Amazingly, the two groups of dancers – each numbering about two hundred – didn't interfere with each other's enjoyment although they virtually merged into one. The two 'dance floors' though, were sections of the concrete quay on slightly different levels, separated by three small steps so that the group dancing to the live band was about a foot higher than the first lot grooving along to the CD player. Something about the acoustics of the concrete and possibly the oily calm water of the river allowed the two music sources to live in harmony only a few metres apart. I doubt if the open area had been constructed with this in mind. More likely, a piece of open air sculpture had been earmarked for it, but the salsa mafia had moved in and occupied the space and now with no advertising, no admission charge and no formal organisation, these salsa sessions had become a Paris tradition, with all the famed French disregard for matters of health, safety and public liability.

The band was about ten strong, though its membership fluctuated as musicians turned up, did their party pieces and ceded their places to a new arrival. The nucleus was a double bass, three rhythm guitars including a Tres, the Cuban guitar with three pairs of strings, every size and shape of conga drum possible and a fluctuating brass section of three trumpets, a trombone and at one point a flautist. There was also an electric piano with a power cable which disappeared off into municipal hedging and was probably tapped in to a municipal power source. Just about every skin tone was covered by the band and I heard at least eight different languages in the breaks between numbers including what I think was Mandingo from West Africa.

'This is better,' I said into Cassandra's ear. 'Keep music live! I used to have a bumper sticker saying that.'

'You play?'

There was a look in her eyes which, in another world, would have had me wondering how big her boyfriend was and how long it would take us to get a room. And it even occurred to me that we already had rooms, two of them, which was surely overkill even for Paris.

'Not as well as you dance,' I said diplomatically.

'You asking?' she grinned.

'No, but he is.'

Behind her, a young French lothario with impossibly skinny hips squeezed into tight jeans tucked into alligator cowboy boots, was offering to partner her as the band hit the opening of its next number.

She raised an eyebrow and I nodded and she took his hand and he swung her away into the crowd. He was wearing a black leather waistcoat over his bare chest and he might not yet be old enough for body hair, but he could certainly dance. As could the next four partners which picked her up as each tune ended. She seemed to be loving it and was having such a good time, I was sure she would tell me anything I wanted to know, if I could think of anything significant to ask her, and if she remembered I was there at all.

I was sitting on the steps near the band, watching

the swirling frocks showing generous proportions of female leg when the smell of French black tobacco tantalized my nostrils. I noticed it because it was rare these days, the *Gauloises* and *Celtiques* having been replaced by mass marketed *Mariboros*. But not, it seems in some of France's former colonies. The guy sucking on the cigarette was a giant black man, one of the trumpet players on a break. He saw me eyeballing him and reached automatically for the blue packet of *Caporal* he had just stuffed into his shirt pocket.

'No thanks,' I said in French, 'I don't smoke any more, I just like the smell.'

'We have something which smells even better if you prefer it,' he said with a thick accent which I could only guess at being Senegalese.

'Not tonight,' I grinned at him. 'But I'll borrow your trumpet if I may.'

He held out his battered, but still shiny B-flat trumpet with one hand as if to make sure he had understood me.

'You want to play?'

'If it doesn't upset the musicians' union,' I said, indicating the rest of the band.

'I'll say you are with me,' he said, puffing out his chest. He was so big and well built, I was happy to be on his side. 'As long as you play well.'

'I'm a bit out of practice,' I admitted, 'but, hey, it's salsa. Everybody makes mistakes.'

'Thank God,' said the African giant as he handed over the horn. Then he held up a finger telling me to wait while he pushed behind one of the bongo players and reached into a much travelled brown trumpet case.

Returning to stand in front of me, he opened his huge hand to reveal a small plastic bag. At first I thought he was offering me a wrap of some interesting but illegal substance, but as soon as I focused I could see that what was in the bag was a spare trumpet mouthpiece. He took back his instrument and removed the mouthpiece he had been using, slipping into his trouser pocket, and let me fit the new one.

'It's been sterilised,' he said shrugging his shoulders. 'You cannot be too careful these days.'

'Thanks,' I said. 'Good thinking.'

'What do you want to play?'

I had thought only to join in on a couple of the choruses but the band seemed to be settling into a pattern of the more traditional Cuban *son* tunes which I was relatively familiar with.

'Do they know *Ritmo do Mi Son?*'

'The old Chocolate Armenteros number?'

'That's the one, but I don't want the first solo.'

'Take the third. I'll tell the others. Hey, I know some of the words to that one.'

'It's salsa, you only need *some* of the words. Anyway, who's listening to the words?'

I doubted if any of the dancers were, so caught up were they in their own hip-swaying worlds. Certainly none of them seemed to notice me warming up in the background to the number the band was riffing to a rapid conclusion.

I took my place in the semi circle formed by the two other trumpeters and the trombonist and we nodded to each other as musicians do, just like boxers. My giant African mentor exchanged words in several languages with the guy playing

225

the electric piano and the percussionists and then counted us in. I licked my upper lip, took a deep breath and blew.

The opening chorus was brash and easy enough, with plenty of leeway for fluffed notes, and the big African made a fair fist of singing two verses in what I assumed was Spanish, but without a microphone it was difficult to tell, though he seemed to be enjoying himself. Then three short trumpet solos, with me taking the third. None of us had the technique to threaten the version recorded by the legendary Alfredo 'Chocolate' Armenteros, but neither did we screw up and we could relax and look smug whilst the pianist took over with three choruses in his own percussive style, before everyone came in on the last final flourish and we ended more or less together.

So we hadn't exactly set the world on fire and our audience didn't mob us, rush the stage area or even applaud. In fact, most of them didn't seem to realise we had stopped and then slipped effortlessly into the next number for which the guitarists were already laying down the rhythm.

I couldn't see Cassandra's red hair or red dress anywhere in the throng of bodies but the big African could have, as he towered head and shoulders above me. I thanked him in English as I handed back his trumpet and he handed me a business card out of his shirt pocket. It had only three words on it:

Youssef Cissoko
African

It was succinct and no doubt accurate, if not exactly informative. Without thinking, I fumbled

226

out one of mine and dealt it to him.

'Thanks, Fitzy,' he boomed. 'See you around.'

The music, and the dancing, continued for nearly another hour until darkness fell and the only light came from street lights on the opposite Right Bank and from the traffic on the Quai Saint Bernhard above and behind us. With so many gyrating bodies only inches away from a sheer three-metre drop into the oily Seine, it made good sense to pack up before it ended in tears for someone. In any case, the band were dying to get away for a few drinks and/or a few smokes, and I was tempted to join them, but I had to justify my expenses and stay on the job.

Cassandra was flushed and, to be honest, rather sweaty from her exertions. She had danced with at least six different partners that I'd noticed whilst I could only claim two as well as her, a Japanese teenager who apologised beautifully every time she stood on one of my feet, and a chic Frenchwoman who could have been anywhere between 40 and 65 (how do Frenchwomen do that?) and I was *definitely* on a promise with her, had I wanted to be, until she caught the eye of Youssef, my new best African buddy. It turned out he could not only play the trumpet and sing, but he had a pretty good sense of natural rhythm. Who'd have thought it? The last I saw of them was walking off together towards the Latin Quarter. Youssef had his trumpet case in one hand, the woman in the other and what looked like a huge seven-skin joint in his mouth.

Cassandra changed her high heels for her

trainers for the short walk back to her hotel. If nothing else, that convinced me that my virtue was not going to be compromised tonight. That sexy red silk dress ending in the comfy pink trainers was body language even I could understand without an illustrated dictionary.

'I'm knackered,' she said, hefting her shoulder bag, which was another coded signal if I needed one.

'Come on, I'll walk you back to the hotel,' I said like it was my best offer.

And that is all that happened. We found some steps up to the boulevard and took our lives in our hands as we crossed it, dodging the traffic which was dangerous enough in daylight but took no prisoners after dark. Five minutes later, we were in Reception at her hotel, where Cassandra said: 'Thank you for a splendid day. Maybe I'll see you back in Cambridge?'

'You never know,' I said.

She collected her key from a reception desk manned by a surly old waiter who couldn't wait for his shift to end.

She was halfway to the lift when she turned to me.

'Did I see you playing up there with the band tonight?'

'Guest appearance. One night only.'

'I thought it was you. Good night.'

Now in my time I've had more brush-offs than the red carpet at the Savoy, but this one ranked high. The woman must have a degree in ignoring people. As the lift doors closed, I asked the ancient waiter on the desk if Prisca the receptionist was

228

around and he said no, she'd gone for the night. I told him that was a pity, and told myself it was probably just as well.

It was only just after ten o'clock, the night young and still warm, as I walked – alone – back to my hotel, getting even more depressed at the sight of a busy McDonald's on the corner opposite the station. I was ten yards short of the hotel before I remembered it didn't have a bar and automatically did a sharp right turn into the Terminus Bar next door, for a quiet night cap.

Over several Belgian beers, I met a family from Brittany who were holidaying in Paris as payback for the invasion of their home village by thousands of Parisians each summer; two illegal immigrants from Bulgaria hoping to remain unnoticed until Bulgaria joined the European Union in a couple of years' time; an Irish truck driver who had parked his juggernaut in a lorry park for the night and couldn't remember exactly where; and a pair of female Spanish back-packers whose back-packs were bulging with Spanish cigarettes which they were trying to use in lieu of currency.

So all in all, an interesting end to the evening and proof of my Rule of Life number 7: No day is wasted. As I weaved my way out of the bar and back to the Hotel Austerlitz all of ten feet away, the only thing on my mind was to try and remember to buy some fresh t-shirts before I went home so that Amy wouldn't detect the smell of Spanish tobacco.

Breakfast at the Austerlitz was a self-service buffet affair, with the usual selection of slightly stale bread rolls and croissants and individual micro jars of jam, almost all of them apricot flavour. There was also a huge plate of smoked cheeses and warm soft boiled eggs wrapped in a tea-cloth, which suggested they got a lot of German visitors. I helped myself to about a pint of orange juice and two cups of coffee, grabbed the last *pain au chocolat* to eat on the hoof and hit the Sunday morning streets.

I had the Jardin des Plantes virtually to myself and the streets around the Roman amphitheatre were so quiet it was possible to cross them without being splattered by a speeding Citroen.

If I had a plan at all it was simply to turn up and ask Cassandra if she fancied another day of playing tourist. I had sunglasses on and carried a camera, so looked the part. It was a technique I was honing for a chapter in the *Private Eye Handbook* on how to follow someone by standing right next to them; and it would have worked for the second day running but for one minor detail. Cassandra had disappeared.

But it's better to be lucky than good and it was young Prisca behind the reception desk again who took such an obvious delight in telling me that '*Madame* Quinn' was out, that I could tell she had more to divulge.

'Did her boyfriend turn up?' I asked casually.

'No, but he telephoned,' she said primly, trying to suppress a smile. 'About half an hour ago.'

'And then *Madame* Quinn left?' I was going to have to grind it out of her.

'Almost immediately. She seemed very happy. Perhaps she is in love.'

'She's in Paris; I thought it was the law.'

Prisca frowned at that (though it doesn't sound that corny in French) and made to put a finger in her throat, pretending to throw up.

'Okay, okay,' I conceded, 'that was excessive, but I think you are right. And I need to know where she is before she does anything stupid.'

'I don't think she intends to do anything stupid,' said Prisca as if thinking aloud to herself. 'Not this morning, anyway...'

She left it hanging there and I let the suspense drag out until honour was satisfied.

'What makes you think that?'

'Because she's going to church,' Prisca said sweetly. 'A very particular church. Strange, because she doesn't sound Russian.'

After her phone call, Cassandra had asked for directions to a Russian Orthodox church at the bottom end of the Boulevard St Germain, for which Prisca had supplied a simple city plan. If she didn't get lost, it was a twenty-minute walk; a good hour if she took in the sights and did some window shopping, or two hours if she stopped at a café on the way. I had the feeling that she would go straight there and she had a good fifteen minutes start so I set off following Prisca's instructions down the Rue Monge to the junction with St Germain.

I was paranoid that there were relatively so few people about, then realised that Sunday morning was, traditionally, a popular time for church-going in a Catholic country. I had been worried that Cassandra walking down the Boulevard somewhere in front would turn and see me following her before I spotted her. Then I thought: why worry? She knew I was in Paris; I had just as much right to be on the Boulevard St Germain as she did; and anyway, she was hurrying to meet her boyfriend, not looking over her shoulder.

In fact she was looking every which way when I spotted her, but she didn't see me.

The Russian church was where Prisca had told me and I approached on the other side of the Boulevard. There were a lot more pedestrians around now and the traffic had thickened up, particularly outside the church, where so many cars were stopping to drop people off or collect them, I thought at first it was a taxi rank.

Cassandra was dressed in a tight white t-shirt, jeans and her pink trainers and once again she carried the large shoulder bag which probably contained the rest of her wardrobe. She was sitting on the low wall outside the church and she was smoking nervously, but exactly what that meant I didn't know.

There was a café on the other side of the street (there usually is in Paris) with tables on the pavement and on one chrome chair, someone had left a copy of *Le Figaro's* week-end magazine. I sat down, hid behind the newspaper and ordered a coffee from a passing waiter. This was more like it – covert surveillance at its best. My target conveniently was not going anyway whilst I sat in the morning sunshine unwrapping sugar cubes and dunking them in my coffee before popping them in my mouth for that satisfying crunch and caffeine rush.

The small courtyard in front of the church gradually filled with worshippers coming out of the church and others arriving all the time. Soon it looked as if there were more bodies outside the church than could possibly fit inside. Most of them were men, talking in small animated groups and smoking furiously and at one point about twenty of them congregated around an old Renault 18 estate car which had pulled up to the kerb. In the back of the car were what looked like washing machines, certainly some form of white goods, and wads of money began to change hands.

Cassandra was observing all this with increasing puzzlement, as I was, as was my waiter, standing – as waiters on Paris pavements always do in quiet moments – as if checking the buildings opposite for snipers.

'Gangster market,' he growled as he put down a saucer containing the bill for my coffee. 'Every Sunday morning. You can buy anything you want there. Bloody Russians.'

I wondered if it was the sort of market where you could buy an instant face lift in the form of a Botox injection. I didn't think it likely, but I placed Amy's camera as unobtrusively as I could on my table and lined up a couple of general shots, making sure that Cassandra was there in the distance.

And then she was moving, and moving quickly, throwing down her cigarette and bustling her way into the crowd around the church doors. I moved the camera slightly, operating the zoom and watching her on the tiny monitor screen, but before I could take a shot, she disappeared into the throng. Then she reappeared, being carried off the ground by the man whom she had just wrapped her legs and arms around, her face glued to his like she was determined to suck the life out of him one way or another.

I put some euros down on the saucer, including a good tip, in case I had to leave quickly, remembering to keep the bill for my expenses and automatically scanning the other tables to see if any previous customers had left them behind, before going back to concentrate on the action across the street or at least the four million pixels of it that were shown on the camera monitor.

The man Cassandra was trying to suffocate with her lips and strangle with her thighs, had absolutely no trouble walking out of the churchyard and on to the pavement carrying her, his hands clamped on to her buttocks. Their behaviour didn't shock anyone, in fact several people applauded them and when he eventually prised Cassandra loose and her feet hit the ground, he had a big smile all across his big, weather-beaten face.

In fact most of him seemed big. He towered over Cassandra and was easily able to kiss the red hair on the top of her head without stretching his neck. He was well built, even a tad overweight, and his mane of white hair and bushy sideboards gave him the air of a jovial Viking.

They went back to the low wall where I'd first seen Cassandra, sat down on it and 'Michel' produced cigarettes for them both. They sat there gazing into each other's eyes and blowing smoke into each other's face talking animatedly and grinning like idiots. What I really needed was Frank Lemarquand with one of his telescopic microphones, though I didn't really think I was missing much, just the inane chit-chat of lovers who hadn't seen each other for some time. Though I did wonder how long they'd been apart and indeed why they were apart. She had a good job and probably a house somewhere in Cambridge. He was – well, I didn't know a thing about him except that he met her in a salsa club in Barcelona.

I did know that he was waiting for something. You don't meet your girlfriend after an unspecified gap, knowing that she's up for it and has a hotel room and it's Paris, and then sit on a wall all morning looking at your watch. Maybe he was playing it cool, but it was behaviour which wouldn't have impressed Amy, for instance, not while the shops were open.

They sat there for twenty minutes, laughing and smoking and then a small, khaki brown car drew up to the kerb beside them, blocking off my sight line. 'Michel' jumped to his feet and threw his hands in the air to welcome the car and its driver, then he pulled Cassandra to her feet, her face a picture of that dark place women go when they don't know whether to laugh or scream.

Cassandra couldn't take her eyes off the car. Neither could most of the pedestrians on both sides of the street, nor the congregation still milling about outside the church, nor drivers passing by, several of whom tooted their horns – some out of affection, most out of sympathy.

And I have to say, I was fairly hypnotised myself. I had only seen one or two before in my life and never one in such immaculate condition and obviously still going strong at age thirty if not forty. You just never saw them these days, but there was no mistaking the distinctive outline and sheer ridiculousness of what used to be East Germany's engineering pride and joy, the Trabant P601, sometimes referred to as 'the little wonder', but more often 'the plastic bomber'.

My waiter had been proved right.

You could buy anything at the Sunday morning Russian gangsters' market.

Chapter Twelve

Over three million 'Trabis' were made in Eastern bloc Europe before the collapse of the Berlin Wall turned them into collectors' items for very strange collectors. Most came from the Sachsenring factory in Zwickau in former East Germany but I had heard of ones made at the Zaporoshetz works in Soviet Russia which were powered by tank starter motors. The famous P60 version dated from 1964, its outer body parts made of Dura-plast, a reinforced resin plastic like Formica or Bakelite, hence the affectionate nickname of 'plastic bomber', though the 'bomber' part was pure optimism given its 594 cc two-stroke engine. The Trabant was a legendary car for all the wrong reasons. There was a famous joke from when Germany re-unified and engineers from the Trabi plant at Sachsenring were invited to Munich to the BMW factory. There they were shown the final quality control test on a new BMW saloon. The works cat was shut in a production line model and if the cat passed out after five minutes, it meant the bodywork was airtight. (Naturally, the cat was then removed.) When the BMW engineers did the return visit to the Trabi works, they found the same test on the production line there, except that with a Trabant, if it took the works cat more than five minutes to get out of the car, then it had passed quality control.

And yet here was a car with everything against it – it was old, uncomfortable, unstylish, unfashionable, Communist and German – and it was causing cars to slow to a crawl, heads to turn and jaws to drop on one of the most fashionable streets in the most fashionable capital in Europe.

And much to the obvious concern of Cassandra (obvious to everybody watching), the love of her life was about to buy it with a thick bundle of euro notes which he didn't seem to mind anyone seeing.

Anyone who has dabbled in the used car market in Britain, as I have, knows that the last thing you do in public is flash a large wedge of cash. If it is a cash transaction, it's best done under a viaduct, at night, preferably a moonless night. Broad daylight on a Sunday morning in the middle of Paris within sight of several key government buildings? Duncan the Drunken would have a coronary when I told him about this.

'Michel' was oblivious to such concerns; he seemed to love the attention as a small crowd from the church gathered round him and the

Trabant, admiring it, laughing at it and offering him advice. I almost felt sorry for Cassandra, who looked lost in this sea of Trabi fans, all of them male and most of them probably speaking Russian, though I couldn't tell for sure from my café table.

Even though I couldn't hear the soundtrack, I could follow the action. The driver of the Trabi was a young, bearded hippy type born long after the Trabant P60 was, but he was holding out for a certain price and 'Michel' was making him sweat for it, insisting on opening the passenger door and looking in and then doing the same in the tiny boot and even getting the bonnet raised to look at the engine, a sight which reminded most people of their lawn mower.

This pantomime went on for so long that my waiter, who was also enjoying the show, started shuffling his feet behind me, indicating that perhaps I ought to buy something else. I ordered a beer just to keep him happy.

No sooner had he plonked it on the table in front of me than the little drama across the Boulevard reached a sort of climax. With much nodding of heads and shaking of hands, 'Michel' handed over some, though not all, of his roll of bank notes and the young hippy student type pocketed them, but then he got back in the Trabant and drove off, even giving his audience a polite toot to show that the horn still worked.

'Michel', with a big grin on his face, turned to Cassandra and bowed slightly, then offered his crooked left arm to her. She threaded her right arm through it and they set off together, heading

238

towards the river.

I didn't have time to reflect on the curious incident of the man who hadn't bought a Trabant, or at least only enough time to drink half my beer, before I was back on the case, tailing my prime suspect, utilising all my years of professional training watching old, black-and-white RKO movies on daytime TV.

The tourist crowds were thickening and the restaurants putting out their menu boards for the lunchtime trade, so following Cassandra and her tame Viking at a discrete distance was dead easy, for although they blended in perfectly with the rest of the sightseers, the Viking was head and shoulders above most of them.

They crossed on to the Îl de la Cité using the Pont Neuf, made famous by a wartime photograph of Parisians doing what Parisians have always done: manning the barricades, on that occasion, in August 1944, to encourage the departure of some German visitors who had outstayed their welcome. When they did that, I assumed they were heading for Notre Dame, but instead, they kept going over the Seine on to the Right Bank, turning west along the embankment. I stayed on the bridge and let them get a good lead before following at a discrete distance.

They kept to the lower level, right down by the river, walking hand-in-hand, blissfully uninterested in me, the crowds of Sunday strollers around them, or the attractions of the Louvre and the Tuileries just up the quay to their right. I was almost convinced that they were just walking aimlessly to work up an appetite for lunch, but about a hundred metres beyond the Pont du Carrousel they called at the kiosk which sold tickets for The Louvre Batobus stop and joined the queue forming at the river's edge.

There was no way I was getting on the damn boat with them. As you climbed into a Batobus at the front end, all the passengers on there got a good look at you, so that was out. But once they got on that boat, they could go anywhere. No they couldn't: they could only go in a big loop, it wasn't as if the Batobus could leave the city, it was on a fixed schedule. It was just a question of guessing where they would get off.

By catching the river bus at The Louvre stop on the Right Bank, their only choices were stops at Champs Elysées and the Eiffel Tower, then the route was upriver along the Left Bank as far as the Jardin des Plantes, where Cassandra would certainly head eventually either for another salsa session or to her hotel.

The Batobus was approaching when I decided I had a fifty/fifty chance of being right. I turned back and hurried along the embankment until I spotted a way up to the Quai des Tuileries and crossed the road with a crocodile line of American tourists looking for the Louvre Museum, most of them clutching copies of the *Da Vinci Code*. Once safely across the road I peeled away from the crowd and scoured the traffic for a taxi. The third one I hailed actually stopped.

I asked the driver for the Pont d'Iena, the nearest bridge to the Eiffel Tower and from then on it was just a gamble as to whether a Paris taxi taking the longer land route could outpace a

Paris river bus. It wasn't much of a gamble.

I was on the bridge in the shadow of the Tower, looking down at the Batobus stop and the pavement artists and Algerian kids selling bottles of water (which was probably tap water, but then Paris tap water is perfectly fine these days) when Cassandra and her Viking stepped ashore. It had been quite exhilarating, chasing a boat on the Seine in a large Peugeot taxi driven by a psychopath along the Right Bank, the sort of thing that would look good in a film and a damn sight more realistic that the Robert de Niro car chase in *Ronin*.

But now I had done the exciting bit, what else could I do? Once they got into the crowds milling around the entrances to the Tower I could lose them unless I got close to them, in which case they'd spot me. Alternatively I could risk waiting around for two hours, skipping lunch, while they did the touristy bit and hope to pick them up on their way out of one of the four entrances. This tailing suspects business suddenly seemed fraught with difficulties, not to mention being a bit dull.

The guy dressed all in black like a ninja, stepping off the Batobus about twenty metres behind them seemed to be enjoying his work, though.

I noticed him because of his clothes: a loose black short-sleeved shirt and black combat trousers, accessorized with a plain black baseball cap and wrap-around sunglasses. Bad dress sense, in itself, is not normally threatening or suspicious, even in Paris. It was the way the guy moved that was suspicious and from my vantage point on the

bridge, I had a bird's eye view of him as he followed the young lovers, stopping when they
stopped to look at the work of the street artists, but
always keeping the same distance behind them. As
they approached the wide stone stairs which
would bring them up to the bridge and the ap-
proach to the Tower, he was still there behind
them, hugging the wall. If only I had a copy of the
Private Eye's Handbook. There was bound to be a
chapter in there which covered this situation, but
as I didn't it looked like I would have to improvise.

As Cassandra and her boyfriend started up the
stairs, I started down, a big smile showing lots of
teeth fixed across my face. At the halfway point,
I skipped a step to my right so I was directly in
front of them and did a little jazz hands routine
in welcome.

'Cassandra! Fancy seeing you here!'

'Michel' was really called Mikail Golubev and he
wasn't a Viking, he was a Russian, and his family
name came from the word for 'pigeon', and did I
speak any Russian? Only a few swear words, I had
said, though I did now know the Russian for
'pigeon'. Cassandra called him Misha, the diminutive of Mikail, or Michael; he called her Sassy
and after she had introduced me, they both called
me Ray. And we all agreed it was a small world, if
not a small city, running into each other again like
that.

It was a bizarre meeting, there on the steps, but
Cassandra didn't seem worried or disturbed, not
even surprised.

'Ray here looked after me yesterday,' she told

Misha, hooking an arm around his waist.

'So you were the one dancing with my girl, eh?' he growled, looming over me.

'No, I was the one trying to keep up with her.'

He thought about this and then allowed his face, which I suppose was handsome even if it did look like it had been carved out of seasoned oak, to break into a grin.

'She's a good little mover, isn't she?' he said, then flinched as Cassandra gave him a squeeze. 'You want her to give you salsa lessons? I can do you a good deal.'

I was sure he could. I'd seen him trading at the gangster market.

'Be nice to Ray, you big bear,' Cassandra scolded him. 'Ray showed me the sights and took me to some really interesting shops.'

'She made you go shopping?' he said with mock horror. 'Sweet Christus, I have to buy this man a drink!'

And that was more or less how we ended up having a beer and a sandwich in l'Altitude 95, the café on the first floor of the Tower, Misha having dismissed the second floor Jules Verne restaurant as 'too touristy'.

'I haven't seen my girl for two months and when I get one day's shore leave in Paris we have to spend it playing the tourist and visiting the bloody Eiffel Tower,' he had announced loudly.

Cassandra gave me the eye and gently kicked my ankle, but spoke to Misha.

'But I've never been here before, my little bear.'

I could take a hint and I knew when to play along.

'So, shore leave. Are you a sailor, Misha?'

Who said I couldn't cut it as a detective?

Misha put two fingers together and slapped his right eyebrow with them in a mock salute.

'First Mate Golubev, of the *Akademik Schtein-mann,* but not reporting for duty until he's fucking well ready.'

'Your English is very good,' I said.

'It is idiomatic – is that right? Or are you just being patronising?' he said smugly.

'It's perfect compared to my Russian, which consists solely of *blyad, suka* and *tvoju mat.*'

Misha roared with laughter and a dozen or so genuine tourists enjoying their lunch visibly flinched.

'Who taught you that? The pronunciation was very good by the way.'

'A hooker from St Petersburg.'

That brought forth another guffaw and he actually slapped his thigh. Much more of this and he would be giving me a bear hug and trying to adopt me.

'What did he say?' Cassandra hissed at him, nudging him in the ribs.

'Ray here knows some of the most important words in Russian,' Misha told her quietly, then lowered his voice to a whisper. 'Including those for shit, fuck and son-of-a-bitch.'

Cassandra was shocked, or at least pretended to be.

'Oh, and *spacebo* – thank you. I know that as well.'

'Did you learn that from the Petersburg hooker?' he asked, right on cue.

'Oh yes, she said that a lot.'

With a bit of rehearsal we could do the comedy club circuit at this rate.

'That's enough – you,' said Cassandra in the way only women can say 'you' to their men folk, which is really shorthand for: it's time to stop enjoying yourself and do what I want to do.

Which reminded me that I wasn't there to enjoy myself either, although I had the feeling that over several more beers, Misha could become a really good, if dangerous, mate.

'So what kind of ship is the Academia?' I said, changing the subject.

'The *Akademik Schteinmann*. It's what we call in Russia a Deep River ship and what you would probably call a freighter.'

I lifted my sunglasses and made a point of looking out towards the Seine snaking away beneath us.

'And where have you parked it?'

'On the coast, at Le Havre, it's too big for this river. But while she's being unloaded at the docks, I get to take my girl here to the top of the world.'

He stroked Cassandra's arm and then pointed a finger straight up, meaning the top of the Tower.

'You can probably see Le Havre from up top,' I said. 'What is your ship loading?'

'Unloading,' he corrected me, 'some timber, aluminium and zinc ingots, fish meal and cattle feed; usual things.'

'And then it's back to the Baltic?'

'Hell no, then I come over to England to see my best girl for a few days.'

This was a good excuse for them to paw each

other some more.

'I was going to make Misha buy me a nice dinner tonight before he goes back to his ship,' Cassandra said dreamily. 'Can you recommend anywhere, Ray? Funnily enough, I have a whim for Italian food.'

'Italian food?' mugged Misha. 'Have you got the right city, my crazy little woman?'

She might be smaller than him, but I didn't think she was crazy.

'Actually, I do know an excellent one...'

It was strangely flattering that Cassandra wanted to recreate with her boyfriend the day we'd spent together: Batobus trip, Eiffel Tower and then dinner at *La Castafiore;* the added spice being that he didn't know she'd done it already. It was a strange feeling, being an unwitting accomplice in her deception, but I couldn't see how it could be anything but innocent. People in love do the weirdest things.

Though it did make my life easy. As they went off to queue for the lift to the very top, I reflected on the luxury of knowing more or less exactly where the suspects I was following were going to be for the next five or six hours, so I could take the afternoon off. I was almost sure Cassandra would even drag her Russian bear shopping in the Marais district, before ice-cream at Berthillon's and then dinner at Edward's place. It was a given that they would end up at the open air salsa session before Misha went back to Le Havre to join his ship, though he hadn't said how he intended getting there.

The hell with it. As far as I could tell they had no intention of doing anything illegal, except maybe to each other, that afternoon, or at least not involving quantities of Botox stolen from the man paying my expenses. Which left me free to do what every red-blooded male in Paris, alone on a hot summer's afternoon, should do. Wander the streets looking at the women and occasionally pausing for refreshment.

As Misha and Cassandra headed skywards courtesy of Gustave Eiffel, I came back down to earth to mingle with the afternoon crowds and automatically headed for the Batobus dock, fancying a float upriver back to the Latin Quarter. I bought a two-stop ticket from a very pretty blonde in the Batobus kiosk and sat on a concrete bench soaking up the sunshine to wait for my boat. I thought to myself: where could you feel this relaxed waiting for a bus in London without being stoned?

It wasn't until the boat had arrived and I had climbed aboard and occupied one of the plum seats at the back, that I realised that the Man In Black, who had been following Misha and Cassandra before lunch, was now following me.

I was fairly certain about this, otherwise of all the boats and all the floating gin palaces on all the rivers of all the world, what was he doing on mine?

I had to make sure, though, and the Private Eye's professional code probably insisted I give him the run around and as I had nothing else to do I decided to enjoy it.

My stop was St Germain des Pres on the Left Bank, but I waited until all the disembarking passengers were on the concrete landing and the boarding ones were just about to be let on board by the crewman acting as tour guide for the day, before I stood up and raced for the exit, passing within eighteen inches of the man in the black baseball cap, who was studiously gazing at the concrete lining of the Seine.

I pushed my way up the jetty steps, apologising to the queue of people trying to board whilst concentrating on not falling ignominiously off the quay and on to the sun-roof of the boat or into the water. I resisted the temptation to look back but from the swearing I could hear from behind, I was pretty sure another late disembarkation was taking place.

The embankment here resembled a market, with temporary stalls selling books, prints and cheesy mirrors advertising the Moulin Rouge, various beers, the cartoon character Betty Boop or, oddly, Ovaltine. Every other square metre of space was occupied by a sketch artist with an easel and a fistful of charcoals or pens, using chat up lines in dictionary English like 'You have, sir, a most peculiar face' to try an win an instant commission.

Even with a sales pitch like that, one of them struck lucky. I selected him not for his artistic skill or the fact that he wore a collarless shirt with so many paint splatters it could pass for a Jackson Pollock, but because of where he was positioned on the quay, he had an excellent view of the Batobus landing stage behind me.

Keeping my voice down and speaking rapidly in French, I told him not to draw me but the Man In Black somewhere over my shoulder, without him noticing.

'Why?' he whispered.

'Because I fancy him and because I want to give you forty euros,' I whispered back, after noticing his sign which offered portraits in two minutes for twenty euros.

'Fifty,' he said out of the corner of his mouth.

'Go for it.'

It was no masterpiece, but the artist did his best and as rapid charcoal sketches of a man thirty metres away wearing sunglasses and a baseball cap went, it had a certain charm. I handed over fifty euros and folded the drawing carefully before slipping it into my jacket pocket and sauntered casually along the quay, stopping at every book stall to examine the merchandise.

Almost all the second-hand books on sale were, naturally enough, in French, and though there was the odd guidebook in Dutch or German, there was nothing in English, the nearest thing being a French edition of an Ian Rankin crime novel which proudly declared it was 'translated from the Scottish'. I settled instead for a badly foxed paperback of a Jean Bruce 'OSS 117' thriller and, tucking it under my arm, I sauntered off to find a pavement café and a nice cold beer or two, over which I could see how rusty my reading skills were when it came to French pulp fiction.

What I really wanted to see, of course, was just how long I could try the Man In Black's patience. Whilst I sat in the shade of an umbrella advertising Kronenbourg beer and sipped one out of brand loyalty, the MIB sulked in the sunshine on the other side of the street. He was good, I'll give him that. I would look up from the book at irregular intervals and three times out of four I would see no sign of him. After an hour or so, I felt as bored as he must have been, so I paid my tab, pocketed the receipt, and left the paperback on my seat hoping it might appreciate its freedom and return to the wild. My plan was to stroll around for an hour or so, soaking up the afternoon heat, and then it would be time for ice-cream.

I sauntered down the Left Bank quays and chose the smallest of the Seine bridges to cross on to the Île de la Cité and the forecourt of Notre Dame where hundreds if not thousands of tourists were patiently lined up waiting to get in to the cathedral. The ones who weren't taking photographs were counting the statues of saints above the doors, trying to work out whether the architecture was symmetrical.

I turned away from the cathedral and headed for the edge of the pedestrianised area where a flight of stone steps descended into the ground under a sign saying *Crypte Archeaologique*. I was surprised that there were no queues here at all, as it was probably the coolest place on the island now the afternoon heat was turned up full and the Algerian kids selling bottles of water were doing a roaring trade.

Stepping down into the crypt, I remembered to take off my sunglasses just before colliding with a tinted glass door leading to the ticket hall of the crypt and allowed my eyes to become accustomed to the gloom before paying my 3.30 euros entrance fee and collecting my official explanatory map. The crypt is an open plan museum built around the site of a 1960s archaeological excavation, and not the entrance, as many think, to the crypt of Notre Dame cathedral. In fact the crypt ends at the foundations of the sixth century cathedral of Saint Etienne, which predated Notre Dame, and the whole area was known as the Rue Neuve Notre-Dame, until demolished by the city planners in 1745, no doubt as part of some mad urban regeneration scheme.

Around the sides were free standing exhibition boards explaining things and some of the bronze and pottery finds of the archaeologists, in sealed plastic cases lit from below. The central area was as the archaeologists had left it; the remains of the earliest buildings of Paris, from Roman houses with their trademark hypocaust central heating systems through the medieval period and the foundations of sixteenth- and seventeenth-century houses. There was even a set of steps leading down to where the Seine would have been a thousand years or more ago.

At first I thought I had the place to myself, but then through the gloom I noticed a young couple with two children on the other side of the crypt walking behind a chunk of ancient wall. I wondered if this might deter my Man In Black from following me in, preferring to wait outside by the only exit. I was happy to let him wait and began a leisurely cruise of the exhibits, taking care not to fall over the random blocks of stone left out as touchyfeely exhibits or perhaps resting places for the weary tourist.

My shadow was cleverer than I had bargained for. Cleverer, quieter, and in his black outfit, perfectly camouflaged in the poorly-lit subterranean museum. He must have entered quietly and taken the anti-clockwise route around the Roman ruins, while I was casually walking clockwise. We met near a man-sized exhibition case containing a reconstructed Roman *amphora*. He stepped out from behind it and was suddenly there, in my face, only a few inches in front of me. I noticed that he too had taken off his sunglasses. It was the last thing I noticed clearly for several minutes.

I think I noticed that he was balancing on the balls of his feet like a boxer and that his hips were turning to add power to his punch, but I never saw the punch itself coming. I certainly felt it, though, a well-placed right hook up into my stomach which must have lifted me off my feet as the next thing I knew, my knees hit the stone floor.

In movies, or on TV, they always try and choreograph fist fights and always for too long. In the real world, punch-ups between two adult males are usually frantic, flailing affairs and are, thankfully, short.

I didn't think they were supposed to be this short, though. This was going to be a one-punch knock-out. I had never felt anything like it. It was as if I had been hit with a battering ram. I couldn't breathe, I could taste vomit and I was sure I had bitten my tongue in half. My vision was blurred, but I managed to pick out the shape of his arm as he withdrew it from my midriff. Probably the only reason he hadn't hit me a second time was because I had collapsed against his legs and in doing so I was obviously cramping his style. As his fist swam across my eyeline as he cocked his arm for another swing, I saw the thick brass knuckledusters he was wearing, which went some way to explaining the pain I was in. I remember thinking that I didn't know what the French for 'ruptured spleen' was, then he used his left to grab a handful of my hair and pull my head up before he swung at me again.

That second blow connected on the left side of my head between my left eye and ear, knocking me sideways off my knees. The right side of my face smashed into the reinforced plastic case containing the amphora. The exhibit case had obviously been designed to withstand hurtling bodies and it didn't move, I just slid down it until I lay on the cool, cool floor and I heard something crack underneath me. I knew immediately it was my sunglasses and not a bone, but that was small comfort. I had really liked those fake Ray-Bans.

I may have fainted then, but I wasn't unconscious for long as the Man In Black was crouched over me, prodding my shoulder with his armoured fist to get my attention, although the pungent body odour he was giving off was acting as an effective smelling salt.

'Who is the girl?' he growled in English with a thick guttural accent.

'I'm sorry, but I don't understand you,' I replied in French, which I thought showed great presence of mind. It fooled him for as long as it took him to grab another handful of my hair and bash my head into the amphora case again.

'Who is the focking girl with Golubev?' he asked again.

'I don't know,' I said in English.

'Yes, you do.'

He was suddenly all relaxed and conversational or maybe my pain-racked brain just wasn't functioning. Quite a few other bits of me had stopped working, my lungs for instance, and I couldn't find the energy to do anything difficult like stand up or even roll out of the way.

But I realised that I ought to be trying to do exactly that as the Man In Black raised himself up and aimed his knuckleduster at my face. I found I couldn't move, either through shock or fear, and the only defence I had was to close my eyes tight shut and listen to the music in my head.

Even at that highly stressed-out moment, I thought it odd that I should be hearing *There's No Business Like Show Business* ringing round my head. And then I realised it wasn't in my head. The electronic melody was coming from one of the leg pockets of my torturer's cargo pants.

'*Blyad,*' he said and straightened up, taking out a flip-up mobile phone.

I had been saved by the ring tone, which cheered me up no end, and the MIB was talking rapidly in Russian and the fact that I recognised it as such told me my brain was still ticking over, even if in neutral. Major motor movements still seemed to be beyond me, though, so I stayed where I was.

The Russian finished his call, snapped the phone shut and leaned over me again, pointing a finger at me. Thankfully, he had removed the brass dusters.

'You tell Golubev we know who the *kotenochek* is and if that focking *kontrabandist* tries to screw us, then we'll screw her. OK? Tell him that from Vovchik, you understand? You tell him.'

He kicked me hard on the right knee just to make sure I had got the message.

'I'll ... tell ... him...' I gasped, trying not to cry.

'Do that,' he said and then he kicked me on the left knee for old times' sake and disappeared towards the exit.

I don't know how long I lay curled up on the floor of the crypt, but the fact that not a single visitor stepped over me told me it must be nearing closing time for the museum.

Fighting off the waves of nausea, I hauled myself up the side of the amphora display, my hands slipping on the casing in what I suspected was my own blood. Once I had mastered the art of standing on my feet and I was only swaying slightly, I managed to focus, with some difficulty, on my pale reflection in the display case. With the lighting in there and my vision, I couldn't see too much, which was probably just as well. Head wounds bleed a lot but they are usually worse than they look.

I took off my jacket and pulled my shirt over my head, bunching it up and dabbing gingerly at my head, but it seemed as if the worst of the bleeding had stopped. I gave the amphora case a quick wipe to get the worst of the smears off as I didn't want one of the museum cleaners having a heart attack on my account. Then I put my jacket on again, fastened it over my bare chest and staggered towards the exit.

I climbed the steps up to the square in front of Notre Dame, almost totally blinded by the sunlight, with my bloody shirt scrunched up in one hand, and walked as fast as I could for the formal gardens which ran to the right and behind the cathedral. A young lad with a bucket of melted ice in which he stored half-litre bottles of mineral water saw into view. I gave him a ten euro note for two bottles and didn't wait for change. He gave me a funny look.

Stepping over a knee-high box hedge into the gardens and away from the bulk of the crowds still waiting in their droves by the cathedral doors, I sat down on the grass and used the bottled water to pour over my head in an attempt to clean myself up. When I couldn't see any fresh spots of red on the shirt, I got to my feet again and stumbled in the direction of the Pont St Louis which connected the Île de la Cité to the Île St Louis, dropping my shirt, the empty water bottles and the two halves of my broken Ray-Bans into a litter bin on the way.

At no point, as I navigated my way around one of the most popular tourist attractions in Western Europe, did anyone stop me or ask if I needed help, so either I didn't look as bad as I felt or the locals just assumed I was an English football fan still trying to get home.

On the smaller of the two islands, the tourists were already heading towards Berthillon's for their early evening ice-cream, but for me, *La Castafiore* was nearer.

Edward was sitting at one of the tables, doing the books and didn't look up as I walked in, just said, automatically: 'We don't open until seven.'

'Can I get a drink while I wait?' I asked in English.

'Angel! You look like shit,' he said, looking up at me.

'I look like *blyad*,' I agreed.

Chapter Thirteen

'Who the fuck is Vovchik, Misha?'

Edward had allowed me to use the restaurant's toilet in which to clean up and hadn't bitched too much about the state of the towels afterwards. His kitchen staff had made me an ice pack out of a clean, crisp linen napkin and found me some Urgos – French versions of Elastoplasts – for the cuts on my knees. They had also offered me a white waiter's shirt and the shiny black trousers to match. I accepted the shirt but declined the trousers on the basis that jeans torn at the knee were still fashionable – just.

I greedily accepted a very large brandy to calm my nerves while Edward, wearing yellow washing-up gloves, parted my hair to examine the cut in my scalp, pronouncing that it probably needed a stitch or two but the bleeding seemed to have stopped. I told him I had no intention of checking into a French hospital, but I would see a doctor when I got home tomorrow. In the meantime, the shirt would cover the black-and-tan bruising on my stomach and a hat and some sunglasses would have to disguise the lump on my head and the black eye that was shaping up nicely on my left side. Neither item was a problem; any popular restaurant in a tourist hot spot has a wardrobe of items left by satisfied customers (satisfied until they got home and realised they'd left their fur coat somewhere). A soft brown felt fedora was produced, which made me look faintly chic in a 1950s gay way, but the sunglasses made me feel distinctly self-conscious. The only pair they had big enough to cover my darkening eye were really large, square, tortoiseshell framed jobs which maybe only Sophia Loren could have got away with. To boost my confidence I had another huge brandy and chomped six paracetamol tablets to ward off the headache that was surely coming.

As a fashion statement, I looked ridiculous, but as a disguise it worked perfectly. Just after 7.30 p.m. Misha and Cassandra bounced into the restaurant, still arm-in-arm, and walked right by the table I was slumped over.

Edward greeted them and nodded towards my table and as they turned, their faces changed: Cassandra's to an expression of bewilderment, Misha's to a huge grin as he recognised me under the fedora and behind the sun glasses.

'Ray! Whatever happened to you?' squeaked Cassandra.

I made them sit down and spun them a yarn about falling down the steps of the *Crypte Archaeologique,* not really caring if they believed me or not. Misha insisted on buying a medicinal drink, so more cognac arrived for us whilst Cassandra splashed out on an orange juice.

As I had arranged with him, when Edward

brought the menus he insisted that Cassandra accompany him to the kitchen where the chef was preparing something special and always insisted on doing it in front of the evening's most beautiful customer. She swallowed this act completely and with a little girl giggle, she followed him through the swing door by the bar.

The tall Russian-Viking opposite showed me the palms of his hands and shrugged his shoulders as if to say 'Women ... huh?'

I took off the sunglasses and glared at him with one-and-a-half good eyes.

'Who the fuck is Vovchik, Misha?'

'Vovchik did that to you?' he responded calmly.

'Yes, and before we had been properly introduced. So who is he?'

'You don't want to know, Ray.'

'Probably I don't, but I'd like to know why you're not surprised.'

'I'm surprised he didn't kill you,' he said, grinning madly. 'He could have, if he had wanted to.' He paused as if giving the matter serious thought. 'Maybe he didn't want to today.'

'I'll make sure there isn't a tomorrow, then. I take it you know this psycho.'

'Psycho?' he feigned confusion.

'Madman, maniac, hit-man, thug; don't piss me about, Misha.'

As I was ranting, he relaxed even further into his chair and his grin became even broader. I could cheerfully have put my glass of brandy in his face, but it would have been a waste of good liquor, not to mention the fact that he would probably have punched my lights out.

'Why should I tell you anything?' he said with a smug smile. I hardly know you.'

'Then you won't mind if I tell this Vovchik all about Cassandra? Next time I run into him, that is?'

That didn't remove the smile from his face, but it stopped it growing.

'He asked you about Sassy?'

'It was all he could talk about. He called her your little *kotenochek*. That's 'kitten' isn't it?'

'You know more Russian than you let on,' he said slowly but he wasn't exactly breaking sweat.

'He called you a *kontrabandist* and you don't have to be a cunning linguist to know that means 'smuggler'. What's his interest in Misha the smuggler and his girlfriend? Is Vovchik KGB or something?'

Now he laughed.

'Vladimir? KGB? Hah! Anyway, KGB is now called the FSB and is much better at public relations. Do try and keep up with things, Ray. No, Vovchik is not FSB. He's one of the bad guys.'

'Russian mafia?'

'No, not *avtoritet* a much smaller fish. What we'd call a *banduk* – a bandit. You'd say gangster.'

'Well I knew he wasn't a social worker. You know him?'

'Oh yes. His name is Vladimir Kozlov. His friends call him Vovchik or Kozel, which means goat. It's also a slang word for someone who is a nasty piece of work and stupid with it.'

'That's him alright.' I had thought of several words for my Man In Black, but I hadn't thought of goat.

'So what did you tell him?'

'I didn't have to tell him anything. He took a call on his mobile phone and immediately lost interest in me. He said to tell you he now knew who the girl was and that if you screwed him, they'd screw her. So now I've told you. Care to let me in on what's going on?'

He linked his fingers and pushed out, stretching his arms. He almost yawned he seemed so bored.

'OK, yes I know Vladimir Kozlov. Vovchik and I were – are – sort of partners in a little import-export business and he thinks I'm taking more than my fair share. I'm not, but once he gets an idea in his brain, it stays there forever. I can handle Vladimir, don't you worry about him.'

'I'm not, but I think you should be. Exactly what sort of import-export business are you in?'

I didn't really expect him to 'fess up on the spot to stealing Botox from Tyler Pharmaceuticals with the aid of his chemist girlfriend. Neither did I expect the answer:

'Trabants.'

'Trabis? The car? You smuggle Trabants? The cars the East Germans couldn't give away?'

Misha sighed loudly and rested his elbows on the table as if he was about to explain a very simple joke to someone even more simple.

'Ten years ago, Trabants were a joke, but ten years ago it was a different world, a different Russia. As communism 'withered on the vine' – a nice expression, don't you think? – the old state-run industries were sold off. How did you call it? Privatisation?'

I nodded.

'One of Margaret Thatcher's truly great ideas, but in Russia it became known as the fire sale of 1996. Whole industries going cheap, state assets moving into private hands. We had the 'oligarchs' as we say: the super-rich businessmen and the economy seemed to boom, at least for some. Moscow is now the biggest capital city in Europe with 15 million people. Not all of them are rich, but a number are *very* rich. Last year, Rolls Royce opened a showroom. Ferrari and Bentley are already there. Rich people like cars. Rich people like toys. When you can afford five or six Ferraris, what bigger joke than to arrive at some fancy party in a Trabant? In immaculate condition, of course.'

'You are joking, right?'

'No, I am not. The Trabant has become a cult fashion accessory for the oligarch who has everything. It has a rarity value because they don't make them any more, so people like me have to search the west for survivors from the bad old days of the German Democratic Republic. You'd be surprised how many I've found in junk yards or in peoples back gardens.'

'So you buy them, ship them back and restore them? That sounds as if it could be a legitimate business.'

'It would be, if we paid tax on it.'

'Ah, I see.'

'Our government in Russia is getting very enthusiastic about such things and even one of the oligarchs can find themselves in prison, these days.'

'In the Matrosskja Tishina,' I said, which impressed him.

'You've heard of the Matrosskja Tishina prison?'

'I make a point of knowing stuff like that. It mean's "sailors' tears" or something in Russian, doesn't it?'

'More accurately "sailors' quietness" – a strange name for a prison in Moscow.'

'Probably a bad place for a sailor to end up.'

He considered this.

'I hadn't thought of that, but this is one sailor who has no intention of trying the black bread and buckwheat porridge they serve there.'

'It does sound a bit of an extreme way of dealing with dodgy second-hand car dealers,' I admitted.

'We don't deal in second-hand. All our cars are "pre-loved".'

'I got the impression that was how Vladimir thought of you: pre-loved.'

'Vovchik has a lot of issues. I'll talk to him; straighten him out, keep him sweet.'

'You do that,' I said firmly.

'So there's no need to mention anything to Sassy, eh?' He put his head on one side and tried to look reasonable.

'If it's got nothing to do with her, no.'

He held up a hand like he was in court.

'Absolutely nothing,' he said.

I didn't trust him as far as I could throw him, but then Cassandra was coming out of the kitchen laughing, with Edward leading her by the hand and it was time to order dinner. I chose the most expensive things off the menu and the wine list and said how kind it was that Misha had offered to pick up the bill. After all, we were almost total strangers.

The salsa crowd on the Left Bank didn't have live music to get sweaty to tonight as the band seemed to have the night off, so they were all doing their thing around the CD player which had its volume control turned up to Eleven. Despite the distortion from the tiny speakers, the disk playing was unmistakeably one by the Congo super group 4 Etoiles, so somebody had taste.

Cassandra and Misha couldn't have identified the band, or cared less. The rhythm had caught them and with only a brief pause while Cassandra changed her pink trainers for the dancing shoes in her shoulder bag, they had jumped into the throng, forgetting I was even in the same city.

I drifted around the edge of the melée of dancers to the upper level where the band had been the night before. Nobody noticed me or even looked twice at my crappy disguise. I decided to ditch the sunglasses as it was now after dark and I had almost stepped off the concrete quay and plunged into the Seine. I kept the hat, though, hoping it made me look mysterious, and sat down on the quay dangling my legs over the edge, watching the twinkling lights on the far bank and the harsher beams of cars as they disappeared into the underpasses.

How many famous artists, writers and philosophers had walked the very Left Bank I was sitting on, having regular miraculous flashes of inspiration and mind-expanding ideas? Whereas all I could think of was how much trouble I was going to be in with Veronica over my expenses, and with

Amy for simply being in Paris when she wasn't, and why on earth didn't I have any cigarettes.

True, I had kept a close watch on Cassandra Quinn, my one and only suspect, but she hadn't mentioned Botox, or even her job working with it, let alone trying to hawk illicit supplies of the stuff around the private cosmetic surgeries, of which there were dozens listed in the Paris phone book. I had met her handsome hulk of a boyfriend who cheerfully admitted to smuggling Trabant cars back to Russia as toys for the new rich kids on the block, but had remained unruffled by the news that his psychotic compatriot was beating up complete strangers.

What was it with these third division Russian gangsters? One was a compulsive salsa dancer and the other had a mobile phone with *There's No Business Like Show Business* as a ring tone. I'd never heard that one before and suddenly I could hear it again. Faintly, and only because the CD player was changing tracks, but out there, somewhere in the crowd, that tinny electronic trilling was unmistakeable. Like no other ring tone I know.

I saw him before he saw me because I had an advantage. I was standing on tip-toe looking for a man trying to take a phone call in the middle of a salsa carnival, and he probably wasn't looking for me. He was leaning away from the crowd, phone clamped to one ear, hand slapped over the other, and he seemed to be shouting into the mouthpiece, but I don't lip-read Russian.

Vovchik was only about ten feet away from me but he was looking away from the river, up the embankment to the road where, under a street light, a lone figure was standing, with his right hand pressed to his right ear. When Vovchik waved a hand in the air, the man under the streetlight returned the wave, then took the phone away from his ear. Vovchik did the same and it was as he put his phone away in one of this combat pockets, that he turned and saw me.

Before his phone had hit the bottom of the pocket, he was striding straight towards me and unless I fancied a moonlight swim across the Seine, I had nowhere to go to avoid him.

He came right up to me to make sure I could hear him above the music; his face in my face, so close I could feel his breath. I had kept my eyes on his hands and though he had made fists of them there was no sign of the knuckleduster. I was also acutely conscious that my heels were only a matter of inches away from a twelve-foot drop into the river. He could push me and be lost in the dancing crowd before I hit the water. If he got any closer, I would probably jump just to get away from his body odour.

'Why do we keep meeting like this?' he asked, not expecting an answer, just using it as an excuse to poke me in the chest with a finger. 'What's your connection with Golubev?'

'Misha?' I said wincing as he poked me again, I had absolutely no idea how to get away from this guy and I had absolute confidence that he could beat me to a pulp before any of the salsa dancers noticed anything. I seriously considered that my safest course of action might be to step backwards into the Seine. In the meantime, all I could do was talk. 'I've never met him before today. I'm here because of the girl.'

That got his interest as I knew it would, considering he'd been asking about her – quite violently – only a few hours before.

'She is his contact, right? Golubev's supplier?'

I nodded enthusiastically as if I knew what he was talking about.

'She's a chemist,' I said, which was both true and vague.

'So what are they doing in Paris?'

'You mean you don't know either?'

It was the wrong thing to say. He stabbed me in the gut with straightened fingers with such economy of movement that I never saw it coming let alone any of the nearby dancers. Once again he had taken my breath away and I clutched at his arm to stop myself buckling at the knees.

'Is Misha selling the stuff here in Paris again?'

I heard the words hissed in my ear but it seemed to take an age to formulate an answer.

'He's not selling anything, he's buying up old cars...'

Another wrong answer and this time he pressed the knuckle of his left forefinger into the lower part of my neck, whilst his right hand went behind my head to hold it in place. I didn't know what the medical description of such an action was, I just knew it was both incredibly painful and paralysing at the same time. Vovchik knew it was too and seemed to take comfort from the fact.

'You don't really know anything, do you?' said Vovchik, increasing the pressure as I flapped my hand ineffectively at his arms which seemed to be made of steel.

I couldn't argue with him, I couldn't plead with him. I was having trouble even breathing and I felt my knees begin to go. If I was lucky I might just manage to throw up over his shoes before I passed out.

And suddenly he had a third arm, moving across my face.

'Is there a problem here, Fitzy?'

The deadening grip on my neck eased and I felt instantly lightheaded. In front of my face was Vovchik's left hand being squeezed by another hand; a giant one; a black one.

I took in a deep breath. Vovchik was still so close to me I could smell him.

'Not any more, Youssef, my man, not now you're here.'

Youssef Cissoko ('African' as it said on his card), showed that not only did he have a noble loyalty to a fellow musician and an immaculate sense of timing, but also a ferocious grip. Vovchik was finding that out as Youssef squeezed hard and forced his hand downwards. Amazingly, Vovchik didn't panic and certainly didn't look half as scared as I would have been if a black giant had appeared out of nowhere and started to break my fingers. To add to the unreality of it, all this was going down with hundreds of dancers shaking their booties within inches of our little tableau. Potentially a couple of hundred witnesses, if any of them had been taking the slightest bit of notice.

'Watch out for his other hand,' I said to Youssef as Vovchik reached down with his right hand to the cargo pocket on the leg of his trousers.

Youssef increased the pressure and Vovchik winced for the first time, but still didn't make a sound. The guy was either very tough or very stupid, possibly both.

I reached into his pocket and pulled out the brass knuckle-dusters.

'You want a free shot?' asked Youssef. 'Go ahead, he's not going anywhere.'

It was tempting, but unless I killed the guy, there would always be another day when Vovchik could turn up and Youssef wouldn't be around. So I shook my head slowly and threw the brass dusters over my shoulder where they made a satisfying *pop* as they hit the water. Then just for the hell of it, I took his mobile phone and threw that, and its irritating ring tone, in as well.

'What now?' said Youssef.

I didn't have a clue but I was saved from admitting that by the arrival of Misha and Cassandra, hand-in-hand out of the throng of dancers.

'Vovchik! Ray! My two good friends!' he shouted over the music. 'Are you having a good time?'

When he got up to us, he clapped an arm around both Vovchik and me and said: 'And who's this?'

Youssef quietly released Vovchik's hand.

'This is a good friend of mine,' I said, 'Mr Cissoko.'

'Pleased to meet you, sir,' said Misha with a huge smile, 'but it has to be hello and then good-bye. Vovchik and I have a boat to catch, don't we, Vovchik? So why don't we go together? I know, let everybody come and see my latest investment. I insist. We can walk my lovely Sassy back to her hotel on the way. Come, come.'

He wasn't going to stop talking until we went and as a group we moved towards the steps up to street level, Vovchik not taking his eyes off Youssef me not taking mine off Vovchik and Youssef quite openly giving Cassandra the once-over.

At the top of the stairs, on the Quai Saint-Bernard, under a street light was the man I was pretty sure had been the one who had called Vovchik on his mobile. This close, he looked vaguely familiar and I realised it was the bearded hippy type who had delivered the Trabant to the Russian Gangster Market that morning. It was yet another surprise and I hate surprises, so I was comforted by Youssef's giant footsteps just behind me.

'Mariusz!' boomed Misha. 'My old friend! You haven't crashed my car have you?'

The hippy looked startled and immediately made eye contact with the sullen Vovchik so I knew I had been right about the phone call.

'This is Mariusz Gorniak,' Misha announced, giving the startled hippy a bear hug and several slaps on the back. 'He's Polish, so you'll have to excuse him, but he has a good nose for sniffing out a bargain when it comes to cars.'

Mariusz was swept along with the rest of us in Misha Golubev's entourage as we crossed the boulevard and marched down the road to Cassandra's hotel, nobody saying much except Misha though no one except maybe Cassandra was listening to him.

Parked outside the Hotel du Jardin, right outside the front door, was the Trabant Misha had bought that morning. With a whoop of delight he skipped the last few metres and beat a quick drum roll on the roof.

'Mariusz, the keys please!' he shouted and caught them one-handed as the Pole tossed them over the car.

How times had changed from the days when even their East German designers had joked that you didn't need to lock a Trabi as who in their right mind would want to steal one? Misha unlocked his door and leaned in to open the passenger side.

'Do you want to drive, Vovchik? Or shall I? We'd better go if we're to catch the tide.'

Kozlov gave him the evil eye and grabbed the door handle, then he turned and gave me the evil eye and exchanged brief, silent nods with the Polish hippy, before climbing into the car. Since we had faced each other off on the river bank, he hadn't said a word.

'And goodnight to you, my dear,' Misha, completely unruffled, was saying to Cassandra. 'I'll see you in England.'

He made to get behind the wheel of the Trabant and then with a great showy gesture, he slapped his forehead and moved away from the car to the girl, taking her dramatically in his arms and kissing her until I thought she would pass out. Then he straightened up, leaving her rocking back on her heels, her face flushed, and waved to the three of us left on the pavement.

'Goodbye my friends, I'll be seeing you.'

It would have been more impressive if the Trabant had started first time, but at the third attempt the engine spluttered into life and the car pulled away and putt-putted off into the night.

Cassandra stared down the street until, long after it had gone from our sight, the sound of the two-stroke engine faded away. Only then did she turn to Youssef and me, beaming like the Cheshire Cat.

'Well, goodnight, all,' she said sweetly and skipped into the hotel foyer.

Youssef and I looked at each other and then, at the sound of running feet, we turned to see Mariusz scurrying down the road in the general direction of the Latin Quarter.

'You have some crazy friends, Fitzy,' said Youssef.

'A strange bunch of people,' I admitted. 'But we do have one thing in common.'

'What's that?' he asked.

'We'll always have Paris.'

The next morning, in the bathroom mirror of my hotel room, I examined all my wounds. The fist-shaped impression on my stomach was still good enough to take fingerprints off and the lump above my left eye was a faded blue rather than black now and the size of a quail's egg rather than a goose's. I managed to wash my hair carefully using the hotel's little plastic bottle of free shampoo on the principle that it was already so watered down it wouldn't sting. Then I packed my bag, filled up on coffee and croissants in the breakfast room and checked out.

I suppose I should have checked on Cassandra but I simply couldn't be bothered. I had spent two days tagging her and had learned precisely nothing except a few new words of Russian. She had shown absolutely no sympathy for my injuries, incurred by her boyfriend's mate, in fact she hadn't even noticed them. Nor had she been disturbed or even mildly curious about the little farce that had been played out at the salsa session last night. She must have tunnel vision to be able to ignore what was going on around her like that. It was probably a condition for which there was a fancy name, but basically it was a form of selfishness. Some people were just so self-centred it wasn't true.

I spent the rest of the morning shopping over on the right bank, taking some more photos for Amy and calling in at *L'Eclaireur Homme* on the Rue Malher where they specialise in designer labels for macho lads. I paid an obscene amount of euros for a Dries van Noten white shirt with embroidery on the collar and felt confident that Veronica wouldn't be able to decipher the fancy handwritten receipt. I felt it only fair as I had sacrificed a perfectly good t-shirt in the line of duty.

I treated myself to a long lunch in a family-run restaurant near the Pompidou Centre and from my table out on the 'terrace' (a fancy name for the bit of pavement they claimed sovereignty over), I used my mobile to ring the office.

It was the first time I had switched it on and I was pleasantly surprised to see that it actually worked in Paris. Indeed, there seemed to be quite a number of messages, all from Amy, for me, probably a shopping list of things she'd forgotten to tell me to bring back.

I made a mental note to get to them eventually and sipped a very fine chilled Chablis while waiting for someone to answer my call. It was Laura. Or Lorna.

'Hi there, you,' I said, playing it safe. 'How's tricks?'

'Where are you?' said the voice, deeply suspicious so I guessed it was Lorna.

'Still working the Paris end of the case,' I said confidently, 'but I need some help from your end. Got a pencil handy?'

'Why would I need a pencil?' she asked, tempting fate. 'I've got my lap top.'

'Fair enough. I want you to check out a ship for me. It's a Russian vessel I think, called the *Akademik Schteinman*.'I spelled it for her. 'It probably left Le Havre sometime this morning. See what you can find out about it.'

'How am I supposed to do that?'

'I don't know, you're a detective aren't you?'

Did I have to do everything myself?

'I'll see what I can do,' she sulked.

'Everything quiet back at the ranch?' I said, hoping she picked up the inference that some of us had been working over the weekend.

'We're managing without you – somehow. Oh, by the way, have you any idea where Frank Lemarquand is? He seems to have disappeared.'

Chapter Fourteen

The train was late, of course. Three hundred kilometres an hour going across the sunny Pas de Calais but as soon as we emerged from the Tunnel into overcast and chilly Kent, then it was leaves on

274

the line at Ashford, or signal failure or track maintenance or some such and our speed dropped to a sluggish crawl all the way in to London. If Thomas the Tank Engine had been running, he would have overtaken us going 'Toot! Toot!'.

I didn't have any transport at Waterloo, so I slummed it with the rush-hour mob on the Northern Line as far as Tottenham Court Road and then switched to the less crowded westbound Central Line to Shepherd's Bush.

Even though it was after six o'clock, Veronica had the Thompson twins slaving away at their desks, though Laura was the only one who seemed pleased to see me. I knew it was Laura because she said:

'Hi there, Angel, had a good time in gay Paree? Lorna said you wanted the shipping news, so I got press-ganged into doing it. Actually, you don't look so good. That's a nasty bump. Nice hat, though.'

She stroked her cool fingertips over the left side of my face with great gentleness and an expression of genuine concern on her face.

'When you've a minute, Angel!'

Trust Veronica to spoil a magic moment, glaring at us through the open door of her office like a Staffordshire Bull Terrier in a kennel.

I gave her a limp wave then dug into my bag and produced the large block of Lindt white chocolate which I'd bought on the way back at Waterloo Station.

'A present from gay Paree,' I said with my best smile. 'And for doing all that research for me, you can have the hat too.'

275

I transferred the fedora to her head and she instinctively tidied her hair under the brim. It was several sizes too big for her, but I didn't think I'd left too many blood stains on it and she did look cute in it.

'Thank you, kind sir,' she squeaked. 'How did you know I liked chocolate?'

'Are frogs waterproof?'

'I'll gorge it all at one go. It'll be so wicked.'

'Eating chocolate's not wicked,' I said.

'In the bath,' she whispered, fluttering her eyelashes.

'So what did you find out for me?' I asked, if only to get her mind, and mine, off chocolate and bubble bath.

She sat down at her desk and worked her keyboard with one hand whilst holding the chocolate in the other, tapping the edge of the block against her teeth.

'It's not that difficult to track shipping,' she said, 'and I've got pictures and a deck plan of the *Akademik Shteinman* if you want me to print them off. Basically, she's an ageing coastal freighter, a pretty small one by today's standards; not a container ship or anything like that. I e-mailed a very nice man at Lloyd's List and he said she was built about fifteen or sixteen years ago to a standard Soviet design for what they called 'deep river' work. The ship is 5,000 tons, though I'm not sure what that means exactly. It is 124 metres in length, 16 metres in the beam and it has seven hatches. My contact at Lloyd's said it has seen better days, probably before it was launched somewhere on the River Volga. The *Shteinman* goes regularly from

St Petersburg to various EU countries, mostly Spain and France and then back home again.'

'Barcelona? Does it call in at Barcelona?' I asked, remembering something Cassandra had said.

'It used to, regularly. More recently it's doing a shorter, triangular run. Russia to France, then England, then back home. Crew of about fourteen; cargoes usually sawn timber, coal, aluminium and zinc ingots, cereals, cattle feed and fish meal on the way out; consumer goods and oil field tools and equipment going back.'

Not to mention some of the ugliest cars ever manufactured and possibly supplies of boot-legged Botox though I had no idea how.

'That's brilliant, Laura, you're a real diamond geezerette.' Doughnuts and chocolate were good for morale, but to get the best out of your staff you had to praise them occasionally. 'Is there any way you can find out where the ship is now?'

Laura looked at her watch, a small, square sparkly affair on a thin bracelet.

'It docked in Harwich about an hour ago.'

'You're a star, girlfriend. Take the rest of the day off and go run yourself a bath.'

She looked up at me from under the brim of the fedora, tapped the chocolate bar against her teeth again and said: 'I might just do that,' as if she'd only just thought of it.

I had almost forgotten that Lorna was in the room, watching all this and refining her glare, not to mention Veronica breathing heavily in her office.

'I have to get Veronica to sign off on a few things before I go home, so if you want to see her,

277

do it now, will you?' she said haughtily. 'Oh, and I'll take back your spare euros.'

'My what?'

'The currency in euros I advanced you on Friday. I have to put the spares back into the petty cash box.'

'It was the word "spare" that threw me. 'You expected change?' I said it with a smile and to soften the blow, I added: 'I've got lots of receipts, but you'll have to give me a day to sort them out. How good's your French, by the way?'

I didn't get a chance to find out.

'Angel! Now would be a really good time.'

'I'm here for you, Veronica, ready to help out in any way I can, just tell me what your problem is.'

'Well, it's you, mainly, but also Frank Lemarquand. We've been using Frank's company for five years and he's given us a perfect service. Until, that is, he goes off on a job with you.'

'And the problem is what exactly?' I took the chair opposite her. Women are not good at shouting and having to look up at the same time.

'The problem is,' she said through gritted teeth, 'is that I didn't know where Frank was and I haven't known since last Thursday when he went waltzing off to Cambridge with you. I didn't even know if he was working on a job for us at the moment.'

'Frank's a big boy, he can take care of himself.'

'Apparently not,' she said, relishing the moment. 'At least, not according to the nurses at the hospital.'

'What hospital?'

'Addenbrookes' in Cambridge, the Accident

and Emergency department.'

'What's he doing there?' I asked stupidly.

'I was hoping you'd tell me.'

'I've no idea, Vonnie. Last I saw of him he was in fine health. What happened?'

'Some sort of car accident they think, but they don't really know and he can't say much as he's broken his jaw.'

'Poor sod.'

'And his right knee cap ... and his wrist.'

'Bloody hell, how fast was he going?'

'There seems to be some mystery about that.'

'Surely the cops have a theory?'

'There were no police involved. Frank drove into the hospital on Saturday night and admitted himself, just before passing out, which was the sensible thing to do in the circumstances. What we all want to know is what he was doing in Cambridge on Saturday night.'

I sprang to my feet and started for the door.

'Where are you going?' she yelled.

'I'm off to see Frank. We can't leave him stuck out in the sticks without so much as a bunch of grapes. I'll bet you lot haven't even sent the poor old sod a card...'

'We only heard where he was this afternoon,' she said defensively.

'Well don't you worry, I'll take care of Frank, but you'll have to ring Olivier Zaborski.'

Veronica sat up as if stung.

'*Why?* Have you made progress?'

'Of course. What do you think I've been doing all weekend? Enjoying myself? Ring Zaborski on his private mobile number and tell him we – no, you

– have a very strong lead and ask him if any of his Botox has turned up unexpectedly in Spain.'

'Spain?'

'Be specific, say Barcelona. I bet you he'll be impressed.'

'Will he now?' she said to herself and was beaming so much she didn't notice I'd gone.

I took a black cab home to Hampstead, a strange though oddly comforting experience, to find the house empty and both Amy and the Freelander missing. I dumped my bag in front of the TV so she could go through it looking for contraband booze and cigarettes and perhaps be pleasantly surprised by the jar of candied chestnuts in the brown paper bag from *L'Epicerie* on the Île St Louis, one of her favourite foodie shops.

Wherever she was, she had taken the only decent vehicle and so I was relegated to driving the Peugeot, which was depressing but I felt I owed it to Frank. If he'd ended up in hospital because of my little moonlighting job out at Comberton Manor, I would never forgive myself.

But then 'never' is such a vague concept and I was certain he'd have insurance.

Once clear of London it took me just under the hour to get to Cambridge, which wasn't bad for the Peugeot and the fact that the Road Angel had beeped a warning on two occasions to slow down and avoid speed cameras.

At Addenbrookes hospital I negotiated a parking space, which involved taking a ticket, getting it validated and then paying a fee somewhere before I left, a procedure only slightly less fraught than an Afghan applying for an American visa.

Naturally, when I eventually got to A & E and found a nurse willing to admit that Frank was a patient, I couldn't get in to see him. The nurse, a pleasant, plump Filippino smelling deliciously of cigarette smoke, told me he was heavily sedated which was the best thing for him in his condition. I suspected she had one eye on the time as it was after 9 p.m. and by ten, A & E units everywhere liked to be clear of civilians in preparation for pub closing time and the influx of new customers.

She did let me look at Frank from a distance, though, one leg and one arm up in traction and a gruesome wire cage around his lower face.

'I heard it was a road accident,' I said to the nurse, whose name badge read 'Gabriella'.

'I don't know about that, I'm sorry.'

'Have the police been?' I asked casually.

'No. Our own security staff knew about the van and they were going to move it themselves.'

'So he got here in his own van?'

'I think so. It was late on Saturday night and he just walked in.'

'With a broken leg?'

'I've seen worse things.' I was sure she had if she worked for the NHS. 'And anyway the security staff spotted the van on Sunday morning on their television cameras. Mr Lemarquand had the keys on him.'

So, good old Frank caught on CCTV. That ought to be worth a few beers when he was up and about.

'So where's his van now?' I tried.

'I don't know, I'm sorry.' It had been a long shot, expecting her to know. 'I think his daughter came and collected it this afternoon.'

Sitting in the Peugeot in the hospital car park I tried Frank's mobile number, just on the off chance. My own phone was flashing at me from the second I switched it on. I think it was telling me that I had so many messages the memory was full but they would just have to wait.

A female voice answered Frank's phone.

'Oh ... er ... hello, is that Frank Lemarquand's phone?'

Which was a bit of a stupid thing to say as I'd dialled the number.

'Yes it is. Hello there, Mr Angel.'

That stumped me for a minute and I automatically glanced around the Peugeot to see if there was a candid camera somewhere. Then I realised that Frank's phone would have me in the address book and 'Angel' would have come up on the display when I rang.

'And you must be Frank's daughter.'

'Daughter and business partner.'

'I didn't know Frank had a partner.'

'Add it to the list.'

'Eh? What list?'

'The list of things you don't know,' she said, rather harshly I thought.

'Look, I'm sorry about your Dad. I'm still in the dark about what happened to him.'

'What happened seems to be that you left a 70-year-old man who wouldn't hurt a fly, on his own late at night miles from anywhere. Left him to get the shit beaten out of him. He could have died, you know. The shock alone could have been enough.'

'Seventy? He's seventy? He looks very fit for seventy,' I said before I could stop myself.

'Not today he doesn't.'

She had a point and I was racking up stupidity bonus points every time I opened my mouth.

'But don't worry about anything,' she went on, with real steel in her voice. 'I've listened to the disks and worked things out. I'll take care of things from here on.'

'If you mean the recordings in the van, then I think we should meet up and let me explain what Frank was doing.'

'Don't bother, I'll find the bitch that did that to him and I'll see she gets hers. *I'm* taking care of business now.'

'Veronica?'

'Is that you Angel? What are you doing ringing at this time?'

'I'm still on the case, working overtime, boss. We do get paid overtime, right?'

'Not in your case.'

'Gee, thanks.'

'What is it, Angel? I'm busy.' I knew she wasn't. She was at home and in the background I could hear a TV set and then, quite distinctly, the ping of a microwave oven.

'Why didn't you tell me Frank Lemarquand had a daughter?'

'What, Alice? You never asked. She was the one who told us where he was. The hospital found her number in Frank's wallet.'

'And she's in the family business?'

'Well, she works with Frank; I don't think she's an official partner, though.'

'But she knows all about spyware and bugging people and stuff like that?'

'Of course she does. Don't tell me you think it's an unsuitable job for a woman?'

'Let me get back to you on that one. Do you know where Alice is now?'

'I should imagine she's gone home, somewhere in Clapham I think. She was in Cambridge when she rang me this afternoon.'

'At the hospital, right?'

'No actually, she'd just come from there, she said. She was at Tyler Pharmaceuticals.'

Oh bugger.

'Why?'

'Asking what Frank had been doing last week. Their security man ... what's his name?'

'Sutton.'

'That's right, Peter Sutton. He sounded nice. He rang and asked me to vouch for Alice's credentials, so of course I did. *Why,* what's wrong?'

'I think Alice may have got the wrong end of the stick about what happened to her father. I'll have to try and sort it out with her.'

Before she did something silly and violent.

'Oh, by the way, Mr Zaborski said you were right about Barcelona. Small quantities of his Botox turned up there last year. He was very impressed. "Good work" he said. I presume all this will be in some sort of a report at some point?'

'Yeah, probably.'

284

At least I had scored one success. Things were looking up.

'I suppose you'll want time off to go to the hospital,' Veronica was saying.

'No, Vonnie, I'm at the hospital now, I'm phoning from the car park.'

'Not Addenbrookes, you idiot,' she snapped. 'Colchester Hospital.'

'Why the hell would I want to go there?'

'To see your father. That's where they took him when he had his stroke. Don't you ever check your messages?'

The Freelander was in the drive in front of the house when I got back to Hampstead in record time. Amy was lying on the sofa holding the jar of candied chestnuts she had found in one hand and a spoon in the other.

'Guess where I had to go this evening,' she said in her don't-mess-with-me-voice before the front door had closed behind me.

'Colchester?' I said faintly.

'That's right, Sherlock! Bloody, bloody Colchester. I had to duck out of a *Vogue* party at The Ivy for Christ's sake, in order to drive to bloody buggering Colchester to play Florence Fucking Nightingale.'

I could have said that it was obviously for her bedside manner, but thought the better of it. After all, she was armed, if only with a spoon.

'And all because I couldn't be arsed to turn my mobile phone on,' I said.

'Yes!' she shouted.

'I just thought I'd say that before you did, that's

285

all. How is my father?'

'It was very interesting, *meeting him for the very first time,*' she said, dripping acid, though I probably deserved that one. 'Though the circumstances were far from ideal. The man's had a stroke, for God's sake.'

'Is it bad?' I asked meekly.

'I don't think there's such a thing as a good one. He's lost the use of his left arm and his left leg and his speech is terribly slurred and his face seems to have ... *sagged,* but then I've seen you like that after a night down Gerry's Club.'

'Come on, fair play, be serious.'

'I was. If you didn't know you'd just think he was incredibly pissed, but the nurses there say the chances for some sort of recovery are good. They're doing scans and tests and things, but the odds are the stroke was on the right side of the brain, which controls the left side of the body. Left-sided strokes are worse, affecting the memory and speech, sometimes permanently. And they think it could have been a blood clot rather than a bleed.'

I must have looked lost; I felt it.

'Don't ask. Just take it that a right-sided clot is far preferable to a left-sided bleed. It's called avoiding the very bad bullet in America. Anyway, he's not ga-ga or anything. He knew I was there and knew who I was and when I mentioned you he snarled, so there's nothing wrong with his memory.'

'Who else was there?'

'No one as far as I know.'

'No sign of my mother?' She shook her head.

'Or a nineteen-year-old topless model?'

'Sorry to disappoint you, but no. I'm the only visitor he's had, and I was only there standing in for you because you were God knew where. He'd put your name and our phone number down when they'd admitted him and asked for his next-of-kin. I don't think they know who he is, you know.'

'What do you mean?'

'I don't think they have any idea he's a peer. He's just down as plain 'Mr Angel', but at least he's got a room to himself.'

'Thank God for that. That's a great relief.'

'That they don't know who he is?'

'No, that he's got a private room. That means he won't be able to fleece the other patients at poker.'

'Look, when you go down there, *try* and play the loving son, would you? Just for the day. I know it will be almost impossible for you to pull it off but you will try, won't you?'

'When am I going?' I sighed.

'Tomorrow morning, of course, first thing. You can take the Freelander. I've got a meeting at Colditz but they'll send a car.'

'Colditz' was her nickname for the head office of a well-known department store chain in the West End. There was a time when she wasn't admitted to the tradesman's entrance, now they sent cars for her.

'Then I'm going to turn in, I'm shattered.'

'Yes, Paris is so tiring, isn't it?'

She hadn't even noticed my bruises.

'Did you see the stuff I left you from the estate

agents?' I said, to make the point that I had been working really, really hard lately.

'Yes I did,' she said, spooning another chestnut. 'I quite like the look of the old pub.'

'The Old Rosemary Branch?'

'That's the one. All the others are much of a muchness. Dining room, library, hall, conservatory. One of them's even got a billiard room. They sound like something out of a game of bloody *Cluedo*.'

Chapter Fifteen

I must have been worried as I woke up at 5.30 a.m. and there were no car alarms going off in the street. Leaving Amy snoring gently, I sneaked downstairs and as soon as I had made coffee, I fired up the computer and went on the internet, determined to give myself a crash course in stroke and dealing with stroke. There is a maxim somewhere which runs that every situation can be handled successfully if you have sixty per cent preparation and fifty per cent inspiration. The other twenty per cent being down to luck and good maths.

It wasn't good, that early in the morning, to discover that typing the word 'strokes' into a search engine produced a whole raft of hits with the 'adult content' warning sign – and did I wish to continue? Well, of course I did, which is why it was 7 a.m. when I finally left the house and headed for the M25 and round to the A12 which followed the line of one of the first roads in the country from the lawless, Dodge City that was Londinium in Roman times to Colchester, which was then the capital of Britannia.

When I got to the Colchester turn-off, I couldn't help but be reminded by the road signs that Harwich was not that far away, so maybe I could look in on the *Akademik Shteinman* and claim the whole trip on expenses. I was also conscious that the road continued on to a little coastal village and failed artists' commune called Romanhoe where my mother, and my father's former wife, had 'found herself' several years ago. I had an instant and very frightening vision of him having his stroke whilst up here having an argument with her. But I quickly cleared my head of it. If my mother had it in for my father, he would never have made the hospital.

It still begged the question as to how he got to hospital and what he was doing in Colchester, but then I was supposed to be a detective now, wasn't I?

There was a woman in bed with him.

Well, sitting on a chair by the side of his bed to be absolutely accurate. And the woman was wearing a dog collar, so it wasn't as interesting a situation as I'd first thought.

'Hello, there,' she said. 'I'm one of the hospital chaplains.'

I looked down at the bed and locked eyes with my father.

'Did he send for you?'

'Well, not exactly. On his admissions form he was asked about his religious faith and he put 'None – Church of England' but I thought I had better check.'

I struggled to keep my face straight and I returned the twinkle in his eyes.

'That's very good of you, vicar, but I'd better take it from here.'

'If you should need me...'

'We know who to call,' I assured her.

When she'd gone, I took her seat and edged it closer to the bed.

'OK, Dad, let's cut to the chase. When do we get to read the will?'

He drew in a big breath, which seemed to take a lot of concentration, and then he said, very slowly and deliberately: 'I, being of sound mind and body, have spent the fucking lot.'

I felt a sudden rush of something, I wasn't sure what, but I knew then that he was going to be fine.

He was in a small side room just big enough for a bed, a chair and a wall-mounted television, which was across from the main ward where most of the patients seemed to be asleep. I guessed that the hospital routine was wake 'em up, get 'em washed and get them back in to freshly-made beds for the rest of the day so they didn't make the place look untidy if there was an inspection by the team management task force or whatever they called themselves. It also made the patients easier to find in the unlikely event that a doctor might visit the ward.

My father was lying on top of his bed, wearing

red silk pyjamas, which he now probably regretted buying, a white terrycloth robe, which I suspect was hospital-issue, and brown leather slippers. Above his headboard was a notice on which had been printed: 'Mr Angel (Kit). Dedicated Nurse: Sally'.

I bet myself they hadn't got his full name out of him, never mind the titular 'Lord'. He'd picked up the nickname 'Kit' when he'd been made a peer because it had an acceptable, gentleman's club ring to it. Even that late in life he's been embarrassed by his full monicker of Christopher Carlton Cleves Angel, which he said looked like a stutter when he did his signature. I always blamed him for taking his revenge on his children, especially my poor brother Finbar and sister Finnoula, though we don't talk about her.

I was still holding the massive bouquet of flowers – pink things like anaemic carnations – and the big box of Quality Street chocolates I'd bought at the hospital shop on the way in and I waved them in front of his face.

'For me?' he said, though it took considerable effort.

'No,' I shook my head and pointed at the sign above his head. 'For Nurse Sally.'

He nodded and held up a thumb in agreement, then pointed to the bell-push on the end of a dangling white cable.

Nurse Sally appeared within a minute, fresh-faced and smiling. I knew that if my father stayed in here for more than a week it would take more than a bunch of flowers and a box of toffees to buy her silence.

'I'm Mr Angel's son,' I glanced at him and he nodded approval at the 'Mr', 'and I just thought I'd come and see what he's up to. I was out of the country until yesterday, you see.' She smiled politely, no doubt having heard all the excuses before. 'And came as soon as I could,' I ended lamely.

'Your father seems to be going for Perfect Patient status. He admitted himself and seemed to know exactly what was happening to him. Even had an overnight bag with him,' Nurse Sally said proudly.

I wasn't surprised by that. He worked in the House of Lords, he must see people having strokes all the time.

Nurse Sally filled me in on the details while my father grunted occasionally. Amy had been right: his face had a definite slump on the left side and he wasn't moving his left arm.

He had been driving up the A12 (and I suspected I knew why) on Saturday morning and somewhere short of Colchester he realised something bad was happening to him. With amazing presence of mind he turned off and followed the signs for A & E, parking his car and presenting himself to the front desk before collapsing in a heap. By later that day, he had all the tell-tale signs: unable to speak, unable to stand up and he could only use his left arm to do a Dr Strangelove impersonation. He had spent the night in the Medical Assessment Unit, which the Americans call 'Triage' and most British nurses refer to as 'the Twilight Zone', and then moved to the Stroke Unit.

Plus points, as such, were that he seemed to

have no trouble swallowing, in fact he'd already complained about the food, his vision wasn't affected and his speech was returning rapidly. He'd even responded to a first session of physiotherapy by referring to his two physios as 'Bambi' and 'Thumper'. Nurse Sally assured me that his progress was good but recovery came in quantum leaps separated by long spells of frustration where isolation and depression were the main enemies. She needed to talk with me about after-care before I left, also the possibility of moving him to London to be nearer his family.

Plenty to think of there, I told her and she must have noticed the concern on my face.

'Try not to worry. The word "stroke" often scares people more than it should,' she said.

I didn't tell her it was the word 'family' which terrified me.

As soon as she'd left us alone, my father glanced over to the other beds to check that the occupants were still sleeping, then he grabbed my arm with his right hand and gripped hard.

'You – have – got – to – get – me – out – of – here,' he growled. 'It's full of old people. I see old people.'

'There's a sluice room down the corridor. I'll start the first tunnel from there if you distract the guards.'

He raised his right thumb again to show he approved of the plan.

'What the hell were you doing driving up here?' I asked, though I suspected I knew the answer.

He held up his right hand again, this time showing the index and little fingers in the Italian 'evil eye' representation of the devil's horns.

'You were on your way to see Mother?'

He nodded.

'Did you get my message on your answer-phone?'

He shook his head slowly and furrowed his brow.

I felt relieved. At least my news about Amy's condition hadn't brought the stroke on. It was much more likely that the thought of seeing my mother again had done the trick.

'So what was the occasion?'

He crooked a finger this time, signalling me closer before he tried to speak. He always had been paranoid.

'I was going to invite her to the wedding,' he whispered.

The only sound in the room was that of my jaw dropping open.

I patted the mattress next to where my father lay. 'Move over, I think I'm having a stroke.'

I met with Nurse Sally at the reception desk for the Stroke Unit and we went through the paper-work. To begin with, she very tactfully asked me to 'confirm' my father's age. What could I do? If he'd said he was 57, then he was 57. Did he have any allergies? Probably not. Did he have a history of high blood pressure? How would I know? Who was his regular doctor? I had no idea: someone in London. Didn't I live in London? Yes I did, but it's a big place. I gave her my address in Hampstead and confirmed that my father lived alone in his flat in Morpeth Terrace, SW1. Was there a Mrs Angel?

Good question. Yes, there had been a Mrs Angel but they'd been divorced for over ten years. I thought it best to leave it at that. (Amy would kill me if she wasn't the first to hear the gossip.) Was there anyone who should be notified? No, I would take care of all that; it seemed I had been volunteered.

I asked if there was anything practical I had to do and what the likely timetable of events was. Nurse Sally reassured me that my father had 'got off lightly' and things could have been much worse. He'd shown excellent signs of recovery in the first fortyeight hours, which often happened, but it could be days, weeks, months or sometimes a year, before he was back to near normal. Of course, she said 'normal' was a relative term. I had to think of a stroke as a sort of 'brain attack'. Some of my father's brain cells would have short circuited and burnt out. They couldn't be replaced, so it was a question of the brain learning to do ordinary things a different way. He would need care, exercise and probably medication for the rest of his life, but there was no reason why we shouldn't hope for a good recovery. Did I have any questions?

While she had been talking, I had scanned the racks of public information leaflets displayed on the wall, mostly published by the Stroke Association. I picked a copy of *Sex After Stroke* from the rack and handed it to Nurse Sally.

'Make sure he gets this, would you? It might cheer him up.'

I made a note of the Stroke Unit's direct line number and said I would be in touch before my father drove everybody on the ward mad.

She smiled thinly and said: 'We're used to that. Thanks for the flowers, by the way.'

As I was leaving the Unit, I held the swing doors open for two fit young women in green uniforms, both blonde, both in their early twenties. They were chatting together and didn't seem to notice me, but I noticed them as they walked away from me.

I wondered which one was Bambi and which was Thumper.

Outside in the car park, near the helipad used by the local Air Ambulance, I phoned Amy's mobile. She didn't mind in the slightest that I caught her in the middle of a meeting; not when I told her my father's news.

'Jeeesus! You are kidding me, right? You are pulling my chain. He's marrying Kim McIntosh, the model?'

'So he says.'

'But she's nineteen.'

'No she's not. He says she's actually twenty-five, just looks younger. She was nineteen when she did most of her topless portfolio.'

'Oh well, that's okay then.'

'Now, now, let's not be bitchy.'

'I'm not worried,' she said, 'she won't be *my* stepmother.'

'She'll be your mother-in-law,' I retaliated.

'I've already got one of them. And did you know that mother-in-law is an anagram of "Woman Hitler"?'

'No, but it makes a sort of sense.'

'So has he told Bethany?'

Amy had always known my mother by the name she'd adopted after the divorce and moved into the Bohemian lifestyle, turning out wonky pottery and charmingly inept seascapes in water colours. Ominously, she and Amy had always got on rather well.

'He was on his way there when it happened. Mother doesn't know yet, neither does Kim – about him being in hospital, I mean.'

'How long's he in for?'

'They don't seem to know. He hasn't seen the consultant yet. If it's any length of time, I'll have to try and get him transferred to London.'

I let the implications of that hang on the air waves.

'Has he got private medical insurance?'

There were times when I was grateful for practical women.

'Not a penny's worth, but the situation's worse than that.'

'With your family, it just has to be.'

'He's broke.'

'How broke?'

'Flat broke. Skint. Bereft of funds. Lacking in assets. If he hadn't paid off the mortgage on his flat, he'd be selling *Big Issue* in Parliament Square.'

'No savings?'

'Nothing; which is exactly what's in his will and he's not kidding. He's sold all the shares he ever had and cashed in all his insurance and pension policies. He hasn't even got an income at the moment.'

'What about the House of Lords?'

'Working Peers get an attendance allowance of £64 a day but if you don't attend, you don't get the allowance. They don't do sick pay.'

'I take it your mother doesn't know that either.'

'I shouldn't think so, nor will his new fiancée.'

'Where is she at the moment?'

'Dad says she's on a fashion shoot in Italy for a week, so that gives us a bit of time.'

'Bit of time to do what?'

'Work out how we're going to tell her.'

'*We?*'

She didn't miss much, Amy.

'Well, I've got a lot on my plate just at the moment. I've got to get over to Cambridge now, sort things out there. I don't know what time I'll be home, there's so much going on at work. God knows what'll happen when Dad gets out of hospital. He might need looking after.'

'Don't worry about that. We can always hire a care nurse or home help for him.'

'Or maybe a Swedish au pair?'

'Don't push it.'

I didn't head for Cambridge straight away, though, I found the A120 and headed further east towards Harwich, getting there in the Freelander in twenty minutes. On the outskirts of the town I took the road to the Parkeston port area, the horizon dominated by the huge crane rigs used by the container ships, but very quickly any view of the port disappeared behind high security fences and the road I was on suddenly ended in barriers across both lanes with a Security Point in the middle staffed by men and women in blue kit to make them look as much like police as possible.

A middle-aged women wearing huge and hugely unfashionable glasses came out from the central control box, talking into a radio at her collar, her right hand resting on a torch clipped to her belt, pretending it was a gun. She made no move to raise the barrier, so I pulled up and lowered the window of the Freelander and looked down at her, really glad I wasn't in the Peugeot looking up.

'Can I help you, sir?'

'I was looking for somewhere to park so I could have a look round the port,' I said with a polite smile.

'Do you have business here?'

'Well, no, I just wanted a look round.'

'A look round, eh?'

I could tell I was going nowhere; it even sounded weak to me.

'I'm afraid the port is restricted to pass holders,' she said in a quite motherly way. 'You could go into Harwich, into the old town for a look round. There are shops and things.'

I realised that I was wasting my time and whatever I said would only convince her that she had a nutter on her hands and make sure I was remembered. If they knew their business, security cameras would have photographed both me and the Freelander's number plates by now. If they didn't have such a system, perhaps Frank and I could sell them one.

'Yeah, I think I'll do that,' I told the lady guard and began to turn the Freelander around. I even gave her a cheery wave as I set off for my sight-seeing and shopping trip around old Harwich.

Naturally, as soon as I was out of sight, I turned west, roughly in the direction of Cambridge, and put my foot down.

I had to concentrate. Things were falling apart around my ears and I needed to prioritise my time and target my efforts and all the other stuff people with proper jobs had to do. What was it Amy always said? Set yourself S.M.A.R.T. targets: Specific, Measurable, Achievable, Realistic and Time bound. Or had I got that from the VCR's programming instructions? I wished I had paid more attention.

After about twenty miles, I had my smart target: get to Cambridge and play it by ear.

Peter Sutton, the security man, was waiting for me at Tyler Pharmaceuticals with the look of a man itching to tell me something whilst not looking too keen. He was an ex-policeman after all, and they never give information away free.

'Was Dr Sanger expecting you today?' he asked as he ushered me into his control room.

'Not really. I just needed to check something, tie up some loose ends, before I report in to Olivier Zaborski.' It never hurt to drop the name of the big boss. 'Is Dr Quinn back at work?' I asked, making it as casual as I could.

I was pretty sure she was as I had seen her VW in the car park. I had also, automatically, looked for Frank's Mercedes spy van, but that was, ominously, missing.

'Yes, Dr Quinn came back this morning after her long weekend. Clocked on early, actually. Seems keen as mustard today. She's working in the wash room. Did you want to see her?'

'No, don't disturb her.'

'I meant do you want to *see* her?' he said, pointing to one of the closed-circuit TV monitors and there was the back view of Cassandra's white coat, her hair clipped up out of the way, as she busied herself transferring clear liquid from one set of vessels to another using a glass pipette just like the ones in school chemistry lessons where you always ended up with a mouthful of something unspeakable.

'Popular girl this week, our Cassandra,' said Sutton. He wasn't going to contain himself much longer.

'Somebody else been asking if she's in?' I prompted him.

'Yesterday, talking to Doc Sanger about her. A friend of yours, or should that be a colleague?'

'Oh, you mean Alice?' I played it cool.

'Yes, Alice Lemarquand. Said she was standing in for her father who is ill it seems.'

'That's right, he's in hospital. I went to visit him last night.'

I seemed to be doing a lot of hospital visits these days.

'So this Alice is Frank's daughter?'

'Yes, and she's in the business with him. I haven't seen her myself today.'

Like I couldn't care less; like I didn't have a really bad feeling about Alice.

'I knew I knew the name,' he said, clenching a fist in triumph. He was now dying to tell me something, but it wouldn't be something to my advantage.

'Remember it from somewhere?' I sighed wearily.

'I told you Lemarquand rang a bell. A case in the Channel Islands, fraud job. Only it wasn't Frank Lemarquand; it must have been Alice.'

'Are you sure? I mean it doesn't sound very likely does it? She's a partner in Frank's business, which is a highly respected company and my firm have used them for years.'

'I am talking five or six years ago, but I'm sure about the name,' he said, but I thought I detected just the hint of a slight doubt in his voice.

'They're probably all called Lemarquand in the Channel Islands,' I said confidently. 'I mean, what are the chances of a convicted fraudster setting up a business as a security specialist? She'd never have got through the Disclosure process at the Criminal Records Bureau.'

'Oh come on,' he snorted. 'We all know of people who have slipped through the net of www. disclosure.gov.uk. Everybody on the Force knows that the CRB and the Police National Computer system are years behind with their data in-putting.'

Some of us did know it; some of us relied on the fact.

'So what was Alice after? She was probably just tying up loose ends that Frank forgot.'

'Like I say, she asked to see Dr Sanger and said she wanted some personnel details. Naturally I checked with your office to see if she was kosher, and your Miss Blugden said you already had electronic versions of our staff files, so young Alice said okay, fine, sorry to bother you, and disappeared.'

'That was it?'

'Yes, but it was then it clicked about the Channel Islands' case.'

'Any idea what details Alice was asking about?' I said, trying to look unconcerned.

'Oh yes, she wanted Dr Quinn's home address.'

Oh bugger.

I sat in the Freelander in the car park and phoned the office with a shaking hand.

I was pretty sure it was Lorna who answered.

'It's Angel.'

'Oh, is it?' Yes, definitely Lorna.

'I need you to go into the Tyler Pharmaceutical personnel files that were emailed to us last week. Just find me one thing, that's all: Cassandra Quinn's home address.'

'36 Wyvern Road, Cambridge.'

'That was quick.'

'I have an excellent memory. Once I've been told something I never forget it.'

Now there was a challenge, but I didn't have the time.

'So who told you that address? And when? And why, come to that?'

'Actually, I told Veronica. She asked me to pull up the files yesterday afternoon while she was talking to someone on the phone.'

Alice.

'Put Veronica on, would you? Now, please.'

'She's busy. She has the accountant with her.'

'Which bit of "now" don't you understand, Lorna?'

I heard a snort and a huffing noise but the next

303

voice was Veronica's.

'Angel, I'm in a meeting.'

'And I'm in a car park. Don't try and impress me, woman, I just want to know why you forgot to tell me that Alice Lemarquand has a record as long as my arm?'

'Oh, for Heaven's sake, Alice Lemarquand is no more a criminal than you or I are, well, me anyway. She's just trying to do the best job she can to support her father in a very male-dominated world. She deserves all the help we can give her.'

'But there was actually the small matter of a fraud charge, wasn't there? A few years ago, in the Channel Islands? Is this ringing any bells?'

'Well there was that,' she said hesitantly, 'but she's paid her dues on all those crimes.'

'*All*? How many is "all", Veronica?'

Sutton had only mentioned financial fraud. Something about unsanctioned electronic withdrawals – the sort of thing banks do every day.

'She was very young and highly strung back then, and her mother had died when she was a child. She's calmed down a lot since then. She's not at all violent these days.'

'*Violent*? Veronica, exactly what is on Alice's criminal record, and how many pages does it run to?'

'There's the fraud charge, but that was eventually dropped by the banks as they recovered all the money and didn't want the publicity.'

'So Alice didn't actually go to jail?'

'I'm afraid she did, but it was for aggravated assault on the arresting officers from the Fraud Squad, not for the fraud.'

'Oh, that's all right then, isn't it?' I said, but the sarcasm was lost, as it usually was on Veronica.

'And I think the other charge,' she continued, 'was to do with grievous bodily harm on another prisoner while she was on remand. But I don't think they pressed that as no witnesses came forward.'

They were probably too scared.

I know I was.

Chapter Sixteen

Wyvern Road was in the part of Cambridge which students used to call 'The Kite', reflecting the shape of the area of terraced housing, the technical college and a cemetery in the geometrical figure formed by Mill Road and East Road. I remembered it from the days when the college was just 'the Tech', and not part of Anglia Polytechnic University, and when pubs like The Tiger played host to aspiring poets and budding novelists who all went on to become well known, and also to student radicals who went on to become Home Secretary (And at least one of them still owed me a pint.)

I cruised Wyvern Road in the Freelander until I identified number 36, a mid-terrace two-up, two-down late Victorian house which had been modernised and then 'improved' thanks to the influence of the torrent of home and garden design television shows.

There was no sign of life from the outside as I crawled by, unable to stop anywhere as parked cars filled every inch of one side of the narrow street. I drove for about ten minutes before I could find a place to turn around and started a trawl the opposite way. It was only then, as I glanced down one of the small cul-de-sacs off Wyvern Road which ended at the cemetery, that I noticed the outline of a Mercedes Sprinter van.

I dumped the Freelander three streets away. Not because I was worried about it being seen (nobody associated me with the vehicle) but because there was nowhere else to park. The Mercedes was where I had seen it and I took up a position by the back doors so I could not be seen from any direction unless she came out of the cemetery. It was, I thought, the perfect ambush until, that is, the side door suddenly slid open and with two steps she was there, right in front of me, nearly scaring me to death.

'You're Angel, aren't you,' she said, without requiring an answer.

'Possibly, if you're Alice.'

'My dad didn't tell you about me, did he?'

'And I can't think why not. Did he tell you about me?'

'Oh yes.'

We stood glaring at each other. I guessed she was about thirty, but she looked younger, fresh-faced, with a freckled complexion and short light brown hair overdue for the blonde highlight treatment. She wore a pink sweatshirt bearing the legend: *Give Me Chocolate – Or Somebody Gets Hurt.*

'I saw your dad yesterday. Any news since then?' I asked when I was fairly sure she wasn't going to hit me.

'He's come round a bit, but he's still groggy and they're keeping him doped up to the eyeballs for the pain.'

'Has he said anything to anyone?'

'About what?'

'About what happened. Hey, look, don't play coy. You were going flippin' mental yesterday on the phone.'

'Oh, about the fact that some crazy bitch crippled an old age pensioner with a length of lead piping and then left him in a hospital car park on the off-chance somebody might find him? Did I let that upset me? I am soooooo sorry.'

'You seem to know more than the hospital does. They think it was some sort of accident and Frank drove himself to Addenbrookes.'

'There was no accident. The van hasn't a scratch on it. See for yourself.' I was, after all, leaning on the damned van and I suppose a better detective would have looked for any incriminating damage. Alice had.

'The passenger seat, though, was soaked with blood. I think she caught him out in the open or yanked him out of the cab, beat the crap out of him then somehow loaded him back in and drove to the hospital. Then she just left him there and thank God he came round enough to walk into Casualty.'

'You seem pretty sure of all this,' I said, but not before gauging the distance to her fists.

'Addenbrookes security men found the keys in

307

the ignition. My dad would never have left them there if he'd been driving. It's just not possible.'

'So there were no marks on the van and the keys in. I suppose the hospital security guys didn't bother to look in the passenger side, so they didn't automatically think it was a road accident and they didn't call the cops? Is that it?'

'For which I'm sure the Cambridgeshire constabulary was very grateful at midnight on a Saturday. Far worse things go unreported.'

'A good point. So the cops aren't asking any questions yet?'

'No, but I'm going to, just as soon as that Quinn bitch gets home.'

'Now, Alice, it's take-a-deep-breath time.' I took a step back into the road just in case. 'Because I think you might be slightly on the wrong track there, about Cassandra Quinn, I mean.'

She put her hands on her hips. Her jeans, tucked in to suede Rocket Dog boots, were so tight I was pretty sure she wasn't carrying a concealed weapon.

'Oh yeah? I've been listening to the recordings Dad made and reading up his case notes.' Notes? You were supposed to make notes? 'I know you were concentrating on this Quinn woman as your prime suspect at Tyler Pharmaceuticals.'

I held up my hands in the T for Time Out sign.

'When was you father attacked?'

'Some time on Saturday night.'

'Cassandra Quinn was in Paris on Saturday night. I know, I was following her. I was with her.'

I thought it best not to mention the salsa dancing.

308

'So who the fuck was the woman who hit him?'

'How do you know it was a woman?' I asked, suddenly waking up.

She looked at me like she was dealing with an idiot child.

'Because Dad took a picture of her as she was hitting him.'

It wasn't a very good picture, but then it had been taken under exceptional circumstances with a camera no bigger than a box of matches, at night, whilst being thrown around like it was in a tumble dryer. It was the camera Frank had given me; the one he paid about eight quid for down The Gadget Shop and which was small enough to fit on a key ring. In fact that was exactly what Frank had done. He had clipped it to the ignition keys of the van and so when he got out – or was pulled out – of the cab, he would have had the keys in his hand and started snapping without his assailant even realising he had a camera. Or that was Alice's theory anyway.

However it had happened, Frank had got off three shots which showed something, although exactly what was debatable. In the back of the Mercedes (Alice had said 'Shall we step into my office?') she plugged the camera into a lap-top computer and with a bit of tweaking managed to put three very dark, grainy images on the screen.

'I reckon the light source is the headlamps of the van,' Alice explained.

Which was just about the only thing clear to me. The images were mostly grey and the focus point, more by luck than judgement, was a horizontal bar of a darker grey with a pink blob at one end; the pink blob had specks of red in it.

'That could be anything,' I said, though I had no idea what.

'That's a piece of lead piping coming right at the camera, like a police baton.' I wasn't going to argue with her as she sounded as if she was speaking from a position of personal experience. 'And that's a female hand wielding it. Note the red nail polish.'

'And you think that hand belongs to Cassandra Quinn?'

'Dad was on her case, wasn't he? I don't know what the case is, but she was the target. He's got audio and visual recordings of her from virtually every day last week. I figure that he followed her after work and she jumped him.'

'Alice, you must believe me. Cassandra Quinn was in Paris when this happened to your dad on Saturday night. Technically, your father wasn't on that case any more.'

'So what was he doing in Cambridge?'

'He was doing a little job for me, a bit of a favour. Out at a place called Comberton Manor. Come on, let me pick up my car and you can follow. I'll show you.'

Fortunately she agreed, which was a relief as I didn't want her in the vicinity of Wyvern Road when the unsuspecting Dr Quinn got home from work. I had known this was the safest course of action from the moment I had seen the baseball bat lying on the floor of the van next to the extra batteries which powered the recording equipment. It was a new baseball bat, still with a JJB Sports price label and barcode stuck on the handle and I didn't think it was the sort of thing Frank would leave casually rolling around in the back of his van. I reckoned Alice had bought it specially, when she couldn't find a shop that did lead piping.

She gave me a lift to Amy's car and I automatically checked the passenger seat for Frank's blood but she had done a good job of cleaning up, and destroying evidence along the way.

'Frank – your dad – he'll be up and about in no time, just you see,' I said as she drove because I thought I ought to say something.

'You're not having much luck around fathers today are you?'

'How did...?'

'Veronica told me when she rang to warn me you might be looking for me,' she said, eyes on the road, concentrating on her driving.

'Oh she did, did she? All girls together is it?'

'Something like that. I think she always fancied me to take over the business when Dad finally retired. Saw me as a fellow female professional. I think she told me because she was worried about you. Thought maybe the news about your father would make you a bit ... irrational.'

Irrational? Me? I wasn't the one looking for justice with a baseball bat.

I pointed out the Freelander and she pulled up behind it and then she followed me out to Comberton and it was slightly uncomfortable to see her in my rear-view mirror all the way there, never allowing another car to come between us and sending out a mental vibration that she would actually enjoy it if I tried to outrun her.

The Manor house still looked like the Bates motel the day after the Christmas decorations had come down and from the outside there was absolutely no sign that anything untoward had happened here. I was beginning to doubt the wisdom of bringing Alice out here. True, I had got her away from Cassandra, but now I had nothing to show her, I hadn't even got a key to the house, and here I was, miles from anywhere, out in the sticks alone with her.

In my mirror, I saw her pull into the drive and park the Mercedes behind me, get out and stride up to my door.

'This was the place Dad was bugging?' she asked me when I lowered the window.

'Yes.'

'At night?'

'Yes.'

It seemed to be all she wanted to know. She looked around her, checking out the landscape, then set off towards the house without another word. I did notice that she had a black bum bag around her waist which hadn't been there before. As I couldn't think of anything else to do, I followed her and by the time I caught up with her she was standing in the hall inside the Manor.

'How did you do that?'

She patted the belt pouch over her hip. 'Same way I got into Cassandra Quinn's house. Say something.'

'What?'

'Anything and walk about a bit. That way we trigger the microphones and any cameras Dad planted. It's quicker than trying to find them.'

I did as I was told, striding around the hall, opening and closing doors and stamping my feet.

'This is an unusual property, built by a madman in 1852 originally as a bicycle shed for the Third Cambridgeshire Foot and Mouth mobile infantry. After several years as a sanctuary for wounded carrier pigeons pensioned off after the Crimean War, it was converted into a family home at a time when a billiards room and a library were essential to middle-class designer living, but bathrooms were thought of as rather flippant luxuries.'

Alice was drawing a finger across her throat.

'That's quite enough for a sound check,' she said striding towards the door. 'I wouldn't want you to waste your best material. Let's go back to the van, see if that set anything off.'

As we walked back out towards the driveway I decided it was time I contributed to this investigation.

'Frank wouldn't have been parked there on Saturday night,' I observed, 'not where he could be clearly seen from the house. What if he was using the directional microphones in the roof-rack?'

'So he showed you his new toy, did he? Their range isn't that great, seventy or eighty yards maybe, but he could have been parked out there somewhere in the lane, I suppose.'

'Let's take a look while the light holds,' I said, realising that evening was coming on, even the country pubs were open and I was hungry.

We went left out of the Manor drive because the road, not really much more than a country lane, curved into a long left hand bend bordered by a tall hedge and an overgrown drainage ditch.

Twenty yards down the lane and a parked car, or even a van as big as the Mercedes, would not be seen from either the entrance to the drive or the Manor house itself.

Alice trotted up the side of the road, eyes down, looking for signs like Hawkeye with me stumbling along behind as the Last of the Mohicans. When she stopped in her tracks, still looking towards the ground, I almost collided with her, but there was no way I wanted to give her grounds for sexual harassment.

'He was parked about here,' she was saying to herself, 'facing towards the house. He wouldn't have had the lights on, so the light in the pictures he took could have been the headlights ... of ... her car...'

'How do you know he was here?' I asked as her voice tailed off. 'A blade of grass out of place, perhaps? Or fresh spoor?'

She gave me a killer look and pointed to something in the shallow ditch by the hedge. It took me a minute or so to work out what it was; a scrunched up ball of greaseproof paper.

'Dad's sandwiches. He also liked them wrapped in greaseproof. I make a batch each week and leave them in his freezer for him.'

'And very good sandwiches they are too,' I complimented her. 'Are you sure that's Frank's litter, though?'

She shrugged her shoulders.

'Pick it up.'

I did, stumbling and putting one foot in the ditch as I did so. I unfolded the paper and offered it to her but she shook her head.

'Is there anything written on it in pencil?'

'S and K,' I read.

'Sausage and ketchup. One of mine.'

That seemed to make it an open and shut case, but there were other interesting things in that ditch. I knew because I was standing on them.

'Well look at this,' I said gingerly holding up a white plastic carrier bag.

'What's that?' asked Alice.

'I think it's called a clue.'

The bag contained two items, one of them a length of old rope wound up like a cowboy would wind in his lasso around his hand and elbow, then tied with a piece of garden twine in the middle so that it formed the shape of the number 8. I guessed that the rope was actually an old clothesline, the sort that has long been replaced by multi-coloured nylon affairs which you can't tie a decent knot in. There again, who uses clotheslines since they invented the tumble drier?

The other item was an old fashioned finger-screw adjustable wrench, coated in rust; to use it you would have needed another wrench to loosen the screw.

'That's not a clue,' said Alice, 'that's fly-tipping.'

'No, I think these are connected to the assault on your father. In fact I think whoever hit him with the lead pipe was carrying these as well.'

'Are you on some sort of medication? You're not making any sense. Why would Cassandra Quinn be carrying around a piece of old rope, a rusty spanner and a length of lead piping?'

'She wasn't. I keep telling you, it wasn't her. It

wasn't her carrying them.'

'Then who the fuck was?'

'Mrs Peacock, Mrs White or possibly Miss Scarlett,' I said smugly.

I must say, Dr Black has a fine house here and I suspect he keeps a good cellar, eh what?...

I suspect you are right, my dear Colonel, but tell me, why do you think such an eminent anthropologist and man of letters would invite us all here to his country home on such an inclement night?...

Inclement? Oh yes. It is a filthy night out there, quite a storm brewing if you ask me... Has he lived in this part of Hampshire for long, do you know?

Oh, very good. No, I hardly know Dr Black at all, except of course by reputation. How about you, Vicar? Have you ever met him?

No, Professor, I've not had the pleasure. Perhaps one of the ladies...?

Not all the ladies are here yet, Vicar. Only Mrs White has arrived so far. We are still awaiting our two other divas and then the evening's entertainment can commence.

Well I'll have some more champagne then whilst we wait.

Certainly, Colonel. A fine idea. Will you join us, Reverend Green?

'Oh, my, God,' said Alice taking off her set of headphones. 'They cannot be serious.'

'I think they are,' I said, taking off mine and straightening up until I hit my head on the roof of the van. Alice went the other way, sinking down until she was sitting cross-legged on the metal floor.

'Pass me the first aid kit,' she ordered and I un-clipped the green plastic box from its mounting behind the driver's seat and handed it to her.

'No, you open it.'

In the small plastic compartments which nor-mally house thumb bandages, surgical lint and those funny shaped scissors which are always blunt, was a generous selection of cannabis resin (Moroccan Black), some leaf and seeds mixture, a packet of hand rolling tobacco, an open pack of green Rizla cigarette papers and a Bic disposable lighter.

'Vazz me up a big one,' said Alice. 'I need to chill.'

'Hey, I know it's been declassified, but...'

'It's been *rescheduled* from a Class B drug to a Class C. Which basically means don't get caught selling, or smoking it near a school. Anyway, it's not mine, it's my dad's.'

'It is?'

'Yeah, he takes the odd toke for his arthritis. Swears by it.'

'So this is purely for medicinal purposes, then?'

'Absolutely. That's why it's in the first aid box.'

'Of course, how silly of me. Would you happen to know if it helps stroke victims?'

'I've no idea.'

'Can't harm, though, can it? I'll vazz up a spare for later if you don't mind.'

I used the shredded leaf as it would be weaker than the resin and added a few seeds just for the fun of watching them explode. It had been a while, but the old skills came back to me.

'Help yourself. Can you believe those people?'

317

'I'm afraid so.'

'You know who they are?'

'I've got a very good idea.'

I gave her joint a final twist and passed it to her with the lighter.

'That was smooth and quick.'

'Beginner's luck,' I said.

'How did you get on to them?'

'I didn't really put two and two together until tonight when we found that bag.' I thought the 'we' was really rather diplomatic, and so did she, for she handed over the joint as she exhaled. 'And then there was that recording of course.'

'But you suspected something daft like this. You never thought it was that Quinn woman.'

'I keep telling you, she was in Paris with me at the time. Jesus! If I'd wanted to take a woman to Paris on the quiet, everyone would know, but when I openly admit to being there with one, nobody believes me.'

She held up a hand, wiggling her first two fingers. I slotted the joint home.

'But these people,' she said quietly, holding her breath, 'must be seriously disturbed.'

'Well one of them is,' I agreed. 'The one who attacked your father, but I think they're mostly harmless.'

'What put you on to them, Mr Detective?'

She was smiling broadly now. I made a mental note to pinch some of that grass if I got the chance; it looked like the good stuff.

'It was something my wi– something somebody said whilst we were talking about houses.'

I don't think she noticed the slip.

'Houses?

'Yes, funnily enough, houses and estate agents.'

'Oh,' said Alice blowing a perfect smoke ring and then giggling about it.

'Which is why you've got to let me come up with a way to sort this out. To your advantage and mine.' I realised I'd better not light up the second joint. 'I mean your father's advantage, of course.'

'You'd do that for us?' she asked sweetly; a little too sweetly.

'Yes, I would, because I like Frank and I want to do business with him in the future.'

'And not because you want to get Cassandra Quinn off the hook because you fancy her?'

'I keep telling you, she's not on the hook for this. Your dad will tell you that when he comes round. Cassandra is not, repeat not, in the frame for this.'

'But she is in the frame for something, isn't she?'

I didn't like the way Alice's eyes had cleared and she wasn't doing her sweet little girl lost act any more.

'Yes, but for something else entirely.'

'I knew it!' She took another huge draw on the joint. The air in the back of the van was blue now, so solid I felt I could step on it and climb over into the driver's seat.

Eventually Alice exhaled.

'I knew she was dirty,' she said.

'Dirty?'

'Strange, spooky, odd, possibly sick and definitely weird.'

'You've been checking up on her?'

'No, I burgled her house and planted a bug – sorry, recording device – this afternoon. Just before you arrived actually.'

I must have straightened up again as I seemed to be hitting my head on the roof.

'And do you know what?' she said, sounding drunk now, waving the joint at me.

'What?'

'She's a really, really, really strange woman.'

'She's a scientist, a chemist. They're all strange.'

'This one is *really* strange.' Alice lowered her voice and, I swear, she glanced around the van to make sure no one could overhear. 'You know she wears kinky underwear, one of those basket things, those corsets that nip your waist in and make yer tits stand up and beg.'

'Basques?'

'That's the one. Them things.'

'Lots of women wear them,' I said unconvincingly.

'On your planet, maybe, but the craziest thing is she keeps hers *in the fridge*. Now how fucking strange is that?'

'That is strange,' I said, adding as an afterthought: 'Are you going to smoke that all yourself?'

Chapter Seventeen

I got back to London and the Hampstead house at about ten-thirty; sweaty, hungry and emotionally drained, but elated that I had, in a funny sort of way, solved my first case. And it was all thanks to a chance remark by Amy, my partner, my soul mate, my rock, my inspiration.

'You've been smoking; I can smell it on you from here!'

'I was on a stake-out, trapped in the back of a van with a chain smoker.'

'Stake-out? Where did you get that one? The Rockford Files?'

I clasped my hands as if praying.

'Please; give me a break. It's been a long day.'

'Okay, get yourself something to eat and then I'll give you your instructions for tomorrow. There's food in the oven.'

'In the oven?'

'Yes it's that hot thing with a window in the door in the kitchen. I cooked earlier. Don't look like that. I can cook you know.'

'It's not anything odd is it, like a chocolate and charcoal soufflé?'

'No, it's not,' she said patiently. 'I'm not getting cravings yet and when I do you probably won't notice. It's *osso bucco* actually, and very good it is too.'

And it was. I ate a plate of it sitting in the kitchen and Amy even poured me a glass of white wine as she talked.

'I made a few calls today and I think we can, and should, get your father transferred to the Devonshire.'

'The Devonshire Arms? The pub?' I said automatically.

'No, you div, the private hospital over near Baker Street. They've a terrific reputation and excellent physiotherapists, and it's convenient for his flat.'

'Expensive?'

'Very, but what's the alternative? Is his girl-friend going to be his full-time carer, or pick up the bills? I think not. I think as soon as she hears, she's offski.'

She jerked a thumb to illustrate how a nine-teen-year-old supermodel might hit the highway.

'That's harsh, Amy,' I said.

'Harsh but fair, that's me. Or would you rather he came to live with us, right in the middle of a major life change and a move out into the country? Just how much upheaval can you handle?'

'I could give up my job; spend more time at home,' I offered.

'Forget that,' she said. 'I think the Devonshire is the solution, at least until we see how his recovery goes. I'll pick up the bills, so tell him not to worry about that.'

Knowing my father, the fact that someone else was picking up the bill wouldn't cause him to lose any sleep at all.

'So one of your first tasks is to get him to agree to that. Then we need to talk to his doctors in Colchester and arrange the transfer. I'm busy most of the day tomorrow but we could drive up and see your father tomorrow night. I'll need the Free-lander. I trust you brought it back in one piece?'

'Of course, but you could always take the Peugeot.'

'Hah-ha. Funny guy. That can be your task number two: get rid of that bloody car, it's litter-ing up the driveway and I've put the house on the market, so we can expect prospective buyers wandering around.'

'I didn't notice a For Sale sign.'

'This is Hampstead, we don't put up signs. I've given a set of keys to the estate agents and they'll handle everything. All you have to do is keep the place tidy, which basically means keep out of the way.'

'Ah, now, talking of estate agents...'

She held up a finger to silence me.

'I think this place will go pretty fast, so I need to start looking at some properties myself. I told you, I liked the look of that *Rosemary Branch* place, so task number three is to fix up a viewing for me. Then we start haggling on the price.'

'You think the price is too high?'

'I've no idea what the price is, you just haggle automatically.'

'I can fix you a viewing, I have a very good contact up there and I have to go to Cambridge again tomorrow.'

'You're spending more time there than you are in your office,' she said suspiciously.

'I go where the work is; wherever my clients need me and my professional expertise, I'm there.'

'Yeah, right.' I got the impression that she wasn't impressed. 'Just how long are you spinning out taking the Zaborski shilling?'

'That case is still on-going, but I have wrapped up another, minor, case, thanks to you, and funnily enough, it involves estate agents and you wouldn't believe...'

'I looked at those tapes, you know,' she interrupted, not hearing a word I had said, and me trying to lavish praise on her for solving the case for me.

'What tapes?'

'The ones you left here last week. It's closed-circuit stuff from Zaborski's laboratory. People in white coats with test tubes and stuff.'

I had totally forgotten the security tapes Frank had given me to study.

'And then I had a look at the digital camera and the pictures you took in Paris. Quite a few had the woman from the lab on.'

'Dr Quinn. She was in Paris. That's why I was there.'

'Interesting,' said Amy, letting it hang tantalisingly in the air until I just had to ask.

'What is?'

'It's interesting that while your Dr Quinn is working in the laboratory, she's an obvious size 16 yet when she's gadding about the shops of Paris she's a size 12 if ever I saw one, and I know about these things.'

Oh shit!

She'd done it again.

In the morning, I arranged to meet up with Amy at five that afternoon, so that we could drive to Colchester hospital together that evening. I had decided to drive straight to Cambridge, on the assumption that if I went in to the office, Veronica would just delay me with ridiculous questions and I had a feeling I was going to be fending off quite enough of them as it was.

Alice Lemarquand had told me she would be visiting her father in Addenbrookes this morning, and I had made her promise not to do anything rash until I touched base with her. I hadn't told her the whole story – such as I had pieced it together – and certainly not any specific names. I wanted to tell Jane Bond first, partly because she would know what to do and partly because I liked her and thought she could do with a good laugh.

I didn't fully trust Alice and when I reached the big roundabout on Hills Road, I crawled around it trying to spot the Mercedes van in the Addenbrookes car park, but I didn't and I couldn't drive any slower. Cyclists were overtaking the Peugeot as it was.

At the house which served as the head office of Symington & Sedgeley, I deliberately parked next to Jane Bond's Aston Martin just because it made me feel better. Inside, she was on duty at her desk under the stairs, wearing a low cut flowery print summer frock which suggested that she got the sun-bed after the divorce. When my parents had split they had argued most over a leather sofa and two wing-backed chairs, which went into family legend as 'the bitter suite'.

'Mr Angel, what a surprise,' she greeted me.

'A pleasant one, I hope, Mrs Bond.'

'Oh yes, you can visit any time. You're responsible for a certain gentleman now being known as 'our huckleberry friend' throughout the firm, although I've taken all the credit for it. Coffee?'

'Yes please. Make a large pot and break out the biscuits, because I want to tell you a story, and if you think "huckleberry friend" is good, wait until you hear this.'

'You've got an even better name for darling Devon, the bane of the boardroom?'

325

'How about "Professor Plum"?'

Jane Bond, estate agent, smiled cruelly and wiped the last of the tears from her eyes.

'That is the best thing I've heard since the divorce settlement. You must let me be the one to tell old man Julius. Please, pretty please. Let me tell him, right now when I take his coffee up. Aw, go on.' She raised an eyebrow and tugged suggestively at the neck of her dress as if she was overheating. 'I'll make it worth your while.'

Then she burst out laughing again and held an arm out, pointing at me.

'You should see your face!' She opened her fist and a set of car keys dropped on to the desk. 'I meant,' she said haughtily, 'that you could take my car for a spin.' Then she went all coy. 'Whatever did *you* think I meant?'

'Nice to see you, Mr Angel. We must owe you some money by now, don't we?' Julius Symington greeted me warmly. What a gentleman.

'I've just given a preliminary report to Mrs Bond here. I think it would be useful for her to put it in context.'

'And why is that?'

'She knows the firm and the personnel.'

Mr Julius sank into his office chair and began to massage his temple with the fingers of both hands.

'You're going to tell me something unpleasant about my great nephew, aren't you?'

'How did you guess?' I asked, genuinely curious.

The look on Jane's face. The last time I saw her

looking so happy was when Devon was thrown in to the Cam during a Gay Rights demonstration.'

'Don't get the wrong idea,' Jane said quickly. 'He was thrown in by the other gays on the march. They found him too embarrassing.'

'So what's the gobby little shit-bag done now?' Julius said wearily and I let Jane, who was straining at the leash, tell it.

It had, perhaps, been going on for a year. Devon Sedgeley and some fellow members of his amateur operatic society had been indulging their passion for the game of *Cluedo*. But not content with the board game, they had been playing it out for real. They had access to costumes and make-up already. All they needed was someone to provide a country house to stand in for the 'Tudor Hall' in the game, and Devon, being a partner in a posh firm of estate agents, had plenty of those on his books, and the keys to them. Most people, normal people, would of course think of this as a fairly harmless pastime, albeit a childish one, on a par with train spotting or Morris Dancing. But not, as Jane gleefully pointed out, if you consider the issues of: trespass, possible criminal damage, the insurance situation if there had been an accident and the betrayal of the vendor's trust, not to mention the fact that Devon had deliberately kept four or five valuable properties effectively off the open market for months, possibly giving the vendors grounds for a professional misconduct charge. And he'd even encouraged Mrs Symington to believe the houses were haunted. Now that, was unforgivable.

Ridiculous? Well, yes, it did sound a bit off the

wall, but people got hooked on computer games and things like Warhammer or role-playing Dungeons and Dragons, and these were people who already liked dressing up and going on stage. They were probably falling over themselves to play Professor Plum or Colonel Mustard or the Reverend Green. It was not unlike the murder weekends put on at country hotels in the off-season. They hadn't even been particularly secretive about it. Devon had cheekily introduced me to a Colonel Colman (as in Colman's Mustard) in the pub, not to mention two females known as Gilly White and Scarlett Smith. So confident were they that their Cluedo roles had become their public nicknames.

'Arthur Colman?' Mr Symington interrupted. 'I know him, he's in the Rotary Club, but I don't think he was ever a Colonel. This is all terribly embarrassing, or it would be if it got out. But it's people being silly, that's all it is.'

That was all it had been, I told him, up until Saturday night when Frank Lemarquand had stumbled on one of the game players, or more likely they had stumbled on him and taken exception to being spied on. A task, I pointed out, he was doing on behalf of Mr and Mrs, don't forget Mrs Symington, to prove the houses weren't haunted.

'There was never any formal contract between us,' he said sharply.

'Julius!' hissed Mrs Bond. 'Really!'

'No there was not,' I agreed with him, 'which is why, under the Association of British Investigators' Code of Ethics, clauses three and, I believe, four, no state of client confidentiality exists between us.'

'So you'd be free to go to the Sunday papers with this?' he said, his eyes narrow, but a faint smile on his lips.

'Like a shot,' I said.

'Angel!' snapped Mrs Bond. 'Behave!'

Julius Symington leaned back in his chair and let his face crumple and his eyes sparkle.

'That would scare the shit out of Devon Sedgeley for sure. He doesn't mind coming across as the screaming queen he probably is, but to be ridiculed and laughed at for playing dressing-up games with his sad little friends from the amateur dramatic society. He would be seen as a real... What's the word I'm looking for?'

'Loser?' I suggested.

'That'll do. Oh no, our Devon couldn't stand to be branded a *loser*. Which makes it almost worthwhile you going to the newspapers, Mr Angel, but then I have to think of the firm and mud sticks, you know, and the firm doesn't need that. So, is this the point where I get my cheque book out?'

'Not just yet. My man Frank Lemarquand is in Addenbrookes just down the road. I don't know how well he'll recover, whether he's insured or whether he'll work again. He might even want to press charges for assault. There may be a need for specialist medical treatment, rest and recuperation.'

'I think I follow,' said Julius. 'Will you trust me to take care of him?'

'Your word is good enough for me, Mr Symington.'

He nodded politely.

'And you on your part won't go to the press?'

'Only on condition that I get to tell Devon that the game's up. He may get the impression that his future with the firm is no longer secure. Would he be a terrible loss to the business?'

Mr Symington pursed his lips and studied the question for a minute.

'Put it this way,' he said slowly. 'There could be a bonus in it for you and Mrs Bond will have the champagne chilled for your return.'

'Bugger that!' she said. 'I'm going with him.'

I asked Jane Bond to ring Devon Sedgeley at the firm's Shelford office and tell him that a client wished to meet him over morning coffee in The Square and Compasses. I thought it a good choice, as he might need a drink afterwards. Whilst she was doing that, I tried to raise Alice on her father's mobile and when she didn't answer, I left a message for her to touch base with me. I had an uneasy feeling that she could still be a bit of a loose cannon in all this and I thought I would be happier knowing where she was and what she was doing.

Mrs Bond asked if I wanted to claim my free drive of her Aston Martin but I told her I would wait for a better opportunity when I could enjoy it more and make sure I had a proper audience.

So just to show me what I was missing, she let me leave first, but made sure the Aston was parked outside the pub, with her casually leaning against the offside wing with her legs crossed at the ankles, by the time I got there. I offered her my arm and, linked together, we entered the pub.

Devon was already there and he had the place to himself, sitting alone at a table, spooning brown sugar into an espresso coffee. He was wearing another expensive suit, in a bottle green linen mix, over a t-shirt again, this one bearing the famous 'Ascot Races' shot of the Divine Audrey as the posh version of Eliza Doolittle, the same image I had seen on his shoulder bag.

As he saw us together, he let his jaw drop and put his free hand to his cheek, mouthing 'Oh my God!'

'So this is your secret client, Janey, you dark horse, you. Well hello, Roy. You're getting quite the *personal* service, aren't you?'

He put the sugar spoon into his cup and offered me a handshake without making a move to stand up. When I ignored it he said: 'Be like that, then' in a stage whisper.

'Shut up, Devon,' I said, scraping a pair of chairs up to the table.

'What did you say to me?'

'I said to shut up. You should try a new thing every day, it's good for the soul.'

'I'll get us some coffee,' said Mrs Bond, seeing the landlord looming behind the bar. 'Start without me.'

'Start what? Has that old witch been slagging me off behind my back?'

'You don't need help in that department Devon, or should I call you Professor Plum?'

'Aw, fuck!' he shouted and brought the flat of his hand down on the table so hard, his cup jumped clean out of its saucer, spilling coffee

331

everywhere but mainly over Eliza Doolittle's face.

As she sat down to join us, Jane Bond handed him an inch of paper napkins from a pile on the bar.

'Have I missed anything?' she asked with an angelically innocent smile.

'Devon was just telling me he's thinking of a career move,' I said. 'Into the theatre, perhaps.'

I thought that might cheer him up but he seemed more concerned with the stain on his t-shirt.

'It would be suited to his talents,' said Jane Bond.

'Absolutely. I've got a recording of one of his performances which he could use as a demo tape.'

He flashed me a killer look at that and gradually stopped dabbing his chest with the wad of napkins as I continued.

'And I've got a bag of props which include a length of rope and a wrench, not to mention photographs of a piece of lead pipe actually being wielded in anger. Devon himself introduced me to Colonel Mustard – I'm sorry, Colman – and a Miss White and another young lady called Scarlett. The only suspects missing are the Reverend Green and Mrs Peacock, but I shouldn't think they'll be hard to find. They're probably fellow members of the Shelford Light Opera Society. Then we'll have the full cast of characters and we can start a real, live game of *Cluedo,* assuming we can find a deserted country house to occupy for the evening. All good clean harmless fun, really. People like dressing up and nobody actually gets murdered. Except somebody did get hurt this time, didn't they, Devon?'

'That old man was spying on us; he was a filthy perv.'

'He was working for Mr Julius, Devon,' Jane Bond said gently.

'He was? It was me who took him to hospital, you know. I didn't have to do that,' he responded peevishly.

'You drove him to the hospital but you didn't stay to see he was all right, did you? You just left him in the car park.' I could tell from the way his eyes went down that I was right. 'You were caught on the Addenbrookes security cameras.'

That was a lie, but I thought he deserved it.

'Is he better now?'

I felt there was a real danger of Devon regressing to childhood, the way his lips were quivering.

'He'll live, but he was hurt bad. The police might have to get involved. Who actually attacked him?'

'Miss Scarlett,' he said automatically. 'I mean Scarlett Smith. That really is her name. She was late arriving and she saw that van in the lane and the old man had headphones on so she thought he was spying on us.'

'He was.'

Devon shrugged. 'Anyway, she lost it big time and went for him, then she came running up to the house, covered in blood and screaming like a fishwife.'

'I know, we have a recording,' I said.

I didn't know whether we had or not, I hadn't listened that far into the disk Frank had recorded on Saturday night, but Devon wasn't to know that.

'So what happens now?' he asked me, putting on what he obviously considered to be his puppy dog face, but aiming it at me, not at Mrs Bond. He knew better than to look for sympathy there.

'I think you start looking for a new career, right now. Possibly in another county if not another country.'

'But we didn't damage anything!' he protested weakly. 'In the properties, I mean.'

'Mr Julius thinks that if this gets out into the press, the firm will have serious trust issues with prospective vendors,' said Jane Bond, 'and I have to agree with him. Plus, we'll be a laughing stock locally. *That's* damage.'

'What about Scarlett?'

'Good question,' I said. 'What happens to her depends on how well Frank does.'

'Who's Frank?'

I almost gave him a slap for that.

'The man she nearly crippled. What happens to Scarlett is up to him, when he recovers. *If* he recovers.'

Unless, that was, Alice Lemarquand found her first.

'She could take a gap year,' Devon was speaking rapidly, close to babbling. 'She's talked about it often enough. She says that if they're banning fox-hunting in this country, then she'll start up a business in France and organise cross-Channel hunts.'

Now I placed 'Miss Scarlett' as the horsey one in the Barbour with riding boots that I had met briefly in this very pub.

'Is Scarlett Smith related to Mr Justice Smith, the Circuit Judge, by any chance?' Mrs Bond asked him.

Devon nodded, glad to be helpful for once.

'She's his youngest daughter and he keeps her on a tight rein she says.'

'Not tight enough. I think a gap year for Miss Scarlett would be a very good idea. I'm sure you can talk her into it. And as far away as possible. Argentina's nice so I'm told.'

'Do you want these coffees or not?'

The pub landlord was behind the bar with a cup in each hand.

'Sorry, I forgot,' said Jane, grabbing her handbag and going to collect them.

While she was at the bar, I leaned forward and spoke softly and quickly to Devon.

'Before you hand in your resignation, you're going to make one last sale, so you can go out on a high.'

'I am?'

'Either later today or early tomorrow, a lady called Amy May will ring asking to view *The Old Rosemary Branch* and you'll show her round, give her the full works, whatever she wants. If she likes it she'll put in an offer on the spot but she'll want to knock about 50K off the asking price. You will use all your considerable skill to persuade the vendors that this is a good offer, right?'

'I can do that,' he said, then his face lit up. 'Did you say Amy May? Amy May the designer?'

'Yes.'

'I just *love* her clothes.'

'He didn't look as *crushed* as I'd hoped he would,' Jane Bond said as we stood outside the pub.

'He was crying inside,' I soothed, 'but he knows he's got off lightly. Taking him away from his amateur dramatic chums will be the biggest blow. He'll miss being a big, brightly coloured fish in a small drab pond.'

'You let him off very lightly, you know, and you could have strung old Mr Julius along for ages, or at least taken him for some exorbitant fee, but you didn't. Why not?'

'I like the area; I may be moving down here and Mr Symington may think positively about putting some clients my way. It might be useful to have him on my side, him being a pillar of local society.'

'Was that it? Was that the only reason you helped out?'

'There was Devon. The role-playing *Cluedo;* well, that was just a bit of a laugh, until Frank got hurt, of course, and the outrageous camp act didn't bother me at all. But when he's rude in public to beautiful women with outstanding taste in cars, then I feel obliged to make sure his life ends in misery and ruin. That's what I call job satisfaction.'

'Are you sure you're married?' she asked coyly.

At that moment, my phone rang and I gave her a limp smile as I reached for it.

'Story of my life,' Mrs Bond said under her breath.

'Angel?'

'Alice? Where are you?'

Mrs Bond looked at me questioningly and

336

pointed to the wedding ring finger of her left hand. When I shook my head she flicked her eyebrows suggestively and leaned over my shoulder, pretending to listen in.

'I'm in your girlfriend's house in Wyvern Road,' said Alice.

'Cassandra Quinn is not my girlfriend,' I said forcefully, and then had to put up with Mrs Bond's expression changing from mock horror to severe disapproval. 'What the hell are you doing there?'

'I'm taking out the bugs I planted yesterday before she notices them.'

'You bugged the place?'

'Of course. It's what I do. Guess what I found out.'

'She's not the one who attacked your dad, you know.'

'Yes, I know. Dad told me this morning. He's conscious if a bit groggy. He says the woman in question is some friend of a poof friend of yours.'

'I wouldn't put it quite like that...'

'Whatever, if Dad's cool about it, I'm cool. He says he's going to sort things out with you. Or maybe that was 'sort you out', anyway, do you want to guess what I found out about Cassandra or not?'

'That she keeps her underwear in the fridge?' I said, more to enjoy the look on Jane Bond's face. 'You told me that already.'

'Apart from that,' Alice was saying. 'I meant what I picked up on the listening device.'

'Which was?'

'She got a phone call yesterday evening.

Sounded as if it was from a boyfriend, 'cause she went all luvvy-duvvy on him, calling him Mishy or something like that, then she got all in a panic and he had to talk her down. I was only getting one side of the call you understand. Then there was stuff about change of plans and bringing the timetable forward due to events beyond his control. And she said she'd do it somehow but it was risky taking so much in the same week, whatever that means, but she would do it and not get caught and it would be worth it because she'd be with him tomorrow and for always. That's today. Does that make any sort of sense at all?'

'Oddly enough, it does, thanks Alice.'

'There's more.'

'There is?'

'Oh yes, she then makes a call to her landlord.'

'She rang a pub?' I said, biting my tongue as I did so.

'No, the landlord of her house. She tells him sorry, but she's leaving earlier than expected, but the rent's on direct debit until he can find another tenant. And of course, he didn't argue with that.'

'So she's leaving town?'

'In a blitz, in a blitz. She's packed and ready to go, suitcases in the hall. Travelling light and fast. Though she still has that kinky corset thing in the fridge here.'

'I think you should get out of there, Alice.'

'I'm leaving as we speak. Your girlfriend is something else, though.'

'She's not my girlfriend! But, by the way, what was that corset in the fridge made of?'

Now Mrs Bond was seriously considering moving away from me.

'Rubber. I thought I'd said. Anyway, she must like wearing them because after she'd talked to her landlord, she rang her supplier and asked if they had another one in stock. When they said yes, she went straight round there to collect it. The place she rang, she called it 'Indiscipline'. I checked it out this morning. It's a sex shop on Mill Road near the Salvation Army Hall.'

'What was that name again? Indiscipline? You're sure?'

I felt Mrs Bond's hand tugging on my arm.

'It's a sex shop on Mill Road,' she said, 'near the Salvation Army Hall.'

Chapter Eighteen

Mrs Bond explained that 'Indiscipline' was really a shop cleverly branded 'indiScIpliNe' so that the letters SIN spelled out its true purpose. How subtle was that? It was, she said, like most serious sex shops outside of London, successfully disguised as a fire-damaged Indian take-away and I had to look carefully to spot the notice which said 'Licensed Sex Shop: Adults Only'. But the owner/manger was a very nice man called Ken, and I could mention her name if it helped.

Before I left her, she gave me a kiss on the cheek and an envelope which she'd had in her handbag all the time.

'Mr Julius wanted me to give you this on account, he said. It's £500.'

My first fee. I felt so proud. But I wouldn't tell Amy, she'd want commission.

Then I kissed Mrs Bond and said:

'I'll see you around.'

'Will you?'

'Depend on it.'

I hadn't had my free drive of her cool car yet.

In Cambridge I found Indiscipline easily enough as I knew what sort of place I was looking for. On the door they did indeed spell it: indiScIpliNe, with the S-I-N picked out in red ink and beside the lettering, just so you got the point, was a logo of a horned red devil complete with trident, satanic leer and stockings and suspenders covering his cloven-hoof legs. There was also a handwritten note saying 'Press bell for service', but the rest of the door was sheeted plywood and the window of frosted glass had a steel mesh over it, so there was no way you could see in.

I opened the back of the Peugeot and rummaged amongst the things I had transferred from Armstrong when I had left him in the care of Duncan the Drunken. I put on the brown Flying Tigers leather jacket and the aviator sunglasses I had kept as an emergency pair in one of the zip pockets. Now I was dressed, as I saw it, as the average lunchtime user of a Cambridge sex shop ought to be. I pressed the bell and expected service.

There is actually so little that is sexy about the inside of sex shops that I'm surprised they don't

340

get prosecuted under the Trades Descriptions Act. There are never any women in them for a start. Not real ones. Yet most of the goods on show were made with a woman in mind.

There were racks of underwear deliberately designed not to keep out draughts; masks; ticklers – some so big that you could do the dusting if you got bored; handcuffs with felt linings; chains; collars; limp whips; more prosthetic rubber body parts than the costume department of *Lord of the Rings* and a spectacular range of vibrators, batteries not included. So; nothing unusual there.

I was the only customer. Again, nothing unusual. Hence the old saying in Soho: good customers come in ones, but often.

'You Ken?' I asked the man behind the counter.

'I'm the proprietor,' he said warily.

He was about fifty, with grey hair and wore a cardigan with two military looking medals pinned to it. He probably had a very interesting story to tell as to how he got in to the sex shop business, but I didn't have the time.

'I'm looking for a special item, probably customised; you might call it a rubber basque. Ring any bells?'

'We have a range of rubber wear, some on show, some in stock. Would sir like to be more specific?'

'It's for a friend, who has had one before from your ... emporium. Perhaps they were a special order?'

'I'm still not sure what sir is on about,' he said, straight-faced.

'Look, this might sound crazy.' I don't know why I said that, given the nature of the merchand-

341

ise surrounding me. 'Would it be possible to pur-
chase an item, a corset say, or a basque, which can
hold liquid? Just go with me on this one.'

'Can I ask if sir was sent here by anyone?' he
asked politely.

'A Mrs Bond sent me.'

'Ah yes,' he breathed, 'a most valued customer.'

'She is?' I exclaimed.

'Well, her husband used to be, and she has
maintained his account. Very decent of her, really,
all things considered.'

Right on, Mrs Bond. Go, girl, go.

'But this wasn't an item for her, it was for
another lady, and very recently, like last night
perhaps?'

'I am sure sir understands I cannot divulge
specific customer information.'

'Understood completely.' I pulled out the
envelope Mrs Bond had given me and plucked
out three £20 notes, laying them on the counter.

'Do you have anything sexy in a size 20 you can
send to an address in London?'

'Split-crotch panties are always popular,' he
offered calmly.

'Excellent. May I borrow a pen? A range of
colours, please, to this address. Oh, and a receipt
if possible.'

I scribbled a name and address on a square of
paper he provided and let him pick up the money.

'I think sir was thinking of a specialist German
line, they mostly seem to be popular in Germany,
these items,' he said as the money disappeared.
'The inflatable rubber basque can hold up to
three litres of warm liquid. The manufacturers

warn against boiling water for safety reasons. It is commonly used in what I believe are called 'water sports' or in providing 'golden showers' – those types of activity. In this country they are a fairly specialised item. They have to be ordered in. I've only ever sold three and two of them were to the same customer, the last one, as I think sir already knows, last night. But I can order another...'

'No, that won't be necessary. You've been very helpful.'

'I think I have a leaflet somewhere about how they work, if sir can read German, that is. Although I believe it's a simple siphon process, with a small rubber bulb and tube arrangement to – shall we say – *regulate the flow.*'

I declined the offer of an instruction manual.

There was such a thing as too much information.

'That was amazingly quick,' said Dr Sanger, 'I only called your office like two minutes ago.'

'It shows we're on the ball,' I bluffed. 'What's the problem?'

I had driven out to Tyler Pharmaceuticals to make sure Cassandra Quinn was where we could keep an eye on her as I had a very bad feeling that she was about to do something unexpected and I've always hated surprises. Even so, I got two within seconds of arriving there. Firstly, Dr Mark Sanger was waiting for me in the entrance lobby and an angry looking Peter Sutton was coming out of his office to join the welcome committee. The second surprise was that Cassandra's brand new, shiny red VW Beetle was nowhere to be seen in the company car park.

'It's Dr Quinn,' they said together.

'I thought it might be. Has she not turned up for work?'

'Oh no, she was in here an hour before her shift started this morning and did a four-hour stint in the wash room before taking a break. We all thought she might be going for an early lunch, but she just got in her car and drove off. There's no response from her home and her mobile's turned off.'

'You're not in a panic just because she's gone for an early lunch are you?'

'Of course not,' said Sutton, 'but you've done nothing but point the finger at her since you got here, so we've been watching her like a hawk this week.'

'And?'

Sutton started to blush but Sanger answered for him.

'We had a new bulk delivery of fermented toxin from our facility in Wales this week, as well as some residual wash from the fermenters, which all needs careful handling before chromatography.'

'You're losing me,' I said.

'OK then, idiot's version: the toxin has be pure, obviously, and concentrated before its diluted. Now that sounds pointless, but it's all about dosage. If you screw up your calculations on the dilution, you produce a dose of Botox which could paralyse the patient, so you have to start with the purest concentration and know what that concentration is, so measuring and evaluating a new delivery is crucial.'

'And this chromatography process? That needs to be done in the lab?'

'A competent chemist could do it in the kitchen sink, after they'd done the dishes,' he scoffed.

'So, if somebody walked off with five or six litres of this concentrate, they could do the business with their toy chemistry set and then dilute it to produce a sellable dose of own-label Botox?'

'A *lot* of doses. And a fancy clinic can charge $300 an injection just to get rid of those unsightly crow's feet.'

'Hang about, you two, just hold the bloody phone,' said Sutton as. though he was breaking up a fight. 'I've been watching that wash room on the monitors all morning and nothing, I repeat nothing, has left there.'

'Except Dr Quinn.'

'She wasn't carrying anything,' he blustered.

I pulled down the Aviator sunglasses to the end of my nose and peered over them.

'Did you check her underwear?'

Cassandra Quinn had been absent without leave for just over an hour, but if the management of Tyler Pharmaceuticals had been suspicious before, they were downright spooked now. I told Sanger to contact Olivier Zaborski and ask what he wanted done.

'What do you mean? He'll want his Botox back of course.'

'Look, I might find her, I might even find she has some chemicals she shouldn't have, but I can't arrest her. You'll have to see if he wants the

345

police involved.'

I wasn't sure I was being paid enough to go through a woman's underwear if she didn't want me to. I wasn't sure I was being paid at all.

'I'll call Zaborski, but he may want to talk to you direct, so turn your damn phone on.'

Did everyone have to nag me about my damn phone? If I thought for one second I would hear something to my advantage, I would keep the thing on 24/7. But for once I did turn it on, and used it as I steered the Peugeot back towards Cambridge, hoping that the Cambridgeshire constabulary took the same attitude as their brothers in Essex towards phoning whilst driving, and looked the other way. (Unlike their cousins in the Avon and Somerset or South Wales forces, who took a really dim view of the practice.)

Alice Lemarquand answered immediately.

'It's Angel. Are you free and clear of Wyvern Road?'

'I left ages ago; I don't hang around where I'm not wanted.'

'Where are you now?'

'In the cafeteria at Addenbrookes having a bite to eat, then I'll be visiting with Dad. Why? You need any help?'

That was a very good question.

'Hope not. There was no sign of Cassandra Quinn at the house, was there?'

'Well she didn't come back while I was there, but she is coming back at some point.'

'How do you know that?'

'The suitcases in the hall and the make-up bag on top of them. A woman can run; a woman can

346

hide; but she won't do either without her make-up bag.'

'You're good,' I said, 'you could teach me things about this detective business.'

'And I've got a feeling you could teach me a lot about why women like her keep their rubber underwear in the fridge. Like I need to know that.'

So cynical and yet so young.

Cassandra Quinn's brand new shiny red VW was parked at the top end of her road, well away from the front door of number 36. There was no sign of a driver and the street itself was deserted. I had no long term plan, but I wouldn't have a better opportunity than now to make sure she didn't do a runner on me.

Amongst the things I had transferred to the Peugeot when I had said goodbye to Armstrong, was my new toy, a JCB impact wrench, which looked like a cross between an electric drill and a hair dryer. Plugged into a dashboard cigarette lighter socket and with the appropriate socket attached, the wrench could loosen the wheel nuts of any car wheel in seconds, if you wanted to do a speed change like they do during a Formula One race. For anyone with a brand new car, where the wheel nuts have been put on in the factory with hydraulic pressure, an impact wrench is essential these days as flat tyres are impossible to change with the pathetic tools the car makers supply.

The impact wrench comes with about four metres of cable, so that you can reach all four wheels. Of course, you're not really supposed to undo the nuts on all four wheels at once, and you're probably not supposed to undo the wheels of somebody else's car which you just happen to have parked next to.

I flipped the flashy VW hubcap off her front offside wheel and with a series of high pitched buzzes, had all four nuts off in less than thirty seconds. I rolled them down the street and kicked the hubcap under the car parked in front of hers, then moved in a crouch to the back wheel and did the same to that one. With the hubcaps missing it was glaringly obvious that something was wrong with the wheels and hopefully she wouldn't be stupid enough to try and drive on them. I didn't want to kill her, although I would have been interested to see how far she got before the wheels fell off.

I threw the wrench into the back of the Peugeot and pulled slowly away, certain that nobody had seen me. So much for the Neighbourhood Watch. They had enough on their hands with illegal parking by non-residents like me and I ended up dumping the Peugeot near the cemetery fence where Alice had parked.

I adjusted the Aviator glasses for maximum coolness and strolled in the direction of Dr Quinn's house, formulating an intricate and cunning plan to literally talk her out of her kinky underwear. How hard could that be?

I was concentrating on my cast iron plan so much that I didn't see it until I was almost on top of it, and when I did see it I couldn't actually accept what it was.

Parked right outside Cassandra Quinn's front door was a pink car.

I wasn't sure it was the shade of Roman Pink Devon Sedgeley had sprayed his car, but it was close. It was certainly a respray job. That colour pink would never have been sanctioned in communist East Germany on the Trabant production line.

It was a thirty-year old, two-door, two-stroke, *pink* Trabant.

'Ray, my friend! Do you like my car? It's a piece of shit and it does not work very well, if at all. But I'll sell it to you!'

'Hello, there, Misha, fancy seeing you here,' I gasped whilst panting for breath as he enveloped me in a bear hug. 'Didn't you buy one of those in Paris?'

'I buy them everywhere I can, I am the bespoke supplier of Trabants to the oligarchs of the new Russia! And me, an honest trader, is taken advantage of by your unscrupulous English car dealers! Pah!'

He launched a savage kick at the bodywork of the Trabi, without taking one arm from around my shoulder. I thought his combat boot was going to go through to the engine block, if there was one.

'Has this one been 'pre-loved' a bit too much?'

'Pre-loved? Is fucked to buggery and beyond.'

His English really was very good.

'Man delivers it here as arranged, takes my hard-earned money and disappears. I think him and his friend pushed it the last few metres. It's dead, completely dead. But you didn't come here looking for Trabis, did you Ray? Are you hanging around my girlfriend again?'

I felt the pressure on my shoulder increasing.

'Absolutely, Misha, but only because I thought you were miles away.'

He laughed at that, but didn't let go of me. He was wearing a black leather jacket over a waxed wool sweater and there was a strong smell of engine oil and also fish meal about him. The sweater was rough against my chin as he hugged me to his chest.

'She's inside, Ray, my old friend, just waiting for you to seduce her. Come inside, but you'll have to be quick. We are about to leave.' He put his lips to my ear. 'We're eloping! To get married! I'm going to make an honest woman of her. What do you think of that?'

I thought he was far too late, but I didn't say anything, just let him push me gently towards the open door of number 36.

The front door led directly into a lounge area, the original Victorian 'front room'. Beyond that was a kitchen/dining area with an open tread staircase up to two sizeable bedrooms. I mentally kicked myself for thinking like an estate agent.

Cassandra Quinn was standing in the kitchen with two suitcases and two large sports bags at her feet. She had her hair tied up and wore a red trouser suit and, oddly, black leather cut-away driving gloves.

'Look who has come to see us off and wish us well,' said Golubev behind me.

Cassandra just looked blank. Not shocked, surprised or angry, just blank. Come to think of it, she was one of the most expressionless women

I had ever come across. I tried to remember when I'd seen her laugh.

'You haven't really, have you?'

And for someone with so many degrees, she was really slow on the uptake. Maybe that was what being in love did to you.

'Naturally I wish you a long and happy life together, but you seem to have sprung this on your employers at rather short notice,' I said as gently as I could.

'Oh yeah, I keep forgetting you work for the company. You're a company spy really, aren't you? I forget because you don't strike me as one. I mean you're not very good at it are you?'

To this day I don't know if she was trying to wind me up or just stating a fact as she saw it.

I gave her my most winning smile.

'You must tell me the secret of your diet, my dear; I mean, you must have lost five or six pounds since this morning alone. How do you do it? It just seems to fall off you, probably into those bags there.'

Her face remained a blank almost as if she'd overdone the Botox and frozen all her muscles, instead of just the wrinkles. I think she realised that she'd been rumbled, but she wasn't going to let her brain accept it yet; if ever.

'Cassy darling, go and get the car,' Misha was saying.

Like a zombie she walked by me, paused to brush a gloved hand against his cheek and then was out of the door. Misha closed the door behind her.

He stood between me and the door. He was a

lot bigger and harder than I was, but he was smiling. I thought that might go in my favour.

'I was going to take the Trabi,' he said, 'before I knew I had bought a dog. The man swore it was in working order, but I've found you cannot trust anything in that newspaper. Your *Exchange and Mart* – it's full of lies. Now we have to take Cassy's car and it will be quite a squash I think.'

'With all this luggage, I would think so,' I said, breathing deeply. 'Let me give you a hand loading up.'

I took a couple of steps into the kitchen and picked up one of the sports bags, hefting it to feel the weight, which was not inconsiderable. As I did so, I thought I heard a creaking sound but couldn't work out what it was.

I turned to face Misha. I was holding the bag. He was now holding a gun, a bright shiny automatic and he was pointing it at me.

'You're not going to shoot me, Misha,' I said as bravely as I could.

'Probably not,' said Misha. 'But he might.'

Coming down the creaking staircase was Vladimir 'Vovchik' Kozlov.

And he had a gun, too.

I decided that ignoring the guns was my best option, if not my only option. Everything in the situation pointed to Misha and Cassandra doing a runner, so that the last thing they would want to do is complicate their escape with a shooting; or so I reasoned. Vladimir, on the other hand, knew very well he could hurt me without resorting to gunfire.

'So you two are working as a team now?' I asked

Misha, making no sudden moves, but lowering the bag to the ground.

'Reluctant partners, thrown together by circumstances, I think you'd say.'

'I've known women like that,' I said and that got a laugh.

'I like you Ray, you know that? I really do. You were polite to Sassy when she was all alone in Paris. You didn't have to do that. You could have taken advantage of her.'

'Nothing was further from my mind,' it was a relief not to have to lie to a man with a gun. 'She only had eyes for you, but I thought Vovchik here was showing an unhealthy interest in her.'

'That is because Vovchik was not then part of the loop, as we say. He is now.'

'So how did he go from out of the loop to a partner in three or four days?'

'Powerful friends in St Petersburg and Moscow,' said Misha, apparently unconcerned as to whether Kozlov was following this or not. 'Very powerful friends, who happen to be my best customers. You might say that Vovchik is here to protect their investment.'

'Awful lot of trouble to go to over some beat-up old Trabants that don't work.'

'The Trabis are just my little side-line. I think you know this is about more than some "classic cars" I think the phrase is. Sassy never thought you would be the one to catch her. She said you hardly showed any interest at the laboratory.'

'My methods remain a trade secret,' I said, 'but it was her fashion sense which let her down. That and her taste in underwear.'

Behind me, Kozlov said something in rapid Russian.

'Vovchik is right, you are cleverer than you appear. Were you going to arrest Sassy?'

I couldn't help but laugh at that.

'I'm not a policeman,' I said, 'I was just hired to stop the leakage of pharmaceuticals.' I waved a hand at the bags at my feet. 'I think I have done that. I mean, there won't be any more leaks, will there?'

'Not from this laboratory,' Misha said with a sly grin.

'Do you mind if I have a look?' I asked, indicating the sports bag I had been holding.

He gave permission with a casual wave of his pistol.

I went down on one knee and unzipped the first bag. I felt Kozlov move to stand right behind me. As if to make sure I knew he was there, he touched the back of my neck with the muzzle of his gun.

I concentrated on opening the bag. There was only one thing in it, a bloated black rubber corset, distended like a hot water bottle with the liquid inside it. It was cold to the touch and there were fine beads of condensation on its surface. It looked like a piece of discarded body armour or, in a bad light, an enormous shiny black beetle. There were two small-bore clear plastic tubes coming off it, one ending in a squeezy rubber bulb, the other sealed with small metal butterfly clip. When she was wearing it, the open tube would have run down the sleeve of her loose-fitting lab coat and when handling the Botox concentrate it would have been easy enough to slip the tip of the tube into a container then produce a vacuum with the squeezy pump, sucking the liquid into the double lining of the basque. Where most women paid good money to have milligrams of the stuff injected, Cassandra Quinn had been walking about with litres of it next to her skin. The security had not seen a thing. Only Amy's eagle eyes had spotted the changing shape of her figure and if she'd worn less flattering off-duty clothes a size or two bigger than she needed, even Amy might have missed it.

'Not very sexy when they're like that, are they?' I said looking up at Misha, delighted to see he had put his gun away.

'But what's inside them makes me really horny.'

'How much?'

'There's enough in each garment to make 600 doses, Cassy says. A dose can fetch $300.'

'That's $360,000 all together,' I said, doing some rapid maths.

'That's retail prices,' Misha said reasonably. 'Maybe we'll clear $200,000.'

'That's a lot of Trabants.' He laughed at that.

There was the sound of a key entering the front door lock and I felt the cold gun barrel disappear from my neck.

The door opened and Cassandra stood there, for once, with a real expression on her face.

'What is the matter, Sassy my dear?' soothed Misha.

'Bloody vandals!' she wailed. 'Somebody's been trying to steal the sodding wheels off my car. It's useless. What are we going to do now?'

For some reason, everyone seemed to be

looking at me.

I suppose I should have felt frightened, or at least threatened, by being kidnapped and forced to drive two armed men and a coldhearted female thief on their getaway, complete with their loot; but we were all crammed into my grotty little Peugeot so I mostly felt just foolish.

With Cassandra's car out of action and the pink Trabi Misha had bought that morning incapable of any sort of motion, they elected to use mine – before they had seen it, of course. Even when they did, they had no shame. Any self-respecting bunch of crooks would have gone out and boosted a BMW. This lot had to insist on cramming four people, two sports bags and two suitcases into a car interior hardly big enough to wear a hat in.

There was no debate about it, as they were on a tight timetable. The *Akademik Shteinman* had altered its schedule and was sailing from Harwich on the evening tide at 6 p.m., the crew supposedly reporting in by 5 p.m. That gave them – us – less than three hours to do the sixty-odd mile run. Even the Peugeot should do that, albeit uncomfortably, despite my protestations that I hadn't had lunch and was starving and that I was due in London by five that afternoon to visit my stroke victim father in hospital. This got me no sympathy, just a gentle clout around the ear from Kozlov, who was still holding a gun over my head, though I don't think that fact registered with Cassandra.

I didn't mention the fact that my father's hospital was directly on the route we would be taking nor that Amy was likely to put me in hospital for standing her up. Knowing my luck, she'd probably overtake us somewhere near Colchester.

Perhaps Dr Sanger had got Zaborski's permission to call the cops and perhaps SWAT teams were on their way to Wyvern Road already. Then again, he might have decided to tick the 'No Publicity' box, cut his losses and write off the product Cassandra had stolen against his insurance.

With Misha and Cassandra squashed in the back (Misha's knees feeling as if they were coming through the back of my seat and into my spine), and the sullen Kozlov sitting next to me with one hand permanently in his jacket pocket, I headed out of Cambridge until we picked up the A14 dual carriageway and headed east. Already the road signs were directing us to Ipswich, Felixstowe, Harwich and the Continent. It was not a comforting thought, but at least they had taken me along. They could have left me behind in Wyvern Road, permanently. I was pretty sure that some of the banter in Russian between Misha and his new partner had covered that point. As long as Misha was the senior partner, I reckoned I was safe. As safe as anyone could be aiding and abetting an armed gang of thieves carrying several litres of a chemical concentrate made from botulinus contained in two elaborate pieces of fetishtic underwear.

I decided to talk to them. We had over an hour to kill, we were all sharing the same small space and I didn't want them getting bored and repeatedly asking 'Are we there yet?'.

'How did you come up with the idea of the kinky rubber corsets?' I asked Misha over my shoulder, but watching him in the driving mirror. He had his arm around Cassandra's shoulders and she was gazing up into his eyes with the sort of expression you get all the time from spaniels, but never from cats.

'I got the idea in a club in Hamburg,' he said.

'It had to be Hamburg, didn't it?' I said and out of the corner of my eye I saw Kozlov smirk.

'What sort of club, Misha?' Cassandra asked him, genuinely innocent.

'That's not important, my love. What is important is that they worked without you getting caught.'

He was getting close to the icky-sticky gooey baby talk that new couples somehow find endearing but anyone still in their right mind finds irritating. If the big oaf showed any sign of going down that path and calling her 'my little shnuckums' or crap like that, I'd have to ask Koslov to shoot him.

'Didn't you ever wonder, Dr Quinn, what those corsets were used for?' I tried.

'What do you mean "used for"?'

'They didn't strike you as odd? I mean, we men sometimes have a thing about getting our women to wear sexy underwear. There's even the old saying: "How do you get a woman to stop wearing stockings and suspenders?"'

'Marry her,' said Misha automatically, then burst out in a huge guffaw at his own joke.

'Exactly,' I said. 'But there's a bit of a difference between a glimpse of stocking top and customised rubber garments with liquid retaining capabilities.'

'What is he talking about, Mishy?' she asked him.

'Ray is just joking, my little one,' he said, hardly noticing the 'Mishy'.

'Didn't you ever wonder what on earth somebody wanted a close-fitting, liquid-retaining piece of rubberwear for?'

'Insulation? Body heat retention?' she said, as if I was questioning her in a foreign language. 'They make excellent hot-water bottles.'

I let out a quiet groan.

'Is there a valve somewhere for emptying them and have you noticed where it's positioned?'

'What is Ray talking about, Misha?'

'Cassandra is innocent of many things, Ray, and we should help her keep her innocence. It's part of her charm,' said Misha trying to keep a straight face.

Innocence? Charm? She had two postgraduate degrees, for God's sake. She had no right to be either innocent or charming.

'Has anybody got a cigarette?' I asked.

'I didn't know you smoked, Ray,' said Misha.

I didn't, but Ray did.

Chapter Nineteen

We stopped once at a petrol station on the A14 to fill the Peugeot with petrol and us passengers with sandwiches and chocolate bars. Misha even helped himself to a couple of cans of Coke and graciously allowed me to pay the cashier. As I waited for my receipt (Olivier Zaborski was definitely paying for this trip), I looked up into the closed circuit camera above the till and mouthed 'Help, I'm being kidnapped'. I didn't know whether it would do any good, but I knew the fore-court cameras would have already recorded the number plates of the Peugeot. They do it auto-matically to all vehicles, just in case you drive off without paying.

'You should drive faster,' Misha instructed me. I hated having a back seat driver who was only about two inches from my neck, and armed. 'That machine there, it tells you if you are speeding, doesn't it?'

His arm brushed the side of my face so close I could smell his armpit, pointing at the Road Angel.

'The speedometer tells you if you're speeding, *that* tells you if the police are waiting round the corner to give you a ticket.'

'Useful. There could be a market for them in Russia.'

'How's the market for Botox in Russia?'

'Flourishing. Our Russian women are getting richer, but they are getting older and they need all the help we can give them.'

'So are you two setting up as cosmetic surgeons or beauty consultants or whatever they call them in the new Russia?'

Cassandra giggled. The sort of self-conscious look-at-me-I'm-a-girlie type of giggle which deserves a slap.

'Tell him, Misha. It's safe enough to tell people

360

now, because it's – going – to – happen! It's coming true!'

She was, by turns, breathless and hyperactive and I saw her burrowing into Misha's sweater pretending to be some sort of tiny mammal. A wool-eating rat perhaps.

'Sassy and I are going to start up a salsa school!' he said proudly, making her squeak and giggle some more. 'The first in St Petersburg. We already have a website designed: www.salsaruss.ru. You know, Ray, that Petersburg is called the Paris of the North and also the Venice of the North? We will make it the Havana of the North. We have a place picked out overlooking the Fontanka Canal and real Cuban musicians for live music. There is a lively scene in Petersburg these days. You'd love it there.'

'Is it true that that there's a real Communist kitsch restaurant where the waitresses all dress as Young Pioneers?'

'Oh yes,' he laughed. 'The *Zov Ilicha,* named after Lenin, but the food is cheaper at the Café Idiot, where they play jazz.'

'Thanks for the tip,' I said cheerfully. 'I was wondering why you had decided to cut and run. You seemed to have quite a sweet operation going with the Botox.'

'It's been good to us. Tell me, Ray, what made the company send you to investigate?'

'Some of their Botox turned up in Paris and they don't sell there. Also some in Barcelona.'

'I knew it!' He screwed up his face in disgust. 'Those fucking drug companies have spies everywhere. We only sold small quantities, just to pay our expenses. Then we found a buyer in Moscow prepared to deal in bulk and we went for one big hit. That business is too dangerous for me and my little Sassy. Those drug corporations, they hold grudges, you know. From now on, I'm sticking to Trabants and salsa!'

He laughed again and Cassandra giggled again.

What worried me most was the way Kozlov, staring straight ahead out of the windscreen, was smiling.

Smiling like a wolf.

About a mile short of the Parkeston Quay turn-off to the Harwich docks, Misha ordered me to pull over into an empty lay-by and told everyone to get out of the car.

'I'll drive from here,' he said. 'You, Ray, get to cuddle my lovely Sassy in the back. I hope I can trust you, my friend.' Then he smiled down at her. 'But can I trust you my love?'

Much more of this and I would throw up over her.

'Why should I?' I protested and Kozlov, who had remained almost mute for the entire journey, began to look interested in the proceedings.

Misha put a hand on my shoulder and gently pressed down, showing me that there was much more pressure available if he needed it.

'Ray, Ray,' he said gently, 'I have a boat to catch, so please don't piss me about. Vovchik and I are registered seamen, so we have passes for the docks. You and Sassy do not, so we hide you under the bags and cases and some coats and Vladimir and I drive straight in. They will not stop us. Our passes are in order and they are very used to me driving into the docks in strange cars. They'll think your little Peugeot is part of my one-man export drive.'

I stared him down.

'But I don't have a boat to catch, Misha. I've brought you far enough.'

Misha's fingers tightened their grip on my shoulder and behind him I could see Vovchik lurking, his hand in his jacket pocket. On the road, articulated lorries juggernauted their way into and out of Harwich, none of their drivers giving our little drama in the lay-by a second glance.

'Ray, Ray, listen to me. I don't want Sassy to have to see you hurting.'

'I'm not wild about the idea either,' I said.

'Of course you're not. You are not mad, are you? So don't give Vovchik any excuse, hey? If we leave you here, you could have the police or Customs crawling over our boat before she sails. Once we cast off, you call who you like. Actually, you'll probably be arrested by the police for trespassing in a restricted dock, but I'm sure you can talk your way out of that one. Come on Ray, you know it makes sense.'

I glanced over towards Kozlov and saw the look on his face.

I got in the car.

If there was anything more embarrassing than driving that damned Peugeot, it was riding in it, crouched on the floor in the back, with a suitcase and Misha's leather jacket over my head, trying to breathe through a mouthful of Cassandra's hair. At least she was in as uncomfortable and ridiculous a position as I was.

We went through the security gates with frightening ease. We slowed right down but I don't think we actually stopped at any point. I could hear the muffled sounds of Misha calling out to and joking with the security guard: probably the woman who had refused me entry the day before.

And then the car was accelerating and the luggage was bouncing off my head and Cassandra was writhing around underneath me trying to suffocate me with her hair.

I saw one of the sports bags right in front of my eyes and thought that I could be in line for a free and possibly massive Botox face job.

'Is this stuff safe?' I hissed at her.

'I wouldn't advise drinking it, and it needs to be put in a fridge as soon as possible, but it should be safe enough. You haven't seen a leak have you?'

'No, your underwear is intact as far as I can tell.'

The car stopped, doors opened, seats were pulled forward and bags lifted and we were able to uncramp our legs.

Yesterday I had told the security guard that I just wanted a look around the docks. Now I had got my wish.

The Peugeot was parked on a dock, about a yard from the edge where, in perfect parallel parking, there was a ship. At first it seemed huge, its blue-painted hull close enough to touch, the cranes on its deck leaning over drunkenly and the name picked out in white lettering on the prow in

Cyrillic letters: *Akademik Shteinman.* One of the Thompson twins had told me how long she was and from where I stood on the dock looking up, I was willing to believe anything from one to two miles, but I knew that was crazy, and a quick glance across the harbour to where the container ships were being unloaded by gigantic cranes sliding on fixed hoop frames, made me realise that in fact the *Shteinman* was little more than a tramp steamer compared to those juggernauts.

'Come aboard, Ray, and have a drink,' boomed Misha. 'It's a Russian tradition never to start a journey without a drink.'

There were two or three crewmen on the deck looking down at us as we climbed the metal gangway which lead to the white bridge and accommodation quarters near the stern, where the single funnel and radio masts were. There were lifeboats there too. I recognised them but that just about exhausted my nautical knowledge.

The crew seemed pleased to see Misha and they whistled and even applauded when they saw Cassandra, no one seemingly bothered that two complete strangers were coming aboard.

'Doesn't the Captain mind us coming aboard?' I asked, but I might as well have been talking to the seagulls.

'The Captain will be in his cabin drunk,' said Misha with a grin. 'He's the sort of Russian who likes a drink at the start, the end and all through the middle of a journey. This ship runs itself but I suppose I'm in charge.'

From the bridge area the view was impressive across the estuary and the mouths of the rivers

Stour and Orwell. On the Harwich side, the flat horizon seemed to have ships parked everywhere, mostly container ships and at least one large passenger ferry, but relatively few small craft. I suppose that was part and parcel of being a modern port: most things came in and went out in bulk.

Which is why the *Akademik Shteinman* was such an oddity. It was one of the smallest vessels in the harbour and probably the only one carrying five ancient Trabant saloon cars on its deck. Two had French number plates, the other three none at all.

Misha shouted orders in Russian to two of the crew on deck. One of them laughed and gave him a mock salute, then went and shouted at the man operating the nearest, dockside, deck crane. The ship had four of them, used to fill the holds which were now closed. Only the one crane remained upright and functioning, the other three had been lowered and chained to the deck, and it swung its boom out over the dock, a series of chains hanging from the tip.

The two crewmen on deck were loading themselves with other, lighter lengths of chain and heading for the gangway.

I knew instantly what they were doing, and why Misha hadn't bothered to unload his sports bags full of Botox from the Peugeot.

'You bastard! You're nicking my car!'

'Fair exchange is no robbery,' said Misha and with a big smile he held out a two tarnished metal keys on a thin metal. 'You can have the Trabant at Sassy's house.'

Oh great. Now I had to tell Duncan the Drunken that his cruddy Peugeot was somewhere in Russia and that he was the proud owner of a pink Trabi which didn't actually work.

'I never liked it much, anyway,' I said sulkily.

I know they don't have to set the mainsail or fire up the boilers and suchlike any more, but it still surprised me how quickly the *Shteinman* was made ready to depart after the Peugeot had been swung on board and dropped, not too gently, on to the deck.

Misha had meant what he'd said about the drink. We were squashed into his cabin drinking lemon vodka out of plastic cups when the engines started throbbing, somewhere beneath the metal floor under our feet.

I proposed a sort of toast:

'Here's to the salsa school of St Petersburg.'

We drank and Cassandra raised her cup again immediately.

'And our wedding!'

I drank to that; Misha looked embarrassed; Cassandra glowed. Vladimir Kozlov, lurking quietly by the cabin door, surprised us all by bursting into a high-pitched giggle, only silenced by Misha growling 'Vovchik...' at him.

'It must be time for me to say *do svidanya,* isn't it?' I said, cutting the silence.

'Some one will come and tell us when we are about to cast off,' said Misha and right on cue, there was a knock on the cabin door.

I didn't like the way Kozlov moved away from the door but never even glanced at it. His whole body language said that he knew who was on the other side.

He did know him. So did Misha – he'd bought a Trabant off him in Paris, where Cassandra and I had both seen him: it was Kozlov's look-out man Mariusz Gorniak.

Mariusz didn't look all that happy to be there; and we weren't happy to see him as he was holding a small revolver, albeit rather shakily and this seemed to prompt Kozlov into getting his gun out again. I had been rather hoping we'd got passed all that posturing.

Mariusz spoke to Kozlov so quickly I couldn't tell if it was Polish or Russian, then Kozlov aimed his gun directly at Cassandra's head and began to speak to Misha, saying more in about ninety seconds than I had heard him speak all day. This time, I didn't need a translator. He kept his gun pointed at Cassandra's forehead and held his left hand out, palm up, towards Misha. With one arm still around her, Misha reached carefully into his jacket pocket and brought out his gun, holding it with fingertips, and handed it over.

'What's going on, Misha?' Cassandra asked in a very tiny voice.

'I would have thought it was bleeding obvious,' I answered for him. 'Your boyfriend's been hanging with the wrong crowd, a right bunch of pirates. And I think they've just staged a mutiny.'

'Not a mutiny,' growled Misha. 'It's a take-over bid and Vovchik here has just made himself the senior partner.'

'So much for the Pirate Code. I presume I'm not going ashore now?'

'Not until we reach St Petersburg; or unless you fancy a swim.'

Kozlov and Mariusz the Pole took all the guns and left, locking the cabin door behind them.

'Are we prisoners?' Cassandra asked him.

'Only until we're out of sight of land,' said Misha, totally deflated and not even bothering to comfort her.

I hoped he was right. The idea of a three day sea journey in a small cabin with the love-struck Dr Sassy No Brain was too horrible to contemplate. Besides, I was supposed to be meeting Amy and visiting my sick father this evening, not cruising the North Sea.

'Won't they miss you on deck?'

He shook his head. 'The Captain stays in his cabin. The crew like to keep him drunk. Vovchik has a First Mate's ticket and he's done this run before on other ships, so he knows what to do and he will have paid the crew well. They'll give him respect if they think he's working for one of the big *avtoritet* bosses.'

'Mafioso?'

'The Russian variety,' he conceded.

'The ones you were going to sell the Botox to before they decided to cut out the middle man?'

'Something like that.'

'They never really trusted you, did they? That's why they sent Vovchik and the Pole to Paris to hang on your coat-tails.'

'I wanted to protect my source, my little Sassy. I let them think I was getting the toxin from Paris. Vovchik insisted on joining the ship at Le Havre.

Gorniak must have come over on the train and got on board this morning when we were in Cambridge. Vovchik would have fixed it. The Pole is low-level scum; it's Vovchik who's the problem.'

'So if Vovchik was out of the way, you could handle the ship?'

Misha looked me in the eyes.

'The next stop is St Petersburg. Now we've left the dock, there is no way this ship will turn round and go back.'

Of course there wasn't; not with the chance the police might be waiting.

'Who said anything about stopping or turning round?'

I really had his attention now.

'How do you think you're going to get off this boat now we are under way?'

'I'm going to need your cigarette lighter – and my car keys,' I admitted.

I didn't tell Misha exactly what I had in mind, as I still wasn't sure I could trust him, but I did stress that what was going to happen had to happen before we were more than eight miles offshore, which meant we had less than an hour to get things organised.

After twenty minutes, I told him to start stirring it up. Through the cabin porthole we could see the Suffolk coast in the distance, hopefully far enough away for Vovchik to feel safe.

Misha used the cabin's internal phone to call the bridge, one level above our heads, and demanded to speak to Kozlov. He talked in rapid Russian, sticking, I hope, to the script I had outlined for him, insisting that we had to get the botox out of the bags in the Peugeot and into a freezer before it deteriorated. I had no idea whether or not you could contaminate the stuff by leaving it in it dark rubber containers, but then neither had Kozlov. With a final snapped command, he hung up the phone and gave me the thumbs up.

'He bought it,' he said.

A few minutes later we heard the lock of the door open and Kozlov beckoned Misha and I to follow him, but signalled Cassandra to stay in the cabin. He wasn't waving a gun around, which was something, but he was probably confident he could take Misha if it came to rough stuff. He knew he could take me.

We followed him out on the metal gangway which ran around the forecastle. That gave us a view down the full length of the deck, or Misha's private car park, with the Trabants furthest away and my sad little lime green Peugeot nearest to us, its nose pointing towards the bow of the ship. Three crewmen were moving in and out of the Trabants, dragging chains and blocks to tie the cars down to the deck. I hadn't thought of that, but fortunately they hadn't got round to the Peugeot.

Kozlov said something and Misha nudged me towards the metal steps leading down to the deck.

'He says to go get it.'

'We have to get him down on to the deck,' I whispered.

Misha lead the way and I followed, leaving Kozlov looking relaxed and confident that we were

371

not going anywhere, leaning on the gangway railing, looking out over the dead calm sea. There was only a slight chill in the air, otherwise it was a fine evening to go sailing.

As we clambered over the deck, Misha shouted out to the crewmen and they laughed at whatever he said to them. Under his breath he said: 'Bastards!' so only I could hear. From the moment we started climbing down the steps, I had been scanning the deck's surface for obstructions. There were hatch covers and clamps and hoist rings and joists all over the place, any one of which could rip the tyres off the Peugeot, but like I had told Misha, I'd never liked it.

I opened the hatchback and began to tug at the luggage piled in there. Misha took one of the sports bags in one hand and casually walked into the middle of the deck and dropped it at his feet.

He went down on one knee and unzipped the bag and when he stood up, he was holding the ungainly and distended rubber corset in front of his chest, almost as if he was modelling it. The crewmen who saw what he was doing started wolf-whistling and Misha turned to play to the crowd. I couldn't get over how obscenely ugly the thing looked, pregnant with liquid. And Misha got the biggest cheer when he turned on one of the hose valves and showed us all the purpose for which such a strange garment had been constructed. Squeezing the body of the corset like the sack of a set of bag-pipes and using the hose as – well, as a man would – Misha began to spray the deck with a clear, slightly oily liquid.

There was a roar of outrage from above us as

Kozlov realised he was watching anything up to $100,000 wash down the deck, giving the *Akademik Shteinman* an expensive and unnecessary face-lift.

I didn't stop to see his reaction, as I was busy creating diversion number two.

At the side of the Peugeot I unlocked the petrol cap and threw it over the side, then I piled in, started the engine, dropped it into first gear and floored the accelerator even before I released the handbrake.

The deck of a ship at sea is probably not the best place for a car chase, but the car I was chasing was stationary and only about sixty feet away. Even so, I felt several teeth-jarring bumps and almost lost control of the wheel as we hit a hatch cover before we ploughed successfully into the rear half of the nearest, oldest and rustiest of Misha's Trabants with a satisfying crunch of metal.

I shook my head to clear it and felt blood on my lip where I'd smashed my nose into the steering wheel. That would teach me not to forget my seat belt in future.

I looked behind me through the still open hatchback. Down the other end of the ship, Misha was staring at me in horror, but whether out of concern for me or his cars I couldn't tell. Kozlov was frozen half-way down the stairway, speechless with rage.

I put the Peugeot into reverse and revved the engine. Metal screamed as the little car pulled back from the Trabant, leaving a large hole in the rusty bodywork as if a giant fist had punched it.

The driver's door of the Trabi fell off with a loudly metallic screech and thumped on to the deck.

At this point in the plan, I was to have used Misha's disposable lighter to ignite the ruptured petrol tank of the Trabant so that it and the Peugeot could go up in a Viking funeral pyre which could be seen from miles around. And indeed there was an unhealthy smell of petrol in the air.

But at that point I became conscious of a series of short sharp cracks behind me and a glance in the skewed driving mirror told that Kozlov was reacting quickly and effectively to the situation as a good First Mate should.

He had his gun out and had already shot Misha and now he was running down the deck shooting at me, aiming into the open hatchback, coming right at me, gun first, in the mirror.

I already had the Peugeot in reverse, so I put my foot down and shortened the distance between us; rather quickly.

Too quickly for Vovchik. To avoid being decapitated by the edge of the hatchback door, he tried to dive to one side but the corner of the car took him on the hip, batting him across the deck and head-first into the lip of the hull. In lazy slow motion I saw the gun fly from his hand and as it landed on the deck it went off, the bullet sparking the trail of petrol that now ran from the wrecked Trabant to the seriously damaged Peugeot with its petrol tank open to the elements. A small blue flame appeared on the deck, turned orange and then raced towards the smashed Trabi. A second later there was a gentle *whoof* and, now I didn't need it, I got my funeral pyre.

As the flame started to travel towards me, I decided it was time to abandon car. 'He shot my sexy underwear!' roared Misha, with an idiot grin. 'It's better than a bullet proof vest!'

He was holding up the rubber basque, from which the last trickles of liquid were pouring from two holes even the designers in their wildest dreams had not imagined.

'Is this stuff dangerous?' he asked, still laughing, splashing in a pool of the stuff with the toe of his boot.

'I don't know. You'd better ask your girlfriend. And if you want to come out of this with any sort of profit, you'd better get some guys to put those fires out.'

The Trabi I had hit and the Peugeot were burning nicely, but petrol fires out in the open are more show than substance. I've seen lots of burnt-out cars where the tyres have hardly been singed.

'How is Vovchik?'

'Badly hurt I hope,' I said, 'as he's my ticket out of here.'

Misha couldn't resist raising his head and scanning the horizon just to make sure we were still surrounded by sea.

'You know, Ray, I thought for a minute you were intending to drive home.'

'I can't drive that thing,' I said, 'it's a wreck.'

'So ... how?'

I unzipped the breast pocket of my Flying Tigers jacket where I kept my mobile phone. They had never seen me use it, nobody had searched me and

I'd had no annoying incoming calls to give away the fact I had one, because I had it turned off until now.

'Me? I'm calling a cab.'

'Emergency services? I'm going to need an ambulance. There's been a traffic accident. Location? As near as I can estimate, latitude 51 degrees 57 minutes north, longitude 1 degree 19 minutes east, about six miles off Harwich. Yes, that's right, on a ship. Oh, I see. Could you put me through to the Coastguard, then? Thank you ever so much.'

The crew put the fires out before they had singed Vovchik too badly and somebody thought to pull him out of range of the Peugeot's petrol tank. He wasn't treated gently and at least one crewman kicked him and shouted *'Tvoju mat'* at him, just to show his loyalty to Misha, now re-instated as First Mate. Of Mariusz there was no sign, but Misha said he had locked himself in a toilet.

We got Cassandra, armed with the ship's medical kit, to take a look at Vovchik even though she protested she was neither a nurse nor a doctor. I told her she was a chemist and that was near enough. Vovchik wouldn't mind. He was unconscious from where he'd hit his head on the side of the ship, obviously had a broken right arm and, I suspected a broken hip from where I'd hit him with the car.

'Should I give him this?' Cassandra asked holding up a phial of liquid and a hypodermic syringe in a sterile pack.

'What is it?'

'Morphine hydrochloride. The dose is usually 10mgs.'

'Give him twenty,' I said. 'I don't want him coming round in the helicopter.'

The Coastguard helicopter crew were brilliant. I'd gladly pay taxes to support guys like that. They lowered a man down on the winch and we helped him strap Vovchik on to a metal stretcher. While the stretcher was being winched up, the paramedic looked at the blood on my face and held up two fingers.

'How many..?'

'Four,' I said, possibly a little too quickly.

'You'd better come with us,' he said.

'I was going to suggest it. My friend there doesn't speak much English and I have his papers here.'

I patted my jacket pocket. Misha had supplied me with Kozlov's passport and merchant seaman's papers, along with his wallet which was fat with American twenty dollar bills. There might even be enough to keep Duncan the Drunken happy when I broke the news that his Peugeot had made the ultimate sacrifice.

And then they sent the winch down with the strap webbing and the paramedic helped me into it, telling me to just relax and not to struggle and his mate in the chopper would haul me aboard.

I was winched up very gently: it was all rather exciting really, watching the rusty deck of the *Akademik Shteinman* sink away beneath me. One of the crew, totally bemused by what was going on, even waved goodbye.

I shouted 'Have a nice life!' to Misha and Cassandra, but over the roar of the helicopter rotors I don't think they heard me.

Chapter Twenty

In the chopper they gave me a helmet and got me to use the intercom system to counter the noise. Each of the three-man crew wanted confirmation that I really had sent a distress signal by dialling 999 on my mobile and I acted like it had been the natural thing to do.

I knew what they were thinking and it had worried me. The new generation of digital phones simply didn't work, like the old analog ones did, more than about eight miles offshore unless you were lucky enough to be in the vicinity of an oil rig which hosted a booster station for the signal. That was why I had been anxious to move quickly; plus the fact that I was now over two hours late meeting Amy and that sort of fear is a great spur.

I congratulated the crew on turning up so quickly and one of them said they hadn't had far to come as they worked out of the MRCC (Maritime Rescue Co-ordination Centre) at Walton on the Naze, just down the Essex coast.

'That's near Colchester, isn't it?' I asked innocently.

'Yeah, that's right. In fact we'll get the Essex Air

Ambulance to meet us and they can fly your mate direct to Colchester General Hospital.'

'Can I go with him?'

'Don't see why not, if you can help us do the paperwork on him. He's in no fit state, is he?'

I tried not to look too pleased.

At this rate, I might even beat Amy to the hospital to see my father, plus I had one pocket stuffed with Julius Symington's pound notes and another with Kozlov's dollars. I was getting two free rides in helicopters and I'd seen the last of that grotty Peugeot.

All in all, not a bad day at the office.

In the bright yellow Air Ambulance chopper, I told the crew how my very good friend Vladimir Kozlov, acting First Mate of the *Akademik Shteinman,* had been injured in a valiant attempt to secure shifting deck cargo which had then caught fire, and I wanted to be there for him when he woke up.

'Is he a citizen of the European Union?' one of the crew asked.

'No, but I am. Does it matter?'

'Not to his treatment. We'll treat him, but there'll be paperwork.'

'That's what I'm here for,' I said solidly.

The chopper drew a small crowd of visitors and nurses going off duty as it landed on the hospital helipad. The crew sprang into action and Kozlov's stretcher was turned into a trolley and he was wheeled away with incredible speed. If I saw a collecting box for the Air Ambulance, I would stuff some of Kozlov's money into it; it was the least he could do.

I followed the trolley to the entrance to the hospital, where the doors swung open automatically, letting it get further and further ahead of me, then I turned on my heel and headed in the opposite direction, following the signs to Gainsborough Wing and the Stroke Unit.

Near the hospital shop, which was closed by this time, there was a litter bin and I slipped Vovchik's passport and papers into it without breaking stride.

In the Stroke Unit, as soon as I asked for Mr Angel, all the nurses went quiet and looked at me with a mixture of respect and awe, the kind I was not used to. At first I assumed that they had somehow discovered my father had a title, albeit a threadbare one, but then one of the senior nurses said, in a hushed voice: 'He has a visitor with him.'

'Can he have another one?'

'Of course, though it is getting a little late and he's had a busy day with the physiotherapists.'

He'd had a busy day?

'Is his visitor a relative?'

'We're not sure. Do you know Miss May?' she asked me.

'Amy May, the designer?'

The nurse nodded enthusiastically.

'I've heard of her.'

'You're late. Bloody late. How did you get here?'

My father was lying in bed, the covers up to his waist. Amy was in a chair at his side. She'd slipped off her shoes and was popping grapes into her mouth from a cellophane bag.

'And good evening to you, dearest. I got a lift; and how is Papa?'

'I – was – doing – fine – and then you ... showed up,' he slurred.

He stretched out his right hand and clasped one of Amy's. His voice was clearer and his complexion healthier than yesterday but his left side remained inert.

'Amy's been appointed chairman of the escape committee,' he said slowly and deliberately as if counting his words in case he had forgotten any.

'I've arranged a transfer to the Devonshire just as soon as he gets the All Clear to travel from the doctors here,' Amy said, patting his hand. 'They'll look after you really well. And I've booked a firm to spring clean your flat for when you get out of there. I'm also checking out a few agencies for day-care home nursing and physiotherapy.' Then she looked up at me. 'Have you done anything useful today?'

'Not really,' I admitted.

'Shall we tell him the news?' Amy said coyly. I wished she wouldn't try that. Amy doesn't really do coy.

'I've got a job, Father,' I said loudly and proudly.

'For God's sake, he's had a stroke, don't give him a heart attack as well! *Our* news.'

But my father was already using his good right arm, patting his stomach and then jerking a thumb at Amy.

'He says you've put on weight,' I said.

Now father's hand was a wagging finger.

'You leave her alone,' he said firmly. 'She should take it easy in her condition.'

'He seems to know our news,' I observed, just to prove my detective skills were still in place.

Amy just gave me one of those looks she normally reserves for customers who try and tell her the cheque is in the post, and Jehovah's Witnesses.

'Have you told Kim about me yet?' my father wanted to know.

'I have actually been rather tied up today,' I said knowing no one in the room was going to believe me. 'But I'm due a day off tomorrow, so I'll do it then. In fact, I'd like to do a deal with you. I'll ring Kim, I'll even go and reassure her personally. I'll tell her you're fine, you're being looked after, you'll be home soon, whatever you want me to say. I'll do all that, and you tell Mum she's going to be a grandmother.'

It took him almost a minute to get the words out, by which time his complexion had a purple tinge to it. I thought it was a regression to the swallowing problems and slurred speech which accompany stroke, but in this case it was sheer temper. When he did find his voice, he found a roar.

'You call *that* a good deal?'

The publishers hope that this book has given you enjoyable reading. Large Print Books are especially designed to be as easy to see and hold as possible. If you wish a complete list of our books please ask at your local library or write directly to:

Magna Large Print Books
Magna House, Long Preston,
Skipton, North Yorkshire.
BD23 4ND

This Large Print Book for the partially sighted, who cannot read normal print, is published under the auspices of

THE ULVERSCROFT FOUNDATION